Lutz, Lisa.
The Spellmans strike again /

Meijer Branch
Jackson District Library          6/08/2010

S0-AEV-839

WITHDRAWN

CON PAR
HAN SAR

# THE SPELLMANS
# STRIKE AGAIN

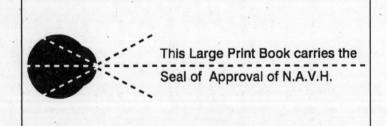

This Large Print Book carries the
Seal of Approval of N.A.V.H.

# THE SPELLMANS
# STRIKE AGAIN

## LISA LUTZ

**THORNDIKE PRESS**
*A part of Gale, Cengage Learning*

GALE
CENGAGE Learning™

Detroit • New York • San Francisco • New Haven, Conn • Waterville, Maine • London

GALE
CENGAGE Learning™

Copyright © 2010 by Spellman Enterprises, Inc.
Thorndike Press, a part of Gale, Cengage Learning.

**ALL RIGHTS RESERVED**
This book is a work of fiction. Names, characters, places, and incidents either are products of the author's imagination or are used fictitiously. Any resemblance to actual events or locales or persons, living or dead, is entirely coincidental.
Thorndike Press® Large Print Core.
The text of this Large Print edition is unabridged.
Other aspects of the book may vary from the original edition.
Set in 16 pt. Plantin.

**LIBRARY OF CONGRESS CATALOGING-IN-PUBLICATION DATA**

Lutz, Lisa.
   The Spellmans strike again / by Lisa Lutz.
     p. cm. — (Thorndike Press large print core)
   ISBN-13: 978-1-4104-2636-9
   ISBN-10: 1-4104-2636-X
   1. Private investigators—Fiction. 2. San Francisco
(Calif.)—Fiction. 3. Domestic fiction. 4. Large type books.
I. Title.
PS3612.U897S69 2010b
813'.6—dc22
                                 2010007907

Published in 2010 by arrangement with Simon & Schuster, Inc.

Printed in the United States of America
1 2 3 4 5 6 7 14 13 12 11 10

Lutz, Lisa.
The Spellmans strike again /

Meijer Branch
Jackson District Library

To all my friends from
Desvernine Associates:
Des, Pamela, Pierre, Yvonne, Debra,
and Gretchen. But not Mike.

# PROLOGUE

## Phone Call from the Edge[1] #28

**Morty:** What's new, Izzele?

**Me:** If I told you, you wouldn't believe me.

**Morty:** Never stopped you before.

**Me:** I wouldn't know where to begin.

**Morty:** It's true. You tell stories funny. You always start in the middle.

**Me:** Here's a headline: Rae committed a felony and might actually have to do time in a juvenile facility.

**Morty:** That is news. What did she do?

**Me:** Something very bad.

**Morty:** Usually felonies are. Feel like sharing?

**Me:** I'm not ready to talk about it. Let's switch subjects.

**Morty:** Okay, how's your Harkey investigation going?

**Me:** Nowhere.

1. Miami, specifically.

**Morty:** Your brother still seeing the hooker?

**Me:** I explained this to you before. She's not a hooker.

**Morty:** Sorry, I got confused. I'm not even going to ask about your Irish boyfriend.[2]

**Me:** Good. Don't.

**Morty:** I didn't. That's what I just said.

**Me:** Don't you have some news for me, Morty?

**Morty:** That's right, I haven't told you yet. We're moving back to San Fran.

**Me:** Say San Francisco, not San Fran.

**Morty:** Why? Life's short. No point wasting it on extra syllables.

**Me:** It makes you sound like a tourist.

**Morty:** You're grumpy today.

**Me:** You have no idea what the past few days have been like for me.

**Morty:** True, because you haven't told me.

**Me:** Later. You'll hear all about it, later.

**Morty:** Don't wait too long. I'm old.[3]

**Me:** I am well aware of that.

**Morty:** I got the shirt, by the way.

**Me:** What shirt?

**Morty:** The blue shirt that says "Free Schmidt."

2. Ex-boyfriend #12, Connor O'Sullivan, bartender by day, bartender by night.

3. Eighty-five years old, to be exact.

**Me:** I didn't send you that shirt.

**Morty:** Who did?

**Me:** Rae.

**Morty:** It came with instructions. A typewritten note that told me I should wear it in public at least twice a week. Who is Schmidt?

**Me:** A man inadvertently responsible for one of the most traumatic events of my life.

**Morty:** So, I take it we don't want to free him?

**Me:** No, we want to free him. Definitely.

**Morty:** Should I wear the shirt?

**Me:** Wear it, don't wear it, I don't care. I just don't want to talk about Schmidt anymore.

**Morty:** Okay. How's the weather?

**Me:** Excuse me, isn't there some real news to discuss?

**Morty:** Are you referring to my forthcoming return to San Fran?

**Me:** Ahem.

**Morty:** Cisco.

**Me:** Yes. Give it to me straight, Morty. How on earth did you convince Ruthy to move back to the city?

**Morty:** Let's call it divine intervention.

■ ■ ■ ■

# PART I:
# CASE WORK
## (THREE MONTHS EARLIER)

■ ■ ■ ■

# FAMILY CAMPING TRIP #2

*Why????* we all asked when my father broke the news. A family disappearance/corporate retreat/camping trip all rolled up into one. *Surely* it was a bad idea, I suggested. The sentiment was reaffirmed by Rae with her constant references to the Donner Party and repeated inquiries as to which one of the Spellmans plus guest would most likely be consumed first (should it come to that). The third time this particular line of inquiry rolled around, my mother sent Rae to her room.

If all of this is confusing you, perhaps I should give you a quick refresher course on the Spellmans. Although I highly recommend reading the first three documents[1] if

---

1. *The Spellman Files, Curse of the Spellmans, Revenge of the Spellmans* — all available in paperback!

you want a true understanding of what is really going on here.

My father is Albert Spellman, a onetime cop turned private investigator who really likes lunch. He is happily married to Olivia Spellman, my mother and co-owner of Spellman Investigations. Mom is an extremely attractive woman — although lately people have been adding the disclaimer "for her age," which has started to get under her skin. Other than my mom's mild vanity, her most obscene characteristic is that she seems to think meddling in her children's lives is an Olympic event. Her training regimen is positively brutal.

Albert and Olivia have three children. The oldest is my brother, David, thirty-four: Formerly a poster boy for the all-American corporate male, currently an out-of-work human being. I'm the middle child. Isabel, thirty-two, if you didn't catch it already. My MO from fifth grade until my midtwenties was that of the problem child. The "student" the principal knew by name, the neighbors feared, and the pot dealers counted on to stay afloat. Also, in the interest of honesty, there were a few arrests thrown into the mix — two (or four, depending on how you're counting) as recently as two years ago, which I guess means that I can't argue that my problem years were confined to my youth or even my twenties. But it's important to note that I've come a long way. Therapy helped, and I'm big enough to admit it was court ordered.

About six months ago, after years of doubt about my future with Spellman Investigations, I committed to the job completely and agreed to slowly begin taking over the business from my parents so they can retire and learn to do macramé[2] or something. My father likes to say the seeds of adulthood have been planted. He's just waiting for them to take.

There's only one other Spellman to speak of — Rae — and I'll mostly let her speak for herself because you might not believe me otherwise.

I suppose the most defining characteristic of my family is that we take our work home with us. If your family's job is investigating other people, you inevitably investigate each other. This single trait has been our primary point of conflict for most of my life.

Finally, to round out the players on this unfortunate camping trip, I should mention

2. The parental unit claims to have plans for their retirement, but so far none sound even remotely plausible.

Maggie. Maggie Mason, girlfriend to brother David. Maggie is a defense attorney who used to date Henry Stone (that's a whole other story I don't really want to get into right now, okay?), who happens to be the "best friend"[3] of my now seventeen-year-old sister, the briefly aforementioned Rae. Henry is a forty-five-year-old police inspector and Rae is a senior in high school. They're an unlikely duo. Rae met Henry when she was fourteen and I guess she decided that they were kindred spirits. However, on the surface (and beneath the surface) they have nothing in common. At the start, Henry endured Rae. Then he got used to her. Then, when Henry was dating Maggie and Rae went to supernatural lengths to sabotage their relationship, Henry cut Rae off completely. Now they have found peace. At least that's what I've heard. I don't get involved anymore.

After Maggie and Henry broke up, over half of the Spellman clan vetted Maggie and determined that she was a quality human, the kind of person that the Spellman circle sorely needed. After an appropriate amount of time passed, the matchmaking plans for Maggie and David were successfully en-

3. Her words, not his.

acted. The couple had only been together about two months at the point of this camping trip, but since Maggie is the only person we know who can make fire from a flint, can pitch a tent, can use a compass, and actually owns bear spray, we thought it wise for our own personal safety to bring her along. That and David refused to come unless she accompanied him.

Now picture me in the predawn hours, in the middle of the woods, in the middle of the Russian River, in the middle of nowhere, sharing a tent with my much younger sister, Rae, who had spent the past two days either trying to get cell phone reception, complaining about the mosquitoes, or "sleeping," during which time she carried on lengthy conversations about . . . well, honestly, I couldn't tell you. I caught phrases like "I've been sworn to secrecy," "Not in this lifetime," and "You'll find the treasure at the bottom of the gorge." I might have been able to sleep through her babbling if she weren't a nighttime thrasher and kicker. And so, once again, there I was, sleep deprived, trapped with family, waiting for the nightmare to come to an end. My life in a nutshell.

On the morning before our return-home date, I gave up on sleep, knowing that this was my last full day in the wild. When I exited my tent, my father was trying to make coffee and failing miserably. He appeared glad for company since my mother was still slumbering in their tent.

"What am I doing wrong?" he asked.

"Strong-arming your family into a cruel and unnecessary nature excursion," I suggested.

"*No,*" Dad replied. "What am I doing wrong with the coffee?"

"You don't stick the coffee in the pot and boil it with the water, Dad. Are you brain-dead? You just boil the water first and use the French press Maggie brought. Weren't you watching her yesterday?" I replied with too much hostility.

My father tried to lighten the mood with the only joke he had in his arsenal this weekend.

"Why don't you take a hike?" he said for about the thirtieth time.

"I'm going to dig a grave for that line and you're going to bury it, Dad. I swear to you, if you say it one more time —"

"Maggie!" Dad shouted with way too much enthusiasm for waking hours. "Thank God you're awake."

Maggie smiled, approached the campfire, and took over the coffee making. Already the morning had improved. But the purpose of the trip had not yet been realized, and eventually we had to accept that this wasn't simply a bonding experience for the Spellmans and friend, but something even more bizarre.

I should mention that no Spellman child had gone AWOL or refused to participate in the excursion since "business" was not to take place until the final day and, frankly, we all wanted our voice to be heard, even if it was heard above the buzz of mosquitoes. Also, I should mention that my parents said they would refuse to give a raise to anyone who didn't participate in this bonding exercise. As for David, he was only there because he thought Maggie needed more quality time with the family, as a kind of cautionary lesson.

I suppose it's time we get to business.

### THE FIRST ANNUAL SHAREHOLDERS' MEETING OF SPELLMAN INVESTIGATIONS, INC.

[The minutes read as follows:]

**Albert:** Here, here. I call this meeting to order. Are all ye present?

**David:** Dad, we're not in old England. These are just shareholders' minutes. State the date, the location, and the parties present.

**Olivia:** Isabel, are you recording?

**Isabel:** Yes. And I'd like to put on record that we could have had this meeting in the comfort of our own home.

**Olivia:** Rae, what are you doing?

**Rae:** Making s'mores.

**Olivia:** It's ten A.M., sweetie.

**Rae:** What's your point?

**Olivia:** S'mores are not breakfast food.

**Albert:** Excuse me, I'm trying to have a meeting here.

**Rae:** Who's stopping you?

**Isabel:** Put the skewer down, Rae.

**Rae:** This is seriously the most torturous experience of my life.

**Albert:** Hello? Do I need to drag out the cowbell?

**David:** Dad, if you do, I'm walking right now.

**Albert:** David, your presence here is necessary. I need you to draw up the minutes.

**David:** You are aware of the fact that many small companies have minutes created without a meeting.

**Rae:** Oh my god, now you tell us!

**Albert:** We have actual business to conduct.

**David:** Dad, you wanted a family vacation and used the threat of business to make it happen by refusing to give a raise to

20

anyone who didn't attend. You got your camping trip. Why don't you just make your announcements, we'll go for one last hike, and then we can get out of here.

**Isabel:** I second that motion.

**Olivia:** Stop scratching, Rae! You'll get scars.

**Rae:** Why haven't we rid the planet of mosquitoes yet? If we can practically wipe out the ozone layer, I don't see why these tiny bloodsuckers can't be systematically destroyed.

**Maggie:** Put some calamine lotion on and then wait a minute or two. You should be fine.

**Isabel:** Can we start the meeting already?

**Albert:** That's what I'm trying to do.

**Olivia:** Who's stopping you?

**Albert:** Quiet. Okay. Where was I? Okay, I call to order the first annual shareholders' meeting of Spellman Investigations, Incorporated. Now what, David?

**David:** We have already discussed the basic issues. On paper, Isabel is now vice president and owns 25 percent of the company. However, for the next few years Isabel, Mom, and Dad will run the firm together and will take a three-way vote if there are any disputes.

**Isabel:** I know how that vote will turn out.

**Albert:** I don't always agree with your

mother, Isabel.

**Isabel:** Right.

**Rae:** Let's get to the whole reason we're here. What's our cost-of-living increase?

**Isabel:** I should point out, Rae, that you don't even pay for your cost of living.

**Olivia:** Let's just go over our plans for the year, Al. We don't need to drag this out any more than we have.

**Albert:** Oh, so now you're turning on me too?

**Isabel:** I would really like this "meeting"[4] to begin so that it can eventually end.

**David:** Here, here.

**Albert:** I thought you told me not to use that language.

**Rae:** I'm going to kill myself.

**David:** Maggie, please step in.

*[Maggie gets to her feet in front of the campfire and takes control of the room, so to speak.]*

**Maggie:** What's the first order of business?

**Albert:** We've started a retirement fund for Isabel and she gets a 5 percent salary increase. Same for Rae.

**Isabel:** That's not fair. I'm more important than Rae.

**Rae:** Excuse me?

4. Finger quotes.

**Olivia:** Rae's entire raise will go into her college fund.

**Rae:** I quit.

**Maggie:** Next order of business.

**Isabel:** I'd like my mother to stop harassing my boyfriend.

**Olivia:** I haven't harassed him. I checked on his immigration status and I pay him a visit every now and again and ask him what he's been up to.

**Isabel:** Can you just leave him alone?
*[Long pause while mother pretends to be concocting a plan she has already concocted.]*

**Olivia:** I'll make you a deal. Go on a blind date with a lawyer once a week and I will pretend that Connor does not exist.

**Isabel:** Mom, that's ridiculous.

**David:** Yeah, Mom, that's kind of weird.

**Olivia:** Once every other week.

**Isabel:** I said no.

**Albert:** Once a fortnight.

**Olivia:** Al, quiet. Isabel, I really think you should accept my offer.

**Isabel:** Why do you hate him so much?

**Maggie:** Next order of business.

**Olivia:** Sorry, Maggie. I don't believe Isabel and I were through with our negotiations.

**Isabel:** We were through.

**Olivia:** Every other week, I'd like you to go

on a date with a lawyer or another professional. Then I'll leave your boyfriend alone.

**Isabel:** I think Connor would have more of an issue with me dating other men than with you harassing him. If that's how you want to use your time, I guess I can't stop you.

**Olivia:** Do you remember Prom Night 1994?

*[Dead silence.]*

**Isabel:** What are you getting at?

**Olivia:** I have pictures of you in that green dress with the puff sleeves and the tulle petticoat. The one Grammy Spellman made you wear.

**Isabel:** Why don't we talk about this later?

**Olivia:** Great. Then we can iron out the details.

**David:** Fifty bucks.

**Albert:** Seventy-five.

**Rae:** Eighty.

**Isabel:** What are you guys going on about?

**David:** We're bidding on those prom pictures. How come I've never seen them?

**Olivia:** That's enough, everyone. Let's get back to the meeting. Any other orders of business?

**Rae:** I'm going to work for Maggie part-time.

**Maggie:** Rae, remember what we talked about.

**Rae:** More like an unpaid internship. But I thought everyone should know.

**Olivia:** I think that's an excellent idea.[5]

**Isabel:** Me too. I guess when you're independently wealthy you can afford to work for free.

**Rae:** I took a beating in the stock market this last year.

**Olivia:** What will you have her do?

**Maggie:** I'm going to have Rae help me review some pro bono cases I'm thinking about taking on. Preliminary research.

**Albert:** That sounds very educational.

**Rae:** Don't try to ruin it for me.

**Isabel:** Speaking of pro bono work, when are we going to start investigating Harkey?[6]

**Albert:** I don't think now is the right time.

**Isabel:** Why not?

**Olivia:** He'll fight back, Isabel.

**Isabel:** He already did. Do you think that audit last month was random?

---

5. Excellent for two reasons: 1) Business is a bit slow and so there's not that much work for Rae anyway; 2) Mom wouldn't mind another person with a graduate degree in the family.
6. An evil PI who needs taking down.

**Olivia:** My point exactly. I was the one who had to spend three weeks pulling together two years of financial data.

**Isabel:** So you're just going to let him get away with it? Is that what I'm hearing?

**Albert:** This is not a good use of your time, Isabel. In this economy, we should be focusing on keeping our business afloat, not taking anyone down. Besides, we don't even know if Harkey was behind the audit.

**Isabel:** You're kidding, right? The timing was impeccable. I run into Harkey at the liquor store, suggest that maybe he should watch his back, and the next thing you know the IRS is knocking on our door.

**David:** Who goes around threatening people like that?

**Rae:** Isabel *loves* to threaten people.

**Isabel:** Shut up. Back to the audit. Harkey started it, Dad.

**Albert:** Listen, Izzy, business is slow. Do you really want to waste our resources on a witch hunt?

**Isabel:** I do. We know he's crooked. If we can put him out of business, that cuts our competition by about 20 percent.

*[Albert shakes his head, still undecided.]*

**Albert:** He won't just roll over, Isabel.

**Isabel:** I'm ready for him.

*[Olivia whispers in Albert's ear; Albert nods*

*his head.]*

**Isabel:** Maggie, is whispering allowed at an official board meeting?

**Maggie:** I don't take sides with you people.

**David:** "You people"?

**Maggie:** You know what I mean.

**Olivia:** Okay, we'll make you a deal, Isabel. You accept now or we shelve this conversation for a later date. One, the Harkey investigation cannot take you away from your regular work, and two, you may not use more than $200 a month in company resources.

**Isabel:** Deal.

**Maggie:** Any other orders of business?

**David:** I hope not.

**Rae:** One last thing. I request that we never do a group camping trip ever again.

**Isabel:** Better than the threatened cruise.

**Rae:** It's still torture.

**Isabel:** At least you didn't have someone kicking you all night long and shouting conspiracy theories.

**David:** If that's all, I call this meeting to a close.

**Albert:** I wanted to do that.

**David:** Then go ahead, Dad. It doesn't actually matter.

**Albert:** Maybe to you it doesn't.

**Olivia:** Al, enough.

**David:** [to Maggie] I hope you're paying attention. Nothing about this morning has been out of the ordinary.

**Maggie:** Relax, David. I'm fine.

**Albert:** As president and CEO of Spellman Investigations, I call this meeting to a close.

**Rae:** I really do think people can die of boredom.

# Rule #22

Sometime during my employment contract negotiations and the redrafting of the Spellman bylaws (which are hardly as professional as they sound — they're simply the codes of the family's personal and work ethics put into writing to prevent arguments at a later date), my mother came up with a new Spellman dictum: the daily rule. It can be written on the whiteboard next to the copy machine by any family member (including David), and so long as no more than two parties object to it at one time, it remains law, punishable by trash duty for the week.[1]

## RULE #22 — NO SPEAKING TODAY! (AUTHOR: OLIVIA SPELLMAN)

After the excess of quality time on our camping disappearance, we'd all had quite

1. Yes, we think of everything.

enough of one another and the hum of bickering filled our domestic and office space. My mom wrote the rule on the board the night before and there was not a single veto. We communicated through e-mails, text messages, and the occasional pantomime. Rae suggested that we do this all the time. That suggestion was vetoed, even though typically we don't veto suggestions.

My mother sent an e-mail to inform me that in line with me being the new face of Spellman Investigations, she had decided I should take the meeting with one of our repeat clients, Mr. Franklin Winslow, scheduled for tomorrow afternoon. Apparently my mother's primary concern with the meeting was my sartorial choice. My mother made it clear that a dress was in order and wanted to be sure that one still remained in my closet.

The e-mail was followed by an instant-message exchange:

Olivia: What *exactly* are you planning on wearing?
Isabel: Remember that periwinkle bridesmaid's dress from cousin Sandy's wedding?
Olivia: There's no way it will still fit you.

Just remember to err on the conservative side.

Isabel: Don't you worry, Mom. I plan on erring.

The phone rang, so I ended our chat.

Isabel: Nice chatting with you, Mom. Let's not make a habit of it.

I picked up the phone.

"Hello?" I said, which felt strange after four hours of silence.

The voice on the other end of the line was awkward, formal, and extremely familiar.

"Hi, Isabel. It's Henry."

"Rae's not here. She's probably at school."

"I'm not calling for Rae."

"My mom just stepped out of the office. You can try the house line."

*Sigh.* "I'm not calling for your mother either."

"Is it Dad you're after? Because, frankly, I'm running out of people who can be found at this number."

"Nope. Don't want to talk to your dad."

"Has someone else moved in that I don't know about?" I asked.

"I was calling for you," Henry said, impressively containing his annoyance.

"Huh," I said. I tend to say "huh" when I'm not sure what else to say. Some people rely on more classic nonresponses, like "I see" or "Interesting" or even "Oh." But I say "huh" and so far it's worked for me.

This might be a good time to elaborate just a bit on the awkward telephone conversation, even though I shouldn't really have to elaborate if you've read these documents in order.[2]

Henry Stone, once my sister's best friend, then enemy, then BFF again, has been tangled in the Spellman web for over three years now. A few years back, he was the lead investigator on a missing persons case — the missing person being Rae. (The conclusion: She staged her own kidnapping.) Since then, Henry has been around and I have gotten used to him being around. And last year I got so used to his whole being-around-ness that I started to think that it was something more than just that, if you know what I mean. If you don't, you'll have to figure it out because I'm not in the mood to dig up the details.

Anyway, when I got this idea into my head, I couldn't get it out, which makes it like most ideas I have. Eventually I made

2. Like you're supposed to!

my feelings known to Henry and he made his nonfeelings equally well known. And that was the end of that. I then got used to him not being around. Not that he wasn't around. He and Rae had settled their primary disputes and continued their bizarre friendship. My parents still invited him over for dinner and consulted him on cases, and he and my mom even have lunch now and again, exchange Christmas presents, and once went shopping together.[3]

As for me, I see Henry as little as possible. I find it's healthier for my ego. When you're thirty-one years old and someone tells you you're not a grown-up, it stings. Now, at the age of thirty-two, the worst of the sting was gone.

Besides, I had matured considerably in the intervening months and was about to take over the family business. In fact, at that very moment I was wearing a tucked-in shirt that was relatively wrinkle free, and my hair was combed. I could certainly handle a simple telephone conversation.

"Isabel?" Henry said into the receiver. I guess I had been silent awhile.

"Sorry. What can I do for you?"

3. Don't ask. I didn't.

"I'd like to speak to you."

"Isn't that what we're doing?"

"In person."

"Why? Are the phones tapped and I don't know about it?"

Sound of throat clearing. "Meet me for a drink after work."

"I'll be at the Philosopher's Club[4] at —"

*"Not there!"* Henry said too quickly and with a buzz of hostility.

"Then you better be buying, because I've grown accustomed to free booze and I have to pay rent these days."

"Yes. I'm buying," Henry said, sounding like he was regretting this entire conversation.

"Okay. Where?"

"Edinburgh Castle."

"I thought that place was too divey for you."

"It is. But I want *you* to be comfortable."

"How kind."

"Six o'clock?"

---

4. My regular bar for years. Now with the added perk that I'm dating the barkeep, so my drinks are almost always free. Except when he's mad at me, which is fairly often. Let me recalculate: My drinks are free about 60 percent of the time.

"Six thirty," I replied, only to assert a share of control.

# Unhappy Hour

It was still light outside, even though the fog had rolled in, but the interior of the bar felt like the night was nearing its end. I spotted Henry at a booth in the back. He was easy to spot, being the most well-groomed patron in the establishment.

He'd already started drinking, but there was a glass of some kind of whiskey and another glass of ice waiting for me.

"I ordered for you," Henry said. "Hope you don't mind. I just got the booze you usually steal from your brother's house.[1] Wasn't sure what you wanted."

"The question is: What do *you* want?" I said.

I took a sip of the excellent whiskey and studied Henry, trying to get an angle on him.

1. Thirty-year-old Glenlivet. If you're not paying for it, go for the best, is my motto.

"All I want is to have a drink with a friend," he said.

"Then you should have called one."

"We were friends."

"Were," I repeated.

"Well, I would like to be friends again. What will it take?"

I drained my bourbon and contemplated the scratched wood table for the answer. It wasn't there.

"Another drink wouldn't hurt," I replied.

Henry slid a twenty across the table and told me to order whatever I wanted. He still wasn't halfway finished with his whiskey, so I didn't even take his order.

At the bar I considered the most expensive options, but then I chose the house label, because I didn't want Henry to think that his bribe had worked. I returned to the table with ample change.

Henry sniffed my drink and instantly got the message.

"How can we work this out?" he asked.

"My brother says I should start making friends my own age."

"Ouch," the inspector replied with mock injury.

"We're not enemies," I offered, thinking that was friendly enough.

"I want to be more than enemies."

"Archenemies? I suppose we could head in that direction. But you'd have to do something pretty awful for us to drive down that road."

"I was thinking in the other direction," Henry answered, not amused.

"We can be friendly acquaintances," I suggested, realizing that I had found myself in the midst of negotiating the terms of a friendship. How odd. Although it's something my sister and Henry have done on numerous occasions.

"No," Henry flatly replied.

"Well, that's my best offer," I said.

"No, it isn't," Henry said with an interrogation-room stare.

I was unprepared for this type of meeting. I figured I held all the cards. Therefore, I would control the conversation. Something was going on here — the power had shifted but I couldn't trace when it had happened.

"I'm going to leave now," I announced.

"See you soon," Henry answered.

"Not that soon."

I left my half-empty drink on the table and Henry opened the book he had been reading when I entered. He made no move to leave, which I found odd since this wasn't his kind of bar and at the moment the smell of hops mixed with something sour was harsh. When I exited, it was dark outside. I didn't have to adjust to the light and therefore didn't have to adjust back to the darkness when I returned to the bar five minutes later.

I stood beside Henry, casting a shadow over his literature. He looked up and smiled.

"Forget something?"

"I want my keys and my wallet back," I demanded.

"Have a seat," Henry calmly replied, "and we'll talk about it."

"No," I said. "Just give 'em back."

"Or what. You'll call the cops?" Henry chuckled at his little joke.

I sat down in a huff and glared at him.

"Have you gone mad?" I asked.

"Nope," Henry replied. "I've just figured out the Spellman way of doing things."

It was then I realized that this particular tactic — the coercion/blackmail/threat technique of reviving a friendship — was exactly what Rae did to return to Henry's good graces. It had worked on him; why wouldn't it work on me? I had to admit that I was both impressed and intrigued that Henry would do something so out of character just to keep me around. If I'm honest with myself, which if you know me you know I'm not all that often, I missed Henry too.

Henry slid a fresh drink across the table. I took a sip and realized it was the good stuff again.

I wasn't sure what to say, so I waited for my captor to speak.

"Now tell me, Isabel. What's new?"

# A Gentleman's Gentleman

Before my meeting with Mr. Winslow, my mother insisted I drop by the house for a personal inspection. Mom took one look at the dress I was wearing, pulled out the iron and ironing board, and told me to take it off. I stood in just a slip and heels in the foyer while she reironed my dress. Just as the lingerie show was ending and I was slipping the dress over my head, one of our lawyer clients, Gerard Mitchell, exited the office.

"Hi, Isabel," Gerard said nonchalantly as he departed.

After he left, my mother whispered, "Recently divorced."

"So?" I replied.

"So, I'm thinking he should be your first lawyer date," Mom casually replied.

"Mom, I have a boyfriend. I'm not going to go on dates with other men."

"I think you are," Mom replied. "I know

it was a long time ago, sweetie, but I don't think we need the events of Prom Night 1994 to see the light of day. Do you?"

"You wouldn't," I replied.

"I would," Mom answered. "I've been holding on to this nugget for Rae's entire lifetime, just waiting for the perfect opportunity."

My mom's threat must have drained the color from my face.

"You could use some blush," she added, scrounging through her purse.

I swallowed, trying to get rid of the lump in my throat. While blackmail is standard fare in the Spellman household, most of my misdeeds had already been exposed. Honestly, I had almost forgotten about this one. And this one was probably the worst of all.

Mom put some color on my cheeks while I batted her hand away. Then she gave me the lowdown on my impending meeting.

"Remember, Izzy. This is important. Mr. Winslow has been our client for seven years. He might be suffering from the early stages of dementia — it's really hard to tell with him. But he is always polite, usually serves some food and drink at meetings, and he always pays his bill on time. Don't fuck this up, sweetie."

■ ■ ■ ■

I arrived at Mr. Franklin Winslow's obscene mansion in Pacific Heights at precisely twelve fifteen P.M. I pulled into his driveway, delighting in one of those rare occasions when parking is not a challenge.

I was greeted at the door by the wary housekeeper, Mrs. Elizabeth Enright. Only Enright and the absent valet, Mason Graves, have been in Mr. Winslow's employment for more than eleven months. The housekeeper had logged five years and the valet eight — relatively brief employments considering how old Mr. Winslow is and how long he has resided at that residence. His previous valet had been with him since he was in his early thirties and died at the ripe old age of eighty-five. I gathered it was a crushing loss, but one that was tempered by his employment of Mason Graves, whom I gathered had been a solid replacement.

Judging purely by the scowl on her face, the housekeeper wasn't pleased to see me. Since that's a phenomenon I'm not unfamiliar with, I wasn't offended. Otherwise I might have taken issue with the scones she served, which I'm pretty certain were scrounged from the back of the freezer and probably baked when I was still in my twenties. In the interest of full disclosure, I ate them anyway because I was starving.

I waited fifteen minutes for Mr. Winslow to make an appearance, which was just enough time to take the edge off my hunger and catch Mrs. Enright peering in on me surreptitiously, although not that surreptitiously, since I spotted her.

Mr. Winslow was old, as I expected, and dressed in a mismatch of evening wear, business clothes, and something that I can only assume is called a smoking jacket, but my familiarity with that fashion statement was limited to stoned viewings of *Masterpiece Theatre* (or maybe it was parodies of *Masterpiece Theatre* from reruns of *The Muppet Show*). One could hardly call me an expert, is my point. Aside from Mr. Winslow's complicated, mismatched ensemble, I would discover other incongruities to fill the time.

As Winslow descended his circular staircase, I got to my feet out of courtesy. He was tall and slim and seemed to be gray all over, including his clothes. I estimated his age to be in the midseventies, but his gait was that of a much younger man. Some might say he was in sore need of a haircut, but I couldn't decide if that was his foppish style or negligent grooming. He was too thin and I found myself considering that I'd lose my appetite too if a rude woman were serving me stale scones all the time. But he didn't exactly look malnourished, just Peter O'Toole, I'd-rather-have-a-drink thin, and Mr. Winslow's posture was exquisite. But then I think English people haven't taken to slouching the way North Americans have.[1]

When Winslow finally reached me, he said, "My dear, a pleasure to see you," and then he kissed my hand, looked me up and down, and wrinkled his brow. "You look so young and big and well fed."

"Thank you," I hesitantly replied, since "What are you getting at?" would have sounded unprofessional.

"Sit down, sit down," Mr. Winslow said, waving me back into my chair. "You've done something different with your hair."

I hadn't, but it's best not to argue with clients, especially on the first meeting. "Something. I've definitely done something with it."

"Well, it's a pleasure seeing you again, Olivia," Mr. Winslow said, and then I solved my very first mystery of the day.

1. I'm speaking of people from the U.S. I'm not commenting on the Canadians. I wouldn't dare lump us into the same category.

"Mr. Winslow," I interrupted. "I'm Is-a-bel Spellman, Albert and Olivia's daughter."

Mr. Winslow stared at me for an uncomfortably long time, shook his head sadly as if fighting tears, and said, "I couldn't find my glasses this morning."

"They're on top of your head," I replied.

Mr. Winslow relocated his glasses and took me in one more time.

"I see it now. You are not Olivia. Your mother is a very beautiful woman."

He said it plainly, not rudely, but sometimes the content is more relevant than the delivery.

"I hope you're not disappointed," I replied, insulted but holding it in. "I believe my mother told you that I would be meeting you today."

"Without Mason, I'm afraid that my entire life is in disarray."

Mrs. Enright hovered with more tea. Mr. Winslow waved her away with a look of distrust and suggested we move into his study, where our meeting could be more private. I suddenly realized why my mom enjoyed these Winslow meetings so much. It was like briefly inhabiting a life-sized game of *Clue*.

Mr. Winslow has employed Spellman

Investigations throughout the years to investigate bad domestic help so that he can clean house with a clear conscience. The problem is he's *always* cleaning house, with the exception of his absent valet, Mason, and Mrs. Enright. No other current employee had lasted longer than a year, which meant that no one — other than Mason, the unspoken head of the household — fully understood how to keep this compound running. And now the house, the staff, and its owner had found themselves living in a state of chaos. Although I have discovered that chaos is relative. Nothing in Winslow's home seemed amiss to me besides Winslow himself.

Ultimately, my client's primary problem was the absence of his not-so-longtime "gentleman's gentleman," Mason Graves. Recently Mason's mother had taken ill and Mason had to return home to England for a few months to care for her. In the meantime, Mr. Winslow was sharing his home with a furtive housekeeper and a handful of strangers.

When it came down to it, Mr. Winslow wanted me to find him a temporary valet, but not just any valet: a valet/spy who could make sure that the support staff wasn't plotting against him at every turn and that the house and the man of the house were kept in working order. When I left Mr. Winslow's home, I had just the valet in mind. I also had two messages on my voice mail, followed by a text message that read: "If the heat doesn't kill me, the boredom will." I decided I should save a life before tackling my next line of business.

# PHONE CALL
## FROM THE EDGE #17

One of my best friends is old — like, really old. And you could say we have nothing in common except a mutual interest in keeping me out of jail. He was my pro bono attorney. I'd met him on a random surveillance and he later helped with some pesky harassment charges. Once the case was closed, we started having lunch. Then I had his driver's license revoked and then I persuaded Morty to move to Florida against all his wishes, since it was the only thing that would keep his marriage (a long and solid one at that) together. If you look at just the bullet points, I guess I don't sound like the kind of friend you'd want on your side. If you want more information, you know what you need to do.

Three months earlier, Morty had moved to Miami. As with our previous lunches, we rarely went more than a week without having some form of communication. I should note, however, that in the dozens of conversations we'd had so far, I hadn't heard any bright lights mentioned about his recent move other than the blazing bright light of the sun, which still doesn't shine as much as you'd think, what with the rain and humidity.

Our conversation on this day went something like this:

**Me:** When did you learn to text-message?

**Morty:** What else am I supposed to do here?

**Me:** I'm so proud of you.

**Morty:** Don't be. It took me a total of fifteen hours to figure it out. I actually timed myself so the next time Gabe tries to get me to learn some of this new cockamamie technology, I'll have evidence that it's not the best use of my last days here on earth.

**Me:** When did you start counting in days?

**Morty:** Since my doctor pointed out that I'm already nine years past the average male lifespan.

**Me:** Morty, I'm going to start ignoring your calls if you keep talking like this.

*[Sound of teeth-sucking.]*

**Me:** Would you stop that!

**Morty:** You can hear that?

**Me:** Yeah, Morty. Teeth-sucking isn't like rolling your eyes. It can be heard over

50

phone lines.

*[Long pause.]*

**Me:** You're rolling your eyes now, aren't you?

**Morty:** They don't roll like they used to.

**Me:** I doubt I'd even see it through those Coke-bottle glasses of yours.

**Morty:** Still with that Irish guy?

**Me:** Yes. Can we change the subject?

**Morty:** You're always changing that subject.

**Me:** Because you always ask as if you're surprised.

**Morty:** I am.

**Me:** So how's life at Sleepy Palms?[1]

**Morty:** They're dropping like flies here.

**Me:** Do you suspect foul play?

**Morty:** It's almost always the cancer or the ticker.

**Me:** Just say "cancer." You don't have to say "*the* cancer."

**Morty:** What are you, a doctor?

**Me:** No. But I know that you don't need to insert an article before the word "cancer."

**Morty:** When did you become a linguist?

**Me:** I'm just giving you some helpful advice so your new friends don't make fun of you.

**Morty:** I don't have any new friends, but if I did, they'd say "the cancer" too.

1. The unfortunate name of Morty's retirement community.

51

**Me:** Forget it.

**Morty:** Forgotten.

**Me:** How's the Northern California vacation plan coming along?

**Morty:** It could be better. Ruthy thinks I'm going to go AWOL, so we're still negotiating.

**Me:** You wouldn't do that to her, would you? *[Dead silence.]*

**Me:** Would you?

**Morty:** Speaking of the devil. Ruthy just got home from the market. I got to help her with the bags. Or should I just say "bags"? "I got to help her with bags"? That doesn't sound right.

**Me:** Good-bye, Morty.

# Undercover Butler

I was halfway across the bridge when my phone call with Morty ended, just in time for me to phone my friend Len and warn him about my impending arrival.

"Hello," he answered, having no idea that this phone call was going to change his entire life — or at least his immediate life and bank account.

"Isabel here. I have a proposition for you."

"Oh, Isabel, why is it that all your propositions are either illegal, ethically questionable, or at the very least offensive?"[1]

"Are you still an unemployed actor?"

"Are you implying that unemployed actors have no right to integrity?"

"No. I was merely making sure you weren't busy, because I have an acting job for you."

"*You* have an acting job for me?"

1. See previous documents for examples.

"Mostly."

"Do I get to keep my clothes on?" Len asked skeptically.

"Oh, yes. In fact, formal wear will be mandatory."

I was across the bridge and at Len and his lover Christopher's Oakland loft in an hour (although it should have taken only forty-five minutes). Christopher had just returned home from work; he's a decorator at a tiny firm in the city. Like Len, Christopher was once an actor (they met at ACT), but reality set in, which included news from his wealthy mother in England that she would no longer be supporting their "habit," as she liked to call it. On the surface Len and Christopher are quite similar — black, lean, handsome, with impeccable taste and manners. But their backgrounds could not be more different. Christopher was brought up in the English boarding school system and his childhood home had *wings.* Len, by contrast, lived in the San Francisco projects on and off and was once a drug dealer (by financial necessity more than choice).

Len, aka Leonard Williams, and I met in high school. Our relationship began, like so many of mine, with a secret. I accidentally discovered that Len was gay and kept it to myself. The longer the secret remained a secret, the more Len realized that he could trust me. Other than the secret, we had nothing in common. This seems like a fragile beginning for any relationship, but for whatever reason it stuck. Even as Len grew to become a respectable member of society and my maturity level flatlined, we remained friends. Eventually his secret came out. (Did it ever.)

In the past, I've asked Len and Christopher to put their considerable acting skills to questionable uses, but this time my request was legitimate. I was offering real money and a true test of his craft. And from the looks of things, Len needed a break from his life of leisure.

I found my old friend swathed in a luxurious bathrobe, being warmed by a cup of tea and an old Bette Davis movie on television. There was a scent of lavender in the air, as if a bath had recently been run, and I could catch the smudge of a face mask on the edge of his forehead. Len was clearly well rested, well groomed, and the picture of idle good health. Christopher, just home from work, observed the same particulars (using the set of detective skills that seem to come with any intimate relationship).

The partner with the job instructed Len

to get me a drink from the kitchen — the traditional domestic roles firmly in place, in part because one person had spent the day doing nothing at all. Len hopped to his feet, happy for the company and the diversion. Christopher got off his feet and looked at me with a note of pleading.

"Tell me you've got a real job for him and not one of your nonsense, no-pay pranks."[2]

Once I'd provided a feature-length version of the assignment, both Len and Christopher were entirely on board, even though the job was Len's alone.

"Can I use my British accent?" Len asked.

"Mr. Winslow was raised in London, so I wouldn't use it unless it's really good," I cautioned him.

Len turned to Christopher for his approval.

"It's good. We'll have to determine which dialect would be the most appropriate, but I think you can pull it off."

I handed Len Mr. Winslow's card with the time of his appointment and added my final instructions: "Remember, this is a full-time valet position, although you can come home

2. Come to think of it, I never did send a thank-you card for Fake Drug Deal #1.

at night. Don't take it unless you're up for it. The pay is fifty dollars an hour. Spend the weekend reading up on what modern valets do — don't just watch a marathon of *Jeeves and Wooster,* okay? Your job is to take care of Mr. Winslow and keep an eye on the help. Make sure nothing is amiss; report to me every few days. If I drop by the house at some point to meet with Mr. Winslow, you don't know me. Got it? You're in there undercover."

"Anything else, boss?" Len asked with a wink.

"Yeah," I replied. "Lose the soul patch."

"Thank god!" Christopher exclaimed, as if it was a long-fought battle and the victory was finally his.

# Ex-Boyfriend #12

Connor phoned me as I was crossing the bridge.

"Where are ya?" he said with a rough edge.

I told him.

"Where are ya headed?"

"I thought I'd drop by the bar and surprise you."

"It's not a surprise if ya do it almost every day."

"Well, would you like a different kind of surprise?" I said, not liking the tone in his voice.

"For instance?"

"Me changing the locks on my apartment," I suggested.

"Don't you sass me after the day I've had," Connor said, and for some reason I could pinpoint the exact source of his agitation.

"Did my mother happen to drop by the bar today?"

"She *certainly* did," Connor replied. "And you, young lady, have some explaining to do."

An hour and a half later, and forty-five minutes into the explaining, the conversation hadn't taken any turns, for better or for worse.

"Let me get this straight," Connor said. "You will be dating other men while you're seeing me, but I'm not allowed to see other women."

"You've got the basic idea down," I said, "but somehow when you say it, it sounds unreasonable."

"It is unreasonable!" Connor shouted.

I should mention that since it was still early in the evening, Connor was the only bartender on shift and so our conversation was pretty much free entertainment for the regulars, primarily Clarence.

"But they're not real dates," I calmly replied. "I don't want to go on them either. But if I go, I think she'll leave us alone for a while. At least that's what she promised."[1]

"She didn't leave me alone today," he said.

Excellent point, but I didn't mention that.

1. A lie, I know. But I wasn't in the mood to tell Connor about Prom Night 1994.

"Well, she thought if she broke the news to you, she could put a slant on things that would interfere with our relationship."

"I think you dating other men will interfere with our relationship as it is."

"Why can't I get it through your thick skull? They're fake dates. I'm going out with lawyers to improve *our* relationship."

"Why is it that half o' what you say doesn't make a damn bit o' sense?"

"Not half," I replied. "Crunch your numbers again."

"You're right," Connor replied. "More like 60 percent."

"Better than a lot of people in this city," I replied.

"But worse than most."

A long silence followed. I was afraid that Connor would see this last bit in a string of family interventions as his final breaking point. I had to figure out the best way to phrase things.

"Why don't you look at it this way?" I suggested. "For a half hour, twice a month, I'll be having coffee or some other kind of beverage with other men. I should point out that I meet with male clients all the time and we drink things together. And rarely do we end up having sex. *Rarely.*"

Connor didn't respond, but he did this

head-nod, which meant that the fight was out of him. I leaned across the bar and kissed Connor on the cheek.

"You're the best Irish boyfriend I've ever had."

"That's not funny anymore," Connor replied, trying to fight off a smile.

Then my phone conveniently rang.

It was Maggie.

"Hi, Isabel. I need a Rae extraction."

# RAE'S OBSESSION

Twenty minutes later I was at Maggie's modest office near the Bryant Street courthouse, observing a standoff.

"I would like to go home for the day," Maggie said. "Rae would not. And apparently she is accustomed to winning these kinds of simple debates."

Maggie and I stood in the doorway of the file room. Rae had made a desk of the floor and encircled herself with a mass of thick, yellow files. Her attention was so wrapped up in the cases she was studying that my shouting her name elicited only a "Shhhh."

I flicked off the light switch.

"Hey!"

Rae got to her feet and flicked it back on. I flicked it off. She flicked it on again.

Back and forth until Rae said, "What are you doing here?"

"I was called for an extraction," I said.

"I have *work* to do," Rae replied. "Real

work. Serious work. People's lives are at stake here."

"You also have *home*work and Maggie would like to leave for the day."

"All things insignificant compared to this," Rae said, sweeping her hand across the assemblage on the floor.

Maggie tried to reason with her. "Rae, you'll come back on Wednesday and pick up where you left off."

Rae simply ignored her "employer" and returned her attention to one of the files.

"Where's the circuit breaker?" I asked.

Maggie led me into the break room and I flicked off the file room lights. When we returned to the file room Rae had found a flashlight and was continuing her work under its glow.

Maggie is about five foot seven and a hundred and twenty-five pounds. I'm five-eight and more than that.[1] Rae is approximately five foot two and around ninety-five pounds. Suffice it to say, Maggie and I had enough manpower, so to speak, to physically remove her.

After a very brief consultation, we decided that it was the only way.

"I'll take her head. You take her feet.

1. None of your business!

63

Watch out," I said. "She's a kicker."

Fifteen minutes later, in the car on the way back to the Spellman house, Rae was deep into her tirade about the abuses in the criminal justice system.

"False confessions are way, way more common than you think. I'm pretty sure I wouldn't confess to a crime I didn't commit, but you never know. Like, if somebody didn't let me pee for hours and hours, I think at some point I'd crack," she said.

"I'd like to see an appeal on a conviction based on no bathroom breaks," I said.

"It's not just that," Rae replied. "There are so many ways a person can be wrongfully incarcerated: biased police lineups, coerced confessions, bad forensics, misuse of informants — the list goes on, and I'm not even thinking about police corruption, like planting evidence and stuff. Which I won't mention in front of Dad because he'll get all mad, but it happens.

"So, anyway, Maggie shows me the files she has. These are all guys in prison who say they are innocent. She can only work on one pro bono case at a time and she told me to review the files and pick the three most likely candidates. How am I supposed to decide something that important? How? Do you realize that I am holding a man's fate in my hands?"

"Rae, do me a favor: Try not to let your 'volunteer'[2] work turn you into a narcissist."

I pulled up in front of the Spellman house.

"Why are we here?" Rae asked.

"Because this is your home and it's where you eat most of your meals and where you tend to sleep."

"No!" Rae said, shaking her head, annoyed. "I was supposed to go to Henry's house after Maggie's."

"Why?"

"The SATs are in two weeks and he's helping me study."

"Have Mom or Dad drive you," I said, unlocking the door.

"Do you see either of their cars in the driveway?" Rae asked.

She was right. Mom and Dad were out doing . . . I really don't know what they do when I'm not around.

"Where are they?"

"They have a yoga class on Monday evening. Then they go to a vegetarian restaurant afterward."

"When the house starts smelling like

2. Finger quotes are hard to do while driving, but I felt they were necessary.

patchouli, you let me know right away," I said.

"Sure thing," Rae replied. "Now, how about that ride to Henry's?"

Henry's apartment isn't that far from my place, so I agreed. However, I took the opportunity to bring up an issue that had been on my mind.

"You have money, Rae," I pointed out.

"Yes. Do you need a loan?"

"No, but I think you should use some of that money to buy a used car since you are so opposed to public transportation."

"I don't want to use my own money on that," Rae said. "I think eventually someone will buy me one."

I pulled up in front of Henry's house.

"It's been fun catching up," I said. "Let's do it again in six months."

"Aren't you coming inside?" Rae asked.

"Nope."

"You should come inside," Rae said. "I think Henry has some information for you."

"What kind of information?" I asked suspiciously.

"Something about Rick Harkey," Rae said as she got out of the car.

I took the bait, just like a dumb fish.

# The Trouble with Henry

Clearly my appearance in Stone's home had been orchestrated, but the players were so casual about the fact that I didn't see any point in drawing conflict from this particular event.

"I'm starving," Rae said as she entered his apartment and carefully hung her coat on the rack.

"I ordered pizza," Henry replied.

The previous statement, coming from almost any non-lactose-intolerant human, would not come off as borderline insane, but Henry is more than something of a health nut and in the three years I have known him, I have not heard him utter those three magical words.

"What's going on here?" I asked, my eyes shifting around the room for evidence of something seriously amiss, like bandits hiding in the back room.

Rae followed my line of thinking and

explained, "It's not what you think, Izzy. Whole-wheat crust, and he orders it with broccoli and spinach. And he makes you eat a salad on top of that. Feel better?"

"Yes," I replied, and then turned to Henry.

"I hear you have some information for me."

"Have a seat," Henry said. "I'll get you a beer."

"I was just hoping for the information."

"Why don't you stay for dinner?"

"I have plans."

"Your boyfriend works nights and your best friend is in Florida and probably in bed by now. What kind of plans?" Henry asked, sounding nice and all, but it was too pushy to be really nice.

Maybe he didn't want to spend a full evening with Rae and needed to be sure an adult was around for an extraction later. I could sympathize, and since I was in fact hungry and wouldn't mind some pizza, even if it did have broccoli on it, I sat down on the couch, conceding some kind of defeat.

Henry served me a beer, which eased the pain.

The SAT practice began shortly after that, which increased the pain. I asked if I could watch television, but my question was met with glares, so I turned to Henry's bookshelf and picked up a volume that I hadn't seen before in his collection: *The Complete Adventures of Sherlock Holmes.*

Henry noted the selection I'd chosen from the shelf.

"I got it for Rae, but she refuses to read it."

"That book is so prehistoric," Rae said.

"It's a classic," he said.

"That's what prehistoric people say about prehistoric things."

" 'Atavistic,' " Henry said, changing the subject. "Definition and use it in a sentence."

I opted to focus on the words on the page rather than the ones floating around the room punctuated by random bickering. It had been years since I had read anything by Doyle, but while turning those pages, a flood of memories washed over me. When I was thirteen my father foisted the Sherlock Holmes canon on me with a relentless zeal. I rejected it at every turn, merely because it was suggested by an adult. Sometime later, I was grounded and all forms of entertainment were removed from my bedroom. During one of my food-delivery windows (steamed broccoli and brown rice) my father included an old paperback of *The Complete Adventures of Sherlock Holmes.* I spent the first few hours of my house arrest making artwork out of my dinner and trying to plot my escape (all exit routes were carefully contained). But eventually — twelve hours in — I turned to Sherlock Holmes. It was the first time in my life I'd found comfort in a book. Only, as further punishment, my father had removed the final pages of each adventure. So I read the Incomplete *Complete Adventures of Sherlock Holmes* and by the end of the night, I thought I would go mad. When my father finally released me, I rode my bike straight to the San Francisco Public Library to have the endings fully realized. My mother thought this marked a promising literary turn in my adolescence. Sadly for her, that trip was the last voluntary library visit of my teenage years.

As I returned to those pages, I felt a certain comfort in knowing that I was holding an unmutilated book, one that wouldn't deprive me of resolution. I was lost in the last pages of "The Adventure of the Blue Carbuncle," in which Holmes searches for the origin of a goose that was sold containing a valuable stone in its craw. (There's obviously more to the plot, but I don't want to ruin it for you.) I always thought of it as a Christmas story for curmudgeons. Nothing too feel-good about, but I liked how Holmes didn't turn the perp in at the end. Maybe that's the crux of my affection for the fictional detective: his sense of justice wasn't absolute, his codes were flexible, and while that flexibility wouldn't work within police forces in the real world, I tended to agree with Holmes's moral judgments. He made sense to me, that's all. Although even *I* think he took way too many drugs.

I shelved the book and dinner was served. Now it was time to get what I came for.

"I've been patient enough," I said. "What have you got on Harkey?"

"He has a lot of insurance clients. Did you know that?"

"You better start singing some real songs or I'm taking this pizza to go."

"Do you know how he gets them?" Henry asked.

"I know! I know!" Rae said, raising her hand as if we were in English class.

I turned to my sister. "*You* tell me. Your answer sounds more interesting."

"*Schmoozing,*" Rae said, giving the word more length and significance than I thought it had.

"That's how we get a lot of our clients, too," I said.

*"No, we don't,"* Rae replied defensively.

"Yes, we do."

*"No, we don't."*

"What do you think 'schmoozing' means?" I asked.

"Don't you know?" Rae said, lowering her volume and staring at me like I needed a special ed class.

Henry, also closely following the conversation, appeared confused as well.

"Define 'schmoozing,' " Henry said.

Rae rolled her eyes and replied, " 'To chat informally or be ingratiating toward somebody.' But it's code for taking clients to strip clubs and buying them hookers."

"Huh?" Henry and I said in unison.

"Dad told me all about how Harkey got his insurance clients when I was asking Dad why we didn't have more insurance clients."[1]

Henry and I didn't argue the semantics; I was more troubled by the fact that Henry thought this code-word "schmoozing" was the kind of legitimate information that was worthy of my time.

I turned to Henry, growing annoyed. "That's all you got for me? Schmoozing?"

1. Heads of insurance companies, please don't assume I'm implying anything about you as a group.

"Why can't Dad just go to a strip club if it means more high-paying clients?" Rae asked. "Or Mom, for that matter?"

"Shut up, Ms. Work-for-Free," I replied.

While I was waiting for Henry's response, Rae extracted the broccoli from her pizza with medical precision.

"Put it back on and eat it," Henry said like a drill sergeant.

"I'm here for information, not pizza and conversation," I interrupted.

"If I weren't sitting at the ADD table, you would have the information already."

"You have the floor," I said. Then I turned to my own slice of pizza and stripped it of all vegetation. The act was less in protest of broccoli and more for the guilty pleasure of irking Stone. And based on his sharp gaze away from my plate, the irking was happening.

I had a sinking feeling that Stone was going to provide me with knowledge that was already on my radar. A large portion of Harkey's business is insurance investigation. That I know. I also know that insurance cases are easily corruptible from almost any angle you look at them. First there's the individual filing the claim, then the investigator investigating the claim and also the physician or insurance adjuster involved in assessing the damage, and last but not least, the lawyer taking the case. Each part of the system can find a way to rig it to his or her advantage. However, it would take hours of off-the-books surveillance for me to prove that Harkey was faking surveillance reports (which would be how a PI could corrupt the system). This was the kind of case that needed an inside man.

Unfortunately, I blew that chance last year when I went to work for Harkey part-time to access information on another case. It was then that I got evidence of Harkey's corruptibility — recording conversations, a violation of California Penal Code §631(a). However, since I stole the recordings from his office, I was hardly in a position to mete out any form of justice. Now I had to find another way. Hence my two-hour wait for Henry's shred of information.

"Harkey does worker's comp investigations," Henry began.

I interrupted: "Don't tell me I sat through an hour of SAT prep and a garden pizza for that."

"Zip it. There's more," he said, at his wit's end. "Harkey's brother-in-law Darren Hurtt is a worker's comp physician who has been investigated for fraud, but nothing could be proven. He and Harkey are never seen in public together, but they could have a deal going on. If you could show the link, show Harkey's team surveilling a claimant, and then show that same claimant entering Darren Hurtt's office, you might have something there. Although, I do think I should mention that any investigation on Harkey would be extremely time-consuming and maybe unwise. But if you're looking for an angle, it's better than just sitting outside his office all day waiting for one to turn up."

"I did that once, Henry. Just once."

A horn honked outside. Rae cleared her plate from the table, scraped it in the sink, and stuck it in the dishwasher. Henry had apparently taught her well. She turned to her BFF and said, "That's my ride."

As Rae left, she punched Henry in the arm, thanked him for dinner, and said she would see him soon.

Henry replied, "Give me at least forty-eight hours."

"We'll see," Rae said as she slipped through the door. "Bye, Izzy."

After Rae departed, I quickly got to my feet, didn't bother clearing my own plate, and took my coat from the rack.

"Where are you going?" Henry asked.

"I'm outta here," I said. "The only reason I stayed this long was I thought she'd need a ride home."

"That's the only reason you stayed? I thought we were friends now."

"That's your opinion, not mine," I said, making my way to the front door.

"There's only one logical reason why you would be unable to remain my friend," Henry said while blocking my exit through the front door.

"What's that?" I smugly replied.

"You're in love with me and can't bear the thought that I don't reciprocate your feelings."

"I would smack you right now if I didn't think the act would confirm your delusional diagnosis."

"Thank you for not hitting me."

"You're welcome. Please step away from the door."

"Unless you still have feelings for me, logically it follows that we are still friends."

Tossing in the word "logically" must have confused me, or at least slid a confused expression on my face, since Henry elaborated on his logical theory.

"We were friends before. Do you deny that?"

"No," I quietly conceded.

"Did I do something wrong? Did I betray you in any way?" he asked.

"No."

"Is there anything else I did that was so awful that it would prevent our remaining friends?"

There was that unreturned kiss that torched my ego, but of course I didn't mention that. "No."

"Then we're friends," Henry said in an authoritarian tone. "Got it?"

"Got it," I replied. But Henry was still blocking the door. "Friends let friends leave when they want to," I explained.

Henry moved from the door. I was halfway out when I realized that Henry had another piece of information I could use.

"Since we're friends," I said, "and friends give up dirt on other friends, who honked the horn that sent Rae running?"

"Rae's got a new boyfriend. Logan Engle."

"Blech. I hate that name," I said.

"So do I," Henry replied.

And then I finally made my escape.

# RULE #26

Back at headquarters, two weeks after the unfortunate camping trip, my mother watched me as I seconded Rae's veto of Dad's "family book club" rule (Rule #25).

"I'd use discretion with those, if I were you," said Mom. "You only have five total and you're already three down."

"There's no way I'm getting trapped in mandatory yoga [Rule #23 — vetoed], lunchtime power walks [Rule #24 — vetoed], and now a family book club. I'd rather just take out the trash every week."

"Can you do me a personal favor and agree to something your dad suggests? He's starting to get miffed that everyone's nixing his ideas."

"If he comes up with something reasonable, I'll consider it," I replied.

"Thank you," she said.

Then, as if to provide a punitive incentive for future agreeability, my mother planted another rule on the board.

## RULE #26 — ISABEL WEARS A DRESS
## TO WORK ONCE A WEEK

"Huh?" I said, squinting at the board. Then I got to my feet and vetoed the rule.

My mom turned to me and smiled smugly.

"Remember," she said. "You need two vetoes. The odds of finding someone to waste a veto on a rule that only affects you are slim."

"I'd scale back on the bullying, Mom. One day, it might come back to haunt you."

"Are you threatening me?" Mom asked, bemused.

"Whatever you want to call it," I replied.

"How adorable."

Work silence followed (we do indeed do some work along with the interpersonal war games). Mom returned to her billing input and I ran a series of background checks on employee applicants for our main corporate employer, Zylor Corp.

Then the phone rang. My mother looked at the clock and said, "It's for you."

I eyed her suspiciously but picked up the phone.

"Hello?"

"Hi, Isabel, It's Gerard . . . Mitchell."

"Oh, hi."

Gerard was the client who saw me in my underwear the other day. Remember? Well, I do. He's a lawyer with McClatchy and Spring. My dad has done work with their firm for years now and has always been their primary liaison.

"What can I do for you?" I asked.

"Can you meet me for a drink later this week?"

"I guess so. Do you want my dad to come?"

"No. I don't think so."

"Is everything all right?"

"Why wouldn't it be?"

"Well, normally you meet with my dad."

"Oh, right."

Silence.

"This isn't that kind of drink," Gerard said.

"What kind of drink is it?"

"The more social kind."

"Huh," I replied.

"It's my understanding you have a quota to fill. You already know me and I'm fairly harmless. What do you say?"

Long, awkward silence followed while I glared at my mother and she smiled back with cheery delight.

"Isabel, are you there?" Gerard said.

"Yes," I said, responding only to the most recent question but inadvertently agreeing to the date.

"Great. Thursday. Eight P.M. Top of the Mark."

"How about a more low-key place?"

Gerard cleared his throat. "I'm sorry," he replied. "The site has been predetermined."

"Unbelievable," I said. "I hope she's giving you a hell of a discount."

"She is."

Knowing I had no other options, I reluctantly replied, "See you Thursday."

I turned to my mother to engage her in some kind of bitter stare-off, but she refused to meet my gaze.

"We had an understanding," she said, staring at her computer screen. "I'm merely facilitating."

"I get it. But why does it feel like you're always facilitating more with me than with your other children?" I asked.

Then my mother looked up and smiled wickedly.

"Not true. There's a big blonde whom I saw leaving your brother's house last Wednesday at four P.M. sharp. I'd love to know who she is, and based on my track record of accusing your brother of certain things,[1] I'm uncomfortable looking into this matter on my own. Can I interest you in a reciprocal negotiation?"

"What's your offer?" I asked.

"In the future, you can choose half of the lawyer dates on your own — all the even-numbered ones. In fact, any professional will do. I'm feeling generous. Of course I will need some evidence that the date has taken place, but I'm sure we can work something out."

"And what exactly do you want from me?"

"Just tell me who that big blonde is. And if she's cause for concern, take care of the situation, if you know what I mean.[2] I like Maggie. I want her sticking around."

"Don't we all?"

---

1. Namely adultery, when he was married to Petra.
2. Actually, I didn't. But I thought it best not to ask.

# Stakeout #1

Henry's information practically begged me to take a closer look at Dr. Darren Hurtt, brother-in-law of Rick Harkey. For three hours the following Monday morning, I sat in the foyer of a three-story office building, which also housed a dentist, a lawyer, a gastroenterologist, some kind of low-rent advertising company, and one general practitioner — Hurtt. I mentally tagged any individual who pressed the elevator button to the third floor and when that same person departed fifteen to twenty minutes later, I phoned my accomplice.

**Me:** Subject is exiting the building now.
**Accomplice:** He sure doesn't look injured.
**Me:** There's also an advertising agency and a charitable operation on the third floor. His health might be impeccable.
**Accomplice:** Can't you park yourself on the third floor?

**Me:** No. There's no place to sit.

**Accomplice:** Can't you pretend you're lost?

**Me:** I can't pretend to be lost for three hours in a twenty-foot-long hallway without being made.

**Accomplice:** How are we spending quality time together if I'm in the car and you're a hundred yards away?

**Me:** It's a shared activity.

**Accomplice:** A boring activity at that.

**Me:** I told you that surveillance is mostly sitting around waiting for people to do something. How did you think that would be exciting?

**Accomplice:** I tot we'd both be sitting in the car tegeter makin' out.

**Me:** Oh, I see.

**Accomplice:** Tat's not gonna happen, is it?

**Me:** Not right now. Sorry.

I suppose now would be as good a time as any to reveal the identity of my accomplice: Connor O'Sullivan, Ex-boyfriend #12. His odd work hours and my relatively normal ones made quality time outside of a bar virtually impossible. I had hoped this job would bring us together, but most surveillance neophytes can't hack the monotony of the work.

While Connor crunched on the snack

food I left in the car, a man in a neck brace entered the building. His pain was our gain. Spirits improved considerably at this vision of a possible lead.

**Connor:** This bloke sure looks like a Dr. Hurtt patient to me. What an unfortunate name for a doctor.

Two hours and only two more obviously injured subjects later, Connor and I called it quits, mostly because Connor said if I didn't agree to quit, he would take off without me. We did, however, make out for fifteen minutes, while sort of pretending to be still on the job, although during that time no further leads were spotted. Probably because we weren't really looking.

I dropped Connor off at the bar and headed to the apartment, where I donned a navy-blue wraparound dress purchased by my mother (in honor of Rule #26) and a full-length overcoat, because in my experience wrap-around dresses don't stay wrapped around in the San Francisco wind. Then I drove to Mr. Winslow's home to see how his new domestic help was working out.

I pressed the doorbell, which sent chimes throughout the house. Within twenty seconds the massive oak door gracefully opened and I was greeted by a fopped-out, clean-shaven Len Williams in a gray three-piece suit topped off with a cravat.

"Ms. Spellman, I presume," Len said with a posh British accent.

The new incarnation of Len was an assault on all my senses. "I should have had a drink before I came over here."

"Follow me, miss."

Len, not breaking character for a moment, escorted me into the drawing room.[1]

"Mr. Winslow will be down shortly."

I stared at my transformed friend and swallowed hard. I'm sure my face was turning red from the internal struggle to stifle my laughter.

"Can I get anything for you, Ms. Spellman?" Len said, remaining utterly and disturbingly professional.

"A sedative, maybe."

I exhaled, dropped to the couch, and stared at the pattern on what I can only assume was an oriental rug that could have paid my college tuition if, say, I went to college.

"I think chamomile tea is in order," Len

---

1. Yes. That's what they call it. It's just like any other kind of room where you can sit and stuff.

deadpanned.

I turned to him, checked for witnesses, and said, "You need to stay out of the room while I meet with Mr. Winslow. I can barely look at you," I said.

"Whatever you wish, Ms. Spellman."

"I'll call you tonight for a report," I whispered.

Len nodded his head once and exited.

Mr. Winslow entered the room five minutes later, exactly the amount of time it took me to move beyond my urge to double over in a fit of hysterical laughter. I got to my feet and shook Mr. Winslow's hand. His appearance, his mood, and the placement of his glasses had improved since our meeting a week back.

"Ms. Spellman, a pleasure as always. Please sit down," he said, waving me into the nearest seat.

"How is everything working out?" I asked.

"Mr. Leonard is a godsend," Winslow replied.

I coughed to get over the shock of hearing Len referred to as Mr. Leonard. It had a nice ring to it. I decided I would call my friend "Mr. Leonard" for the rest of his days or as long as my joke endurance lasted.

Mr. Leonard, whose posture had improved considerably in the past week, entered the room with a quiet knock and put a plate of cookies and tea on the table.

I immediately ate a cookie, mostly out of curiosity. It was good and tasted like it had been baked this year.

"This one has such an appetite," Mr. Winslow said to Mr. Leonard.

"Indeed," Mr. Leonard replied.

The discussion of my appetite squashed it, so I drank the tea that Mr. Leonard served.

"Will that be all?" Mr. Leonard said to his other boss.[2]

"Yes. Thank you," Mr. Winslow replied graciously.

I could bore you with the details of the perfectly brewed tea and the polite conversation that accompanied it, but suffice it to say Mr. Winslow believed Mr. Leonard was a benefit to his home and his welfare. I asked my host if he had any particular employees of which he was in doubt and he said that was not the sort of thing he kept track of. Mason was far more vigilant in that regard and kept the details to himself to avoid upsetting Mr. Winslow. I asked for

2. Let us not forget that this is an undercover operation and the employment hierarchy should reflect that.

Mason's current contact information, but my client was at a loss for how he would even begin to find it. He did say that he'd received some "letters on the computer"[3] since his departure and he would try to locate them at his earliest convenience.

I drank my tea, ate one more cookie when Winslow wasn't looking, and departed, catching one final glimpse of my friend Mr. Leonard, who said, "Until next time, Ms. Spellman."

## NEXT TIME

After twelve hours of his undercover butlering, I phoned Mr. Leonard for his report. He refused to shake the accent, which I assumed he did to annoy either me or Christopher, but later I would learn otherwise. Anyway, for the proper effect you should imagine this conversation between me and Sir John Gielgud in *Arthur*.

**Mr. Leonard:** Good evening, Ms. Isabel.
**Me:** You can lose the accent now.
**Mr. Leonard:** I'd rather not. I prefer the Method approach.

3. E-mails. Mr. Winslow had an account, but typically a member of his staff would access his e-mail and print the correspondences.

**Me:** Great. What have you got for me, Mr. Leonard?

**Mr. Leonard:** I can tell you that the house was a complete disaster until I got there. That Mason Graves was thoroughly disorganized and had absolutely no idea how to keep his employer looking respectable. Until I arrived, Mr. Winslow dressed himself like a blind man tossed into a closet of clothes that might have been appropriate in the sixties. It was shameful.

**Me:** Do you have any opinions on anything beyond Winslow's closet?

**Mr. Leonard:** For instance?

**Me:** What do you make of the rest of the staff?

**Mr. Leonard:** I believe the driver is doing a fine job. At least he keeps the cars in order and seems to obey the laws of traffic. I have not taken to Mrs. Enright, the head housekeeper, I have to admit. But how can you like someone who clearly despises you? I haven't been loathed with that kind of passion since I stole the part of Sam in Athol Fugard's *Master Harold . . . and the Boys* from Derek Miller.

**Me:** You know that reference was totally lost on me.

**Mr. Leonard:** Yes, I do. You need more culture.

**Me:** Do me a favor and make sure Mr. Winslow finds those e-mails that Graves sent him. Also, find out who his lawyer is. I'm curious about the state of his will.

**Mr. Leonard:** I will take care of these matters promptly.

**Me:** Is there anyone in the house that you find suspicious?

**Mr. Leonard:** Not yet. I suspect everyone was afraid of Mason. At least that seems to be the case since I can barely get any of the staff to talk to me and whenever I enter a room, all conversations are hushed and the parties hustle back to work.

**Me:** Why is that?

**Mr. Leonard:** I don't know. It's simply the roles that have been established. But they fear me. I'm like the evil foreman on a construction site or something.

**Me:** Well, don't let all that power go to your head.

**Len:**[4] Speaking of fear, did you tell Mr. Winslow I was a brother?

**Me:** Um, I don't think it came up. Why?

**Len:** Well, when I first met him in the driveway of the estate, he reached for his wallet as if he were going to hand it over.

**Me:** That must have been awkward.

4. Sorry, it's really just easier to type "Len."

**Len:** We laugh about it now. I'll be in touch, Ms. Spellman.

# MANDATORY
## LAWYER DATE #1

After hours of brainstorming, my mother and I could find no other way to verify my lawyer dates (and confirm that I was not deliberately sabotaging them) other than through digital recordings. Unfortunately, this is against the law in California (unless both parties consent, and that would be hard to explain on any first date), and so once my mother listened to the tape and verified that a date in fact occurred, we would destroy the evidence. My point is, don't tell anyone about this. It's illegal, but it's not like I'm going to use the recordings in a legal proceeding; I'm simply complying with the intractable demands of my mother. Not that meeting these demands precluded subterfuge. Oh no, there would be subterfuge, all right.

The purpose of the recordings was to prove that the "dates" had the feel of dates — the uncomfortable, bio-swapping, dead-silent, ice-clinking, dread-filled feel of a date. As far as I could tell, I only had to be myself to bring about all that and more.

Since my first mandatory date was with a known entity — a valued client who had spent enough time with my parents to know that a few tools in their shed needed replacement, and one who was getting a discount for his troubles — he was a soft target. The others, I should mention now, were a trickier bunch.

After the initial pleasantries (if you don't know what pleasantries are — I didn't for years — they're the "Hello, how are you doing," ordering-drinks part of the introductions), I pulled the tape recorder from my pocket and showed it to Gerard.

"I need to record this for proof," I said.

"Seriously?" Gerard replied.

"She needs evidence. Otherwise she'll accuse me of deliberate sabotage or bribery."

"Bribery?"

"You know, like I offer you twenty bucks or an extra 10 percent off future work if you just tell my mother that we had drinks and a few laughs, but I'm not the girl for you, which is what you're going to tell her anyway."

"I'm confused, Isabel."

"Cards on the table, Gerard."

"Oh, good."

"I have a boyfriend. My mother loathes him. If I date two lawyers a month, she leaves him alone."[1]

"If you don't?"

"She calls the INS, the IRS, any governmental organization with three letters, and then, if that doesn't work, she drops by the bar —"

"The bar?"

"He's a bartender."

"I see."

"She drops by his bar with empty threats, which don't seem empty to people who are not well acquainted with her."

"I guess I should be glad she works for me," Gerard said, appearing mildly stunned and a little bit tired.

Gerard drained his martini; I turned on the digital recorder once I got his nod of approval.

[Partial transcript reads as follows:]

**Isabel:** So, Gerard, tell me about yourself.
**Gerard:** What do you want to know?
**Isabel:** Tell me everything. I want to know

1. No, not the real reason; but if I didn't tell Connor about Prom Night 1994, I'm certainly not going to tell Gerard.

everything there is to know about you.

**Gerard:** Waiter, can I get another drink?

**Waiter:** Ma'am, would you like another?

**Isabel:** Yes, and make that the last time you call me "ma'am."

*[Long pause.]*

**Isabel:** Go on, Gerard. Tell me your life story.

**Gerard:** Two parents. One sister. Primary school. College. Law school. Lawyer. Married. No children. Divorced. Still lawyer.

**Isabel:** Wow. That was succinct.

**Gerard:** I've always admired brevity.

**Isabel:** Me too. Except when I have fifteen minutes of tape to fill.

**Gerard:** Isabel, I'm a lawyer, not an actor.

**Isabel:** If you want that discount my mom offered you, you better become one really fast.

*[End of tape.]*

In the end, after four martinis and two more hours of rehearsal time, Gerard finally stepped up and played the part of a drunk lawyer on an uncomfortable first date.

When I played the evidence for my mother, she furrowed her brow with concern and said, "What did you do to him, Isabel? He sounds drunk and . . . depressed."

"Yes," I replied. "I don't think there will

be a second date."

According to script, Gerard called my mother the next day and said, "We had some drinks, some laughs, but I don't think we're a good match."

As usual, my mother needed more information.

"Why not?"

"Your daughter scares me."

Mom gave Gerard her secret hangover cure and got off the phone.

"Isabel, you better get on board with this."

"I did what you asked," I replied.

"Do it better."

"Why?"

"Because Connor is not the man for you, and I would like you to get out more to see that."

"Mom, I'm thirty-two years old. How is this any of your business?"

"I'm your mother and I have a stake in your happiness. I also have *very, very* serious dirt on you. This is how I want to leverage it."

"You scare me," I said.

"And I love you," Mom replied.

# David's New Friend/
# My New Client

To remain marginally in my mother's good graces and spare Connor an impromptu visit, I decided to investigate what David was doing with all of his free time.

David's mystery woman was indeed blond, curvy, and unnaturally tall — attractive in the vein of a 1940s movie star. Her hips tested the limits of her A-line skirt and the buttons on her blouse were on the borderline of tasteful. Her hair stretched down to her waist in waves — the kind that nature stubbornly refuses to create. Our mystery woman must have spent hours on her appearance every morning.

I staked out my brother's house exactly one week after the day and time my mother had first spotted our blond Amazon. She exited his residence at roughly two P.M. There was no passionate embrace, but I did observe a warm hug that lingered longer than I thought appropriate. I was about to follow the mystery woman when my dad phoned from the office.

"Where are you?" he asked.

"In the Tenderloin, stocking up on a few rocks[1] so I don't have to drive back later," I replied.

I think it's important that the parents of a thiry-two-year-old daughter should not expect to know her whereabouts at all hours of the day.

"When you're done scoring crack, can you please come into the office? You have a three thirty appointment with a new client."

"How come I didn't know about it?"

"Because the call came in on the same day as Rule #22[2] and your mother just put it on your calendar without mentioning it."

"Oh, I should start checking that more."

"I agree."

"Okay, I'll see you in a few minutes. I need to get high first."

My plan to tail the big blonde was foiled and instead I picked up my drugs (coffee) and headed back to Spellman headquarters to have an utterly painful meeting with Jeremy Pratt — screenwriter, filmmaker,

1. Crack cocaine is sold in different sizes of "rocks."
2. "No speaking today!"

painter, video artist, guitarist, freelance reviewer, and Francophile.[3] I didn't ask Jeremy whether his enthusiasm for France extended to speaking the language, mostly because Jeremy was really good at elaborating without any encouragement.

Before I launch into a hearty complaint about my new client, I'd like to file an official one regarding my mother. At Spellman Investigations, like many police departments, the investigator who answers the call has officially "caught" the case. My mother answered Jeremy's call and made an executive decision, based on Jeremy's age and my mother's ability to convince my father to agree with her on almost any subject under the sun, that I should take the case since such a "youthful" client would respond better to a younger investigator.

I entered through the office window in case the client was already waiting in the foyer. I wanted at least the preliminary information from my mother before my first meeting with Jeremy began. Mom made it sound so simple and easy and maybe even fun. But she's evil that way.

Jeremy, as Mom explained, is an amateur screenwriter who used to work with a writ-

3. All on his business card.

ing partner named Shana Breslin. They parted ways over artistic differences and couldn't come to any official custody agreement on the script, and so their contentious collaboration was doomed to fall into the gaping abyss of unproduced screenplays. Or so it seemed, until Jeremy heard rumblings about meetings in Los Angeles and Shana landing an agent. I first asked my mother the obvious question:

"How is an unemployed screenwriter going to pay our fee?"

"He lives off a monthly stipend provided by his well-to-do parents."

"No regular job?" I asked.

"No," my mother replied.

"Not even at a coffee shop?"

"No."

"I hate him already."

"I know," Mom said, smiling wickedly. "Me too!"

I cleared my desk and told my mother to make herself disappear. The layout of the Spellman offices (I should really use the singular form — it's one large room) prevents private client meetings unless the room is vacated by other employees. Mom slipped into the basement, where we hide one desk, a paper shredder, and a DVD player. The room is dark, damp, and depressing; we keep our visits down there to a minimum. When I was a kid, that's where all my punishment hearings were held. But I digress. Back to my new nemesis,[4] Jeremy Pratt.

## THE SNOWBALL EFFECT

I estimated Jeremy's age to be somewhere between twenty-four and twenty-five. He liked to layer his clothes as if a blizzard or a heat wave could attack at any moment. I never saw the very bottom layer, but there was a button-down thrift-store shirt under a blue Adidas warm-up jacket under a brown, orange, and yellow-striped ski jacket that his dad probably wore in the seventies. I offered to take his most outer layer, but that's where he kept his paperwork, so he slung it over the back of his chair and pulled out some pages folded in quarters, unfolded them, and flattened them on top of my desk.

"Before we begin," Jeremy said, "I need you to sign something."

He then unzipped his Adidas warm-up jacket and pulled a gel pen from the breast pocket of his button-down shirt and readied

4. I suppose one should not label someone a nemesis before proper introductions are made, but turns out I was right.

it for me to sign, as if he were some kind of hipster real estate agent and we were closing a deal.

"What am I signing?" I asked.

"I cannot discuss any of my artistic endeavors unless you sign a nondisclosure agreement."

"What is the purpose of this?"

"To make sure that you don't a) steal my screenplay idea or b) discuss it with someone who might steal my idea. I'm afraid we can't continue this meeting unless you sign."

I snatched the pen in a split second.

"No problem," I replied. "I have no show business aspirations."

I did, however, read the contract — fine print and all — just to make sure that I was signing away my rights to his script and not, say, my liver.[5]

I signed and then decided, based on my client's ridiculous dress and even more ridiculous paranoid contract, that this conversation needed to go on record.

"Do you mind if I record this meeting?" I asked. "I'm afraid my penmanship makes note-taking a rather useless endeavor."

5. In the event of my untimely death, I'm happy to donate any or all of my organs, but you might want to take a pass on my liver.

"Uh . . . okay," Pratt replied with mild discomfort.

"Don't worry. I'll burn the tapes when the case is closed."[6]

As for the conversation that followed, I'm only going to play you the best part:

[Partial transcript reads as follows:]

**Jeremy:** Before I tell you anything else, you need to know about the project.
*[Jeremy pulls out a set of notes.]*
**Jeremy:** It's called *The Snowball Effect.*
**Isabel:** I like it.
**Jeremy:** There's this snowball that gets tossed from neighbor to neighbor in a small ski town in Colorado.
**Isabel:** Like in a snowball fight?
**Jeremy:** Yes. Exactly. So, like, the fight goes for like three months.
**Isabel:** Nonstop?
**Jeremy:** They take breaks.
**Isabel:** To sleep and stuff?
**Jeremy:** And they have jobs.
**Isabel:** Doesn't the snowball melt?
**Jeremy:** No.
**Isabel:** Never?
**Jeremy:** First of all, it's winter. But it's a

6. A figure of speech, of course. "Burn" sounds much more permanent than "delete."

magic snowball.

**Isabel:** You should lead with that.

**Jeremy:** Anyway, every time the snowball gets passed to the next person, it makes that person's wishes come true.

**Isabel:** All of them?

**Jeremy:** Just one.

**Isabel:** Okay, I get it.

**Jeremy:** I picture a Christmastime release. A total feel-good movie. Not my usual kind of thing, but you got to get your foot in the door somehow.

**Isabel:** Let me ask you a question. What if the snowball ends up in the hands of someone whose foremost wish is that her husband die in a freak accident?

*[Long pause.]*

**Jeremy:** I hadn't thought of that.

**Isabel:** Makes it more of a feel-bad movie.

**Jeremy:** Yeah. So right now I need to find out what Shana is doing with the script.

**Isabel:** Under the circumstances I'd recommend surveillance.

**Jeremy:** Can't you just look in her garbage?

**Isabel:** That would certainly be another angle I would suggest.

**Jeremy:** I think it's the only angle I can afford.

**Isabel:** I see.

**Jeremy:** If she's actively shopping the script,

she's probably still working on it to put her stamp everywhere, in case I try to dispute it with the Writers Guild. In that case, it'll end up in her recycling. She prints everything out. A total tree waster.

**Isabel:** So we'll start with a simple garbology and go from there.

**Jeremy:** Right on.

# Phone Call
## from the Edge #18

**Isabel:** Hi, Morty.

**Morty:** Hello, Izzele.

**Isabel:** How are you feeling today?

**Morty:** The air conditioner is on the fritz; how do you think I'm feeling?

**Isabel:** Warm?

**Morty:** I'm schvitzing like a three-hundred-pound marathon runner.

**Isabel:** Thanks for that image. Why don't you take a dip in the pool?

**Morty:** That's your answer for everything.

**Isabel:** It's only the second time I've said that to you.

**Morty:** Right. That's Gabe's[1] answer for everything.

**Isabel:** I think you should have an ice-cold beer.

1. Morty's grandson. Current boyfriend to my childhood best friend and brother's ex-wife, Petra Clark.

**Morty:** *That's* your answer for everything.

**Isabel:** What's new, Morty?

**Morty:** I had a tuna sandwich for lunch.

**Isabel:** Please, go on.

**Morty:** You talk. You and the Irish bartender still together?

**Isabel:** I talk to you once a week like clockwork and you ask me that every time.

**Morty:** I'll try to cut back to every other week.

**Isabel:** Thank you.

**Morty:** Got any interesting cases on your plate?

**Isabel:** Nothing that's got my full attention — although I spotted a rather handsome blonde leaving my brother's house in the middle of the day. It shows some promise.

**Morty:** Leave your poor brother alone. She could be the Avon lady for all you know.

**Isabel:** Only she was there a week earlier and I haven't noticed David wearing any makeup.

**Morty:** Hang on — that's my other line.
*[Sound of clicking.]*

**Morty:** Hello. Hello?

**Isabel:** It's still me, Morty.

**Morty:** This damn thing.
*[Sound of clicking. Long pause.]*

**Morty:** Izzele, I got to go. That was Ruthy. The air conditioner repair guy will be here in five minutes. I got to put some pants on. Talk to you later, bubbele.

# FREE SCHMIDT!

Rae phoned from Maggie's office while Maggie was at a dinner meeting. My sister begged me for a ride and said she was out of cash and couldn't take the bus and her boyfriend/driver was busy. I phoned David's cell to see if he could pick her up, but he said he was busy.

"Doing what?" I asked. "Maggie has a business meeting."

"I'll have a popcorn and a Coke," David replied.

"Are you at the movies?" I asked.

"I got to go, Izzy."

"What are you seeing?"

"Talk to you later," David replied, and hung up the phone.

Rather than trouble my parents, who I knew were working a surveillance together, I just drove the few miles to Maggie's office and accepted my fate.

Once again Rae was holed up in the file

room, reviewing case files of the potentially wrongly convicted. The contrast between the sloppy adolescent girl, all denim and unkempt dirty-blond hair, and the single-minded focus of a professional sifting through legal files made for a ridiculous sight. Rae lay flat on her back, her heels hooked on an open file cabinet and her head resting on a stack of files. Without even a single pleasantry, she launched into another lecture.

"Have I told you the story of Levi Schmidt?" she said, not even lifting her head to make eye contact.

"Yes," I replied, hoping for an abrupt end to the conversation. The conversation ended; Rae's brief sermon followed.

"When Levi was fifteen his girlfriend was found murdered after a drunken night of partying. Not an unfamiliar phenomenon for you, I would guess. The drunken part, not the murdered girlfriend."

"I got that."

"The police, convinced that Levi was their one and only suspect, brought him in for questioning. At the time he was drunk, having drowned his sorrows in his parents' liquor supply immediately upon hearing the news of his girlfriend's death. Levi was held for forty-eight hours without being charged, questioned relentlessly, and deprived of sleep. Eventually, he confessed. According to Levi, the police promised that he could go home as soon as he signed his confession. All Levi wanted in that moment was to crawl into bed and stay there forever. He signed the confession, which was stupid, but it was a lie."

"Rae, I understand your commitment to this —"

"The cops convinced Levi that he was going down for the crime. He was the last person to be seen with his girlfriend, and fibers from his clothes were found on her body, which was the DNA evidence of the olden days. Schmidt was charged with second-degree murder and held without bail. The prosecution wanted to try him as an adult. He had no alibi, because all of his friends were passed out in the family basement and no one could say with a hundred percent certainty that Schmidt had been there all night long. Schmidt immediately recanted his confession, but then a jailhouse snitch came forward and claimed that Schmidt had confessed to him while they were in lockup together.

"Schmidt was tried for murder and found guilty by a jury of middle-aged suburbanites who were *so* not his peers. The judge admitted the coerced confession and the jury bought the snitch's story. DNA back then was different, so all they had were fibers. Fibers from his sweatshirt jacket were found on the deceased. Of course they were! She was his girlfriend! The jury found the fiber evidence compelling, and Levi Schmidt has spent the last fifteen years in prison for a crime he did not commit."

I didn't want to make light of my sister's newfound purpose, but I did suddenly realize that my sister's call for a ride home was more of a call to arms.

"I take it that this is the case you and Maggie are working on."

"Yes," Rae replied. "But I can only do so much."

"Excuse me?"

"Minors aren't allowed to interview witnesses in legal cases. Oh, sure, I could be tried for murder as an adult, but I can't have a recorded conversation until I'm eighteen."

"It does seem unfair," I replied. "Okay, let's go," I said, nodding my head toward the door.

"We could use your help, Izzy."

Me: *Sigh.*

"There are others who need our help. Not just Levi Schmidt."

"I appreciate your passion for this cause,

Rae," I said, "but now is not a good time. I'm not independently wealthy. I have to keep the business afloat."

"What about Harkey?" Rae said accusatorily. "You're not making money on that investigation."

"Harkey is my Schmidt, Rae."

"That's the difference between you and me, Izzy. You want to destroy a man; I want to set one free."

"Tomato, tomah-to," I replied.

Once we got in the car, Rae changed her travel plan. She wanted a ride to Henry's house to discuss the case. I obliged since I've discovered not obliging Rae often has dire consequences. She phoned Henry when we were a few blocks from his house.

"I'm on my way over. Important matters to discuss . . . Yes. Izzy gave me a ride. Sure. I got it."

I pulled the car up in front of Henry's apartment.

"Park in the driveway," Rae said. "His neighbor is out of town."

"I don't need to park, just get out of the car."

"Henry needs to talk to you."

"About what?"

"He didn't say. But it could be important.

Also, the way you avoid him is sooo obvious."

"Excuse me?"

"You know. It makes you look like you
can't handle being friends with him because,
well . . ."

"Stop talking," I said with an air of authority that signaled a willingness to escalate to
violence.

"The driveway on the left," Rae said, and
I followed her instruction.

Inside, Henry served me bourbon, handed
Rae her SAT book, and told her they could
talk about the case after she completed a
practice test in his office.

"I heard you had information for me," I
said, once Rae was out of the room.

"I thought we talked about this already."

"Excuse me?"

"Friends don't talk to friends as if they're
meeting in a parking lot in the middle of
the night to exchange top-secret information."

"Some friends do. We could be friends like
that."

"I don't want to be friends like that."

"What if I do?" I said.

"Parking lots are cold this time of year."

"That's not what I meant."

"Why so hostile, Isabel?"

"You pulled a bait and switch."

"How so?"

"You told Rae you had information for me. Where is it? I don't see it anywhere," I said, scanning the room for emphasis.

"Drink your drink, Isabel, and then you'll get your information."

I drank my drink and glared at Henry. I slammed my glass on the table, indicating a second drink was in order. He obliged, even though he was stingy with the bourbon, the way all moderate drinkers are.

"Now," he said. "Tell me about your day. Or would you prefer we chat in the alley using code names?"

My day had been dull, but Henry hung on every word. Eventually I pried that bit of information out of him.

"I've been here long enough," I said. "What have you got for me?"

"Tonight's a full moon," Henry replied.

"And?"

"You should stop and take a look at it. That's all."

I punched Henry in the arm and left.

# THE SNOWBALL EFFECT

My cheap screenwriter client had only one
assignment for me: pick up his ex-writing
partner's trash and see what she was writing and whether her writing was getting her
anywhere.

Spellman Investigations keeps a schedule
of the city's sanitation collection in order to
organize our garbology assignments. The
law is simple. If the trash is left out for collection, we can confiscate it, search it, and
use it however we see fit. However, if the
garbage is kept behind a fence or along the
side of the house or in a garage, it's not legal
to take. So, late at night or in the predawn
morning (and who wants to get up that
early — unless you're a sanitation worker?)[1]
are the only times to get your hands on
someone else's trash.

1. For the record: I love you all. You have no idea
how much you mean to me.

After Henry's place, I drove over to Shana's residence and parked out front to case the neighborhood. It was ten P.M. and I wanted a few more lights on the street to fade before I took a look in the trash bins perched outside her residence. She lived in a three-unit building — not as easy as a single-family home, but also not as nightmarish as a high-rise, which can make garbology one of the worst jobs in the PI playbook.

A half hour later, I pulled a pair of yellow dishwashing gloves from my aptly named *glove* compartment and exited my vehicle. The key to a safe and subtle garbology is a simple grab-and-walk. You pull the most promising bags and deal with the sorting at a later time. Garbology often involves a good news/bad news scenario. For example, the client doesn't recycle, but the client also doesn't own a shredder. In that case, you're stuck going through rank garbage, but at least the paperwork is in one piece. Shana, on the one hand, was an ardent recycler, or at least her building was deeply into the cause. The smell from their compost bin almost flattened me on the spot (and I've been doing this for twenty years), but their recycling contained three lightweight bags of fluff with the unmistakable airiness of shredded paper, which is generally the worst news of all.

I swiftly grasped three bags in my hand, popped the trunk of my car, and took a visual sweep of the neighborhood to make sure that I wasn't made by any nosy neighbor. The coast was clear and I headed home.

Piecing together angel-hair strips of paper is a job I usually leave for Rae. But since she was otherwise occupied and the economy had left us with no choice but to let go of most of our support staff, I had no alternative but to tackle this hideous puzzle on my own.

Four hours later, I'd managed to assemble one inch of one page of a script and had connected approximately ten two-or-three-strip matches on the coffee table. I took a shower and went to bed, hoping that I wouldn't continue reassembling screenplays in my dreams.

I awoke an hour later when Connor came home. I heard him mumble, "Bloody 'ell," which he mumbles a lot, and then I heard a noise that sounded like the rustling of papers. Although, at first I didn't recognize the sound. At least I didn't recognize it until it was too late.

I got out of bed and walked into the living room.

"What are you doing?" I asked, when what I should have done was race across the room and throw myself on top of the coffee table.

"What ta hell is this mess? It smells like rubbish!" he said.

"It *is* rubbish," I said. "Don't touch it!"

I watched as Connor swept his hand across the table, sliding my paper puzzle into a paper bag.

"You're going to pay for that," I said in my most villainous voice.

Connor pulled a quarter out of his pocket and tossed it at me.

"Will that do?" he asked.

I threw the quarter back at him, aiming for his eye. He ducked.

"That was *four hours* of hard labor you just extinguished with a sweep of a hand! I charge seventy-five dollars an hour. You figure it out."

"Why? Because ya can't?" he shouted back.

"I want my three hundred dollars!" I said. Loudly.

"Then I guess I'll be starting a tab for you at the bar. We'll call it even in, say, a week's time."

I scanned the room looking for something to throw. My brain was too tired for any comeback more sophisticated than "You're a dead man." Besides, I've found these empty threats carry no weight. Now, a pet rock, on the other hand . . .

I was angry, but I was also tired and devastated by the idea that I would have to spend another four hours trying to reassemble some obnoxious feel-good movie that had done nothing but make me feel bad. I did what any tough, self-reliant, overburdened, sleep-deprived, seasoned investigator would do: I cried. And, to my delight, I discovered tears were the weapon of choice against Connor. Better than any pet rock known to man.

"Ah, no, Isabel, pleeease don' cry," he said in his most soothing and thick accent. He put his arms around me and walked me back to bed.

A few hours later, Pratt's stupid puzzle nagged at my subconscious. I woke, returned to the living room, and began the painstaking task of reuniting the slices of screenplay. After an hour at task, Connor woke up, turned on the overhead light, and joined me on the couch.

"When I was a lad, I had a knack for any kind of puzzle," he said, carefully sliding shreds of paper out of the bag of recycling.

I kissed Connor on the cheek and for the next two hours we worked in silence and ended up right back where I started. Although this time, we taped the matching strips together. Then we returned to bed and slept through the morning.

The next afternoon, I phoned Pratt and explained that Shana was shredding the scripts and that in keeping with his budget, the best I could do was pick up the confetti and deliver it to him.

Jeremy said that he liked puzzles. If only I'd known that the night before.

# Rule #28 — Mandatory Sunday-Night Family Dinners

AUTHOR: ALBERT SPELLMAN
VETOES: NONE
(UNDER DIRECT THREAT BY MY MOTHER)

Rule #28 originally started as mandatory individual lunches with Dad but shifted when I pointed out that there was something utterly pathetic about essentially offering your children the choice between having lunch with you or taking out the trash for a week. While I didn't necessarily want every Sunday night ad infinitum to be ruled by a meal with my immediate relatives, I figured it was the kind of event I could occasionally miss since other parties could make up for my absence. Besides, Connor worked Sunday nights anyway.

Dad wasted no time in initiating Rule #28. In retrospect, one could view the meal as a collision of varying agendas. My father wanted quality family time. My mother needed information on David's big blonde. David wanted my mother to take a cooking class. Maggie encouraged another camping trip. I wanted more wine. And Rae, Rae wanted to free Schmidt. In fact, she made T-shirts. Navy-blue cotton with yellow felt letters spelling out her slogan.

At this point in the evening, I slipped into the office, grabbed the digital recorder, and turned it on. Sometimes it just makes me feel better if I have hard evidence.

[Partial transcript reads as follows:]

**Rae:** I need everyone to wear their shirt whenever it's appropriate. Obviously, it's not mandatory when you're in court, Maggie, but if you go for a jog that's perfect. It gets the word out. In fact, if everyone could take up jogging, I really think that would help our cause.

**Isabel:** My shirt looks different than the other shirts.

**Rae:** That's because yours was the test shirt.

**Olivia:** Since we haven't done this in a while, I made turkey tonight.

**David:** [loud sigh]

**Olivia:** Do you have a problem, mister?

**David:** No, it's just that your turkey is usually extremely dry.

**Olivia:** Why don't you taste the food before you start complaining about it?

**Albert:** I have an idea: Why don't we go

around the table and share something about our week with each other?

**Rae:** I'll start.

**Isabel:** We all know what you've been up to.

**Rae:** This week I helped Maggie research the wrongful conviction of Levi Schmidt. Maggie is in the process of filing an appeal. We could use some more help, however. I mean, a man's life is on the line. Would anyone here like to help free Schmidt?

**Isabel:** I'll wear the shirt. What more do you want?

**David:** I've been helping, Rae. I do a little free legal research on the side. I just don't go around announcing it to everyone.

**Rae:** Why not?

**Isabel:** Okay, my turn.

**Rae:** I wasn't done.

**Maggie:** Rae, your help with Levi's case has been invaluable. But we all have other work that we need to attend to as well.

**Rae:** How can anyone think about work when a man is rotting away in a prison cell for a crime he didn't commit?

**Olivia:** Speaking of work, David, how is your job hunt coming along?

**David:** I'm not actively looking for work, Mom. I'm still trying to figure out what areas of the law I want to pursue. I'm pretty sure I'd like to stay away from corporate.

**Olivia:** So what have you been doing with your time?

**David:** This and that.

**Olivia:** Just give me a picture of your typical day. How about Wednesday, for example?

**David:** I don't know. I went for a jog. I picked up a new kerosene lamp for our next camping trip.

**Maggie:** Do you guys want to come?

**Rae:** Never again.

**Isabel:** I'm busy.

**Albert:** I could be talked into it.

**Maggie:** Ouch. David, that hurt.[1]

**David:** [quietly to Maggie] We agreed not to invite anyone.

**Olivia:** So what were you doing Wednesday afternoon?

**David:** I don't know, Mom. I don't keep a surveillance report on myself. I admit that I'm leading a life of leisure. However, after ten years of an eighty-hour workweek, I think I deserve a break.

**Olivia:** I'm sorry, David. My question came out wrong. I think you should take all the time in the world to figure out your career.

1. One must assume that David kicked Maggie under the table.

I'm more interested in your hobbies.

**David:** I don't have that many hobbies.

**Albert:** Since you have so much free time, you must come to my yoga class with me.

**Isabel:** I just lost my appetite.

The evening came to its merciful end when a horn honked outside.

Rae cleared her plate and said, "That's my ride. Am I excused?"

I could only assume it was Logan Engle behind the wheel, so I asked the obvious question: "Is he your boyfriend or your driver?"

"Why can't he be both?" Rae replied.

Once Rae departed, I was the next guest to make a beeline for the door, in part because Maggie was too polite to leave my parents' house with a sink full of dirty dishes. I thought I'd made a silent escape, but my mother caught up with me so we could have a private chat.

She brushed a strand of hair off my face. "Are you getting enough sleep, sweetie?"

"Enough," I replied.

"Are you happy?"

"Enough," I replied.

Mom studied my face and then said, "You're getting dark circles. You want me to buy you some eye cream?"

"No. Is there anything else?"

"I want to know who the big blonde is. Get on it."

"Good night, Mom."

# UNDERCOVER BUTLER #2

The following week I dropped by the Winslow residence to check on Mr. Leonard. However, Christopher answered the door, in the same three-piece *Masterpiece Theatre* getup.

"Christopher, what are you doing here?" I said when he appeared before me.

Christopher glanced over his shoulder and said, "Shhhh." Then he took me by the arm and dragged me into the drawing room. "Just call me Mr. Leonard," he said quietly.

"What's going on?"

"Len had an audition. I insisted that he go to it and so I figured a substitute for one day wouldn't be a problem. When I arrived I was going to explain the situation to Mr. Winslow, but he apparently can't tell us apart."

"What about the housekeeper?"

"It's her day off."

"This makes me uncomfortable," I said.

"Why? Because a white man can't tell two brothers apart or because of the deception angle?"

"Both," I replied. "You didn't think to come clean at any point?"

"Well, it seemed easier this way. I do suspect that he needs new glasses. When I asked him when was the last time he saw an eye doctor, he couldn't recall. Also, I did a bit more digging. Hope you don't mind. I'm afraid Len is taking more to the part of butler than that of investigator. You know, some days I think he could do this full-time. That's why I insisted he go to the audition today. I refuse to have a life partner who spends his days pretending to be on a BBC show."

"So far Len has given me nothing; have you got anything that I can use?"

"You could check Mr. Winslow's driver, Bill Cosgrove. Len described his eating habits to me. He hovers over his food protectively and is a little jumpy."

"That means?" I asked.

"Haven't you watched *Oz*? He's probably done time. Hold on, I'll get you his employee file. I found where Winslow keeps his records. I will say that the driver seems to have gone legit. Neither Len nor I have noticed anything amiss."

Christopher climbed the stairs two at a time and I followed him into a small room that was clearly designated office space for "the help."

"We already know about Cosgrove's record. It was for a minor drug charge twenty years ago. But good work. If you found the employee records in a day, what has Mr. Leonard been doing?"

"He's been reorganizing Mr. Winslow's closets and taking him shopping for more suitable attire."

"What about investigating?" I asked.

Christopher sighed and said, "Len thinks Mr. Winslow's only problem was his previous valet. He believes it would be for the best if Mason Graves never returned."

"Has anyone heard from him yet?"

"No."

"Did Len get a copy of those e-mails for me?"

Christopher pulled an envelope out of the desk drawer.

"I printed out the three e-mails I could find on Winslow's computer. There's nothing out of the ordinary about them. I'm still looking for Mason's employee file. You want his Social Security number, right?"

At this point I was wishing I'd given the job to Christopher. At least he had his priorities straight.

"Also in the envelope," said Christopher, "is a copy of Winslow's will. But it's dated 1998, so I'm not sure if it's the latest version. Len needs to get Winslow to check on that. I read through this will and there's nothing out of the ordinary in it."

A quiet beep sounded somewhere on Christopher's body. He pulled a cell phone from his pocket.

"What's that?"

"Len is bringing Mr. Winslow into the twenty-first century. They purchased cell phones last week. And now, instead of shouting or using the bell or fumbling with the intercom, Mr. Winslow sends a polite and subtle text message. Len programmed it for him so all he needs to do is press a button on his cell phone."

Christopher read his message and looked up at me.

"I'm needed now. I suggest you call Len later and remind him about his primary responsibilities."

Christopher spoke with a sharp edge that indicated his problem with Len wasn't left at the office, so to speak.

"Everything all right at home?" I asked.

"When actors perform, there's usually a time limit involved. Once they leave the stage, they have to return to some semblance of their real selves. Len is already speaking with the accent at home, in constant formal attire, and, well, I'd rather not mention what he does with his pinkie when he sips tea. And don't get me started on that ridiculously expensive Gucci smoking jacket that he purchased. First of all, if he's going to go all Method-actor on me, he should know that the help doesn't wear smoking jackets, even when they are off duty."

"I'm sorry to hear about this, Christopher," I said. "I'll try to straighten things out, once I do a little research on these latest employee records."

"Thank you, Isabel. Anything that will speed this investigation along would be greatly appreciated. Must run. It's tea time."

Christopher gave me a kiss on the cheek and told me to let myself out. What he did next, I couldn't tell you. But I was picturing him serving tea and scones. I was feeling hungry and maybe just a little bit offended that I wasn't invited to stay.

# STAKEOUT #2

I didn't bother asking Connor to accompany me on the early-morning shift, since I was switching gears and using my allotment of Harkey investigation time checking out the insurance surveillance his firm was conducting. By following Harkey's lead investigator, I hoped I could connect the dots to one of Dr. Hurtt's patients. In the early hours of dawn, groggy and sleepy eyed, I sat in my car, wishing that I'd gotten myself that cup of coffee that I'd decided against because I was running late and didn't know when Harkey's surveillance guy, Jim Atherton, would be starting his shift. Jim would lead me to the subject of the investigation and I couldn't risk missing his departure.

Atherton's car was still in his driveway at six fifty A.M.; by seven forty-five, he was on the move. The move was short — four miles to Bernal Heights. I parked two cars behind his and tried to pare down the options of houses he was surveilling. Using my laptop I did a reverse address check on the residences and compared them to the list of potential patients I got from my photographs and license plate numbers from the Dr. Hurtt surveillance. Eventually, a name clicked. Marco Pileggi. The thrill of this minor victory was dulled by my caffeine-withdrawal headache. Just as I began searching my purse for an aspirin, there was a knock on my passenger-side window.

I was first startled and then calmed. I unlocked the door and the passenger entered my car with a nice hot cup of black coffee.

"How'd you know I'd be here?"

"I was the one who told you to check the insurance angle to begin with."

"But how did you know my exact location?"

"I'm a cop, remember?"

"And you were in the neighborhood?" I asked.

"It's early. I thought you might need your drug."

I really wanted the coffee and no matter how I tried to wrap my mind around turning it down impolitely, I simply couldn't. I grabbed the cup and said thank you, because that's what you do when a friend brings you coffee. We sat in the car in relative silence until Marco Pileggi exited his house, neck brace still in place.

"I better get to work," Henry said.

"Me too," I replied.

Henry hopped out of the car and I waited until Pileggi drove away followed by Atherton. Then I followed Atherton. I spent the next two hours surveilling one man surveilling another man. When it was time for me to call it quits and return to my own work, no man had done anything that would help me get another man in trouble. Sometimes you just have an off day.

Later that afternoon, I would discover that I wasn't the only person who had an off day.

"How's your day been?" I asked Connor after he served me a drink. Although to be perfectly honest, I was still brainstorming about how to take down Harkey. A new storm shoved my brainstorm out of the way, however, when Connor answered the question with a dose of sharp hostility.

"How's my day been?" he asked. He does that a lot, repeating the question with more inflection before answering it. He answered it, all right.

"It's been a fecken Spellman family reunion in here today."

" 'Fecken.' I'll never get used to that," I replied, hoping to distract him with friendly banter.

"Did you hear me?" he asked.

"Did I hear you?" I said, turning the tables. "Yes."

"Well?"

"Please, go on," I said, since he was going to go on anyway.

"First your sister came in here."

"I thought you liked her."

"I did. But then she asked me to drive her to San Quentin, and when I said no she said she'd be willing to pay for the gas money and followed it up with a comment about how she's heard my people are cheap. And when I told her that's the Scots, not the Irish, she said, *'Same difference.'* "

"Oops. Sorry about that. Then what happened?"

"I refused to serve her just like the sign says and so she pouted in the back booth until that cop fellow with the shifty eyes showed up and they left. Maybe he drove her to San Quentin. If you ask me, that's where *she* belongs."

"No argument from me."

"Then your brother showed up, looking for your sister, but she had already left. He's clearly adopted. He said hello, ordered a drink, tipped well, and departed. Not too long after that, your mother arrived, pretending to be looking for you, but I know better. When I told her you weren't in, that she just missed the young lass, your mom ordered a gimlet, complained about it, and then asked if you had arranged your lawyer date for this week, just to rub it in, I guess."

"Oh, right. That reminds me. I need to get on it."

"I need some sympathy right this second, Isabel."

I leaned across the bar and combed Connor's thick black hair with my fingers. "I'm sorry, Connor. You've got all kinds of sympathy. I swear. Please forgive me and my family."

"I accept your apology. On one condition."

"Name it."

"I want the lawyer date for this fortnight out of the way. His name is Larry. He's in the back waiting for you. An honest-to-goodness lawyer."

"Really? Back there?"

"Don't keep him waiting."

"Can I finish my drink first?"

"Drink fast," Connor replied. "I've already had to prop him up twice this afternoon."

# MANDATORY
## LAWYER DATE #2

Larry Meyers, fifty-four, semiconscious, in a two-day-old suit and three-day unwashed hair (best guess), sank into a corner crevice in a booth in the back room. If he were a vain woman, he would have been pleased with the backlighting that hid his many flaws.

Larry was indeed a lawyer — an ambulance chaser, to be exact. But his client list had dimmed to a flicker in the past few years, beginning at the time of his divorce. I brought Larry a glass of water and hoped that he would be coherent enough to satisfy the lawyer-date requirement. My job was to force the awkward conversation that followed into something that resembled a date. Fortunately, for now, no accompanying photographs were required.

[The partial, but utterly sad, transcript

reads as follows:][1]

**Isabel:** Hi, are you Larry?
**Larry:** If I could be anyone else, I would be.
**Isabel:** My friend tells me you're a lawyer.[2]
**Larry:** I've heard all the jokes. Please spare me.
**Isabel:** I never remember jokes anyway.
**Larry:** Good, because I hate jokes.
**Isabel:** Me too.
**Larry:** You probably don't hate them as much as I do.
**Isabel:** Probably not. Can I get you a cup of coffee?
**Larry:** Stick some whiskey in it this time. That bartender is stingy with the booze.
**Isabel:** I'll be right back.
*[Long pause while I return to the bar. The recorder picks up Larry falling asleep again. The sound of snoring is unmistakable.]*
**Isabel:** Wake up, Larry. I brought you another drink.

1. And you'd definitely need transcripts. Larry's slurred speech was almost beyond recognition. Fortunately, I'm fluent in slur.
2. Have to make sure that employment status is affirmed or the date can be tossed out of the official list.

**Larry:** That was so nice of you.

**Isabel:** It was nothing.

**Larry:** [choking with emotion] Why would you do something so nice for a complete stranger?

**Isabel:** We're not strangers, remember?

**Larry:** Who are you?

**Isabel:** Your date.

**Larry:** You can't possibly be my date. You're pretty. And nice.

**Isabel:** Thanks. You must work too hard. That's why you fell asleep.[3]

**Larry:** Oh. Maybe.

**Isabel:** Drink up. The caffeine will do you good.

*[Long pause.]*

**Larry:** What's it all about?

**Isabel:** What's what all about?

**Larry:** Life.

**Isabel:** That might be too big a question for me.

**Larry:** It's just so full of pain.

*[Sound of crying.]*

---

3. I had to try to come up with a plausible explanation for the slurred words and snoring and the utterly desperate tone in Larry's voice. Otherwise my mother would accuse me of hiring winos to play my lawyers.

141

**Isabel:** Do you have any hobbies?[4]

When I couldn't get Larry to stop crying, I insisted that we head across the street to the Squat and Gobble café and I ordered Larry something they call the Tripple Gobble, which eventually did the trick of sobering him up. I'm not sure that he was any happier sober, but at least he could find his way home. I also managed to work in a few more required date questions, which I played for my mother a few hours later.

**Isabel:** If you could have dinner with any
    person, living or dead, who would it be?
**Larry:** My nana. She was the only person
    who ever really loved me.
*[End of tape.]*[5]

My mother picked up the recording device as if it were a miniature Larry and gestured with it.

"Where did you find this guy?"

"Around."

"Around a homeless shelter? I'm not sure this qualifies."

4. One of the five required date questions. If you're paying attention, you'll catch them all.
5. It looked like Larry was going to cry again, so I figured I'd cut my losses.

"Oh, *it qualifies.* I have a first and last name and his bar number. I spent two hours drinking and eating with him. I even woke him up twice. I asked him what he did for fun. I inquired into his past relationships. It was a date, if you consider a date a bizarre ritual your mother forces you to enact in order to maintain some false idea of control. It was a date according to your definition of one."

# THE BUTLER DID SOMETHING

Mason Graves's e-mails provided no concrete evidence of his current whereabouts. They were formal, banal, and came from a web-based e-mail account. Here's a sampling of the juiciest one:

To: Franklin Winslow
From: Mason Graves
Subject: Greetings

Dear Sir:
   I hope this e-mail finds you well. I feel dreadful for leaving you for so long but hope that you have found a sufficient temporary replacement. I assure you I will be back in no time at all.
   Mother has taken a turn for the worse. She is stubborn and might linger for a while, but I suspect her days are numbered.
   Please take care of yourself and remind

the gardener that he must not overwater the lilies in the back.

Your humble servant,<br>
Mason

In the years we'd had Mr. Winslow as a client, we'd never investigated his valet, since he never gave us cause to. Mason was hired a year before Winslow became a client. But I decided to run a database check on the name Mason Graves in the Bay Area. I found fifteen. However, no one jumped out at me as a plausible match. All but three were employed elsewhere and the rest didn't match Mason Graves's probable age (late forties to early fifties was my best guess). This was cause for some concern, but not as much cause for concern as Mr. Leonard's accent, which had still not returned to normal.

When I dropped by Len and Christopher's home, shortly after nine P.M., the new valet was shining his shoes and laying out his clothes for the following day. Apparently, he had spent almost his entire salary to date on a new wardrobe. Christopher sat helplessly in a lounge chair and pretended to read a book, but I noticed that he didn't turn a single page during my visit. Len answered the door (because that's what he does), gave me a warm greeting, and then adjusted my collar and dusted some lint off my jacket.

"Isabel, a pleasure to see you," Len said very politely, but still in character. I guess I had to see it in context — or rather out of context — to believe it.

"Okay, knock it off," I said.

"Pardon me?"

"I never thought a day would come when I'd miss your Christopher Walken impression."[1]

"Oh, Isabel, you're so droll."

I turned to his partner. "Make him stop!"

"You started it; you make him stop!" Christopher shouted back at me. Then he pretended to be reading his book again.

"I'm worried about you, Len," I said.

"Darling, you mustn't worry. I assure you I am perfectly well. Can I get you a cup of tea?"

"Yeah, you do that," I replied, just to get him to leave the room.

I sat down next to Christopher on the

1. Everyone likes a good Christopher Walken impression, since it's typically the closest you get to the real thing, but Len's overuse could be positively maddening.

couch. His glare was loaded with accusation.

"This is not all my fault," I said. "Would you prefer he lounged around the house all day taking bubble baths and giving himself facials?"

"I'm undecided," Christopher replied.

"What's going on with him?" I asked.

"He hasn't had a decent part in eight months."

"Well, he's only playing one of his parts. That's the problem I'm having here."

"You need to explain it better. It's like *Victor Victoria*."

"Huh?"

"Do not tell me you have never seen that classic. Julie Andrews, James Garner, a positively brilliant performance by Lesley Ann Warren."

"Go ahead and list the entire credits — I've got all night — but I still don't know what you're talking about."

"I keep forgetting you're a cultural retard."

"It's not a crime to miss a single film made in the sixties."

"Eighties, darling. And sorry. I'm in a dreadful mood."

"Was there a point you were going to make?" I asked.

"Yes. In *Victor Victoria,* Julie Andrews plays

a woman pretending to be a man pretending to be a woman."

"That makes no sense at all."

"She plays a drag singer in an old nightclub."

"I'm getting a headache."

"Forget it," Christopher said. "My point is, you didn't emphasize to Len that he was an actor, playing a spy, playing a butler."

"I thought 'undercover butler' explained enough."

"You never gave him a backstory."

"Oh my god. Can you do me a favor? I've had all of the actor-speak I can handle for one night. Discuss Len's motivation with him and then give him this kit. Instructions enclosed. Tell him I want him to gather fingerprints of the entire staff — on the sly, if possible. I just want to make sure there are no surprises. Obviously, not the driver. Since we already know about him. Also, have Len get fingerprints from Mason's bedroom. I doubt we'll find anything, but it's worth a try."

Christopher's face lit up when he got a glimpse of the fingerprinting kit.

"This looks like fun. Can I do it instead? I've always wanted to dust for fingerprints."

"I don't care who does it; just don't send warning signals out to the rest of the staff.

Don't forget to label the prints. Okay?"

Len returned with the tea, served on a silver tray that was once Christopher's grandmother's. While our butler-channeling friend set out the teacups, I lost my appetite for Earl Grey.

I glanced at my watch for show and said that I had to run.

"Where?" Christopher asked suspiciously.

"I need to spend some quality time with Connor."

"Of course," Christopher replied, "because that one is definitely going to last."

"Now I'm leaving for sure."

"What a pity," said Len, as Mr. Leonard.

"You'll live," I replied.

"Christopher, do you want cream and sugar or just cream?"

"I'd like a whiskey and soda."

"Then why did I make tea?" Len asked with the patient understanding of a seasoned manservant.

Who says you can't find good help these days? Christopher walked me to the door.

"What am I supposed to do about Jeeves here?"

From the doorway I watched Len clearing the tray, still in character.

"Perhaps he needs a taste of his own medicine," I replied.

# "QUALITY TIME"

I lied. I went straight home and back to work. I looked at Mason's e-mails again and realized that there might be a way to at least track his general whereabouts. It was eleven P.M., but I phoned Robbie Gruber, Spellman Investigations' tech support guy, since I knew he was awake and would be awake for hours.

"What?" Robbie said when he picked up the phone. That's how he always answers the phone. In fact, I don't think I've ever heard Robbie say "hello."

"Hi, Robbie. It's Izzy."

"I know that. What do you want?"

"Is there any way to track where an e-mail originated from?"

"Yes."

"How?"

"I'd need the e-mail headers."

"How do I do that?" I asked.

"You don't know?"

"That's why I asked."

"I'll send you an e-mail with detailed in-structions."

"You can't just tell me over the phone?"

"No. It will take too long to explain it to you and I don't feel like talking anymore."

Robbie hung up the phone. No good-bye. That's another word I haven't heard him use.

After my phone call with Robbie I went straight to bed. There was no point in stay-ing up for Connor. Considering our sched-ule conflicts, it's a miracle our relationship had lasted this long. Connor starts work at four P.M., doesn't finish until three A.M. most nights, and sleeps until noon. I'm usu-ally at the office by nine A.M. and out cold by midnight. We were together when I visited the bar after work, for a few hours in the morning on Saturday, and as for Sun-day . . . well, Sunday was always decided by a coin-toss. If Connor won, I maimed the morning watching rugby and killed the afternoon drinking beer with stinky, sweaty, dirt-streaked men. When I won, I enjoyed quiet time at home, alone.

As you might imagine, the snippets of time Connor and I shared did not a relationship make. And when you toss in a hostile mother, dates with other men, constant sleep interruptions from both parties, and almost all communication happening in the privacy of a crowded bar, well, things were complicated. We needed more time together (and watching him play rugby is not time together, as I have explained again and again) and since I'm always thinking about my revenge on Harkey, I decided that bringing Connor into my Harkey investigation was a good idea for everyone. Except maybe Connor and Harkey. I had to admit that Connor tried to be a good sport about the whole thing. But when he realized that surveillance was sort of like sitting on a couch and watching TV together, only the television show was really bad and you couldn't tear your eyes away from the set, he lost interest in the endeavor. As with all surveillance neophytes, the first time is always the best; Connor had finally reached his boredom threshold.

The following day, Ex #12 and I were parked together in my car, watching Jim Atherton watching Marco Pileggi, but Connor was trying to get a football game on the radio.

**Connor:** I could be watching football right now, if I weren't doing this.

**Isabel:** But then we'd almost never see each other.

**Connor:** Are you coming to my game on Sunday?

**Isabel:** Maybe. How many points is Declan offering?

**Connor:** Ya can't bet against me again.

**Isabel:** There's no room for sentiment in wagers.

**Connor:** There's no bloody balance to this relationship, Isabel. I come on a bloody boring job with you, I tape pieces of shredded paper together, I endure your family, I lose sleep, I get kicked in the middle of the night, and you get free drinks.

**Isabel:** I always say thank you and sometimes I even tip.

**Connor:** It's time to take a stand, Isabel. I have a few precious hours a day away from the bar; I'm not spending them sitting in a car, taking pictures of people with neck braces. I'm sorry, Izzy. But I quit.

Once again, I was alone in my quest to take down Harkey.

# Rule #31 — Vacate Residence Every Wednesday

## AUTHOR: MOM AND DAD
## VETOES: (N/A)

---

I assumed there was a logical explanation, like maybe the house was being painted or fumigated, but no, the rationale was far more warped.

"Rae, did you pack your overnight bag?" Mom asked.

"You were serious about that?" Rae replied.

"Yes, you'll be spending the night at David's."

"I don't get it," Rae replied.

"Just pack your bag or you'll be late for school."

"I won't step foot out this door until everyone has their shirt on," Rae said as she passed Dad on her way out of the office.

Our shirts were laid out on our desks. We didn't argue, since there wasn't any point. We all simply donned our FREE SCHMIDT! uniforms and continued the conversation.

"Somebody better start talking," I said.

"You need the house vacated for twenty-four hours why?"

"Once a week. Twenty-four hours. No one enters or exits," Dad said.

"Well, we do," my mom added, correcting him.

"You and Rae need to stay out," Dad explained, explaining nothing.

"I'm still waiting for the details, please," I said.

"One day, when we're retired and the house is empty, we need to know that we can handle it," Mom said.

"We're doing a test run once a week," said Dad.

"Huh?"

"Because if we can't handle it, we need to be prepared," Mom chimed in.

"Maybe get a dog or a foreign exchange student," Dad suggested.

"I'm vetoing the foreign exchange student idea right now," Mom said.

I tried to steer the conversation back to some semblance of rationality: "So, you're just kicking us out so you can see what it's like to be alone? Is that what I'm hearing?"

"In a nutshell," Dad replied.

"Why don't you take a freakin' vacation like normal people?"

"Vacations are different," my mom said.

"And we don't actually like them so much," Dad continued.

"We need to see what it's like to be home alone together with no distractions," said Mom.

"And face it," Dad said. "You are all really distracting."

Rae resurfaced with a more voluminous backpack.

"What did I miss?" she asked.

"Mom and Dad need some quality time together, so we have to vacate the house for twenty-four hours every Wednesday at eight A.M. until Thursday same time."

"Why can't you have quality time while I'm here?"

There was a brief pause, which filled Rae's head with probably the wrong idea.

"*Oh my god.* I'm going to be sick!" she shouted, and ran for the front door. "Izzy, drive me to school now!"

My father calmly bellowed to my sister, "It's not what you think, Rae."

A very loud "La la la la" was the only reply he got.

I gathered any work-related items I might need and said, "I'll be taking wagers on which one of you snaps first. Send me a text message if you want in."

In my car Rae took a few soothing breaths

to clear her mind. Then she shivered and shook her head and made this noise that sounded like she was trying to cough up a hairball.

As I drove her to school, I fished for a few pieces of information. I hadn't had time to go fishing in a while.

"How's everything going with Maggie?"

"We're killing ourselves on the Schmidt case. We could use some help."

"I'm asking about Maggie as a person, not Maggie the lawyer."

"The two are closely connected," Rae replied.

"Listen, all I want to know is how things seem between Maggie and David."

"Great, as far as I can tell. He drops by the office all the time. They have lunch a lot. He's brought her flowers once or twice, and candy. I ate most of it, though. He went to that candy store off of Polk. Their licorice is really good. Not stale like you get at the movies or the drugstore."

"Tell me about your boyfriend," I asked.

"He's an excellent driver," Rae replied.

"Is that his best quality?" I asked.

Rae ignored my question and said, "His car is in the shop. You need to pick me up from school this afternoon."

"Is there a bus strike that I don't know about?"

"Izzy, please don't make me threaten you. Just pick me up from school and everything will be cool."

"When was the last time you were actually on a bus?" I asked.

"Can't recall."

"It's been *that* long?"

"I'll see you at four," Rae quickly replied, as if she were trying to change the subject.

Resisting the urge to lecture Rae on the benefits of public transportation, I suddenly had a feeling that I had missed a key moment in Rae's history.

"Did something happen to you?" I asked.

Rae ignored the question and jumped out of the car, but the look on her face after the query was all I needed to know. *Something* had happened.

I circled Rae's school, searching for Logan's car, just to be sure. I couldn't locate the car, but Logan was easy to spot, in his preppy-boy clothes chatting with a carbon copy of himself (albeit with a sloppier haircut) around the corner of the school entrance. I pulled my car over to the side and grabbed my binoculars from the glove compartment and watched their exchange, hoping for some kind of vague insight. It never occurred to me that the insight I'd acquire would be so specific.

Logan's counterpart handed over an envelope. Logan opened it and counted the cash. Logan then slipped something into the other guy's pocket. They bumped fists and parted ways. My mind started wandering, which is never good for anyone.

■ ■ ■ ■

# PART II:
# APPEALS

■ ■ ■ ■

# THE BIG BLONDE

I didn't want to investigate David and the big blonde, I swear. Sure, I wasn't above spying on family members, but I saw a distinction between my underage sister, who could have been associating with a dangerous element, and snooping around behind the back of my perfectly respectable brother — whose back, I should mention, I had snooped behind and come up empty. If it were up to me, I would have liked to have shown David that people can change by doing nothing and letting this big-blonde business work itself out on its own.

Unfortunately, I had a blackmailing mother on my hands, and the mound of dirt she had on me could not be swept under any carpet *I've* ever seen. I suppose the honest thing to do would have been to come clean and erase her tool of manipulation, but after sixteen years I simply did not want the Prom Night episode to see the light of day.

And so I followed Mom's orders. Since I was banned from the office and I had already inadvertently (yes, that's what I call inadvertent) acquired some kind of dirt on one family member, I decided to keep that the theme of the day and deal with the David issue, which I figured was probably not an issue at all.

At two P.M. on a sunny Wednesday afternoon, I parked a few blocks from David's residence and pulled out my laptop, mooching off his neighbor's wireless. I forwarded the e-mail Robbie sent me about gathering e-mail headers on to Len and Christopher and hoped that one of them would see to it that the request was handled.

Then I decided that I had to take more control over my not-so-personal life. I found a website called www.litidate.com, which looked promising. It contained pictures and detailed profiles, and the members' bar memberships were verified in case your mother thought you were pulling some kind of faux-lawyer con. Besides, at least with these guys I could pick the ones I was sure wouldn't want a second date with me. Forty-five minutes later, just as I'd found a few promising candidates, David exited his residence and drove two miles up California, parked on the street, and entered an office building on the corner of Sacramento and Locust.

I parked my car, entered the building, and was delighted to find that there was a security checkpoint and a sign-in form. I saw my brother's name and the associated suite number. I signed myself in and took the elevator to the fourth floor. When the elevator doors opened, I cautiously moved along the hallway until I reached Suite 405 and then I read the sign on the door:

Sharon Tudor, Therapist

As usual, David's intrigue was hardly intrigue at all, and if the big blonde was David's therapist, then maybe I could put my mother at ease and spare David any further meddling. I exited the building and, on my way to my car, spotted Maggie entering the same office building. Huh. This made things more interesting/worrisome, but still, isn't seeking therapy on your own, without an order by the court, simply a sign of good sense?

I grabbed my laptop from the trunk of my car and slipped into a coffee shop with Wi-Fi. After caffeinating myself, I searched for

Sharon Tudor and found her full profile on her business website. She was definitely *the* blonde. She was also something else. Something that made me want to have a drink, a real drink, that very instant.

I found a bar nearby, ordered a house bourbon, and called Morty. I had a feeling he would be around.

Usually when I phone people, I receive a variety of initial responses, which generally fall into the following categories:

"What do you want, Izzy?"

"You again?"

"Why are you calling me this late?"

"Speak."

"Can you call back later?"

"This is bad news, isn't it?"

"How did you get my number?"

You get the idea. In contrast, when I call Morty, his replies fall into the following general categories:

"Izzele, thank God you called. I'm bored out of my mind."

"Izzele, talk to me about anything but your ailing health and I'm all ears."

"Izzele, get on a plane and get me outta here!"

Today's greeting was more subtle, but still, it hit the spot.

[Transcript reads as follows:]

**Morty:** Izzele, tell me *everything* that's new.

**Me:** I have some information and I don't know what to do with it.

**Morty:** I'm all ears.

**Me:** You are, aren't you?[1]

*[Dead silence.]*

**Morty:** Did you call to try out your Don Rickles impression, or are you interested in kibitzing with an old friend?

**Me:** The other thing.

**Morty:** Say it.

**Me:** It's not a word that rolls off my tongue.

**Morty:** Say it anyway.

**Me:** Kibitz. I called to kibitz.

**Morty:** Thank you. Now go on.

**Me:** I think my sister is dating a drug dealer.

**Morty:** Oy gevalt. Your poor mother.

**Me:** Let's not jump to conclusions yet.

**Morty:** You just did.

**Me:** He could be selling term papers or chemistry test answers for all I know.

**Morty:** [sarcastically] And that would be a blessing. He sounds like a thug.

**Me:** He's something. I don't know if "thug" is the word. I have to investigate.

1. Morty's ears are positively enormous.

**Morty:** How's the Irish guy?

**Me:** Nice leap, Morty. We're talking about thugs and you bring up my boyfriend. He's an honest businessman, that's what he is.

**Morty:** There was a lull in the conversation; I switched topics, that's all.

**Me:** There was no lull.

**Morty:** There was most definitely a lull.

*[Awkward silence. You could call it a lull.]*

**Morty:** You've got more in that muddled head of yours, Izzele. Spill it.

**Me:** Here's my real problem. My mother saw a blond woman exiting my brother's house one day. We brokered a deal. I can pick 50 percent of my lawyer dates if I find out who the blonde is. Well, I found out who the blonde is.

*[Long pause as I ask myself why I'm talking about this with an eighty-five-year-old man.]*

**Morty:** [impatiently] So who is she?

**Me:** [mumbled] She's a sex therapist.

**Morty:** A what?

**Me:** A sex therapist.

**Morty:** I still didn't get that.

**Me:** *A sex therapist!!*

**Morty:** Is that like a hooker?

**Me:** NO!

**Morty:** It sounds like a fancy name for a hooker.

**Me:** No, no, no. She's like a psychologist, only she specializes in sex stuff.

**Morty:** Interesting.

*[Long pause. Absolutely a lull.]*

**Me:** I don't want to have this information.

**Morty:** Neither do I.

**Me:** And I don't want my mother to have this information. It's none of her business and David wouldn't want her to know either.

**Morty:** So don't tell her.

**Me:** She explicitly asked me to gather this information for her. I have to return to her with some information or she won't leave me alone. And, honestly, I can't go out with two of her lawyers a month. It's way too much.

**Morty:** You're a grown woman, Izzele. Why can't you simply say no to your mother?

**Me:** I just can't.

**Morty:** That doesn't sound like you. You have a mind of your own and follow it whether it makes good sense or not.

**Me:** I just can't cross her this time.

**Morty:** You did something, didn't you?

**Me:** No. It's not that.

**Morty:** What did you do? Tell me.

**Me:** My battery's dying. I'll call you later.

**Morty:** I wasn't born yesterday, Izzele.
**Me:** Don't I know it.

# THE ENGLE PROBLEM

I put on a black wig in the style of a sharp bob and a tan trench coat and parked two blocks away from Rae's school. I phoned my sister from the car and told her that something had come up and she'd have to find another ride. I suggested David, since I knew his counseling session would be over. I then waited in my car across the street from her school and watched the entrance/ exit.

When I caught sight of Logan Engle, I exited my vehicle and followed him on foot. He circled the school and took his post by the parking lot gate. A younger male student approached him and I observed yet another exchange of goods. Now I only had to find out what his product was.

I approached quickly and quietly. I wore sneakers, not boots, which would have worked much better with this outfit but don't contribute to stealth.

"What are you selling?" I asked.

"What are *you* selling?" he asked, all cocky and young and thinking that the world was at his fingertips, not knowing the frustration and heartache that would eventually beset him. I know I'm being dramatic. But Logan looked to me like the kind of guy who peaks in high school.

I pulled forty dollars from my pocket.

"What will this buy me?"

"Are you a cop?"

"Do I look like a cop?"

"You look like a woman who needs a hairdresser."

"Is my wig crooked?"

"Yes."

"Look, I was in the neighborhood. I've spent the day spying on my cheating ex. I see you in your preppy uniform, swapping goods with a kid, and I think, you're not smart enough to be selling term papers, so I draw a conclusion, because I'm good at drawing conclusions. You're selling weed and I could use some weed right now. I got forty bucks. What will it get me?"

I shoved the bills into Logan's pocket. The kid swept the street with his eyes and handed me a baggy. Bingo. Now that I knew what I was dealing with, so to speak, I got to the bottom of things.

"You know someone named Rae Spellman?" I asked.

"Who are you?" he said, his color fading from fear.

To be honest, I was enjoying myself.

"Here's all you need to know," I said. "I'm not a snitch. It's not my style. But I want to know who Rae Spellman is to you."

"Why are you asking?"

"Enough with the questions. Start spilling."

"She's no one. She's just a thorn in my side."

"She's not your girlfriend?"

"No way. Talk about high maintenance. I already have to wear this stupid shirt all the time."

Logan lifted up his sweater and revealed a FREE SCHMIDT! T-shirt underneath.

"So why are you always driving her places?"

"Because I have to!" Logan said, sounding desperate.

"Why?"

"Because she knows about my side business. She's holding it over my head."

"She's blackmailing you?"

"Yeah."

"Are you stoned when you drive her?"

"Nah. I never touch the stuff. It makes

me paranoid."

"One more question: Does she ever take the bus?"

"I don't think so. I get the feeling something bad happened to her one time."

"You know what?"

"Nah."

"Watch your back, Logan," I said, just to keep him off balance.

Then I returned to my car, took my visual post again, and spotted my sister cozying up to a guy alongside a bike rack. They looked chummy and he looked, well, harmless. No discernible hair gel or tattoos. His khakis said he wasn't too cool or too uncool, and he wore a battered green army jacket over a wrinkled button-down shirt. He had a strap around his right leg, identifying him as a cyclist. Rae said something he thought was hilarious and then he casually put his arm around her and kissed her on the cheek. As I watched them from behind a tree, across the street, David pulled up in his Toyota Prius. The new couple ducked out of view and kissed on the lips. Gross. Harmless boy put on his bike helmet and waved good-bye to my sister. Rae waited a beat so our brother wouldn't connect the two parties and casually walked to his car.

When David and Rae departed, I removed

my wig and decided to gloat about my new-found information. Since I couldn't tell the unit (and it was still Wednesday) I dropped by the police station.

"You know *nothing,*" I said to Henry once I closed his office door.

"What a charming way to begin a conversation," he replied.

"I have some information you might find intriguing."

"How nice of you to drop by."

"Logan Engle is *so* not Rae's boyfriend."

"It's nice to get some good news for once. Make yourself comfortable."

My trench coat was warm, so I took it off and threw it over the chair.

"Can I get you something to drink?" he asked.

"You serve bourbon here?"

Henry ignored me and left his office, returning a short while later with two mugs. Mine had stale instant hot chocolate in it; his contained herbal tea.

"So if he's not her boyfriend, who is he?" Henry asked, leading back to the opening of the conversation.

"He's her victim. She's blackmailing him. He plays *Driving Miss Daisy* and she keeps his secret."

"What's his secret?" Henry asked.

"Sorry," I replied. "I'm no snitch."

"Is it illegal?"

"She has a real boyfriend, you know."

"So why doesn't she make him drive her places?"

"He has a bicycle."

"I like him already," Henry said. "Now tell me Logan's secret."

"No," I replied. "What happened to Rae on the bus?"

Henry leaned back in his chair. He had leverage now and would only squander it on an exchange of information.

"Tell me what she's got on Logan and I'll spill all the dirt I know."

I eyed the inspector carefully. Judging from the expression on his face, the slightly evil eye twinkle, whatever happened to Rae on the bus was worth knowing, but it was not a deep, dark secret. I could get the information elsewhere. I didn't need to bring a cop into Rae's troubles. The last thing she needed in her senior year of high school was to be dragged into a drug bust. I wasn't sure what Henry's legal obligations would be if I told him the truth, so I made an executive decision not to tell him the truth.

"No deal," I replied. "Thanks for the

cocoa, Henry. I'll see you around."

I pulled my coat off the chair and made a prompt departure.

# REEFER MADNESS

I couldn't finish any busy work at the office, my family investigations were done (for the day), the city was cold and wet, and I didn't feel like sitting in my car outside Harkey's office, so I decided to drop by the Philosopher's Club and spend some quality time with Ex #12.

"Is-a-bel," Connor said, "wat er ya doin' here in the middle of the afternoon?"

"Slumming," I replied.

"You're such a sweetheart, you are," he said, pouring me a pint of Guinness without asking whether that was the drink I had in mind. "Can I interest you in stocking the bar for me? You can work off some of your tab."

"It would be my pleasure," I replied, thinking that I ought to do something nice for Connor after betting against his team in last Sunday's game and winning handsomely. Once I'd restocked the bar, which I had done on numerous occasions as an official employee, I used the bar as a desk and got back to work. First I checked my e-mail.

Christopher informed me that he'd dropped by the Winslow residence, and while Len was occupying the man of the house with a new landscaper[1] meeting, Christopher logged on to Winslow's computer, and forwarded Mason Graves's e-mail headers to me. I, in turn, forwarded them to Robbie, glad for the opportunity to avoid direct communication with the social misfit.

A half hour of peace and silence was broken by Connor's cold announcement.

"Izzy, ya haf a visitor, I think."

I turned to the doorway and saw Henry Stone, blocking the now dim light from outside. I couldn't read his expression until he took a few steps in and the shadow previously cast over his face slid away, revealing the severity of his expression. I hadn't seen Henry this angry in months.

He approached the bar.

Trying to keep things light, I said, "Should I make a run for it?"

"I need to speak to you in private," Henry

1. Just a regular landscaper. Nothing suspicious about that.

coldly replied.

"She can talk to you right here," Connor said. "We don' have any secrets."

"Yes, we do," I interrupted. "We have many."

"Nothing is funny about this," Henry said.

Letting up just a touch on my smartass act, I said, "Please step into my office," and guided Henry over to a booth in the back room.

Henry took in the room and, when he was satisfied that no one was watching, slid a baggy across the table right in front of me. It looked just like the baggy that was in my trench coat pocket. Come to think of it, it was probably no longer in my pocket.

"You left this in my office, my office inside a police precinct, inside a criminal courthouse."

"Shit," was all I said at first. I reached for the drugs, but Henry snatched them away.

"What were you thinking?" he said. "What if one of my superiors found it before I did?"

"I'm so sorry. It's not what you think."

"Your pot? Or did you just score it for your Irish friend?"

"I have an excellent explanation and if you keep being rude to me, you're not going to get it."

"This better be good," Henry said.

Five minutes later, after I told Henry the whole story, he agreed. It was good. Unfortunately, we still had a problem. Since I remain ardently anti-snitch and didn't want to force Rae into that role and Henry is, well, a cop, we had opposing agendas. Or so I thought.

"What are you going to do with this information?" I asked.

"What information?" Henry replied, sliding the greens back in my direction. "Make it disappear, and not in an incendiary kind of way."

"Got it. What are you going to do about Rae? Just let it slide?"

"Of course not. Logan Engle is out of her life for good."

"How will you swing that?"

"Through the same means by which their relationship started," Henry replied.

"Blackmail?"

"Yes," Henry replied, "because that's the kind of person you people have turned me into."

"I'm sorry," I said.

"No, you're not," he said with all the conviction my apology lacked.

# Lost Wednesday #1

"So how was yesterday?" I asked the unit the morning after their mysterious twenty-four hours of solitude.

"Fabulous," Mom replied. "We should have started kicking you all out of the house years ago."

"Glad to hear it," I replied.

Then I turned to my father to gauge his reaction. He was oddly focused on his computer screen.

"How about you, Dad? Did you have fun?"

My father looked up at me and smiled evenly. "When your mother has fun, I have fun."

"That can't always be the case," I replied.

"I suppose there are exceptions to every rule," Dad said.

I was going to suggest a few of those exceptions, but we were rudely interrupted by my sister, who stormed into the office carrying what I would later learn was a book inside a paper bag and dropped it with a thud on Mom's desk. Without saying a single word, Rae then approached the whiteboard and authored a new rule.

## RULE #32 — PUT READING MATERIALS AWAY WHEN YOU'RE FINISHED

Then Rae turned to me and said, "Don't even *think* about vetoing this rule."

"What are you going on about?" I asked my sister.

"That's all I'm going to say," Rae replied, refusing to make eye contact with anyone else in the room. Then she departed as swiftly as she arrived.

"Should I ask?" I said, eyeing the book with both fear and curiosity.

"She's such a prude," Mom said.

"Did you ever have the sex talk with her?" Dad asked, deadpan.

"No. I thought you did that," Mom replied.

They were having fun and wanted to draw me into their game. My curiosity, as always, got the best of me and I approached my mom's desk, pulled the book out of its brown bag, and immediately slid it back in its appropriate package.

"I second Rae's rule. You need to put that stuff away when you're done with it."

My glimpse of the "literature" was brief. I saw tangled flesh on the cover and the words "unlocking," "secret," and "sex." I'm pretty sure there were a few other words involved, but I got the gist and averted my gaze, like I might be watching the end of a slasher flick. While leaving this kind of material out in the open seemed dangerous in a household where all the children are fluent in the language of mockery, I suspect none of us wanted to consider the idea long enough to toss out any sarcastic remarks. Besides, I had other family matters on my agenda for that day.

I sent my father an instant message on his computer to keep my mom in the dark:

Me: Dad, you want to go to lunch with me today?
Dad: What's the hitch?
Me: No hitch. And I'm buying.
Dad: Really? That sounds just wonderful. I'm really looking forward to it. Where will we go? Can we try the new Thai place on Polk?
Me: Yes.
Dad: Fantastic!!

Me: It's just lunch, Dad. I didn't buy you a
pony.

"Ready to go," I said to my father at
twelve thirty sharp.

My mother looked up from her desk. "Going somewhere?" she asked.

"Lunch," I said. "I figured you and Dad
could use some quality time apart after
yesterday's marathon of . . . well, whatever
it was you were doing."

"Why don't you ever invite me to lunch?"

"Next week. Your turn," I replied, thinking it might be a good idea to split them up
to see whether they had their stories
straight.

Something about these Lost Wednesdays
needed explaining. Although, honestly, I
wasn't sure I wanted to delve into that
terrain.

At lunch, this was the extent of my delving:

"So, should I even ask about yesterday?" I
asked.

"Ask at your own risk," Dad replied.

"Uh . . . everything's okay between you
and Mom?"

"Yes. It's just a tune-up."

"And you need that because . . . ?"

"Isabel, marriages require work. We have

185

job stress and two high-maintenance children, and we've been married thirty-five years."

"*Two* high-maintenance children?" I asked.

"No offense, Isabel. We don't count David."

"I think Mom would count him."

"What's that supposed to mean?"

"Mom is investigating David again and using me as her proxy. I don't want to do it anymore."

"Just say no."

"I've tried that, but she finds another angle to hook me."

"Not a phenomenon I'm unfamiliar with."

"I need her off my back and I need her to leave David alone. He's fine. Maggie's fine. How do I get myself out of the situation?"

"Can't you make something up?"

"One look at me and she knows when I'm lying."

"There are ways around talking," Dad replied. "That's what the rule board is for."

I thought about it and realized that maybe it could work. Then I switched gears. I wanted to see if Dad could do anything to derail my mother's lawyer-date commandment.

"Don't you think it's creepy that Mom is

making me go on dates with men I don't like?"

"I do," Dad replied, making real eye contact for the first time all lunch, "but it's even more bizarre that you're doing it."

"Excuse me?"

"You could say no," Dad replied. "That's not a word you're unfamiliar with. Sometimes I think it was the only thing that came out of your mouth for fifteen years."

"You know what happens when you cross Mom," I replied.

"I do," said Dad. "But how bad can it be? You live in your own apartment, have your own life, she can't ground you, take away bar privileges, dock your pay. I promise that. So why are you doing it?"

Dad made an excellent point. A point I wasn't prepared to answer. I had to play it cool.

"She has her ways," I answered and then picked up the check and pretended to be calculating the tip, like someone who has never calculated a tip before. I even used my fingers for show.

My dad rolled his eyes and looked at me with concern and a bit of embarrassment, I think.

"Just double the tax, Isabel," Dad mumbled.

"Really?" I said. "Is that how it's done?"

After I paid the check, Dad stared at the table for a minute as if he were trying out some words of wisdom in his head.

"Don't be too hard on your mother with the dating thing."

"Easy for you to say."

"She worries it's her fault."

"What's her fault?"

"How do I phrase this?" Dad said, consulting the ceiling.

"Just spit it out."

"She thinks your trouble with men is her doing. She wanted her girls to be strong. She thinks maybe she took it too far."

"Oh my god. She just wants to take credit for everything, doesn't she?" I said, trying to lighten things up.

I'd asked my dad to lunch to pump him for information, not to have a serious conversation. I was hoping the moment would pass.

"Dad, I'm okay. You need to stop worrying."

The moment didn't pass. Dad stared down at the table, afraid to make eye contact.

"Isabel, have you ever thought about going back to therapy, just to check in on things and stuff?"

Dead silence. How did I answer this question?

"I'm going to let you in on a secret, Dad. I never quit therapy. I still see Dr. Rush once a week."[1]

For once, Dad was utterly speechless and didn't try to fill the void with sentimental aphorisms. He smiled and patted me on the head and said, "That's my girl."

As Dad and I strolled back to the Spellman office/homestead, we passed a newsstand. Dad stopped in his tracks and stared at the women's section of the magazine rack. I figured it was a passing glance, but he stayed put. I slid next to him and tried to follow his eye line.

"Do you want to make him wild in bed or get rid of cellulite for good?" I asked.

Dad grabbed a piece of the gender-specific propaganda off the rack and paid the newsagent. Once the exchange was complete, Dad continued on his way. I followed.

"My gift to you," Dad said with a wicked smirk on his face.

I pulled the magazine out of the paper bag and read the cover blurbs, hunting for the point of this offering.

1. True. But these sessions are personal, so I'm going to keep them that way.

Are you a shoe addict? Take the quiz
White lies: Certain truths
should not be told

And finally, the eureka moment:

The Dating Bible: Ten things you
shouldn't do on a first date

"That is so sweet," I said as I slid the magazine back in the bag.

"You probably don't have to do all ten," Dad replied.

Back at the office, I authored a new rule.

### #33 — COMMUNICATION ONLY BY INSTANT MESSAGE THIS AFTERNOON

I typed the following:

Me: David is fine. The big blonde is a headhunter he was in talks with.
Mom: You sure?
Me: Positive.
Mom: Thank you.
Me: I'm not doing any more dirty work for you. Got it?
Mom: Don't forget, you have a date tomorrow at eight P.M. Drinks at One Market with

a James Fitzgerald. He's blond and will wear a red handkerchief. Err on the conservative side.

Me: Don't worry. I'll err as usual.

Mom: Stop that.

# WAKE-UP CALL

My alarm clock shoved me out of bed and growled, "Bloody 'ell, wake up, Isabel!" Connor was already roused by the digital version of himself, which had buzzed rudely at five A.M. sharp. I had managed to ignore the first wake-up call since I was in deep REM sleep. However, he had only just gone to bed a few hours back and apparently doesn't sleep through anything above fifty decibels. Me, under the perfect set of circumstances, I can max out around eighty.

To avoid further agitating the already agitated and sleep-deprived Ex #12, I dressed quickly and inelegantly and slipped into the kitchen to make coffee. Only, the bag that holds the coffee was empty and after an extended hunt for more of the same, I came up short. I returned to the bedroom and tapped the heel of the sleep-deprived bed-grouch and demanded to know where he hid my coffee.

He muttered something inaudible, which I concluded meant that we had run out and he had not replenished our supply.

I controlled the temper tantrum that would have usually surfaced and said with calm rationality, "You are the worst boyfriend in the history of the world."

Ex #12 lifted his head, smiled sheepishly, and said, "An' yoo arr even worse than that. There's plenty of coffee to be had outside these doors."

"Satan," was my clever reply.

"Will I see ya later?" Connor asked, still thick with a groggy Irish slur.

"No, I have a date tonight."

"Right. Forgot. Now give us a kiss and get the 'ell outta here so I can sleep. I have nightmares to get back ta."

I kissed Connor on the lips. His breath still stank of whiskey. I flicked him on the forehead to remind him that not replenishing the coffee supply is a punishable offense and then I did as I was told. I got the hell out of there.

The notion that coffee can be had anywhere, anytime is a patent untruth. Most decent coffee shops don't open until six A.M. I planned to be at my post before then, so I traveled the two miles to my parents' house, entered the premises through the office window (habit), and quietly started the coffee brewing.

The peaceful quiet of dawn was broken by my sister's whine.

"Why aren't you wearing your shirt?" Rae asked, standing in the doorway of the kitchen, sporting pajamas and tangled bed hair.

I looked down at the wrinkled blue Oxford that I'd pulled from the pitch-dark closet. I thought there was a chance I could lie my way out of the conflict, so I said, "It's under my shirt."

"Prove it," Rae replied, as I knew she would, so it was silly to even try.

"I forgot, okay. It's early. I don't even know what you're doing up."

"Finishing an English paper. I think I have an extra shirt lying around," Rae said. "I'll get it for you."

Rae disappeared while I poured a travel mug of coffee. When my sister returned, she handed me the new Spellman uniform — a blue T-shirt with yellow felt letters unevenly ironed on the front.

Free Schmidt!

I proceeded to unbutton my shirt, planning to layer the uniform under my usual wrinkled attire, but Rae would have none of it.

"Put it on *over* your shirt," Rae said in a whiny, demanding tone.

"No," I said.

"Why not?"

"Because I don't like people staring at my boobs all day."

"It doesn't bother me," Rae replied.

"That's because you're a walking bill-board," I replied.

Rae shook her head with a dramatic sense of disappointment and said, "A man spends fifteen years in prison for a crime he didn't commit and you're worried about people staring at your chest?"

There was no point in continuing the conversation. I threw the FREE SCHMIDT! shirt over my long-sleeved button-down and exited the house with my mug of coffee.

After six weeks of surveilling Dr. Hurtt and Harkey, all I had was a subject they had in common: Marco Pileggi, patient of Dr. Hurtt's and subject of Mr. Harkey's insurance investigation. Without seeing the surveillance reports themselves (which wouldn't become available unless there was a trial) I couldn't be certain that anything untoward was happening with the investigation. Marco Pileggi appeared legitimately injured. He wore his neck brace at all times and didn't do things like climb ladders, hang Christmas lights, or prowl the Tenderloin for hookers. If Marco wasn't doing anything wrong then Harkey could hardly doctor a report saying otherwise. I was staring at the deadest of dead ends and even at that very moment I wasn't ready to admit it.

My cell phone rang at six fifteen A.M., just as I was settling into reading the paper, drinking my coffee, and hoping that Harkey's men would lead me in the direction of a serious violation of investigative codes.

The number was listed as private.

"Hello?"

"I'm watching you, Isabel."

It was Harkey's voice; I would recognize that counterfeit growl anywhere.

"What a coincidence; I'm watching you too, or more specifically, I'm watching Jim Atherton watching Marco Pileggi. Another insurance case, I assume."

"What do you think you're going to find?"

"With a PI as crooked as you, the sky's the limit."

"I'm careful, Isabel."

"You didn't used to be."

"And yet you couldn't prove anything."

196

"Not yet."

"You shouldn't have started this, Isabel."

"I didn't start it; you struck first, actually."

"Like I said before. I had nothing to do with that audit."

"I just hope all *your* books are in order."

"You should stop worrying about me, Isabel, and clean your own house. You wouldn't want to disappoint your parents, would you?"

"I wouldn't worry about that. They're used to it. Besides, eliminating the competition would be great for business."

"I thought you'd be a more worthy adversary."

"What makes you think I'm not?"

"There's trouble under your nose and you don't even see it."

"An empty threat, I think."

"You're wasting your time, sweetheart."

"Maybe. But I'm young. I've got more time to waste than you."

I liked my exit line. It left my threat in the air. But the fact of the matter was this investigation was a total waste of time. If I wanted to find Harkey's Achilles, I'd have to attack from another angle.

Before my lawyer date that night, I decided

to check in on one of my paying cases and see whether any progress had been made. I phoned the Winslow home and caught Len breathless and impatient.

"Len, it's Isabel."

"Darling, I'll call you tomorrow."

"This won't take long."

"We're already late for the theater," Len replied.

"The theater?"

"Yes. Mr. Winslow and I are on our way to see Shaw tonight and we're already late."

"Who's Shaw?"

"George Bernard Shaw, Isabel. We have orchestra seats for *Don Juan in Hell*."

"Is that a play?"

"I cannot *believe* you just asked that question," Len said in the most condescending tone.

"Remember, that accent isn't real."

"We have fifteen minutes to get across town, Isabel."

"Len, have you made any progress on this investigation?"

"We'll chat tomorrow, darling. And I'll tell you all about the play."

"Can't wait," I said, but Len had already disconnected the call.

I thought it was safe to assume that no progress had been made.

# MANDATORY
# LAWYER DATE #3
## JAMES FITZGERALD

---

[Partial transcript reads as follows:]

**James:** So, Isabel, what do you like to do for fun?

**Isabel:** Shopping is my first love.*[1]

**James:** I see.

**Isabel:** What about you?

**James:** In the winter I like to ski. Are you into any snow sports?

**Isabel:** No, but I think some of the outfits are really cute.

**James:** You're a PI, I hear.

**Isabel:** And you're a lawyer. I love lawyers.

**James:** Why exactly?

**Isabel:** They've come in handy a few times.

**James:** Oh.

**Isabel:** And they make tons of money.*

**James:** Not all of us.

**Isabel:** But you do all right, don't you?

1. An asterisk marks where a dating rule from the magazine has been broken.

199

**James:** Uh, I guess so.

**Isabel:** Whew. So, are you a player or do you want to get married and have kids?*

**James:** Eventually, I'd like those things.

**Isabel:** How many kids do you want?*

**James:** I don't know. Not too many.

**Isabel:** I want four. One girl. One boy. And a pair of twins. Is that redundant? A pair of twins?

**James:** Yes.

**Isabel:** Oh well, the English language is so not my thing.

**James:** Waiter, can I get another drink?

**Waiter:** And for the lady? Are you finished with your vodka tonic?

**Isabel:** Yes, keep 'em coming.[2]

*[Long, awkward silence while I work on a new line of defense.]*

**Isabel:** So where did you go to school?

**James:** Princeton.

**Isabel:** Oh, that's one of the good ones, isn't it?

**James:** How about you?

**Isabel:** Garfield High and then I did some time at community college. And then I actually did some time.

2. I know, I was breaking character, but I needed more liquid courage. I found my own performance deeply disturbing.

**James:** Excuse me?

**Isabel:** That was a joke. But a true one.

**James:** What are your long-term goals?

**Isabel:** I'd like to start my own charitable organization.

**James:** What kind of charity?

**Isabel:** I'm still working out the details, but we'll have really great soirees, I know that for sure.

**James:** Sounds like you've got it all worked out.

**Isabel:** There's something I should tell you.

**James:** What?

**Isabel:** I don't know whether I should bring it up on a first date.

**James:** Maybe you shouldn't.

**Isabel:** [whispering] I'm saving myself until marriage.*

**James:** Interesting.

**Isabel:** Now, tell me everything about yourself.

To close the deal, I phoned James an hour after the date was over and told him what a great time I had and hoped we could do it again real soon.*

The following day, my mother phoned me and asked how my date went. Her tone was unfriendly, so I figured she'd already heard.

"What did he say?"

" 'You have a very nice daughter, but I feel like we didn't connect intellectually,' he said. Bravo," Mom said.

"He's a liar," I insisted. " 'Not connecting intellectually' means he thought my ass was too big."

"Not true," Mom replied. "I asked James, and he likes women with a little meat on their bones."

"I think I might be sick."

"I want the evidence, Isabel," said Mom. "Bring the recording to dinner on Sunday."

"Fine."

"We'll talk about this later," she said.

"Make an appointment first," I replied.

# PHONE CALL
## FROM THE EDGE #20

Morty phoned me Sunday morning, while Connor was playing rugby and I was enjoying a few hours of peace before the mandatory family meal.

[Partial transcript reads as follows:]

**Morty:** You know what they call a widower in Miami?

**Me:** No.

**Morty:** A guy with too many girlfriends.

**Me:** Was that a joke? Because it was a bad one and the timing and phrasing are all wrong.

**Morty:** No, it's not a joke, Professor Shecky Green. It's a fact. The old guys here whose wives have passed on are like players.

**Me:** Who taught you the word "player"?

**Morty:** I watch a lot of the television.

**Me:** Just say "television" or "TV"; don't say "*the* television."

**Morty:** I've been speaking for a lot longer than you have. What makes you the expert?

**Me:** I don't want to have the "things change" talk again. Can we agree to switch subjects?

**Morty:** Fine by me.

**Me:** Has your shuffleboard game improved?

**Morty:** That's a very rude stereotype.

**Me:** So, it hasn't improved.

**Morty:** You know the shiksa and Gabe are still together?

**Me:** Morty, her name is Petra.

**Morty:** Right. I'm old. I got a bad memory.

**Me:** You always remember she's a shiksa.

**Morty:** With tattoos.

**Me:** Yes, she has a few tattoos.

**Morty:** I sure hope Gabey doesn't get them.

**Me:** They're not contagious, you know.

**Morty:** Do me a favor and go visit them sometime. I want to make sure that my Gabe doesn't have any ink.

**Me:** Ink? Where'd you learn that term?

**Morty:** From the television.

**Me:** I'm going to hang up now.

# THE RETURN OF
## SUNDAY-NIGHT DINNER

Picture a table of five adults and one seventeen-year-old, all clothed in navy-blue T-shirts with the FREE SCHMIDT! slogan in yellow felt letters across the front. Keep that image in your head as I describe the rest of the meal.

"Isn't Schmidt free yet?" I asked over salad.

"No," Rae replied, emoting with the appropriate shade of social conscience. "You should be helping," she added.

"We've already had this conversation," I replied.

"Even Dad's helping."

I turned to my father, a look of surprise, I'm sure, sliding over my previous expression, whatever that was.

Dad sighed and then spoke. "It's a serious case of police misconduct. A horrible travesty of justice. Whenever this happens it puts a cloud over my whole profession."

Maggie smiled at my dad. "Thanks again for the help," she said.

"Dad's helping with the Schmidt case," said Rae. "Did you hear that, Isabel?"

Then Maggie turned to me as if to absolve me of my sins. "He's just helping interview witnesses. We're getting ready to file an appeal and I want to make sure everything's in order. We have it covered."

I was wearing Schmidt. Did I have to talk about him all night long? It wasn't that I didn't feel for Schmidt, but I was busy with other things.

Fortunately, or not, David decided to change the subject.

"So how was secret Wednesday?" he asked.

"We're calling it Lost Wednesday," I said.

"It was fine. Your father and I had some quality time together," Mom said, reaching over and running her fingers through what's left of my father's hair.

"Yes, we did," Dad echoed.

Rae coughed, as if she were choking on a particle of food, and said, "Please don't talk about it while I'm trying to eat."

David eyed my parents with a dose of skepticism and then asked Mom what else was for dinner.

"Al, will you grab the turkey loaf and the pilaf?"

David made a face when he heard the menu, which my mother caught but ignored. My dad did his best oblivious act and served the food. Once the table began its unchoreographed dance of serving dishes and salt-shaker swapping, the previous line of conversation was revisited.

"What's this Lost Wednesday you're all talking about?" foolish Maggie asked.

"You can retract questions in this house," Rae informed her. "It's in the rule book."[1]

Maggie turned to David for an explanation. "Is it a secret? I don't mean to pry."

"You're not prying," my mother casually replied. "Al and I just feel that at this point in our marriage we need to spend more time getting to know each other."

"Did you know you can plant fingerprint evidence with regular old Scotch tape?" Rae said.

"We call it 'Lost Wednesday,' " Dad explained, "just because we lose a day. We don't work and stuff."

"How do you fill the time?" Maggie asked.

"You *definitely* want to retract that question," Rae said.

"We're creative," Mom replied.

"Did you know," Rae interrupted loudly,

1. Indeed, it is.

"that in the Ice Age giant beavers roamed the earth? Beavers the size of grizzly bears. I can't imagine. Can you?"

"Rae, would you like to take your dinner to your room?" my mom asked. It was a simple question, not a punishment.

"Not this particular meal," Rae replied. "But I wouldn't mind going to my room with other nourishment."

"Fine," Mom said. "Just make sure there's some protein in the mix."

Rae made a run for it to the kitchen, quickly scrounged around so she wouldn't hear any more "Lost Wednesday" chatter, and raced up the stairs.

Some peace and quiet arrived upon Rae's exit, while the remaining diners consumed their bland dinner. It was my mother who broke the silence and also the basic laws of good taste.

"There's nothing wrong with trying to figure out how to put a little spice into your relationship. I mean, even when Al and I were first dating, we had to figure a few things out."

Maybe to you that statement sounds innocent enough. But it wasn't innocent. It was loaded with meaning, which I will now share with you. Apparently Mom didn't buy my text message about the headhunter and did her own investigation on the big blonde, acquiring the same knowledge I did. Judging by the way my father picked and gawked at his hideous turkey loaf, he was clueless and guiltless. However, Olivia had to be stopped before Maggie realized that my mother was essentially trying to talk about sex therapy with my brother's girlfriend of only three months.

There was no time for subtlety.

"Mom!" I shouted. This got her attention.

I slit my finger across my throat.

"Relax and eat your dinner, Isabel. I'm just making conversation."

"Boundaries, Mom. Boundaries."

"I want us to be the kind of family that talks about everything."

"Let's not get carried away," Dad said, still oblivious.

"Mom, if you say one more word on the topic, I will come around the table and tackle you to the ground."

"Am I missing something?" Dad asked.

David then turned to Maggie and said one simple word: "See?"

Maggie chuckled to herself. "So who knows?" she asked, scanning the faces of her fellow dinner companions.

I turned to her. "Just me and Mom, I think. And, I swear, I did everything I could to keep her in the dark. Also, I just want to add, the only reason I was investigating you was because Mom blackmailed me."

"So everybody knows but me?" Dad said, sounding really left out and kind of hurt.

David, once again, directed his words to Maggie: "You need to know what it's like before things go any farther. Can you deal?"

"Can we at least tell them the truth first?" Maggie said, squirming under the four sets of eyes that were gauging her expression.

David turned to my mother.

"Mom, we weren't seeing a sex therapist. We were fake-seeing one."

"What does that even mean?" Dad asked.

"It was a setup," David explained. "Maggie and I are thinking about moving in together and I wanted her to understand that if she did, her expectation of privacy would have to significantly diminish."

"Talk about thinking ahead," I said, trying to break the tension.

"So, you two are okay in the —"

"Not another word, Mom," said David.

"Olivia, can't you just leave the kids alone? They're turning out all right on their own," said Dad. "*Especially* David."

"Hello, I'm sitting right next to you," I exclaimed.

"You win the most-improved-camper

award," Dad replied, smiling his big, goofy no-hard-feelings grin.

During the course of the entire meal I had never seen so many expressions morph across Maggie's face. It was like watching a very subtle silent-film actress in an epic saga about a journey across the globe. But the final expression was one of amusement, not fear, and that meant the night would end as a comedy, not a tragedy.

"Who wants dessert?" Mom said, as if this were just another end to just another meal.

# TROUBLE BREWING

A second Lost Wednesday passed with yet another disturbing result.

Rae, on her way out the door to school, once again approached the whiteboard and drafted another rule.

### RULE #38 — PUT YOUR DVDs AWAY WHEN YOU'RE DONE!!!!!

Once again, Rae tossed a brown-bagged item on Mom's desk and refused to make eye contact. She departed without a single word. It was kind of nice, actually.

I could not contain my curiosity and looked inside the bag. Imagine my shock and horror upon discovering a salsa dancing video. I shook off the image and began my brief interrogation.

"This has to be joke," I said.

"That's what I thought," Dad replied.

"You didn't do this, Dad, did you?"

"No comment," he replied, focusing intently on the computer screen.

"Why don't you mind your own business, Isabel?" Mom suggested.

I ignored her, of course.

"You don't have to salsa if you don't want to, Dad."

"Excuse me, I'm going to make some tea," my father said, making his escape.

"Mom, do you want to have lunch today?" I suddenly suggested.

"Just you and me?" Mom replied.

"I think that would be for the best."

"Love to," Mom replied. And that was the end of that conversation.

Over lunch I tried to delve deeper into the salsa mystery, but I got nowhere. Mom was a dead end.

"We're trying something new. That's all. I don't think you have to worry about us entering any dance contests," she said over a *salade niçoise* at this French place on Polk Street.

"Honestly, Mom. Is everything okay between you and Dad?"

"Yes," Mom said. Only there was something incomplete about the delivery. Mom can lie, but she can't cover up every sparring emotion inside of her. I didn't push at that moment, since I knew I wouldn't get any hard facts. And, to be perfectly honest, it was my goal to trim my extracurricular investigations to a minimum. Some things that transpired between my parents I didn't really want to know about.

Instead, I decided to use my quality time with Mom to see whether I could put a dent in her meddling.

"Mom, how long are you going to hold Prom Night 1994 over my head?"

"I don't believe in long-term blackmail. This incident will be forgotten once you go on, say, twenty lawyer dates."

"How about ten," I countered.

"The best offer I'll give you is sixteen. Since that's the age you were when the incident took place. Don't forget that. I saved your ass."

"Fine, sixteen lawyer dates. Thirteen to go. I want it in writing that we're done after this."

As Mom drafted our agreement on a place mat, I tried to get to the bottom of her brand of meddling.

"What is the point of all this?"

"Connor is not the guy for you."

"How do you know?"

"I know," Mom replied in a tone as solid as steel. Then she asked for the check.

I guessed the conversation was over.

Sometimes you get the feeling that your life is going to take a sudden and alarming twist, but the feeling is vague and you can't put your finger on what might go wrong. Therefore you see signs in everything and remain on guard at all times.

Rae phoned me later that night.

"Izzy?"

"Hi, Rae."

"Something is wrong."

"Please don't ask me for a ride. I'm busy."

"I'm home."

"Then what's wrong?"

"I went downstairs to grab a snack and I caught Mom in the pantry crying."

"Mom was crying?"

"Like really hard."

"What did you do?"

"Nothing. I went back to my room. Should I have done something? What do you do?"

"I don't know."

"Do you think she was crying about the salsa dancing? I know I would."

"I think that probably wasn't it," I replied.

"Is something bad happening?"

"Like what?"

"I don't know, the usual bad stuff. Somebody is sick. She and Dad are getting a divorce."

"They're not getting a divorce."

"How do you know?" Rae replied.

"Who else would have them?"

"Good point. But she was crying really hard, Izzy."

"Sometimes people cry, Rae."

"Yeah, I know."

"Don't worry about it."

"Okay."

"Do you want me to come over there?" I asked.

"No. It's late. But I'm still hungry and I think Mom's still in the kitchen."

"Don't you have anything stashed in your room?"

"No. Wait. Oh yeah. I have those leftover Doritos from the camping trip in my desk."

"You really shouldn't keep open bags of food in your bedroom, Rae. You're going to get ants and then you'll never get rid of them."

"Okay, good-bye."

Most of my conversations with Rae end with that simple cutoff. When she decides a conversation is over, it's over. Was I worried about my mother's flood of tears? Yes. But everyone cries sometimes. I've been known to cry when I can't find coffee. Every once in a while a thought hits you and you're unprepared for it and suddenly it seems like your world is coming to an end. Most of the time it isn't. That's not to say I didn't register this episode as another clue in a vague mystery, but I wasn't too worried. At least, not yet.

Shortly after my conversation with Rae, I got another call that set off sirens in my head.

"Izzeee," Bernie[1] said. That's how he says my name, as if I'm the star member of his favorite football team.

"Hi, Bernie," I said dully. He's not even a benchwarmer on any of my imaginary teams.

"What are you doing?" Bernie asked.

"Nothing," I replied.

"Been there, done that."

"How's everything with Daisy[2]?" I asked, because when things aren't good with Daisy, they're also not good with my living situation.

"Everything's great. We're coming to the

1. Bernie Peterson, ex-cop. Old guy I sublet from. If you want to know more about Bernie, read previous documents.
2. Bernie's ex-showgirl sweetheart. They live in Vegas, in case you were wondering.

217

city next week."

"What hotel are you staying in?" I inquired nervously.

"The Travelodge on Lombard."

"Excellent choice!" I said with a little too much enthusiasm.

"I'm taking Daisy to see *Beach Blanket Babylon.* Can you believe she's never seen it?"

"Yes, I can."[3]

"Maybe we can meet up for some clam chowder," Bernie said.

"Maybe," I replied. Translation: only under the threat of imminent death.

"Catch you later, Izzee."

"I hope not."

Phone calls with Bernie always drain my energy. I like it when Bernie stays in Vegas, because when he does, other things seem to stay there as well. Like trouble, for instance. I couldn't tell you how I knew it — just a feeling in my gut — but nothing good was going to come from Bernie's visit.

3. I'm not saying another word.

# Rule #40 —
## Learn Some Manners

I spotted Rule #40 on the board as I entered the Spellman offices. No one vetoed it, because really, how can you veto manners? My father pretended it was a general reminder, Rae curtsied on her way out the door, and I later inquired as to the specifics.

First you must know something about the Spellmans. We like nuts — cashews, almonds, macadamia nuts, mixed nuts, but especially pistachios. My mother had recently taken to leaving a bowl of pistachio nuts on the bar that separates the kitchen from the living room. This was the first time other than a holiday party that the nuts were just sitting there for the taking. Someone was leaving the shells inside the bowl with the uncorrupted nuts, which really got under my mother's skin. She was so determined to nail the culprit, I found her setting up a hidden camera to capture the evidence. My mother's a private investigator. This is what she does. And, sure, there have been many occasions on which she's used such tactics to uncover benign infractions, like who's left the porch light on or the garage door open, drunk the last of the milk, etc. Our work instincts cannot be left in the office, especially when the office is inside the family home. However, something about Mom was off these days and I wanted to get to the bottom of it.

Later that afternoon, after completing a few hours of work, I tried to launch into a casual conversation. I'm sure you will admire my subtlety.

"You feeling all right, Mom?"

"Why do you ask?"

"How about answering the question?"

"Maybe I would if it weren't presented with that attitude."

"Mom, you're not yourself, and that concerns me because even your normal self is a tad on the unpredictable side."

"What are you getting at?"

"Well, there was that 'literature'[1] and the DVD."

"What your father and I do on our own

1. I used finger quotes, yes.

time is none of your business," Mom replied.

"Okay, what about bringing up sex therapy at dinner the other night?" I said as a reminder.

"I don't want David to screw this up."

"I'd rephrase that if I were you."

"I'm his mother and I have the right to meddle, just as I meddle with you and just as I meddle with Rae. One day I won't be here to meddle and you'll miss me."

"And then the three of us will unite as a band of traveling bank robbers and all hell will break loose."

"Something like that," Mom replied.

After a long pause, enough time for a topic change to not be too jarring, I asked, "Is everything all right with you and Dad?" I asked.

"Of course. We're fine. I have no complaints. Well, I'd like him to drop another ten pounds, but with the holidays coming up, I don't see that happening. And I wish you'd break up with that thug. And I wish that Rae would get a haircut. Well, I have some complaints. But none is all that severe."

"You should take down the pistachio cam, Mom. In this house we don't need any more invasions of privacy."

"Fine," said Mom, "but that's the end of the pistachios."

"I understand," I replied.[2]

My next order of business was to subtly and sensitively inquire into the matter of my mother crying in the kitchen late at night. I assume you've gathered by now that subtle and sensitive are not in my regular playbook. How about an A for effort?

"I heard you were crying in the kitchen the other night."

"How'd you hear that?"

"It was caught on your pistachio cam."

My mother didn't think that was funny at all.

"Sorry," I said. "Rae saw you. It upset her. Then she told me. If it were Aunt Martie[3] I wouldn't think twice. But you're not a crier. So is everything okay?"

2. The pistachio thug turned out to be none other than Jeremy Pratt. I left him in the hallway too long and he got bored, as boys like him tend to. I remember smelling pistachios on his breath. When he emptied his pockets of paperwork, no shells flew out. They had to go somewhere. It took my mom this long to notice the empty shells since Rae liked to replenish the bowl whenever it dipped just an inch.

3. Mom's slightly unstable older sister.

"Yes, yes," my mother said, stopping short of saying more. The thing is, people don't always say more with me, for obvious reasons. I had to push harder and yet with more sensitivity. Not an easy feat.

"If you wanted to elaborate, I would respond in an appropriate manner."

My mother stared at her computer screen, but there were only floating fish to hold her attention.

"A friend from high school died. I got an e-mail about it."

"Who?"

"Martha Givens."

"I'm sorry. Were you close?"[4]

"No. I hadn't seen her in years. But she was in my class and she died of natural causes. A heart attack while she was sleeping. It made me sad, that's all. Got me thinking about my own mortality, which I rarely consider. You were always a perennial teenager. I was always middle-aged. I keep forgetting you're thirty-two. Oh my god, you're thirty-two. Speaking of your shortening lifespan and unmarried status —"

"We weren't actually speaking of that."

"Have you found your next lawyer?"

"Would you look at the time?"

4. See, an utterly appropriate response.

"Wait, don't go. I'll change the subject."

"What?" I said.

"I need you to do me a favor. I have a seven o'clock meeting with the new Zylor HR person. Somebody needs to pick up Rae from Maggie's office tonight."

"How about a bus driver?" I suggested.

"Please, Isabel. Also, I don't know if it would hurt matters if you could maybe say something to Maggie to smooth things over. You know, with Sunday-night dinner and all."

"I wouldn't worry about it," I replied.

"Really?" Mom said, looking for re-assurance.

"There's no way those giant beavers are coming back."

I agreed to pick up Rae from Maggie's office but grew suspicious when I learned that Rae had already arranged for a ride there from school. I decided to swing by Garfield High School to make sure Rae Spellman was no longer using the Logan Engle Car Service.

It was easier to keep watch on the BMW, so I found a post that gave me a clear view of Logan's car. When he got in and drove off alone, my work was done.

Only, as I was driving away, I caught Rae

with that cyclist guy again, and while I had no intention of following them or infringing on their privacy in any way, I did pull out my digital camera, focus with the zoom lens, and take several high-definition shots of the pair looking remarkably cozy. Just as I was pondering how Rae was planning on getting home, David pulled up in front of the school.

When his car came into view, Rae and the cyclist took on the roles of complete strangers. My sister casually walked over to my brother's vehicle and my siblings departed. Briefly I considered that Rae had dirt on David and that was why he was driving her, but I followed them a short distance (just a few blocks; don't judge me!) and realized that they were headed to Maggie's office. Everything made sense now, except for the secret boyfriend. But that was none of my business and I was done investigating family members. For the day, at least.

Maggie and Rae were celebrating over Jelly Bellies and root beer. Their appeal had been successful — Levi Schmidt's case was reopened. The crime lab was currently testing for any leftover DNA evidence. Barring any laboratory or storage mishaps, there was an excellent chance that science could free

Schmidt, although Rae would take all the credit.

When my sister started to appear drunk off the sugar, Maggie cut her off and reminded Rae that she had to refocus her energy on the upcoming SATs. As we were leaving, I asked Maggie if she had any concerns that she needed to voice.

"I'm fine," she casually replied.

It seemed impossible that someone could be casual in the aftermath of Sunday night's dinner, but I took her at her word.

"If you have any problem with my mother, let me know."

Rae, who had taken my car keys, started honking the horn.

"There's only one Spellman who scares me," Maggie said, eyeing Rae through the office window. "That one."

I couldn't argue with her.

# SON OF
# SUNDAY-NIGHT DINNER

It's remarkable how quickly seven days can pass. I had to admit, I was ready to author a rule that limited Sunday-night dinners to every other Sunday. There's only so much bland food and conflict-laden conversation that a person should be expected to tolerate. And since I worked at the house all week, it seemed especially cruel to make me show up on Sunday.

When I arrived, Mom had burned a roast and called out for pizza. Rae, I was told, was in her room celebrating. This seemed as good a time as any to clear up the situation behind Mom's crying jag, so I knocked on Rae's door, although I didn't wait for an invitation to enter.

She was hanging upside down off her bed and in the midst of a conversation.

"All I did was turn up the oven to five hundred degrees for an hour and then turn it down. Voilà, pizza. That's how it's done —"

My entrance interrupted her sentence, but at least now the roast mystery was solved (Mom's roasts are not exactly good, but the woman knows how to follow a recipe).

"Got to go," Rae said, and then she quickly ended the call.

"I knocked," I said.

"Then you wait for an invitation," Rae replied. "That's how it's done."

"I have information," I said. "I figured you'd be interested."

Rae sat upright. "Shoot."

"Don't worry about Mom," I said. "She's okay. An old friend died."

"What friend?" Rae asked.

"Martha Givens."

"From high school?"

"Yes."

"I heard about that," Rae said.

"Well, then, mystery solved."

"No. *Not* solved. I was there when Mom got the e-mail from Aunt Martie. Martha Givens was the superhero of bitches. She and Mom liked the same guy — his name was Benjamin something —"

"Ben Frankel. That's Uncle Ben.[1] You know, the guy who always wears sock garters."

1. We found it amusing too.

228

"Mom and Uncle Ben used to go out?" Rae asked.

"Yes."

*"Oh my god,"* she said, and then she made that hairball face and shivered. "First let me clear that image from my head."

Rae closed her eyes and breathed. Then she continued.

"So after some guy named Ben and Mom started going out," Rae said, "Martha put drain cleaner in Mom's shampoo. But Mom smelled it first, so nothing happened. But then Martha told all these lies about Mom."

"Like what?"

"That Mom put out on the first date. You would have been like the school slut if you lived in Mom's day," Rae said.

"And you'd be in reform school," I said. "Now back to Martha. So, they were *never* friends?"

"They were full-on enemies," Rae replied. "I don't think Mom wanted her dead, but I *know* that crying spree was not for the loss of a woman who tried to make her go bald."

"Huh," I said. Then it occurred to me that Mom was really a spectacular liar. This is a fact I have always known, but sometimes it's good to take notice of a fresh reminder.

"So why was she crying?" I asked.

"I don't know," Rae said with a little too

much nonchalance.

"Something strange is going on in this house."

"Tell me about it," Rae replied.

Dinner was better this time around for a number of reasons: We all like pizza and no one was delving into anyone else's sex life. Although there was an awkward moment when Mom was giving Dad a quick shoulder-rub and Rae suggested they get a room.

The only other notable incident was when David brought to light a minor observation.

"What happened to that hideous light fixture in the downstairs bathroom?"

"We changed it," Mom awkwardly replied after a brief pause.

"I've been asking you to change it for the last fifteen years."

"So we did," Mom said.

"Why is the towel rod missing?" David asked.

"It's missing?" Dad said.

"I took it down," Mom interjected.

"Why?" David asked.

"I didn't like it," Mom replied.

"She didn't like it," Dad echoed.

David studied my parents for signs of misdirection but eventually gave up when no member of the unit offered up their usual tells.

"Maggie, how has your week been?" Dad asked.

"Great. As you know, we won the Levi Schmidt appeal, so now we just have to wait for the DNA evidence to come back. Which takes forever, Rae, so you don't have to keep asking."

"I heard you loud and clear the first five times you said that."

"Well, you didn't hear me loud and clear, Rae. Because if you did, you wouldn't have asked me every single day this week."

"Got it," Rae replied, attacking another slice of pizza.

"Maggie won another case this week too," David interjected.

"Well, that's good news. What was the charge?"

"Armed robbery and aggravated assault," Maggie replied. "A jury of his peers found him innocent."

"Congratulations," said Dad.

"Thanks," Maggie replied. "Too bad he was guilty."

The next Tuesday rolled around and I was back on garbology, which meant a simple trip to Shana Breslin's residence to pick up her recycling and then drop it off at Pratt's place.

The neighborhood was sufficiently quiet; the puffy plastic bags were in their place. I dropped the recycling into the trunk of my car and drove off unnoticed. I phoned Jeremy from the road and told him that I would be stopping by. He lived in the Mission, off Folsom near Twenty-second Street. A one-bedroom apartment, not unlike mine, but newer, cleaner, and paid for by somebody else. I knocked on his door and he answered wearing several layers of cotton T-shirts in various sleeve lengths, topped with a navy-blue short-sleeved shirt that had a skater logo on it, although there was no skateboard in sight. Rae would call him a poser. I would call him a moron. My mother would call him useless. My father would call him a dropout. Grammy Spellman would call him a good-for-nothing, which seems to be the most accurate description. Less-judgmental folk would say that he was finding himself, but some people have the luxury to look; others don't.

Jeremy was on his cell phone when I entered with the "goods." He continued his conversation, interspersed with brief comments aimed in my direction.

"[To phone:] Dude, where are we meeting Friday night? Okay, I'm down with that. [To me:] You can leave the bags in the foyer."

"If that's all, I'm going to go," I said.

"Hang on, hang on," Jeremy said to the phone.

Being dismissed like the help by a twenty-something trust-fund hipster with a failed screenwriting career shot me full of adrenalized hate. Oh, how I wanted to sucker-punch Pratt and tell him to get off the fucking phone if he had something to say.

I kept my tone even and interrupted his other conversation.

"I don't have all night, Jeremy."

I did have all night, but my delivery was delightfully cold and had its intended effect.

"Dude, let me call you right back."

Jeremy flipped his phone shut and turned to me. I could see his attitude like steam coming out of his pores.

"Is that it?" Jeremy said, nodding at the bags on the floor.

"Yes," I replied. "Unless you want to pay an arm and a leg, I suggest you try to piece them together yourself."

"Do people actually do that?" he asked.

"Some do. It just depends on how important it is to you."

"Other options?"

"Surveillance," I replied.

"I'm not made of money."

"It seems you're mostly made of a wide variety of fabrics, as far as I can tell."

"Can we check her phone records?"

"It's kind of hard to do that these days."

"Can I listen in on her conversations?"

"If she's in public, sure."

"No, like, can you tap her line? Or could you put some kind of recording device in her house? I mean, all I'd need to do is listen to her for a few days and then I'd know for sure."

"Sorry, can't do that," I replied. "It's illegal."

"People do it all the time in the movies."

"People fire semiautomatic weapons while

doing somersaults in the movies. Doesn't mean it happens in real life."

Jeremy looked disappointed that I'd wrecked his genius idea.

"Do you want her trash again next week too? We can give each other code names if you want it to be more cinematic," I suggested.

It took him a moment to answer the question.

"See you next week," he said.

"It's been a pleasure," I replied.

It took everything I had not to slam the door on the way out.

As I was walking to my car, my cell phone rang. It was Maggie.

"Everything okay?" I asked as I got into my vehicle and shut the door. "Do you need a Rae extraction?"

"No. She just left David's place about an hour ago. After over an hour of asking her to leave, he actually had to physically pick her up and place her outside the front door. Then she said 'Okay, I can take a hint.' "

"I hope for all our sakes that she doesn't gain any weight. If we lose the physical extraction option, we're doomed," I said.

Usually when Maggie calls me, it's for a Rae extraction. We aren't unfriendly otherwise, but when she began dating my brother,

I thought I should give them their space. The friendship Maggie and I seemed to be forging before that was put on hold, so I couldn't imagine why she was calling.

"Is something on your mind?" I asked.

"Yes," Maggie replied, although she didn't follow up.

"Do you feel like telling me?"

"David asked me to move in with him."

"And how do you feel about that?"[1]

"I'm wondering if it's too soon. We've only been together like four months."

"Don't you practically live together anyway?"

"Good point."

"Thank you."

"What would your mother think?"

"My mother adores you. She'd be ecstatic."

"Really?"

"Yes. Were you worried about her?"

"A little."

"Don't. Just worry about Rae. Are you willing to live in a place that's walking distance from her home?"

"Now *that* I have to think about."

Our call ended a few sage words later. I put the key in the ignition and started the

1. I learned to ask questions like this in therapy.

engine. As I was checking my rearview mirror, I saw the oddest thing: Jeremy Pratt exited his apartment with three puffy bags and stuck them in his recycling bin. Now what do you make of that?

# THE DIALECT WARS

The next day, Robbie Gruber finally got back to me about tracing Mason's e-mails through the headers.

"It looks like the e-mail was sent from the UK," Robbie replied.

"Can you narrow down the location beyond that?"

"No. He's using a web-based e-mail program. You'd need a court order to the service provider to get more details," Robbie said.

"But you're sure he's sending the e-mails from the UK?" I asked.

*"No,"* Robbie replied, loading that single word with truckloads of disdain. "You're not listening. I said *it looks like* the e-mail was sent from the UK."

"What does that mean, Robbie?" I asked impatiently.

"It means the e-mail could have been sent from the UK or it also could have been sent from hundreds of other countries using a proxy."

"How hard would that be to do?" I asked.

"For you, impossible."

"Hey. Remember who's paying you," I said.

"Right, 'cause that fifty bucks is gonna make or break me," Robbie snapped back.

"If you want your car to run tomorrow morning, answer the question."

"Are you threatening me?"

"Yes."

"As soon as this conversation is over, I'm going to file a restraining order."[1]

"Then the sooner you get off the phone, the sooner you can start your legal proceedings. Answer the question: How hard would it be to use a proxy and fake sending e-mails from the UK?"

"Not very hard."

"Thank you, Robbie."

"The bill's in the mail."

*Click.*

That evening, Christopher phoned me and said that he had collected some fingerprint samples from Mason's room. I decided to

1. Don't worry. Robbie threatens this every time we get into a fight. He never follows through.

drop by their loft and see how my Method actor and his partner were doing. I'm afraid I have to report that things had taken a turn for the worse.

Just a quick refresher: Christopher is British; Len (aka Mr. Leonard) is San Francisco born and bred.

This is how Christopher answered the door: "Yo, Izz, where ya been?"

While his accent wasn't perfect, it resembled Baltimore slang à la HBO's *The Wire,* Len and Christopher's favorite show.[2] However, if I missed the point with the accent, Christopher's puff jacket, saggy jeans, and do-rag cleared it up for me.

"Uh-oh," I said.

"Yo, make yourself comfortable."

"Where's Len?" I asked nervously.

"The motherfucker's makin' tea or something. You feelin' thirst?"

"No, I'm fine," I replied, finding a seat on the couch, bracing myself for what might happen next.

When Len entered the room, the contrast reached the point of absurdity. Len was still in his three-piece work attire and he was, as his companion had said so eloquently,

2. Even I have to admit, it's genius. Better than *Get Smart* and *Doctor Who.*

making tea.

"Isabel, what a pleasant surprise," Len said. Yes, still in his valet character.

"Yo, I told you she'd be dropping by for the shit."

"Oh yes, must have slipped my mind," Len said with excessive sarcasm. Then he turned to me as if I'd be his ally. "Can you believe the vulgarity I have to contend with here?"

"Oh my god, what have I done?" I said.

"You want that English shit or a forty instead?" Christopher asked while popping his own can of malt liquor.

"This is what I want. I want the fingerprints and I want both of you to break character and talk like reasonable people about what's going on here."

"I'll get you your shit," Christopher said, heading into the other room.

Len approached and sat down on the couch right next to me, leaning in conspiratorially.

"He won't stop. No matter what I do, I simply cannot get him to stop. I'm absolutely at my wit's end."

"You stop first," I said.

"I'm merely doing my job; what's he doing?"

"Heads up," Christopher said, tossing a

paper bag in my direction.

I caught the bag in midair and made a beeline for the door.

"I'll be in touch," I said.

"Isabel, I beg you, don't go," said Mr. Leonard.

"I have a date," I replied.

"Bitch, you lie," Christopher said, following me to the door.

"This is dreadful," I said.

"Holler if ya need more investigative materials," said Christopher, and finally, breaking character, he mumbled, "I want this case closed."

"Fo shizzle," I replied.

My lie wasn't an entire untruth. I did have a date, with my ever-reliable fingerprint kit. After cross-checking all of Christopher's new prints against the control group, I discovered that Chris had found a fingerprint from every already-identified person currently in Winslow's employ. There were no new prints in the collection. Therefore, there was no chance I would find a match to Mason Graves in the set. This is what happens when you send an actor/decorator to do an investigator's job.

The following day I made an impromptu visit to the Winslow home and found my client to be in great spirits. Apparently, Len had insisted on an eye doctor visit the previous week and his handsome new Gucci glasses had just arrived. Mr. Winslow donned the frames and a whole new world emerged. I had to admit that while my case was stalling, Mr. Winslow was thriving with Len on the job. His skin showed more color, his mood was generally elevated, and I even think he put on a few pounds. I had never seen Winslow smile before, but today he did. Even his teeth didn't look half-bad.

"My god," Mr. Winslow said, glorying in the sight of his backyard terrace, "has it always been this magnificent?"

"Of course," Mr. Leonard replied. "That is why I constantly insist you have afternoon tea out here, weather permitting."

Winslow spun in a circle, taking in his home as if it were brand new.

"I love those candelabra," he said.

"They're gorgeous," Len concurred.

"I really should have gone to an eye doctor ages ago," Winslow said.

Once again, Len agreed in that polite British way. Out of the corner of my eye I spotted the housekeeper scowling, and then Mr. Winslow finally spotted me. There was no mistaken identity this time around.

"Isabel, you look so . . . so much less

blurry than before."

Would it kill the man to throw me a compliment?

"Thank you," I said politely, and then excused myself so that I could speak to Len in private. Winslow hardly noticed, distracted by his new 20/20 vision.

"Christopher found fingerprints for everybody I already knew about. Is there any room that he might have missed dusting?"

"Did he check Mason's bedroom?" Len asked.

"I don't know. Did he?" I asked with a slight edge in my voice.

Len handed me a key. "Third floor, second room on the right."

"Send me a text message if the housekeeper heads upstairs," I mumbled.

"Will do," Len replied.

The room hadn't been aired in weeks. It had a musty mothball smell. To call it impersonal would be generous. It was like a guest room at a lazy man's B and B. A bed, bureau, desk, and lamp pretty much covered the furnishings. There was artwork on the wall — a dreadful amateurish landscape[3] — and the only item of accessory was a day

3. And if I'm calling it amateurish, you know it's bad.

calendar on the desk. I decided to dust the bureau first and found four clear prints right away. I quickly prepped the prints and stuck them in my purse. I looked both ways before I exited Mason's room, locking the door behind me.

I made my way downstairs and covertly slipped Len the key. Mr. Winslow was still in the midst of a mind-blowing tour of his own mansion. Len walked me to the door.

"How are things at home?" I asked.

"Nothing to worry about, Isabel. I promise you."

"You're taking to this a little too well," I said with concern.

"An actor needs to act," Len replied.

And that got me thinking.

# More Detective Work

A few days later, Maggie phoned me again and said that she had a doctor's appointment the following afternoon and would prefer not to leave Rae alone in her office. Something about some embarrassing calls to the district attorney — I didn't get all the details. Anyway, I picked Rae up from school. She did her best to hide the cyclist from me, but I still caught them pretending to be strangers.

I took her to my apartment to help me sort through the fingerprint collection I got from Mason's bedroom.

When we were young — meaning children — and first absorbing the nuts and bolts of the business, even garbology had its moments of delight, but fingerprint collecting had a playground aura of fun around it. In truth, the fingerprint stuff doesn't come up often (that's police work) and when it does, we don't mind so much, even though it's a painstaking process. Rae hadn't worked with the printing kit for years, so I let her prep the prints from Mason's room and then had her cross-check them against all the known prints in the house.

Rae got to work but eventually broke the silence. For once, she had something to talk about besides Schmidt.

"The other day I was looking for candy in Maggie's desk and I found these pills."

"What kind of pills?"

"I didn't recognize them by name, but when I later looked them up, they were antianxiety meds. And according to the Internet, she's on a very high dosage."

"She doesn't seem anxious," I said.

"Well, she wouldn't if she were drugged up all the time."

"Huh," I said, thinking.

"What should I do?"

"You shouldn't be going through her desk," I said.

"But what should I do about her anxiety?" Rae asked.

"You should try not to stress her out."

"How?"

"When she asks you to do something, do it."

"Do you think I'm the cause of her stress?"

"I'm sure you're a top contributor."

Rae seemed to mull that idea over for a very brief moment, but then she shook her head. "Nah, that's not it," she said, and went back to work.

"These don't match any of the others," Rae said after careful scrutiny of our fingerprint samples.

"Finally," I replied, gathering the prints and putting them away safely in an envelope.

Rae then tried to bring up Schmidt again. That's when I told her our work was done. Coincidentally, it was.

As I was driving Rae home, I tried to start a conversation about Rae's new boyfriend and get a few more details on Logan, but Rae and I had decidedly conflicting agendas.

"Were you and Logan ever going out, or were you just blackmailing him?" I asked.

"There are other men and women wrongly incarcerated besides Schmidt."

"It seems like an extreme measure to take just to avoid riding the bus," I said.

"Maggie has many files in her office. You should look at them when you have the chance. It's a better use of your time than obsessing over a has-been like Harkey."

"What happened to you on the bus?" I asked.

"There are people on death row right now who are innocent."

"Who's the new guy with the bicycle?"

"Forget it," Rae finally said. "There's no way to convince you."

I pulled up in front of the Spellman house. Rae hopped out of the car, as did I.

"I don't require an escort," Rae said.

"The world doesn't revolve around you and Schmidt. I need to talk to Dad."

"Whatever," Rae replied.

I followed her inside the house. Rae raced upstairs to her bedroom, as teenagers do. I roamed the residence looking for Dad. In the process, I noticed that the doorknob to the hall closet was missing.

I found my dad parked in front of the television, belly-laughing at some inane program in which a family enters the witness protection program, only to be forced to work at a Frosty Freeze. They can't handle their new lives and so they return to their criminal pasts, using their Frosty Freeze shifts as an alibi, while their handlers try to cover it up, since the family hasn't yet testified against the crime family from whom they are hiding. It's a comedy, I think. Or at least Dad thinks it's a comedy.

I sat down next to him, waited for the commercial break, and asked for the favor

I'd come for.

Only cops and FBI agents and official law-enforcement personnel have access to fingerprint databases. My dad no longer has direct access to this information, but he has a guy on the force who does.

I put the envelope with the prints on the coffee table.

"Dad, will you ask Gary to run these prints for me?"

My father glanced at the envelope and then back at the television, even though only commercials were running.

"I've called in a few too many favors this month. Can you find someone else?"

"Who?"

"Ask your mom. She has her own contact on the force."

"Where is she?"

"In the kitchen."

"Did you know the doorknob on the hall closet is missing?"

Dad paused, sighed, and then said, "Yeah. It fell off."

I went into the kitchen. My mother was in the midst of replacing a handle on the silverware drawer. Unfortunately, it didn't match the other handles in the rest of the kitchen and I could see her scowling over this fact.

"What happened to the other handle?"

"It broke."

"How?"

"I don't know, Isabel."

"This one doesn't match the others."

"Yes. I am aware of that," Mom snapped. "Is there something I can help you with?"

"I need some fingerprints run for the Winslow case. Dad doesn't want to use his source. I was wondering if I could use yours."

"I always ask Henry," Mom said.

"Could you ask him for me?" I said, placing the envelope on the kitchen table.

"Ask him yourself," she replied in that tone that means the conversation is over.

So I drove to Henry's place.

"Isabel, what a pleasant surprise," he said pleasantly.

"I was in the neighborhood," I replied.

"I doubt it," he said.

"I need a favor."

"That's what I figured."

I handed Henry the set of prints. "Will you run these for me?"

"Have a seat. Can I get you something to drink?"

Apparently friends don't just demand police work and run. They sit and chat and maybe drink or eat things together. At least that's Henry's agenda. So I played along in order to push my "favor" agenda. This is simply how the world works. I think. I'm just saying that, actually. To be perfectly honest, I don't know how the world works. Sometimes it seems like it's not working at all.

Henry asked me what I was drinking. I said, "Not tea." He served me a beer and put out a bowl of spelt[1] pretzels. He asked me what was new; I said not much. He inquired into the Harkey matter and I said it was a dead end. He apologized for the insurance information. I told him not to worry about it. It was the only angle available to me. Henry asked me how Connor was doing. I said fine. He asked me whether our relationship was getting serious. I asked him to define "serious." He described serious as "moving forward." I asked Henry where forward might take someone. Henry said that forward usually leads to moving in, engagement, and maybe marriage. I told him that while Connor kept his own apartment, he had practically moved in. I see, Henry said. Then I explained that if Connor didn't practically live with me, we'd

1. Don't ask.

never see each other, what with our opposite hours and such. Henry said, "I see," again. Then he asked if Connor and I ever spoke of marriage. We didn't, but I didn't mention that. What I did mention was that way back my mom had had me sign a legal document promising that I wouldn't marry Connor. I asked Henry whether he thought that document was legally binding and Henry said that he thought it was unlikely.

"Do you want to marry him?" Henry asked.

At this point my beer was finished. I asked for another one instead of answering the question.

The truth: No, I didn't. In fact, I was sure of that one thing. And yet I couldn't tell you why. In case you're wondering: Yes, I've discussed this in therapy, so I don't see any point in going on about it here. As for Henry, the question quickly slipped away when I made it slip away by changing the subject. I casually brought up the far more compelling mystery of the missing fixtures in the Spellman home.

"Isn't that strange?" I asked.

"I guess so," Henry replied. "But it is an old house. Things are bound to break."

For another forty-five minutes, Henry inquired into an assortment of details about my life. Nothing too intrusive, but he got updates on Morty, Mom and Dad's Lost Wednesdays, and even Bernie's impending visit.

"Do you think I should change the locks?" I asked.

Henry said no. Turns out, Henry had never been so wrong.

# My First Holdup

I was supposed to be sitting on a park bench in the middle of the night, waiting for my date. This didn't seem like a wise location for a rendezvous, which I guess was the point.

A man approached. He made no introduction. He then pointed something at me, which I guessed was a gun.

"If you do everything I tell you, no one will get hurt," he said. Then he stared at me with cool confidence.

"Uh, okay," I replied.

"Give me all your money," the man said.

His dress wasn't robber-appropriate, so I had some trouble taking him seriously. But I regrouped and realized that I shouldn't stereotype. Robbers come with a variety of different fashion senses, and he'd probably come straight from work or something.

"I don't have my money with me," I replied.

"Where is it?"

"In my purse."

"Where's your purse?"

"In my car."

"Where's your car?"

"In the parking lot."

"Give me your car keys."

"Uh, okay," I said, and handed him my keys.

He took them.

"A thank-you would be nice," I said.

He rolled his eyes.

"Empty your pockets," he said.

"I'd rather not," I said.

"I'm not afraid to use this thing," the man with no name said, sounding plausibly threatening.

I had on a jacket and jeans, so there were a number of pockets.

"You probably don't want *everything* in my pockets," I replied.

He held out his other hand. "Everything," he repeated.

"Okay."

My jacket pocket held a used tissue, a paper clip, a lost Lifesaver, a parking stub, and a tampon. I tossed the items into his hands. The man with the gun tossed them on the ground.

"If you didn't want them, why did you ask?"

He stared at me and at the bits and pieces on the ground for a while. It looked like he was thinking, but since I didn't know the man, I couldn't tell you for sure what he looked like when he was thinking.

"I can't do this," he suddenly said, dropping his arms to his sides.

"Why not?" I asked.

"Because you're not taking this seriously."

"I am."

"You're not scared."

"I would be if you were scary."

"Oh, so it's *my* fault."

"Nobody's to blame here," I generously suggested.

Finally the teacher, Mrs. Louise Granger, called, "Cut," and our mediocre improvisation came to a halt. Unlike the previous three-minute performances, ours didn't receive even token applause. Not one single clap to break the awkward silence. Perhaps it was my fault. And perhaps, as the teacher suggested later that night, acting classes were not for me. I was fine with all that. I just wanted to play the odds and find a room full of people who might work for free.

When the evening came to a close and I had seen the wide variety of actors available to me, I approached my favorite (or at the very least the most gullible looking): Chelsea Jacobs, twenty-three, blond, skinny, fake tan, your usual actress in the last two years before regular Botox injections begin. Still, she wasn't bad. In her improv, she played a woman trying to return a sweater to the wrong store. I liked her determination and she had some nice comic timing.

Len was right. An actor has got to act. It took me about ten minutes to convince Chelsea that I was legit and not your average San Francisco lunatic.[1] But by the end of the night, she had my card and promised to call. She even had some friends whom she thought might be up for the challenge.

After improv class, I pulled Shana Breslin's recycling, dropped it by Pratt's house, waited fifteen minutes, and watched him stick the same bags back in his own recycling receptacle. I pulled the bags and stuck them in my trunk. That kid was up to something, but for the life of me, I couldn't figure out what.

1. It's a beautiful city, with wonderful residents, but the per capita crazy has got to be the highest in the country.

# Lost Wednesday the Third

I arrived at the offices in the afternoon. My parents were hunched over their desks, drinking coffee, yawning, and struggling to stay awake.

"Too much salsa dancing?" I asked.

They looked at each other, as far I could tell, to get their stories straight. My mom did the talking.

"We went for a hike in Muir Woods. Maybe we overdid it."

"If you're running around on outdoor adventures, then why do we need to leave the premises?"

"Because it's all about spontaneity, Isabel. We weren't sure when we were going to return or what we'd want to do when we did."

"And what did you do?" I asked against my better judgment.

"We watched moves and ate popcorn,"

Dad replied. "Air popped,"[1] he added to get sympathy.

"What movies?" I inquired as I sat down at my desk.

"We had a Mel Brooks marathon," my mother answered, a little too quickly. "*Blazing Saddles, High Anxiety,* and *Young Frankenstein.*"

"Frahnkenshteen," my father said, correcting her per Gene Wilder's pronunciation. I guess you have to have seen it to understand. If you haven't seen it, then you should put down this document immediately and run, not walk, to your local video store. You should also be ashamed of yourself, if you are over the age of eighteen.

Here's the problem with my parents' collective claim to have watched movies all day: I couldn't quiz them on the films since we'd all seen them at least five to ten times each. There was a deeper lie embedded in there somewhere, I just couldn't figure out what.

"There are a few holes in your story," I said.

"There were holes in every story you told from age nine to nineteen," Mom replied.

1. I checked the pantry on my first inspection. No popcorn in sight. And that smell lingers. There was no smell. What do they take me for?

"Why don't you just worry about your own work, and Dad and I will keep our marriage in order?"

"Right," I replied, and focused my attention back on my work.

In the afternoon, when I was grabbing a snack from the kitchen, I noticed the light fixture was missing from the ceiling. This left a raw unfiltered light that was headache inducing. The fixture itself was nowhere to be seen.

When Rae arrived home from school, I asked her where the light fixture had gone.

"How should I know?" Rae replied.

I followed her into the Spellman offices, where Mom was giving Dad a back rub.

"Feel any better?" Mom asked.

"Thanks, dear," Dad replied.

Rae glared at my parents and in complete silence dictated a new rule.

## RULE #44 — NO MORE PDA

Then she departed without another word. My mother approached the whiteboard and vetoed the rule, followed by my father.

While I'm no fan of watching my parents grope each other, I had other topics on my mind.

"Why do things keep disappearing from

the house?"

"What are you talking about, sweetie?" Mom asked.

"There was the towel rod that David noticed, then the doorknob the other day, and now the light fixture in the kitchen is gone. It's kind of blinding in there."

"I was dusting and it broke," Mom casually replied.

"Since when do you dust?" I asked.

"It happens on occasion," Mom replied.

"Okay, if that's your story," I said, and that was the end of the conversation for the time being. However, I decided then and there that these Lost Wednesdays needed some looking into.

In the early evening I pulled the bags of screenplay fluff into the basement and started the long and miserable process of continuing the assembly of the confetti puzzle. Little progress was made in deciphering the text, but based on the three-hole-punch edges and the blank spaces on the sheets, the documents were almost certainly a screenplay. After two hours of time wasting, I decided there might be another way to figure out the mystery of Pratt.

I parked outside his residence for two

hours. He neither came nor went. I made use of the hours by studying astrological charts,[2] but then it occurred to me that my arrests and court-ordered therapy were the consequences of my taking a case too far — often a case that wasn't even mine. I was hired to pull Shana's trash. Why was I wasting hours of my own time trying to understand a client's motivation? I returned to the office and generated Pratt's bill. I decided that if he paid it, there was no problem. If a man wants to throw away his parents' hard-earned money, what's it to me?

2. To be explained shortly.

# DEAD ENDS AND
# NEW BEGINNINGS

Chelsea, my free actress, met me for coffee thirty minutes after her first (and only) meeting with Harkey. The plan was for Chelsea to pretend she had an ex-boyfriend who owed her three thousand dollars in rent from when they'd lived together. After Harkey informed her of her legal options — namely, small-claims court — Chelsea was supposed to bat her eyelashes and ask if there was another way, because she was pretty sure that if she served her ex notice of any sort, he would skip town. If Harkey took the bait, he might suggest that he (or one of his guys) pay a visit to the deadbeat ex and maybe pretend to be a cop and maybe shake him down and scare him into paying up. Such behavior would at the very least be worthy of an investigation from the California Bureau of Consumer Affairs. PIs are forbidden to pretend to be persons of authority. We even had an actor lined up to play the lame ex, but it never came to that. Harkey told Chelsea that her only option was within the legal system. She cried and pleaded. I would have recorded the proceedings if it weren't illegal and I was dealing with an unknown entity (i.e., an actor), so I can't verify the quality of her performance. My uneducated opinion is that it probably sucked.

The last thing Harkey said to Chelsea as she was exiting his office: "Say hi to Ms. Spellman for me."

I decided to drown my sorrows and seek some comfort from my own ex. Specifically, Ex #12. It took only a half a pint to tell him the whole story, and I was drinking fast.

"That's all?" he said.

"I could add some color to it, if you're looking for more information. For instance, Chelsea was wearing a pink sweater and skinny jeans."

"So are ya done now?"

"Excuse me?"

"With this whole Harkey mess. Is it over?"

"I was thinking I just needed a better actor. I went for the looks instead of talent, which is a common mistake it seems."

"Seriously?" Connor said, looking downright grumpy.

"Have you been to the movies lately?" I asked.

"I'm talking about Harkey," he said.

"Well, I don't think giving up is the answer. If I don't take him down, who will?"

"Retirement or death," Connor replied.

My cell phone rang.

"Hello?"

"Morty here. I have news. Big news. The kind of news you might want to be sitting down for."

"Hang on a second."

I went into Connor's office to find a comfortable chair and avoid the distraction of the jukebox.

"What is it?"

"Gabe and the shiksa are engaged."

"Then it's time you started calling her Petra."

"If that isn't a goy name, I don't know what is."

"Do you really think an engagement is sitting-down news? I think the sitting-down imperative should be limited to a more shocking headline."

"I'm old. I like most of my news sitting down."

I did then sit down, for the record. "Well, it is newsworthy. I'll give you that. Although it's kind of weird hearing it from you first, Morty. Don't you think she should have called me?"

"I got off the phone with Gabe only five minutes ago. She'll probably call you any second now."

As it turned out, my call-waiting buzzed through and it was Petra's line.

"That's her," I said.

"Okay, I'll talk to you later. Do me a favor, Izzele, eat an apple today."

"Why?"

"It's never too early to think about your health."

I clicked over to the other line.

"Hello?"

"It's me."

"I know. I have caller ID."

"I know you know. That's why I said 'It's me' rather than my name."

"What's up?" I asked. "It's been a while."

"It certainly has," Petra replied. "Your hair must look like shit."[1]

"It doesn't look great."

"You should make an appointment."

"I will."

"What are you doing right now?"

---

1. Petra is a hairstylist. In the past she's kept my locks within the borders of presentable.

"Uh, nothing, come to think of it."

"I'll see you in a half hour," she said.

On my way out of the bar, Connor said, "Where are ya going now?"

"Haircut," I replied.

"Well, don' cut too much off. I like it long."

His instruction, for obvious reasons, didn't sit right with me. I approached the bar and leaned in so Connor would have to mirror my move. Then I could whisper.

"It's my hair, if you haven't noticed. I'll do whatever I want with it."

As I turned to walk away, Connor said in his lightest leprechaun voice, "I'll see ya later, gorgeous."

"Don't wait up!" I shouted over my shoulder. "I have a date tonight."

That would have been a superb exit line if Ex #12 weren't a bartender who frequently returns home just before dawn. No matter how long the date lasted, I'd still be in bed before him.

Connor laughed mockingly and said, "Have a lovely time."

An hour later, as Petra was hacking away at my hair, she finally broke the news to me.

"Gabe and I are engaged."

"Finally," I said.

"We've only been dating six months."

"The 'finally' was in reference to giving me the news, not the length of your courtship."

"You knew?"

"Morty called me right before you."

"Wow. You and the old guy are tight."

"I guess so."

"Are you sure you want it this short?"

"I'm making a statement," I replied.

Petra kept cutting and then there was a lull. This happens when you haven't seen someone in a few months. History counts for only so much. A lull can happen with anyone.

"You must be happy that they're moving back," Petra said.

"Who?" I asked.

"Morty and Ruth."

"They're moving back?"

"He didn't tell you?" Petra asked.

"No," I replied, trying to figure out what scam Morty pulled to make that happen.

"I just heard the news, so it's new. I'm sure he'll tell you any day now."

"Right," I said.

Then Petra started blow-drying my hair, which dried up the conversation.

After being coiffed I returned to my car

and tried to mess up my hair enough so that I resembled myself. Then I called Morty, hoping for the scoop. But the call went straight to voice mail. Then I phoned Henry to see if he'd gotten those fingerprint results back. Voice mail again. I decided to drive home and change for my lawyer date that night. While struggling with the decision between donning a conservative skirt and sweater set or that potentially perilous wraparound dress, I phoned David for a pep talk. The lawyer date was putting me in a bad mood and I needed a distraction.

"What are you doing?" I asked.

"Try saying 'hello' first and then maybe I'll answer the question," David replied.

"Sorry. I've been working on my pleasantries."

"Work harder."

"So how have you been?"

"Good. And you?"

"Fine. I got a haircut today. Petra's engaged. Rumor has it Morty is moving back to the city."

"That was fast," David casually replied.

"Which of the above are you referring to?"

David thought about it. "All three, I guess."

"Do you have an opinion on any of them?"

"Not that I feel like sharing."

"Come to think of it, you rarely feel like sharing."

"Are you calling for a reason," David asked, "or is this just one of those 'Hey, how are you doing?' calls?"

"So, what are you doing?" I asked again, thinking enough time had passed.

"Reading."

"What?"

"I'd rather not say."

"Is it porn? Because if it is, you shouldn't say 'reading.' I think 'looking' would be the more appropriate term."

"It's not porn."

"Hmmm. I can't imagine why you'd want to keep it secret. Is it one of those *Pot Roast for the Soul* books?"

"No."

"Would you find it in the self-help aisle of your local bookstore?"

"This conversation is nearing its end," David said.

"I can sense that you would like me to switch topics, so I'm going to, because I'm evolving into the kind of person who switches topics when she senses the cue."

"Well done."

"Thank you," I replied, glad for some validation.

"You know that evolution is a constant

process, right? Improving yourself doesn't end when you've stopped getting arrested regularly."

"Are you always evolving?" I asked.

"I'd like to think so," David replied.

"How does that work, exactly?" I inquired, not to mock, but out of genuine curiosity.

"It's different for everyone," David replied.

"But since we're related, maybe your method could work on me."

David sighed extra hard, which meant he was done talking with me on this topic. If I wanted to see how David was evolving, or whatever it was he was doing with all his free time, I would have to find another way to unearth that mystery. For now, I changed the subject.

"How's Maggie?" I asked.

"That was a very clumsy transition," David replied.

"I'm also working on my transitions."

"Good."

"So how is Maggie?"

"She's fine."

"She's not under any unnecessary stress?"

"No more than usual."

"Have you noticed any changes in her personality?"

"Why are you asking?"

"I thought maybe Rae or Mom or somebody else was stressing her out."

"Has she seemed stressed to you?" David asked.

"No," I said. And that was the truth.

"I asked her to move in with me. Could that be causing her stress?"

This is when I realized I'd blown it. I had no idea what was causing Maggie stress, but now I was convincing my brother that he was the source of it.

"I'm sure that's not the reason," I said.

"Maybe she's just not prepared for all this," David said.

"You mean prepared for our family?"

"Yes."

"I see," I replied. Then I felt kind of bad. Like David's relationship might run more smoothly if he and Maggie didn't have all of us to contend with. "Forget I asked the question," I said. "I'm sure everything is fine and if she *is* stressed, I assure you it is Rae's fault."

I've discovered that Rae is the best diagnosis for all stress-related conditions.

"You're probably right," David agreed.

There was a lull and then David surprised me with a question of his own.

"And how are things with you and Connor?"

"Who?" I asked.

"You're hilarious," he replied without conviction.

"Things are excellent," I said. "You know I get free drinks, right?"

"Of course. I forgot. The primary selling point."

"I wouldn't say primary, but it is up on the list."

"Do you think it will last, Isabel?"

"Sure," I replied. "At least through the week."

"Don't you have another lawyer date coming up?"

"Oops. Thanks for reminding me. Talk to you later. Bye."

# MANDATORY
## LAWYER DATE #4

To refresh your memory, lawyer dates with an even number are chosen at my discretion, minus the predetermined standards. I found www.litidate.com to be an excellent site for finding the available barristers in the area. For my particular situation, the best bets were the most attractive and well educated. I figured I could turn off one of those guys within five minutes flat (maybe less on a good day). The key was somehow getting them to go out with me to begin with. I didn't feel like faking my educational background, so I admitted to PI work, but I did claim to be a golf enthusiast,[1] a gourmet cook, and a killer on the tennis court.[2] What I didn't list on my profile but planned to market on the date, which would make my

1. Miniature golf.
2. Not a complete untruth, minus the killer part. I've played tennis before, is my point.

ill-suited-ness more ill suited, was that I was a new-age enthusiast with an astrological chart obsession.

Conrad Frith booked a table for two at Michael Mina[3] for eight P.M. I arrived early to express the eagerness that men so often fear. I smiled too much, looking him up and down, attempting to illustrate approval of the specimen before me. Conrad, I got the feeling, was accustomed to this particular expression of approval. His attractiveness was that standard white-male attractiveness that is typically lost on me. However, I can fake approval with the best of them.

Once we were seated, the gushing phase of the evening commenced. I complimented Conrad's choice of restaurant, then I complimented his tie, his suit, and after looking under the table, his shoes. He ordered a whiskey; I said, "Oh, that sounds tasty. I've never had one before. I think I'll give it a try." Then I returned to perusing the menu.

When the drinks arrived, I took a sip, made a face, and then immediately adjusted to its flavor and downed mine in one quick

3. If there was one thing I was going to miss from these dates, it was the good food and drink. Although I'd have preferred to consume it in casual attire.

shot, calling the garçon[4] over to bring me another. Then we ordered food. While I was pretty sure I had lost Conrad at "Your shoes are *yummy*," I sealed the deal over dinner.

[Partial transcript reads as follows:]

**Me:** What's your full name?

**Conrad:** Conrad Easterly Frith.

**Me:** What a stately name. Are you a third or a fourth?

**Conrad:** No, I'm just a first.

**Me:** Now, down to important matters. What's your birthday?

**Conrad:** July eighteenth.

**Me:** [with palpable disappointment] So, you're a Cancer?

**Conrad:** I guess so.

**Me:** There's no guessing about it. If you were born on July eighteenth, you're a Cancer.

**Conrad:** I don't pay much heed to those things.

**Me:** Well I do.

**Conrad:** I see.

**Me:** I have some bad news for you.

**Conrad:** What?

**Me:** Astrologically speaking, we're a nightmare waiting to happen.

4. Yep, I called him garçon.

**Conrad:** You don't say.

**Me:** It could still work, but we'd be bucking the odds.

**Conrad:** Should we even finish this meal?

**Me:** We already ordered.[5]

**Conrad:** Maybe we should talk about something besides our astrological charts.

**Me:** That's an idea.

**Conrad:** You're a golfer, I believe.

**Me:** Yes. One of my many loves.

**Conrad:** What's your handicap?

**Me:** I think the preferred term is "physical challenge" and I don't have one as far as I know.

**Conrad:** What's your golf handicap? Your profile says you play golf.

**Me:** Oh, *that.* What's yours?

**Conrad:** Nine.

**Me:** No way! Mine too!

**Conrad:** Excuse me?

**Me:** So, aside from golf, what do you do for fun?

5. He was paying.

# THE "FREE SCHMIDT!"
## EXPLOSION

My punishment, after my mother heard the recording of Lawyer Date #4, was playing chauffeur for Rae the following Saturday. At one P.M. Rae's final stab at the SAT would be over, and so would her chance to sway all those Ivy League schools my parents had forced her to apply to.

I waited outside Mission High School (the test center) for fifteen minutes until the exodus of weary, test-addled students began. Out of the corner of my eye, something struck me as off, but I didn't turn my head from the newspaper until it was impossible to ignore.

Picture this: A swarm of close to two hundred awkward and not-so-awkward students of various sizes, shapes, and ethnicities, all in the now-familiar blue T-shirts with yellow felt letters:

Free Schmidt!

279

Just as all penguins look alike to most nonpenguins, I didn't even notice my sister until she approached the car and knocked on the window. Intriguingly, she was accompanied by none other than that secret boyfriend with the bicycle, although he did not have his accessory with him. I unlocked the car door.

"How'd it go?" I asked.

"Only time will tell," Rae vaguely replied.

"You didn't throw it again, did you?" I asked, annoyed. It was a reasonable accusation. She'd thrown the PSAT (pronounced *Psssat*) last year.[1]

"No, not this time," Rae answered.

By now both my sister and the relatively unknown male were safely ensconced in the car. I thought introductions were in order.

"Who's the intruder?" I asked.

And then the fresh-faced young male leaned over the seat and held out his hand.

"Hi, I'm Fred. Nice to meet you, Isabel."

"Fred what?"[2]

"Fred Finkel."

"Seriously?" I said, because if Rae was in

1. For details, see previous document — *Revenge of the Spellmans* — now available in paperback!
2. Always get a last name.

the mood to make up a name, this would be it.

"Do you want to see my ID?" "Fred" asked pleasantly.

"Sure," I replied. "Why not?"

"Fred" presented an authentic school identification card. He wasn't lying.

"I'm sorry," I said, handing it back to him. The apology was less about demanding the ID and more about his unfortunate name. Fred picked up on that.

"It's okay," he replied. "After seventeen and a half years, you get used to some things."

"I like your attitude, Fred."

"Thanks."

"Where's your bike?"

"How'd you know I rode a bike?"

"There's a wear mark on your right pant leg from a leg strap."

"A friend of mine is riding my bike home. But your observation was impressively Holmesian."

"Thank you," I replied, pleased that my fake deduction got its due notice. Fred was growing on me in leaps and bounds. Aside from the company he kept and the FREE SCHMIDT! T-shirt he wore like a uniform, no obvious faults were apparent in this boy. Was it possible that Rae had better taste in

281

men than I did?

"Rae, what have you done to all these people?" I asked, staring at the swarm of blue T-shirts with bright yellow lettering.

"I mobilized them," Rae replied.

Trying to avoid a repeat of the same conversation I'd been having for the past several weeks, I kept quiet and waited for my driving instructions. Because celebrating was in order, and celebrating with the unit is hardly celebrating (especially these days), Rae insisted that I drive the pair to Henry's house. I couldn't imagine what he had planned for the duo, but I didn't bother asking.

"They're everywhere," I said, slowly fighting my way through the traffic of FREE SCHMIDT! fashion campaigners.

"It's not too late for you to join the cause, Izzy," Rae said.

"It looks like you've got it covered."

"Schmidt's not the only one."

"I have my Schmidt, Rae. I don't need another."

"We'll talk about this later," my sister said. And we did. Sort of.

# THE FINGERPRINT FAIRY

I delivered Team Schmidt to Henry's house a few minutes later. He patted the delightful Fred on the back and said, "Dude, how you been?"

"Dude"? Since when did Henry use the word "dude"? Also intriguing: his familiarity with the previously unfamiliar Fred. Before I inquired into professional matters, I needed some background information.

"You know Fred?" I asked with a touch of accusation.

"He's great, isn't he?" Henry replied.

Meanwhile, Fred and Rae ignored the adults and raided the shelf in Henry's pantry that contains my sister's stash of food, all of which lives somewhere in the heavens of the food pyramid — specifically, a blend of salted and heavily sugared items that Henry thoroughly disapproves of and yet agreed to accommodate under the duress of a rather lengthy negotiation.

"He seems more likable than I would expect," I replied, "but sometimes that's a sign of a true con artist."

"No con," Henry said. "He's exactly what he seems: nice, honest, humble, smart, geeky, curious. You couldn't assemble a better kid if you got a kit and made one on your own."

"If he's that great," I said, "shouldn't we be protecting him from Rae?"

"My thoughts precisely."

The subadults spread their food on Henry's coffee table and began their feast. The adults retired to Henry's office to go over the fingerprint results. But before we talked business, I noticed a swatch of dark blue peeking out beneath Henry's charcoal-gray sweater.

"Take off your sweater," I said.

"Excuse me?" he replied.

"You heard me."

"If you insist."

Henry removed his outer layer to reveal what we all know was hiding beneath.

Free Schmidt!

"You too, Henry?" I said, like I imagined

Caesar saying to Brutus (only in Latin, I think).

"He *is* innocent," Henry said, defending his shirt.

"I know," I replied. "That's not the point."

I threw the sweater at him.

"Put it back on," I said. "I've seen enough."

While Henry reclothed himself, he gave me the lowdown on the fingerprints.

"No match," he said.

Now *that* was sitting-down news. After all this fingerprint fuss, I had nothing.

"Really?" I asked, disappointed. It was a stupid question.

"You gave me four prints," Henry said. "Did you cross-check them against each other?"

"No, I just made sure they weren't from any of the regular household staff."

"You gave me duplicates. Two identical thumbs and two identical index fingers, I think."

"Oh," I said, taking it in.

"Were those the only prints you found in the room?" Henry asked, and I could see what he was driving at.

I wasn't exactly thorough since it was Mason's room and the door was locked and I was under a time crunch. I pulled the first prints I found. It never occurred to me that there was anything suspicious about their placement.

Humor me with a short course on fingerprint analysis. While every fingerprint is unique (even with identical twins), there are only seven types of fingerprints — the arch, the tent arch, the loop, the double loop, the pocked loop, the whorl, and mixed.[1] Each individual might have only one type on all ten fingers, or a variety. Had I given the prints a cursory glance, I should have spotted the duplicates and perhaps, based on print size, noted that they all came from the same person.

I thought back to when I was collecting the prints — they were awkwardly located on the bureau. It was like someone had tapped their thumb and index finger on the bureau, then twisted their hand eighty degrees, moved it two inches to the left, and did it again. In fact, standing still in front of the bureau, it would be almost impossible to get your hand at that angle.

What did all this mean? I don't know. My working conclusion: Someone had planted the fingerprints to throw me off the scent. I

1. Which sort of implies that there are more than seven.

decided to go back to the Winslow home and look at where the fingerprints were placed again. Hopefully the room had not been tampered with since my previous visit a week earlier.

On my way out of Henry's place, I found Rae and Fred reading aloud from *The Adventures of Sherlock Holmes* with a gallon of milk and shot glasses before them.

Henry rolled his eyes when he took in the spectacle. I turned to him for an explanation.

"What are they doing?"

"Rae made up a drinking game," Henry said. "You must be so proud."

"How does it work?" I asked.

"Whenever the words 'elementary,' 'indeed,' or 'extraordinary' are used, you have to take a shot."

"How stupid. They're drinking milk."

"True," Henry said with reluctant resignation, "only, poor Fred's lactose intolerant."

# THE BUTLER'S SECRET

Mr. Leonard was unchanged when he answered the door, still Method-acting his way through his assignment.

"Isabel, what a pleasant surprise."

"Where's Mr. Winslow?" I asked.

"Napping."

"Good."

"I agree. I wouldn't want him to see you in that grungy ensemble."

"Be nice," I snapped.

"As you wish," Len replied, leading me into the foyer.

"Something strange is going on here," I whispered.

"Indeed," Leonard replied.[1] "Mr. Winslow is considering repainting the library in glossy coral."

I ignored Len and simply took care of

1. Right about then I could have used a shot of bourbon.

business.

"Can you let me back into Manson's bedroom? I need to look for a few more prints."

I stared at the bureau again, trying to align my hand in the formation that would be required to leave those two sets of prints. It would be impossible unless one was a contortionist.

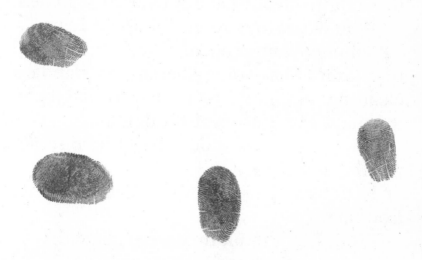

I had no doubt at this point that the prints had been planted. But why? The only logical reason was that Manson didn't want his real fingerprints found, which meant that he was probably in the system.

The second time I searched Manson's bedroom I noticed how utterly unclean it was. The bed was made and no objects were turned over or clothes tossed about the floor, but dust had been settling for months around the room. The patches of clean were what stood out. There was a moon around the light switch where the wall had been scrubbed down to the bare faded paint. You could still see cleaning streaks on the desktop. There were no prints anywhere on the inside doorknob. After dusting for prints in all the obvious locations, I decided I had to be more creative about where I searched.

"Who cleans this room?" I asked Len.

"No one," Len replied. "Mrs. Enright said that Graves has some allergies to standard cleaning supplies and he has always been the maid and master of his domain."

"Then his prints should be in here somewhere," I said.

"I thought you already collected prints from here."

"I did. But I think they were planted."

"The plot thickens."

"Knock it off," I said.

"Knock what off?" Len asked.

"Everything. Where is Mrs. Enright?"

"At the store."

"When will she be back?"

"Any minute now."

"Keep her downstairs," I said. "I need to have a chat with her."

"As you wish," Len replied, and then, with

the straightest back I've ever seen, he slowly descended the staircase.

I scanned the room, calculating my best bet. Where are fingerprints sure to be found but not so obviously noticed?

The furniture in Mason's room was sparse. Every clean surface could have been easily wiped down. In fact, I was starting to think that Mason had planned ahead and cleared his own prints and planted the new set before he left. However, Graves had lived in this house for five years. He couldn't possibly have erased every trace of his fingerprint existence. I bravely donned a pair of plastic gloves and entered the bathroom. Men use toilets. Men lift the seats of toilets. Maybe I would get lucky, although that phrase seemed inappropriate for the job at hand.

I dusted the underside of Mason's toilet seat and found a few partial prints. I attached a wide slice of printing tape to the edge and then carefully flattened it with a credit card over the prints. Once I'd extracted them and attached them to the fingerprint cards with a label, I put them in an envelope and dropped it in my purse. I removed the gloves, washed my hands, and found Mrs. Enright in the kitchen.

"Mrs. Enright, where is Mason Graves

right now?"

"In England, visiting his mother."

"Where is he really?" I asked.

"Excuse me?"

"Why did you plant someone else's fingerprints in his bedroom?"

"There is no plant in his bedroom," Mrs. Enright replied. "I would know because then I'd water it."

Watching the elderly woman scowl and slip about the house, I pictured her as Mason's crafty partner in the perfect long con, but now, with my brief questions answered, I got the feeling the permanent scowl was simply an unfortunate feature that belied the simple woman she was.

Mr. Leonard walked me to the door, glancing back at Mrs. Enright, who peeked out at us from behind the kitchen door. She slipped out of view without an ounce of subtlety.

"That woman drives me mad," Len said, rolling his eyes. "I know she's up to something."

"That woman," I said, "needs a hearing aid. She's trying to hide it. She lurks so if someone calls for her, she can see it."

"You don't think she's in cahoots with Mr. Graves?"

"Honestly, I don't know. Mason kept her

around for a reason — maybe because she couldn't eavesdrop. Mr. Graves certainly liked to surround himself with people whose faculties are compromised."

"Didn't I tell you? Mason Graves has been the problem from the start."

"Agreed. Now we just need to find out where he is and what he gains from his employment here."

I took my fingerprints and ran.

# A QUIET NIGHT IN

I returned to my apartment, hoping for a quiet night in, and discovered Connor there, along with five of his "mates," in the midst of a boisterous, booze-soaked poker game.

"What are you doing here?" I said.

"John's got the bar covered so we thought we'd skip out, playing cards."

"But why here," I asked, "when you have your own place?"

"But I don' have a table like this," Connor said as if he was speaking to a slow child.

It is true that I had a table well-suited for poker games. It was one of Bernie's relics. In fact, I was having a Bernie flashback at that very moment. Cigar smoke snaked throughout the room, the scent of beer came no longer from the open bottles but from the pores of men, and snack food was tossed about like the remnants of a three-year-old's birthday party.

"You could have called first," I suggested.

"Check your voice mail," Connor replied, staring at his hand. He had three kings, two queens. "Love, can you grab me another beer from the fridge?" he asked.

"Yes," I replied.

I could have kicked the men out and made a scene, but I didn't have the energy for it. I grabbed a beer from the refrigerator, popped the cap, and stood behind Connor, checking out his hand. He had just raised, conservatively, in an attempt to slowly build the pot, and had the other players' attention.

I held up three fingers and mouthed "kings." Then I held up two fingers and mouthed "queens." Any player with elementary lip-reading skills would fold.

"See you later," I said, and I was out the door.

While I sat in my car, stewing over Connor's home invasion, I listened to the voice mail messages that I had failed to notice earlier. It was true that Ex #12 had called to inform me of his poker night; however, there was no form of a question in his brief message. A beep followed and then I heard Bernie's unnecessarily loud voice.

"Hey, Izzy," he said. "You want to eat some crab cakes?"

It occurred to me that Bernie had the ability to make everything sound dirty. I deleted both messages and started the car.

Fifteen minutes later I knocked on Henry's front door.

"Long time, no see," he said.

"I was in the neighborhood," I replied. We both knew it was a lie. But who cares? "I have another set of prints for you."

"Come on in," Henry said.

I scanned the living room. All signs of the adolescent takeover were gone.

"You got rid of them," I observed.

"Fred wasn't feeling well," Henry replied.

I handed Henry the prints.

"Where'd these come from?"

"Don't ask."

"Okay."

"What are you doing?" I asked.

"Watching TV."

I approached the muted television set and saw that it was an episode of *Doctor Who* where the Doctor thinks he's human and Martha (his traveling companion) has to convince him he's the Doctor and help him figure out how to get his powers back and save the world.

"I love this episode," I said.

"Me too," Henry replied, taking a seat

next to me and unmuting the sound.

The *Doctor Who* marathon saved my evening from complete disaster. Henry and I sat in rapt silence, taking breaks only for more beer (me) and tea (Henry) and some lightly salted snack food that was probably good for you. It was three A.M. when the marathon ended, but I apparently didn't notice. I fell asleep on the couch; Henry threw a wool blanket over me and I didn't wake up until eight o'clock, when Henry was getting ready for work.

Connor didn't notice until hours later that I was missing.

That night was the last peaceful night's rest I would have for weeks. Everything changed after that night.

I mean *everything.*

■ ■ ■ ■

# Part III:
# Charges

■ ■ ■ ■

# IN THE HOLE

The next morning was business as usual. I drove straight to the office from Henry's house and occupied my morning with dull background research, until the monotony was interrupted by irritation in the form of an e-mail from Jeremy Pratt.

To: I.Spell@spellmaninvestigations.com
From: JP.Prattman@gmail.com
Re: What's up?
Hey Izzy,
   What's going on with my case? All I got so far are some fluffy plastic bags. Are you any closer to figuring out what Shana Breslin is up to?

I replied quickly to abate my annoyance; no point in letting it linger.

Jeremy:
   You agreed that the investigation would

only involve garbology. You've conveniently omitted that fact. Are you any closer to paying your bill?

Warmest regards,<br>Isabel

Mom and Dad entered the office right after I hit the Send button. Before they uttered a single world, I said: "I'm in a bad mood. Don't mess with me today."

I decided to clear my head while tackling the giant shred pile in the basement. However, when I reached for the door, the knob was missing.

"The doorknob is missing," I said.

"Would you look at that," Dad replied.

"What happened to it?"

"It must have fallen off," Mom said.

"Why do things keep vanishing from the house?"

My mom then pulled a spare doorknob from her desk and opened the basement door for me, leaving it ajar.

"Call me crazy," I said, "but I think every door should have a knob."

"Have fun down there," Mom replied.

I tried to get into a zone of mindless shredding, but my mind wandered to all the available objects of disappointment — my foiled investigation on Harkey, my never-ending lawyer dates, Pratt, and my apartment, which I was certain I would find in a state of disrepair once I returned to it. I am all too aware of what happens when you leave men alone overnight playing poker. Then my mind started wandering to the subject of the missing objects in the Spellman home. Why would a doorknob, drawer handle, and towel rack vanish without explanation? Either the grating sound of the shredder or too much thinking was giving me a headache.

I reentered the Spellman offices, sluggishly ascending the staircase. My sluggishness afforded me an overheard snippet of my parents' conversation.

"Have you found them yet?" Mom asked.

"No," Dad replied. "I thought you were on it."

"I've looked. I can't find them," my mother said.

"Well, they have to be around here somewhere."

"They could be anywhere, Al."

"Have you checked the pistachio cam?" Dad asked.

"Isabel made me take it down. By the way, it was that Jeremy Pratt kid who was leaving the shells in the — Isabel, are you there?"

And that was the end of my eavesdropping. I suppose I could have asked my parents what they were talking about, but instead, I just entered the office and said, "I can't shred anymore."

"Why don't you take the rest of the day off?" Mom said. "You look tired."

"What gives?" I asked suspiciously.

"Everybody should have a day off now and again," Dad replied.

"What aren't you telling me?"

"Isabel, go home, go to a movie. Just do something for yourself today," replied Mom.

"Get a hobby. You'll need one eventually," said my father.

On my way out the door, I noticed another doorknob missing from the bathroom just outside the dining area.

"Another doorknob's gone," I shouted.

"We're on it!" my dad shouted back.

I was on my way home when I realized that all home had to offer was the mess to repair from last night's raid of Irishmen.[1]

Instead, for reasons I couldn't tell you at the time, I drove to my brother's house and parked in front. His car was in the driveway, so I knew he was home. But instead of calling or ringing the doorbell, I just sat there,

1. And I'm not saying Irishmen make more messes than any other kind of man.

casing his residence. If pressed, I wouldn't be able to provide a solid excuse for my behavior. I was curious is the best answer I have. David had been unemployed for over six months and I couldn't imagine how he'd killed all that time. It seemed to me that a man who once worked eighty hours a week might go mad with all that empty space in his day calendar. I wanted to see what he did with himself. David has always been the more responsible, useful, reasonable member of the family, and frankly, I wanted to know his secret. Whenever I asked David what he did with himself, he was always vague. His answers fell into the "You know, stuff" category, which really doesn't help if you're interested in duplicating those activities yourself. My point is I was staking out David's residence to discover what his idle activities involved. Unfortunately, I was made within the first fifteen minutes.

My phone rang.

"Hi, Isabel," David said.

"Hi, David. What are you up to?"

"Nothing much."

"What a coincidence," I said. "Me too."

"Would you like to come in?" David asked.

"Why not?"

"I'll see you in about thirty seconds," David replied.

■ ■ ■

I found my brother in his kitchen, wearing an apron, hunched over the chopping block, studying a recipe book.

"Hand me that onion, will you?" he asked.

I tossed David the onion, which he caught in midair without even raising his gaze from the cookbook.

"So, you're cooking?" I said, hoping the question would lead to an explanation.

"Your observational skills continue to amaze me."

"Is this something you've been doing for a while, or is it a new activity?"

"Relatively new," David replied as he skinned the onion and began chopping it with professional precision.

"You look like one of those people on cooking shows," I said.

"I've been taking a class," David replied. "Give me the garlic."

I tossed him the garlic. In one swift motion he grabbed it from midair and then smashed it into pieces on the cutting board.

"Why are you taking a cooking class?"

"Because I'm not the best cook and neither is Maggie and we don't want to be eating out all the time."

"Good answer. What else have you been doing with your time?"

"Why do you ask?"

"Because you have a lot of time and I'm curious how you fill it."

"Let me ask you a question for once," David said.

"Shoot."

"What happened on Prom Night 1994?"

*Sigh:* "Nothing."

"So it's that bad?"

"I have no idea what you're talking about." I said it this time with much less conviction than in the past.

"These lawyer dates. You'd never agree to them unless Mom had a vise grip on you. Damn, you must have done something awful."

"I did. Can we leave it at that?"

"Yes, and you know why? Because you asked me to. It would be really great if you showed me the same courtesy. I'm not a mystery for you to solve. I'm just your brother. I don't have all the answers. All I'm trying to do is figure out what makes me happy."

"Have you figured it out?"

"Not yet."

"I thought you knew things."

"Sorry to disappoint you."

"That's okay. Can I stay for dinner?"

"No, Isabel. I promised Maggie a quiet night in. She's been stuck with Rae all day."

David served me bourbon (the good stuff) and when I was done with my *one*[2] drink, he walked me to the door.

"Maybe I should get a hobby," I said, standing in his foyer.

"I thought you had one."

"What?" I asked.

"Drinking," he replied, amused with his little joke.

"Right. Thanks for reminding me."

I kissed David on the cheek and departed. When I arrived at home, I deloused my apartment for three hours. Then I took a shower and a very long nap. A nap so long, in fact, I wasn't awoken until half past eight in the evening. The phone call came from Rae.

"Izzy, I'm at Maggie's office. I need a ride home."

"Where are Mom and Dad?"

"I think they're at a movie. Please," she said.

"One of these days you're going to tell me what happened on that bus," I replied.

2. It had been stipulated that the David bar closed after one beverage.

"It's a deal."

Twenty minutes later, I was inside Maggie's office.

"Do you need to pee?" Rae asked.

"Not really," I replied.

"Maybe you should go ahead, because I need to make a couple stops."

"Where?" I asked suspiciously.

"It won't take that long, but maybe you should use the bathroom."

"I don't need to use the bathroom, okay?"

"Not even a little bit?"

"No! Now get your stuff together so we can leave."

The door to the unlit file room was open; a sturdy chair rested under the light fixture.

"Even on a chair, I can't reach it," Rae said.

"Isn't there a janitor?" I asked.

"Yeah, but I don't want Maggie to have to deal with that in the morning," Rae replied.

I climbed up on the chair, unscrewed the burned-out bulb, and handed it to Rae. She was texting someone on her cell phone and not paying attention.

"My phone's dead," Rae said. "Where's yours?"

"In my purse," I replied, which was on the receptionist's desk.

Then my sister gave me this meaningful

look and said, "Have you changed your mind about helping with the Schmidt case?"

"No. And I don't want to talk about it anymore."

Rae stuck her phone in her pocket and passed me a fresh lightbulb. Once I'd screwed it in, Rae flipped the switch, which was outside of the file room door.

"Good. You'll need light."

"Why?" I asked, still oblivious.

"Maybe a night in solitary will give you some perspective. Maybe then you'll understand how Schmidt feels."

I was still standing on the chair when Rae shut the file room door. I heard the key go in the lock and a deadbolt lodge into place.

Then I heard Rae exit the office.

After that, all I heard was silence.

I checked the door. Then I checked it again. Then I scanned the room, which was equipped with a bottle of water, a bag of cookies, a stack of files, a legal-sized writing pad with an assortment of pens, and an empty bucket.

The first hour of my false imprisonment was spent overcoming the sheer shock of the situation. Rae was capable of many things, but this, *this* took me by surprise. The shock was followed by the natural need to escape the confined quarters. I banged on the door and screamed for help. I searched the file room for anything that could aid my escape. If I found a hammer, I would have spent the rest of my hours bashing away at the door, hoping it would eventually give. There were no matches, so I couldn't set off the fire alarm, and there was not a single paper clip in sight to play with the lock, although paper clip lockpicking is a long shot at best.

Hour three, I plotted revenge. Hour four, I considered sleep, but I would have had to either bash out or unscrew a steaming hot lightbulb, and frankly, I didn't think sleep was even possible. By the fifth hour, I resigned myself to the situation, knowing that my revenge would take on many forms and I had only five more hours until morning, when someone would free me.

I used that time wisely. But I'll tell you about that later. First things first.

# THE MORNING AFTER

It was Maggie who liberated me at eight A.M., eleven hours after my incarceration began. The moment I heard the rustlings in the office, I began banging my fists on the door and screaming for help.

A startled Maggie shouted, "Who's in there?"

"Isabel!"

Within seconds, the door was flung open. Maggie gawked at me in utter shock.

"What were you doing in there?" she asked.

"Excuse me," I said. "I have to pee."

I rushed past her and used the bathroom. That weird conversation with Rae had started making sense around hour six. When I returned to Maggie's office, her expression remained unchanged.

"What's going on?" she asked.

I was still steaming with emotion and said only, *"Rae."*

"I don't understand."

"Rae *locked* me in there last night."

*"What?"*

"Rae locked me in the file room overnight," I said, spelling it out.

"Why?" Maggie asked, as if it were still possible that there was a logical explanation.

"To let me know what it's like to be innocently incarcerated."

Maggie gawked at me for a moment, but when understanding kicked in, she put her hand over her mouth and gasped in shock.

"Oh my god. I'm so sorry. Are you okay?"

"I'm fine," I replied. "I think."

Maggie reached into her pocket and offered me a half-eaten cookie.

"Are you hungry?"

"No, thanks. There was food."

"Do you need some water?"

"There was water."

Maggie then pulled something from her other pocket.

"Breath mint?"

"I'll take one of those," I said.

I leaned against the file room door and lost myself in revenge scenarios for a moment. Maggie interrupted.

"What are you going to do?" she asked.

"I don't know."

My purse was still sitting on the desk. I looked inside for my phone and car keys and both were missing. Well, one mystery was solved — how Rae managed to get home without taking the bus.

"What can I do?" Maggie asked.

"Drive me to Rae's school," I said. "I need to get my phone and car keys."

Twenty-five minutes later (Maggie and I stopped for coffee) I was in the administrative office waiting for a visitor's pass so I could collect my things. The secretary told me that Rae was in history class and gave me the room number.

I opened the door and got the teacher's attention.

"Hi. I'm Rae's sister. I need to speak with her just for a moment."

Rae was seated in the back of the room. She studied me carefully. I caught glimpses of fear in her expression, but not enough for my liking. As she approached the door, I had a sudden urge to tackle her to the ground and rage over the events of the previous night. I took a deep breath and calmed myself. A brawl wouldn't be punishment enough. I had to be careful how I proceeded.

My sister and I stepped into the hallway.

"I believe you have my phone and car keys," I said.

Rae was prepared for the request and handed them over.

"Where's my car?" I asked.

"In the parking lot," Rae replied, not taking her eyes off of me.

"Thank you," I replied in a severely formal tone.

Long pause.

"You didn't have to use the bucket, did you?" Rae asked.

"No," I replied.

"Good."

"See you around, Rae," I said, and briskly walked away.

My sister was expecting immediate retribution. But this was much better. It kept her off balance and I wanted her to feel that sense of dangerous uncertainty for as long as possible.

The battery on my phone was dead, so I went for a drive while I charged my phone and cleared my head. Without even thinking about it, I ended up in Golden Gate Park, idling my car in front of the acreage that houses the bison. I checked the messages on my phone; a text had come in from Bernie late last night.

*BPeter:*

Izzy, I got a problem. Can I stay at your place tonight?

Daisy kicked me out of the hotel room.

Rae had taken the liberty of replying for me.

*I.Ellmanspay:*

No problem. Won't be home tonight.

Then I listened to the voice mail messages. There were three. I braced myself for what might come. The first was from Connor: *"Bloody 'ell, Isabel. I come home to a fat man in our bed! Where the hell are you? Jesus Christ, somebody could have gotten very hurt here. Call back immediately."*

An hour later, Connor again . . . *"Isabel, where are you? It's five A.M. I'm angry, I'm worried, and I would like someone to vouch for the fat guy who is now on our couch."*

I could hear Bernie shout "Hey" in the background.

The third message was from Bernie, left just an hour ago. *"Sorry, Izzy. When you said you wouldn't be home, I didn't know that meant your boyfriend would be there. He's got quite a temper, that one. I just left your place. He's sleeping. Where are you, Izz?*

*We're worried. If you don't call me back soon, I'm going to call your parents."*

I phoned Bernie right away so that he wouldn't contact the unit. I didn't want them in on this just yet. I needed to weigh all my options. He asked me about the text message. I said that Rae sent it as a joke. He didn't think it was funny and said, "Somebody should teach that kid a lesson."

I agreed.

I finished drinking my coffee in the park. There wasn't another message from Connor, so I assumed he was still in bed. I drove home a little while later, wondering why I'd drunk the coffee when what I really needed was eight hours of sleep.

When I climbed into bed with Connor, he screamed, as if now every time someone crawled into bed with him, it would be an unusually large retirement-age man.

Connor looked at me, not with concern but with annoyance, as if *he* had taken the brunt of last night's nightmare.

"Is this your idea of a joke?"

"No," I replied, too spent to say more.

"I don't think you and I are going to work," Connor said.

"No, we're not," I agreed.

And now I will provide you with Connor's epitaph:

# Ex-boyfriend #12:

Name: O'Sullivan, Connor
Age: 37
Occupation: Bartender
Hobby: Rugby
Duration: Five months
Last Words: "Sharing a bed with a fat man is where I draw the line."

# CONSEQUENCES

I slept out of exhaustion and, in part, to keep myself occupied. It was too soon to take action — not that I knew what action I would take. When I wasn't sleeping, I stayed in bed and watched TV. Phone calls filtered through and I sent e-mails back explaining that I had the flu. My mother asked if I needed anything. I told her that Connor was taking care of me and there was no need for her to drop by. Rae went silent — too fearful, I suspect, to make any kind of move.

The following day, Henry dropped by. When I opened the door, he felt my forehead and handed me a paper bag containing soup — not just any old soup, but a savory Vietnamese specialty called pho.[1] While I like pho it seemed an odd choice for someone claiming to have the flu.

"Chicken soup and ginger ale are the

1. Pronounced fuh, not foe.

generally agreed-upon fluids for influenza," I remarked.

"I just figured you were hungover," Henry said. "And spicy soup is the agreed-upon fluid for that."

"True."

"But you're not sick, are you?" he asked.

"No."

"You don't look hungover, either."

"I'm not."

"So why are you hiding out?"

"I'm thinking."

Henry sat down on the couch. I guess he was planning on staying.

"About what?"

And so I told him. And after a lengthy debate and thoughtful consideration, we came up with a plan. If you've read the previous documents, maybe you think that plan might be a carefully orchestrated revenge plot that would fall flat. But this time around, we acted like the rational adults that we aspire to be and did what we had to do.

I would like to make it clear that we did not make this decision lightly.

I filed a police report that afternoon. Henry and I arrived at my parents' house shortly thereafter and explained the events of the previous days. While my parents took in this alarming information, Henry took in the state of the Spellman home, which was increasingly lacking in small but significant hardware.

"You know, the doorknob to the office is gone," Henry said.

"Yeah, we know," Dad said without much interest. And under the circumstances, who cared about missing doorknobs and light fixtures (the hallway one was now AWOL, I noticed).

The unit had other things on their mind and, frankly, so did I. While we waited for Rae to return home from school, I added another rule to the whiteboard. It's one of those rules you'd think would be implied. But I suppose with the Spellmans everything needs to be spelled out.

## RULE #51 — NO LOCKING RELATIVES IN CONFINED SPACES

When Rae returned home from school, my mother made her change into clean and comfortable clothes and explained that the police would be arriving shortly to take her into custody. Rae turned to every adult in the room with a genuine look of surprise.

"Are you bluffing?" she asked no one in

particular.

My father was too furious to speak. But Mom had a few choice words.

"How could you do such a thing? Lock your own sister in a room for eleven hours. It's despicable. What if the building had caught fire? She wouldn't have been able to get out."

"Those odds were extremely unlikely," Rae quietly replied.

"Don't speak," said my mother. "That's the best advice I can give you."

Rae was arrested at five P.M. on a Thursday afternoon. She spent the night in a juvenile facility, was arraigned the following morning, and bail was set at $2,000. My parents posted bail and brought Rae home, where the real punishment began. Her room was cleared of all items that might provide entertainment and for the next week she was forbidden to leave the house. Mom picked up her schoolwork every afternoon and returned it every morning. Rae went into immediate sugar withdrawal — coercing, negotiating, pleading for some form of sucrose. My mother, out of pity, gave her some dried apricots, but that was it. All her meals were the bland, square variety. My parents didn't speak to her unless it was to reiterate their sense of shock and disappointment.

To be perfectly honest, I was truly surprised that the unit sided with me. But I guess locking someone in a file room overnight is a considerable offense. It was hard for me to have perspective since I had my own substantial rap sheet.

I spent the next few days away from the Spellman fold.

On Friday, I lounged around my apartment in my pajamas clearing out all signs of Connor. I tried to make myself wallow in the breakup, but to be perfectly honest, I barely noticed Connor's absence, and not being woken up in the middle of the night improved my sleep pattern, which then improved my general mood. That is, until I realized that I could no longer frequent the Philosopher's Club. Rather than mourn my loss, I decided to move on. Immediately.

# THE HEMLOCK EFFECT

Saturday afternoon I commenced a bar crawl, anonymously auditioning bars to be my new watering hole.

I started with a beer at the Kilowatt, but then I decided I needed a place closer to the office, in the event of an emergency. I hopped on the Van Ness bus and stopped at O'Farrell and walked a few blocks to The Nite Cap. I made friends within a few minutes and decided I needed a place with more anonymity. I then strolled down to Polk Street, which is like a bar garden — a vast and incongruous mix of flora ranging from weeds, to daisies, to lilacs, to orchids, and even the occasional plain but snobby rose (which I suppose I associate with wine bars — and those were totally out of the question). I dropped into Lush Lounge and ordered a whiskey. I liked it, but somehow the name seemed too fancy for me. I moved on to Edinburgh Castle, but it reminded me too much of Uncle Ray and it made me sad. Still, I stayed for another drink and honored his memory.

When I finally surfaced again, it was night and the cool air sent a chill through me. My audition wasn't complete, so I roamed the street a little longer looking for that perfect flower. And then I found it — the Hemlock, a tavern right off Hemlock Street, walking distance from Spellman Investigations. It seemed perfect considering the mood I was in. I sat down at the bar and I ordered a drink. I made small talk with the bartender, but that was it. No point in things getting personal. I was going to learn to keep things professional. That was the only way this kind of relationship could work out.

By seven P.M. I was tanked, out of cash for a cab, and in no mood to take the bus. Since Rae always asks for rides from Henry, I didn't see any reason why he should deny me.

I made the call.

"Hello. I need a ride."

"Isabel?"

"Yeah."

"Are you drunk?"

"Only a little."

"Where are you?"

"At the Hemlock."

"Where is it?"

"On Hemlock Street."

"Off Polk?"

"Yes. Don't you think it's cool there's a street called Hemlock? It's more like an alley, but I think it's cool. Don't you?"

"I'll be there soon. Don't drink anymore."

I ordered another beer while I waited for Henry. He arrived twenty minutes later, looked at the bartender, and said, "Is she paid up?"

The bartender, whose name I never got because now I'm all into the anonymity thing, nodded his head. Henry took my arm.

"Let's go," he said.

"What are you doing here?" I asked.

"You called me," he replied, annoyed.

I didn't forget calling him, I just felt like being difficult.

"Oh yeah," I said.

"How drunk are you, Isabel?"

"Extremely," I replied.

Can you blame me for drowning my sorrows? In the past four days, I had been locked in a file room for eleven hours, my boyfriend had broken up with me, and I had been directly responsible for having my sister arrested on felony charges. Plus, every single case I was working on was going nowhere. This was definitely not my best week.

Henry pulled his car into the driveway of my apartment building and left a note on the windshield in the event one of the neighbors needed access to the garage. I stumbled up the stairs; he made sure I didn't plummet to my death.

"Is Connor here?" Henry asked.

"Nope."

"You expecting him?"

"Huh."

"Yes or no. That was indistinguishable."

"You like big words."

"It's not that big a word."

"It has many letters. I can't count them right now, but if I did I think you'd be surprised how many letters it has."[1]

"Yes or no," Henry said. Unfortunately I had forgotten the question.

"Huh?"

"Are you expecting Connor?"

"No way, José." (One of the problems with being drunk is that you say things you wouldn't normally, and if you say something like that once, there's always a chance it will pop up again inadvertently.)

I tried to work the key in the door, but it

1. Seventeen.

327

was testing Henry's patience, so he took it from me and worked the lock himself. Once inside, I threw myself down on the couch. Henry busied himself in the kitchen. Then he made me sit up and drink a glass of water. Then he served me a plate of toast and butter.

I seemed to sober up for just a split second and my mind briefly returned to work.

"Where are my fingerprints!" I demanded.

"On your fingers," Henry replied.

"*Noooo*. Not my fingerprints. The ones I gave you. I need them. I need them *now.*"

"You don't need them right now," Henry replied. "Eat your toast."

"Don't try to distract me from my work."

"There's a backlog in the lab and they're not a priority. You'll get them when I get them."

"We'll see about that," I said, which I suppose doesn't really make any sense.

After that brief exchange, Henry made me drink another glass of water, then take two aspirin and have another glass of water, until I flat-out refused.

"Are you trying to kill me?" I asked.

"You'll thank me in the morning."

The next morning, I was in no condition to thank anyone. I got out of bed, ate more toast, drank more water, and went back to bed. Two hours later, I made eggs (loaded with Tabasco sauce) and coffee and once again returned to bed with a pounding headache.

At eleven A.M. Dr. Hangover (Henry) phoned to check on my status. He asked if I needed anything; I said no. At one P.M. Henry dropped by with more pho. And after I ate it, I was at 70 percent. Then Henry handed me a grocery bag.

"I don't approve of this kind of nourishment, but I've heard that it helps with the hangovers."

"Just say 'hangovers'. Not 'the hangovers'. You sound like Morty."

"Whatever. At your age, you shouldn't be having 'the hangovers' anymore."

"Can we have this conversation in about five years? My head still hurts."

"Just take the bag."

I looked inside the offering and saw what appeared to be the entire contents of my sister's junk food stash from Henry's apartment. Potato chips, beef jerky, licorice, dark chocolate malt balls, a variety pack of Jelly Bellies, Tootsie Rolls, and Blow Pops.

"I'll be 85 percent in no time at all."

"Where's Connor?" Henry asked, interrupting my brief moment of happiness.

"Not here," I replied.

"Something you'd like to share?"

"Don't like sharing. You know that."

"Is it over?"

Long pause.

"Yep."

"What happened?"

"Bernie crawled into bed with him while I was locked in the file room."

Henry sat down next to me and choked back laughter. He put his arm around me and said, "I'm sorry."

"That's okay," I replied. "It was over long before that. Do me a favor, though. Don't tell my mom. I'm not in the mood to watch her celebrate."

"It's a deal."

# Phone Call
## from the Edge #28

After Henry left, I devoured Rae's unnatural food stash and watched bad TV. My evening was broken up by Morty, finally returning my call:

**Morty:** What's new, Izzele?
**Me:** If I told you, you wouldn't believe me.
**Morty:** Never stopped you before.
**Me:** I wouldn't know where to begin.
**Morty:** It's true. You tell stories funny. You always start in the middle.
**Me:** Here's a headline: Rae committed a felony and might actually have to do time in a juvenile facility.
**Morty:** That is news. What did she do?
**Me:** Something very bad.
**Morty:** Usually felonies are. Feel like sharing?
**Me:** I'm not ready to talk about it. Let's switch subjects.
**Morty:** Okay, how's your Harkey investiga-

tion going?

**Me:** Nowhere.

**Morty:** Your brother still seeing the hooker?

**Me:** I explained this to you before. She's not a hooker.

**Morty:** Sorry, I got confused. I'm not even going to ask about your Irish boyfriend.

**Me:** Good. Don't.

**Morty:** I didn't. That's what I just said.

**Me:** Don't you have some news for me, Morty?

**Morty:** That's right, I haven't told you yet. We're moving back to San Fran.

**Me:** Say San Francisco, not San Fran.

**Morty:** Why? Life's short. No point wasting it on extra syllables.

**Me:** It makes you sound like a tourist.

**Morty:** You're grumpy today.

**Me:** You have no idea what the past few days have been like for me.

**Morty:** True, because you haven't told me.

**Me:** Later. You'll hear all about it later.

**Morty:** Don't wait too long. I'm old.

**Me:** I am well aware of that.

**Morty:** I got the shirt, by the way.

**Me:** What shirt?

**Morty:** The blue shirt that says "Free Schmidt."

**Me:** I didn't send you that shirt.

**Morty:** Who did?

**Me:** Rae.

**Morty:** It came with instructions. A typewritten note that told me I should wear it in public at least twice a week. Who is Schmidt?

**Me:** A man inadvertently responsible for one of the most traumatic events of my life.

**Morty:** So, I take it we don't want to free him?

**Me:** No, we want to free him. Definitely.

**Morty:** Should I wear the shirt?

**Me:** Wear it, don't wear it, I don't care. I just don't want to talk about Schmidt anymore.

**Morty:** Okay. How's the weather?

**Me:** Excuse me, isn't there some real news to discuss?

**Morty:** Are you referring to my forthcoming return to San Fran?

**Me:** *Ahem.*

**Morty:** Cisco.

**Me:** Yes. Give it to me straight, Morty. How on earth did you convince Ruthy to move back to the city?

**Morty:** Let's call it divine intervention.

# BRIDE OF SUNDAY-NIGHT DINNER

Rae was in Spellman lockdown when the guests arrived, and there she would remain for the rest of the evening and for several days to follow. I was surprised to find my parents persisting with their rigorous punishment regimen. I say that because the last time I'd tried to get Rae arrested[1] (for grand larceny of my car), my parents forced me to drop the charges. This time around, there would most likely be a plea bargain and serious probation — which might interfere with her college applications, which would most definitely interfere with my mother's dreams for Rae's future.

Maggie found Rae a defense attorney named Zack Frank. Rae tried to fire him because she didn't like his two first names, but my mother rehired him and informed

---

1. See previous document — *Revenge of the Spellmans* — now available in paperback!

Rae that she would be making no decisions of her own until she turned eighteen (five months from the date of Rae's arrest).

When David and Maggie arrived, my mother and father's behavior got me thinking that they had heard about the anxiety drugs as well — that and the new rule on the whiteboard.

### RULE #55 —
### BE EXTRA NICE TO MAGGIE

Within the first five minutes, my mother asked Maggie if she was comfortable, if she could get her something to drink. When Maggie said no, my mom said she'd get her a lemonade, rendering the previous exchange moot. My father then suggested that they light an incense stick and do a pre-dinner meditation together. Maggie found this all very amusing, despite the scowl on David's face. When Maggie sat down on the couch, Dad slid over a footstool and suggested Maggie put her feet up. David's scowl remained.

"Such a nice face," Mom said to David, "and that's what you do with it?"

David turned to Maggie and said, "You tell them, or I'll tell them."

Maggie merely rolled her eyes and put

her feet up.

"We are not getting sucked into their world," David said.

None of us knew precisely what he was speaking of, but we gathered it was a general dis on the Spellman clan.

"Hey!" said my dad, not really knowing what he was saying "hey" to.

My mother served Maggie her lemonade and turned to my brother for an explanation.

Maggie sipped her drink and said, "I'm perfectly healthy."

"We're very happy to hear that," my mother replied.

"And?" David said, coaxing her.

"And those pills Rae found in my desk were planted there. Okay? Sorry. I did it so she wouldn't turn on me like she does with you guys."

It seemed that Maggie's stress had imparted stress to my parents, who feared that they or their spawn were the cause of it. So once Maggie's confession was made, the barometer of stress in the room dipped considerably.

"No harm done," my father casually replied. "What's for dinner?" he asked.

In case you're curious, dinner was an only slightly less bland offering than the prison food upstairs (salmon, steamed vegetables, and brown rice vs. a can of generic chicken noodle soup and stale bread).

After dinner, David got up to use the restroom. The doorknob was missing and the latch was taped flat. You could open and close the door by looping your finger through the hole. My parents had attached a temporary flip sign for privacy that said OCCUPIED/NOT OCCUPIED.

"What's happening to this house?" David said at full volume.

"Nothing," Mom casually replied. "We're just doing some home improvement."

"Then why is everything unimproved?"

I studied my parents as David questioned them. Their deceit was taking on an unusual form. It was vague and uncalculated, as if they weren't sure exactly what they were hiding.

"We've been busy. We haven't had time to go to the hardware store."

"Then why didn't you just leave the old doorknobs where they were?" David asked.

"Excellent question," I added. "It's not just the five doorknobs, either. There's a missing light fixture, a towel rod, kitchen drawer handles, and the curtains in the upstairs bathroom. What are you hiding?"

The unit cleared the table and ignored all

further inquiries.

Briefly, David and I convened and agreed to investigate the missing hardware matter more thoroughly. The couple departed shortly after that, but for me, the night was still young.

Over coffee and sliced pineapple Dad said, "In light of your troubles with Rae, we thought we should do something to make it up to you."

"Are you going to buy me a new car?"

"No," Mom replied.

"A pony?"

"No," Dad replied.

"Well I hope it's not a raise, because I was going to demand one anyway."

"You'll get another raise as soon as business and the economy improve," Mom sourly replied.

"I've already lost interest."

"We're granting you three wishes," Dad said, trying to make it sound exciting. "Of course, there are some strict stipulations."

"What are you talking about?" I asked.

"Essentially, you may make three demands upon Rae in exchange for the incident."

"Don't call it 'the incident.' Call it what it is."

"In exchange for locking you in a file

room overnight —"

"Thank you."

"You're welcome. You may make three random demands upon your sister," Dad repeated.

"I'm not dropping the charges," I said defensively, thinking this was some sort of barter.

"No. This is in addition to her official charges. Okay?" Mom interjected.

"Really?" I replied as the evil machinations of my mind began working overtime. Sadly, all my early wishes were nixed on the spot. The nixed list follows:

- I'd like her to shave her head.
- Move her bedroom into the garage.
- Make her audition for *American Idol*.
- Dreadlocks?
- A tattoo that says "Isabel rocks!"
- Five thousand dollars in an offshore account.
- Clean my apartment once a week until she goes to college.
- Make her watch *Scared Straight!* in a forty-eight-hour loop.[2]
- Twenty thousand dollars in an offshore

2. The unit actually agreed to three viewings in a row, but that wasn't enough for me.

account.

- A tattoo that says "I ♡ my mommy."[3]

By the time I'd listed my tenth wish and my parents said no, I had little faith that I would be able to come up with a trio of punishments that would a) be approved, b) make Rae suffer, and c) provide me with a satisfyingly sadistic pleasure. But after careful ruminations, I found my three. I hope you will approve; I did the best I could.

3. Honestly, I was really surprised Mom didn't go for that one.

# THREE WISHES

My parents decided that I should have the pleasure of breaking the news to Rae. She already knew that it was coming and had been warned beforehand to treat me with calm respect. Actually, I think this time around Rae's contrition was not a face she put on but a real understanding that she had gone too far.

"Are you ready for my punishments?" I asked after I entered her room.

Rae took a deep breath and replied, "Yes. And once again I'd like to say how sorry I am."

"Number one: When you return to school, for one week straight you must wear a dress every day."

"I only own one dress," Rae replied. "And it's that black one from Uncle Ray's funeral."

"That still fits you?"

"Mom made me buy it big, just in case."

"In case what, someone else died?"

"I guess so. Do you want me to wear that one?"

"No. I'll have Mom pick out some things for you. She'll enjoy that."

Rae sighed with great sadness and held her tongue patiently.

"Number two," I said. "There's a bag of shredded paper in the basement. I want to know what it is."

"The time frame?"

"One week."

Rae took another deep breath, accepting her fate.

"What else?"

"That's all," I replied.

"Oh," Rae said, looking confused. She was under the impression I had a trifecta of punishments. I did but managed to convince the unit that my final blow had to be a blindside. It also required some careful planning and some hard labor. It would have to hold for a while.

I turned to leave; my business was done for now. But I remembered that there was one last thing nagging at me that I needed to know.

"What happened to you on the bus?" I asked. "I think you owe me that answer now, since you used your 'ride home' excuse to lure me into that trap. Tell me and we'll be mostly even."

Rae stared at the floor for a moment, but she was too beat to argue this time around.

"I was taking the bus home from Henry's — sitting in the back, minding my own business. A frat boy sits down next to me and the next thing I know, he vomits. All. Over. Me. Next to my night in juvie, it was the worst experience of my life."

"Thank you," I replied. I was thanking her for the insight and, frankly, for her new nickname. "I'll see you later, Barf Bag."

# BACK TO WORK

Tuesday night I parked in front of Shana Breslin's home and waited for the trash to be put out front. The garbage bins were already out, but the recycling was nowhere to be found. I got out of my car to see if maybe the bin was empty, but when I checked alongside the house, where the receptacles are stored during the week, the green bin was in plain sight and clearly stuffed with goods.

Even though opening the gate and snatching the bags would have taken less than ten seconds, it was out of the question. This basic law of garbology cannot be broken. It's been drilled into me from the start. The trash must be left out for the public. So I returned to my car.

Out of the corner of my eye, I saw movement in a parked sedan approximately fifty yards away. I scanned the area, trying not to draw attention to my discovery. There was a man in a parked car and he didn't appear to be doing anything but sitting there. At eleven o'clock at night. And he just happened to have a clear view of the apartment and me.

I casually walked back toward my car and then abruptly switched directions and darted directly at the suspicious sedan, running at top speed. When the driver saw me coming, he immediately started the engine and pulled out of the parking space. It didn't matter. I was close enough to get his license plate number and I had a feeling that was all I'd need.

I didn't bother waiting any longer for the recycling. I returned home and went straight to bed.

At work the next morning my mother had the nerve to mention that she'd chosen a lawyer for my next date. I was certain being locked in a file room overnight would gain me at least a temporary reprieve. But she reminded me that appropriate restitution had been made and a deal was a deal. It occurred to me that I might be able to get out of lawyer dates if I informed my mother that Connor was officially Ex #12, but I still wasn't ready to reveal that information, so I continued to play her game. Although I was seriously toying with the idea of coming clean — about everything, including Prom Night 1994.

Midmorning, I went into the restroom and pulled the door closed behind me, linking my finger through the hole where the doorknob used to be. The piece of tape holding the latch shut must have broken, because I soon realized I had locked myself in. I went into an immediate panic and began pounding on the bathroom door and shouting, "Let me out of here!" over and over again. I am happy to report that Dad freed me within seconds.

"What is going on in this house?!" I impatiently shouted when I returned to the office and had both of my parents' ears.

Dad gave me a blank stare; Mom answered.

"We're thinking of replacing all the doorknobs and light fixtures," Mom said. "Only we can't decide on a design theme."

I turned to my father for his reaction. When he saw me looking, he chimed in.

"Decorating is hard," Dad said.

"This is ridiculous. I'm not buying a word either of you are saying," I said.

"Relax, Isabel," Mom said. "It's just a doorknob."

"Here's the thing, Mom. Doorknobs are

useful and I like to come and go as I please!"

Mom promptly walked up to the whiteboard and wrote our next rule:

### RULE #58 — CARRY AN EXTRA DOORKNOB WITH YOU AT ALL TIMES

My dad then opened his desk drawer and handed me an old brushed-metal knob.

"Here," Dad said. "I have an extra."

"Me too," Mom said, pulling her own personal doorknob out of her desk, trying to make it all sound ordinary.

I snatched the doorknob from my dad and glared at him.

Then I returned to my desk and e-mailed my father the license plate from the previous night.

"What's this?" Dad asked.

"Probably nothing, but I need to check. The car was parked outside Shana Breslin's home the other night. I need to see if there's a connection."

"I'll get right on it," Dad replied, as if to appease me after the whole doorknob incident.

My father called in the plate number with his police source and the rest of the morning passed in silence until my dad turned to my mother and said, "Did you feed the prisoner yet today?"

"Al, of course I fed her. I'm her mother. I want her to suffer, not starve."

"When's the meeting with her lawyer?" I asked.

"On Friday," Mom replied. "She's going to plea out. We think she'll get bombed with hours of community service but no time."

"Good," I replied.

"I think some of the anti-Rae[1] faculty at her school might notify the colleges where she applied. I think we can safely say that Yale is out. Berkeley might take her. They like students who have a cause, don't they?"

"Isn't it time for another room check?" Dad asked.

Mom looked at her watch. "Close enough," Mom replied. While Mom was looking in on the prisoner, Dad got a call back from his police source. He wrote down the information and then stared at the piece of paper instead of passing it on to me.

I cleared my throat to get his attention.

Dad looked at me with that quizzical expression I have grown so accustomed to and said, "The car is owned by Wallace

1. There are two camps of instructors at Rae's high school: pro-Rae and anti-Rae. The anti-Rae camp is fairly proactive.

Brown. Doesn't he work for Harkey?"

I was too busy turning this information over in my head to respond.

"Isabel?"

"What? Yes. He does work for Harkey."

"What's going on?"

"I don't know," I replied.

Then the phone rang. I turned to my father and said, "Your turn."

Dad answered the phone, leaving me to my thoughts, but only briefly. No one's allowed to think too long in the Spellman home.

Mom returned to report that the prisoner needed my ear.

"Did she actually use that phrase? 'Need my ear'?"

"Actually, yes," my mother replied.

"Are there any sharp objects in her room?"

"You're not as funny as you think you are," Mom said.

"So I've heard."

I climbed the stairs to my sister's cell and knocked, even though in a true jailhouse situation, there would be no pretense of privacy.

Rae politely opened the door. Inside, the floor, her dresser, and her desk were covered with an assortment of assembled pages from

(I can only conclude) Shana Breslin's recycling.

"You've been busy," I remarked.

"It wasn't easy," Rae replied.

She squinted as if trying to refocus. This kind of work certainly doesn't improve anyone's vision.

"Anything I should know?" I asked.

"Yeah," Rae answered. "This isn't any original screenplay."

"How do you know?"

"It's *Shrek*!" Rae shouted. "Why would someone shred *Shrek*? That makes no sense at all!"

She was right. It didn't.

"Did you find anything else?"

"There's another partial page and I think it's from *Reservoir Dogs*, but I can't say for sure. I know that there's a Mr. White in it and a few lines sound right."

"Mr. White? Could it be a feel-good Christmas movie?"

"I doubt it. I've never seen a Christmas movie that heavy on the F-word. Why would someone shred screenplays that are already made?"

"Don't know," I replied. "But I'm going to find out."

# PRATTFALL

These were the facts: Jeremy Pratt wanted me to do a garbology on recycled screenplays that were shredded just for show, as far as I could tell. On the one night Shana's recycling was impossible to access, a car was following me, a car driven by a man who worked for Enemy #1, Rick Harkey. Was this a coincidence? I don't think so.

I spent my afternoon researching Jeremy Pratt. From his credit file I could pull his last known addresses. The first on record was in San Diego. I followed up with a property-owner search and discovered that the San Diego residence had been owned for the last twenty years by Deborah and Tom Pratt. I then searched for Deborah Pratts in San Diego and matched her credit file to her address. From Deborah Pratt's credit file, I got her maiden name. Harkey.

First, I drove to Jeremy's apartment with my short file of the shredded *Shrek.*

"Hi, Jeremy," I said pleasantly when he answered the door. "Sorry I didn't call first, but I was in the neighborhood. Do you have a minute?"

"Uh, okay."

I entered his apartment without being invited, which is perfectly fine if you're not a vampire.

"Out of curiosity, I pieced together a few pages of the screenplays Shana has been kind enough to shred for you. I won't trouble you with my comment on the sheer wastefulness of it. God knows how many trees have been destroyed for this prank. But that's neither here nor there."

Jeremy looked confused, as if he were only partially in on the con.

"Why don't I make this simple for you?" I said, handing him his final bill. "I'll expect this to be paid in full. Otherwise, you'll be seeing me again, and I don't think you want that."

"Anything else?" he asked.

"One little thing. Can you do me a favor and phone your uncle Rick for me?"

Pratt just stared at me. He didn't make a move.

"Or give me your phone and I'll make the call."

Pratt took his phone out of his back

pocket. Within seconds he had Harkey on the line.

"It's Jeremy. Isabel Spellman is here and she wants to talk to you."

A moment passed and Jeremy handed me the phone.

"Hi, Rick," I said. "How you been?"

"What can I do for you, Isabel?" he replied.

"Let's meet in a public place for a drink. I have a proposition for you."

"Really?"

"Yes."

"Your usual bar?"

"My new usual bar. You'll like it. It's much more convenient. The Hemlock, off Polk."

"I'll see you there in an hour."

## AN HOUR LATER

I arrived early and was already on my second beer before Harkey showed. I find the happy-hour prices hard to resist.

Harkey entered, casting a shadow in the doorway, making this whole meeting seem like a showdown in an old Western. He ordered a drink, not knowing that our meeting would be brief.

"What do you want, sweetheart?"

"World peace."

"What do you want from me?"

"I want you to stop calling me 'sweetheart.' "

"Anything else?"

"A truce, I think, is the best we can hope for."

"You're ready to call off your witch hunt?"

"Did you really think you'd catch me in a garbology infraction?"

"Women with their hormones and all — you never know what they'll do."

"Which is why you want me off your back."

Harkey said nothing at first. He swallowed his shot in one gulp to show me what a man he was. I would have matched him, only I was drinking Guinness and I had almost a full pint left. And I was wearing a clean shirt.

It was Harkey's turn to speak and so I waited patiently. If I tried to convince him a truce was in order, he would hold the power. I needed to see how much he wanted it.

"I think it's time we ended this thing," Harkey replied.

"Glad to hear it," I said.

Then we shook hands. I wished that part wasn't necessary. His hand was clammy and he had that bad habit of trying to crush you with his grip.

"I have a parting gift for you," he said,

getting to his feet.

The human slug handed me a manila envelope and said, "No need to thank me. See you around, sweetheart."

Harkey exited the bar and left me alone with the mystery envelope. I didn't crack the seal right away. For some reason, I knew that what I'd find inside wouldn't be pleasant. I finished my drink so that I could be at least buzzed for the unveiling. Then my patience gave out and I opened the envelope and emptied the contents on top of the bar.

Spread out before me were three eight-by-ten glossy prints of Connor kissing another woman. On first viewing I thought it was the same woman, but I looked again and realized there were three different women. Huh.

# FREE MERRIWEATHER —

I arrived at Maggie's office the following morning. She seemed surprised to see me.

"This is the last place I'd expect to find you."

"Do you mind if I look at something in your file room?" I asked.

Maggie met my gaze, trying to read what was going on in my head. "Sure. I'll even let you leave when you want to. You know where to find me."

I knew what I was looking for, so I made my return visit to the chamber of nightmares quick. I pulled a thick yellow file and brought it into Maggie's office. I slid it across her desk.

"Do you mind if I make a copy of this?"

Maggie looked through the documents and turned to me with a sober expression.

"I don't mind, but you know it won't be easy."

"I know."

"And you know what else won't be easy? Fitting the name 'Merriweather' on a T-shirt."

"Don't worry," I replied. "I'll find a way."

Demetrius Merriweather had a rap sheet a mile long, as the saying goes. Yet his crimes of choice appeared to be petty larceny[1] and marijuana possession. Coincidentally, these were also my crimes of choice, back when I was committing crimes. You could say that I chose Merriweather because he was a kindred spirit, and maybe he was. But I'll tell you the truth right now: My agenda was even more personal than that.

Merriweather, back when he was a free man, liked to steal things — cars, jewelry, guitars, leather coats, computers, bicycles, once a coffeemaker, a ladder, and one purebred dog. He would pinch anything that had a resale value over $15. However, what Demetrius liked to steal most was televisions. And stealing TVs was his undoing.

Currently Demetrius was doing life for the first-degree murder of his elderly neighbor, Elsie Collins, who was stabbed fifteen times in her sleep twenty years ago. Merri-

---

1. Theft of property under $500, typically.

weather had always vehemently claimed his innocence, but since his fingerprints were found in Elsie's house and Elsie's TV was found in Merriweather's apartment, he became the prime suspect and eventually the only suspect. While the cops never found the murder weapon or signs of violence in Demetrius's belongings, they did find a spot of Mrs. Collins's blood on the television,[2] and he was convicted based on eyewitness testimony. Elsie's neighbor had seen Demetrius leave her house, carrying a television, sometime before her body was discovered. Demetrius claimed that all he was doing was stealing her TV. He assumed she was sleeping upstairs. He knew she went to bed at ten P.M. every night. He knew that because he could see the lights in the bedroom turn dark with clockwork precision.

I'm a firm believer in consistency. If a man liked to steal things, and small things at that, what would make him escalate to murder? There was a step missing in between. If a man can lose a murder weapon and all evidence of a murder, why would he keep a television around that tied him to

2. A spot of blood can be found anywhere, any time. Blood is all over the place. Or so I've heard.

the crime? The evidence against Demetrius was unfortunate but utterly circumstantial. He was convicted because he stole the wrong TV at the wrong time, but it was an epic leap to call him a murderer.

In Demetrius's file was a letter from the prison chaplain calling Demetrius a peaceful man who had found God while incarcerated (I know, what a cliché) and seen the error of his ways. But the chaplain insisted that he didn't believe Merriweather could have committed such a crime even before he found God. Merriweather had been a model prisoner from the start and had no infractions against him except for stealing a fellow inmate's rosary beads. But that was at the very beginning.

I drove to San Quentin the following week, after memorizing every detail of Merriweather's file.

He was in a maximum-security cell block, which meant we talked on those phones through a thick plastic barrier. The first question I asked him was this:

"Did you murder Elsie Collins?"

"I've never murdered anyone," Demetrius replied.

Some people know how to lie. They can do it with remarkable conviction. Sociopaths do it best because they believe the lie. It's possible that Merriweather was fooling me, but the moment he answered that question, I believed him and I said so.

"I want to look into your case, Demetrius. I think there might be a way to reopen it. First, I'd like to go over some of the details I found in your file."

"Ask away."

"You admitted to being in Ms. Collins's home the night of her murder, correct?"

"Yes."

"Tell me exactly what you did."

"I climbed through her back window —"

"What time?"

"Around midnight. I unplugged her TV and left through the back door. Couldn't have taken more than five minutes."

"So you left the back door open?"

"Right. I know what you're thinking. If I didn't kill her, I certainly made it easier for the real killer to break in."

"Did she have any enemies?"

"No. Everybody loved her. She was a sweetheart."

"Then why'd you steal her TV?"

"I don't know why I was always stealing her TVs. Her son owned a pawnshop, so I knew she could always replace them, I guess."

"You stole her TV more than once?"

"Afraid so."

"How many times?"

"I'm ashamed to say."

"Spit it out."

"Three times."

"Seriously? Couldn't you have chosen another victim?"

"I knew where she kept her TVs," Demetrius said, shrugging his shoulders with embarrassment.

"Just her TVs? Nothing else?" I asked.

"Back then I smoked a lot of the dope[3] and I really liked watching television when I was high. And eating Cheetos."[4]

"Wasn't one television enough?"

"I only stole more TVs when I ran out."

"What happened to the TVs you stole?"

"My brother stole the first one from me and I pawned the second one to buy my mama a birthday present."[5]

"I see. Did Ms. Collins suspect you had stolen her TV?"

"No. She *knew* I did it. Every time she

3. Notice how I refrained from telling him just to call it "dope," not "the dope." I have more restraint than I am generally credited with.

4. A pastime I have enjoyed myself on occasion.

5. It's kind of sweet, if you think about it.

saw me, she'd say, 'Boy, give me my TV back!' "

"What would you say?"

"I'd say, 'I don't have it no more,' which was true."

"Do you have any idea who killed her?"

"No," Demetrius replied. "I just know it wasn't me."

"According to the police report you claimed to have an alibi — Theresa Barnes — but she didn't back your story."

"That's because they found drugs in her house and threatened her with jail time if she talked. But then she retracted her retraction, but nobody would listen to her no more."

"I need to contact Theresa. Can you get her information for me?"

"Yes, ma'am."

"Demetrius, I hate being called 'ma'am.' "

"Then I'm gonna call you 'Angel.' "

"Or Isabel is just fine."

"Are you going to get me out of here, Angel?"

"I'm going to try. Hang in there, Demetrius. I'll be in touch."

"I knew it, the moment I saw you, that the Lord had sent you to me."

"Listen to me, Demetrius: I'm no angel. You and me, we're not that different."

# Lost Wednesday Again

The missing hardware and Lost Wednesdays were connected. I just couldn't figure out how and I also couldn't fathom why my parents hadn't gotten to the bottom of the situation. As far as I could tell, they knew the identity of the thief but were protecting him or her for reasons that I had yet to determine.

I borrowed Petra's car and a wig from her shop and settled into a day of surveillance on the Spellman household. I parked down the block with a set of binoculars and some snack food. As far as long-term surveillances went, this one was a piece of cake. Our neighbor, Edison Horlador, a retired banker and avid baker, was home most days. He could be relied upon for coffee breaks, cookies, and an available bathroom. One with an actual doorknob on it.

And so I planted myself at the house for a few hours and watched. Eventually three people arrived in the same car. All looked like your average sort. I could have picked them out of a lineup, but there was nothing else I could report about them. They stayed in the house for an hour and then departed. I followed them. Two members of the trio were dropped off at a residence in the Sunset. The woman driving the vehicle returned to her place of employment. None of the parties exited the house with anything more than they had entered with, so one mystery remained unsolved. However, I finally knew what those Lost Wednesdays were about. And let me tell you right now: There was never any salsa dancing.

David, Rae, and I collided at the front door of the Spellman home early Thursday morning. David was returning Rae to her jail cell (she had a twenty-four-hour furlough at David's house, during which I gathered he let her watch TV and eat M&M's). My sister's spirit had been much restored, although the return to her fate of confined spaces and bland food would soon bring her back to her current status quo (i.e., miserable).

"Do you know what's going on here, Isabel?" David asked, taking in the scene.

All the missing doorknobs had been replaced by temporary ones that didn't fit the

Victorian aesthetic. Our previous knobs were made of brass or glass. These were silver, modern, and straight out of a hardware shop.

"I'm still working out all the details," I replied.

"I think we should pay them a visit," David suggested. "And gather some intelligence."

It was seven thirty A.M. and Mom and Dad were still in bed. David knocked on their door.

"What?!" Dad answered, sounding groggy, cranky, and something else.

"We're coming in," David said, and swung open the door.

Inside, my parents' bedroom had been transformed from its previous utilitarian sleeping nook/storage closet to a clean, well-lit, beige bedroom, with the furniture entirely rearranged.

"What happened here?" David asked.

"Feng shui," Mom replied.

"Gesundheit," I said.

"That's so unlike you both," David said, eyeing them suspiciously.

"We got a book," said Mom. "It's important for the marriage to keep clutter out of the bedroom. And the bed shouldn't line up directly with the door and should be approachable from both sides."

David stared at the television set that was still stationed in front of the bed.

"Don't they tell you to get rid of the TV, too?"

"We don't have to do everything the book says," Dad replied.

"Is there something we can do for you?" Mom asked.

"No. We just dropped by to say hello."

"Did you feed the prisoner?" Dad asked.

"Not yet," I replied.

"May I recommend Cream of Wheat? Straight up," Mom said.

"Excellent choice," I replied.

Demetrius had passed on his alibi information through Maggie. We agreed that I would do the hard labor and she would file the appeal, if I could find any new evidence to base it on. While the Schmidt case hinged on compelling DNA evidence, I had to find a different angle because the physical evidence in this case (both Elsie Collins's garments and the clothes they took from Demetrius) was "misplaced" in the evidence room and never recovered.

This didn't leave me many avenues to pursue, but I would pursue them nonetheless. I needed to speak to everyone who was interviewed at the time of the murder to see whether something was missed in the original investigation.

Before I commenced my own investigation, beginning with my first interview with Theresa Barnes (the alibi), Maggie asked me to drop by her office for a chat.

"I'm missing something here, Isabel. I understand that being locked in a file room all night could be traumatic and cause some unusual behavior, but there's something you're not telling me. And I think I should know it."

"I think this case might hinge on police misconduct," I replied.

"They often do. You're not answering my question. Is this an act of goodwill? Are you trying to clear your conscience? Or something else?"

"All of the above?"

"Spill it," Maggie said rather authoritatively.

So I spilled. "Look at the lead investigator on the case."

Maggie perused the file.

"Oh," Maggie said, finally putting two and two together. "Inspector Rick Harkey. Why didn't I see that before?"

"You weren't looking," I replied.

In case you were thinking that I had turned saintly or at the very least developed some kind of social conscience, I hate to disappoint you. I took on the Merriweather case for one primary reason — to finally get at Harkey. If I couldn't destroy his career, maybe I could ruin his reputation.

Well, that's how the whole thing started. But as I'm sure you've discovered yourself, things change, people change, and what drives you to act can turn on a dime.

Theresa Barnes conveniently lived across the bay in El Cerrito. When I phoned her about an interview, there was no hesitation in her agreement. We met in her one-bedroom stucco house. She said she lived alone, but I gathered it was more that she paid rent alone. There were signs of other inhabitants, even though the inhabitants weren't currently around.

I asked if I could film her and she agreed, although she left the room to apply makeup and don a more flattering top. The interview was straightforward, and Theresa was a sound witness — a witness, however, who was once a drug addict who lied to stay out of prison. Her story was exactly the same as Demetrius said it would be, so I won't bore you with the details. The most striking thing I noticed about Theresa was that her remorse was unshakable. According to prison records, she visited Demetrius at least once a month. She had contacted lawyers before, seeking help. In fact, it was Theresa who found Maggie Mason.

Through Ms. Barnes, I got the names of

other individuals who knew Merriweather before he was convicted. Character witnesses wouldn't do me much good at this point, but I was curious, and if the case was ever reopened, they might come in handy.

While my gut told me that Demetrius and Theresa were telling the truth, I've learned to occasionally ignore my innards and instead follow logic. My next stop was Jack Weaver, the ten-year-old neighbor across the street who was the only eyewitness in the case. Jack was now thirty and working for a telecom company. He remembered the case but said he had little to add to his original statement. He never testified in court. He merely said that he saw Demetrius leave Ms. Collins's home carrying a television. It was dark outside but he recognized Demetrius.

I asked him what a ten-year-old was doing up so late. Watching Johnny Carson, of course.

"Do you remember what Demetrius was wearing?"

"The same thing he always wore. A sweatshirt under a denim jacket."

"Do you remember seeing him the next day?"

"I don't know if it was the next day, but I saw him after the murder. We were all standing outside Elsie's house, talking."

"Did he look sad?"

"I think so."

"Did he look guilty?"

"I was ten. I didn't notice."

"Do you remember anything else about Mr. Merriweather?"

"I saw him steal toothpaste from the corner shop once."

"That's it?"

"But what I remember was how he made it look so natural. I think that's why he could take TVs and stuff. He didn't look around all shifty eyed. He acted like he was supposed to take the TV."

"Do you think he murdered Elsie Collins?"

"No. But I know he stole her TV."

# WHAT THE BUTLER DID DO

It's easy to get lost in a cause (or a vendetta), but when you suddenly realize bills need to be paid, well, real cases take priority. At least that's the grown-up perspective on things, and since I've been impersonating one of those recently, I had to go with the plan.

If you recall, we last left the Case of Mr. Winslow's Sort-of-Missing Butler with a new set of fingerprints, which I found under the toilet seat. Henry left a message on my voice mail informing me that he found a match on the prints. He said he'd meet me at my new bar at seven if I wanted the information. Of course, a name, Social Security number, and any criminal record could easily have been provided in either a phone message or an e-mail. But I guess Henry wanted a drink and I wanted information, so I agreed to meet him. I guess that's what friends do: They drink together and exchange information. I was getting used to this relationship. I no longer felt the need to protest.

"Hand it over," I said as soon as Henry arrived.

Henry passed me the envelope and then went to the bar and ordered. I broke the seal and reviewed the contents.

Mason Graves was no Mason Graves at all. He was Harvey Grunderman, born in Missouri and raised in Arizona, where he first did time for check fraud. He was currently serving six months in a minimum-security prison for neglecting to pay child support. Ten years of child support, to be exact. So, apparently, Grunderman also had a kid. I checked the home address listed on his police record and decided I'd check it out the next day.

After I studied the file and finished my drink, I remembered my manners. The fact remained that Henry owed me nothing and using him as a source was a favor. And I knew that later I was going to have to ask him for an even bigger favor. I reminded myself to be extra nice.

"Thank you, Henry."

"You're welcome."

"I'm sorry I forgot to say it five minutes ago."

"It's okay."

"I'm rude."

"I know."

"Can I buy you another drink?" I asked.

"I'm not done with the first one."

"Well, when you're done."

"Okay."

There was an awkward silence while I waited for Henry to finish his drink.

"I don't drink as quickly as you do, Isabel. Don't rush me."

"Right," I replied.

"We can make small talk," Henry suggested. "You need to practice that anyway."

"How's it hanging?" I said, practicing.

"You've never said that before in your life."

"Since we're practicing, I thought I'd give it a whirl."

"Make that its last whirl."

"Agreed."

"How was your day?" Henry asked, identifying precisely what it is about small talk that I don't like — simple, general questions that can be answered in myriad ways. I need specific questions to answer or avoid directly.

"Fine," I said, like I've said since I was

twelve whenever asked the very same question.

"You're horrible at this," Henry replied.

"You are too. Going around asking lame questions and then insulting the person you ask when they answer."

Henry finished his drink in one delightful gulp.

"Now that's how it's done. I'll get you another," I said, returning to the bar and ordering for both of us.

Back at small-talk central, Henry attempted a different line of inquiry.

"Do you have any plans for tonight?"

"Yes," I replied, because I did.

"Care to elaborate?"

"No," I said, because I didn't.

Two hours later, I hit a liquor store for provisions. Then I swung by the Philosopher's Club and found Connor's truck parked on a residential street around the corner. I posed the glossy snapshots (courtesy of Harkey) on the windshield. I searched the area for witnesses, gave myself pitching distance from the truck, opened the carton of eggs, aimed, and then suddenly I lost interest.

Over the years, I'd often found the egging of a car to be the perfect ritual to mark the end of a relationship. But this time around I couldn't muster the energy. There was no point. I simply left the carton of eggs on top of his car — a reminder of what could have been — and left. If that's not evolution, I don't know what is.

# Spawn of
# Sunday-Night Dinner

After ten days of Rae being in solitary confinement, my parents agreed to let her join the general population, just for dinner. However, leaving the confines of the Spellman home was still out of the question. The prisoner was even allowed a visitor, Fred. But I suspect the Fred invitation was more for my parents' benefit than Rae's. As I soon discovered, Fred was universally adored. I noticed, when he arrived, that he ate a few pistachios and then pocketed the shells. That did not go unnoticed by Mom, even though the pistachio cam was long gone.

I decided that this particular dinner was the perfect time to share my new pro bono case with the family. I had shirts made up and everyone donned theirs while Rae was still held captive in her cell.

No matter how hard I tried, I had to hyphenate.

Mom asked me to fetch Rae from her bedroom and to make sure she wasn't wearing pajamas, which she had been for most of her parental internment. I knocked on Rae's door. She opened it within seconds. That's what solitary confinement does to people. It makes them crave the company of those they often try to avoid.

Rae studied my shirt.

"Justice for Mary?" she said mockingly.

"Merriweather," I corrected, pulling my shirt down to make sure she got a full view.

"Oh, I see it now. Merriweather? I think I saw that file. Refresh my memory."

"Demetrius Merriweather. Thief, not murderer."

"Maybe you should put that on a T-shirt," Rae smugly replied.

"Maybe I will."

"Funny how you don't mind people staring at your boobs for Merriweather, but Schmidt was another story. FYI, they're going to stare a lot longer with a name like that."

"My body. I get to decide what I advertise on it."

My mother shouted up the stairs, "Girls, time for dinner."

I shouted back: "I'm thirty-two. Don't lump me in the same category as the prisoner."

As Rae and I descended the stairs, she even had the nerve to say, "I'm going to free my guy *way* before you free your guy."

"That's because you picked an easy guy."

"He's not easy," Rae snapped back.

"You're swimming with flippers," I said. "I'm swimming with dead weights attached to my ankles. These are entirely different situations."

When we reached the dinner table, Rae turned to Fred and smiled.

"You have no idea what's it like in there," she said, nodding her head in the direction of her bedroom. "Now I know exactly how Schmidt feels."

My father sighed and rolled his eyes. "No, you don't, Rae. You are in a comfortable bedroom with clean sheets and allowed to use the toilet without people watching you. Okay? I'd rather you didn't equate being grounded with prison time."

"Yes, but I know what it's like to not have anyone to talk to for a week. It's not easy."

"That's why we let you out," Mom said.

"I got tired of listening to you talk to yourself."

Mom and Dad began loading the serving dishes onto the table.

"You were talking to yourself?" Fred asked.

"I was thinking out loud," Rae replied defensively.

"About what?" Fred asked.

"Random stuff."

"He's looking for examples, Rae," I said.

"Well, at first I was just practicing what I'd say to the judge so I wouldn't have to do time. It was compelling. I'm pretty sure he'll understand. Then I was thinking about escaping through the window and then I got distracted by the glass and wondered who first found glass. Where does it come from? What was it first used for? You took my computer away, so I couldn't look it up. It was driving me crazy. Then as I was getting ready for bed and I was flossing my teeth, I thought about how weird it was that there's this universal rule to floss every day, but that seemed so strange because the cavemen didn't floss. They also didn't have toothpaste or shampoo. If I don't wash my hair for three days, it's unbelievably itchy and disgusting. So, how could the cave people not be totally grossing themselves out? Sure, you can swim in a lake, but that doesn't solve the greasy-hair problem. Oh, and then I was thinking about other disgusting things. Like, have you noticed that whenever a woman takes a pregnancy test on TV, she waves that wand around like it's a lollipop? She just peed on the thing and then passes it off to the maybe-father and then when she's done with the whole thing she never washes her hands. I have never seen an actor accurately portray touching a stick that you just peed on."

It had become clear that Rae's rambling was just the beginning of the deluge that would follow. My father was distracted by the flood of words; my mother was in the kitchen when Rae's little speech began. But something happened at the table when Rae touched on her pregnancy-test issue. Even though no one else was speaking, it was like a hush came over the room. Out of the corner of my eye, I glanced at a silent exchange between David and Maggie. Fred, intriguingly, spotted it himself. Sometimes my instincts fail me. For instance, I missed every warning signal before my file room incarceration. But this time, in a flash, I knew that Maggie was pregnant. I also knew that Fred knew that Maggie was pregnant, and I needed to make sure that Fred knew that this information should not be shared with Rae.

"Mrs. Spellman, will you please pass the potatoes and the spinach?" Fred asked.

"Of course, Fred," my mother replied, and then she gave him eyes like she wished she could adopt him or something. "Rae, did you notice that Fred took a second serving of spinach?" Mom said.

"No," Rae replied distractedly. "I'm still adjusting to being on the outside. So much has changed since I went in."

"Shut up," I said.

"Eat more spinach," Fred suggested. "I've heard fresh produce is hard to come by in lockup."

"Actually, it's very easy to come by," Rae replied.

"So, Fred," Dad said, "what do you do for fun?"

"Dad, leave Fred alone," David said.

Wow. Even David loved Fred.

"I was asking an innocent question," Dad replied.

"You sound like you're on a blind date with him," David said.

Mom said, "Speaking of blind dates —"

"Not another word," I interrupted.

"I don't mind," Fred said.

Then the table went silent.

"Fred, if you want to answer the question, go ahead. But if you don't want to, you have the right to refuse to answer the question. We do it all the time," Rae advised him.

To the delight of the entire table, Fred answered the question.

"I like to go mountain biking and to the movies, listen to music, read books, worship Satan. You know, the usual stuff."

"Don't you just want to clone him?" Mom asked no one in particular.

When the meal ended and "dessert" was finished, my parents turned to Rae and said, "I think it's time you went back to your room, Rae."

Rae gave them a strangely evil expression. If anyone was worshipping Satan, it was her. "Is it?" she said with a sneer. "I thought maybe we all might drink some Sanka and have a chat about a few things."

When I turned to my parents for a re-action, they appeared almost, well, intimidated.

Then my father hardened his gaze at Rae and said, "Say good night, Fred."

Then he actually said, "Good night, Fred."

"Let me walk you out, Fred," I said, walking Fred out.

While the delightful Fred unlocked his bike, put on his helmet, and turned on the light, I decided to see if I could gain his confidence for a little while.

"You might have noticed something earlier at the table, while Rae was talking about pee and pregnancy tests."

Fred looked me in the eye. "I might have noticed something."

"Can you not notice it anymore?" I asked.

"Don't see why not," Fred replied.

"Especially don't notice it with Rae."

"I think I hear what you're saying," Fred said.

"Do you need a bribe?" I asked, because Rae always needs a bribe and by virtue of association, I thought Fred might be the same.

"No. But thanks for the offer," Fred said.

When I returned to the dining room, I heard my father say to Rae in his sternest tone, "Go upstairs and practice your please-forgive-me face in the mirror for an hour. You have court tomorrow."

"But —"

"Not another word out of you, *young lady.*"

Rae stomped up the stairs but followed her instructions — not a single word leaked from her lips.

The rest of the family, drained by the run-

of-the-mill family dinner, dispersed in silence.

# WOULD THE REAL MASON GRAVES PLEASE STAND UP?

The address on Mason Graves's employee file was a one-bedroom apartment in the Tenderloin, which I had assumed was Mason's cheap getaway from the Winslow home. I rang the buzzer and a man answered.

"Hello?"

"Hi, I'm looking for Mason Graves. I have some information for him."

I was buzzed up without any further communication. Apartment 606 was inconveniently located on the sixth floor of a walkup. A large man in his midforties met me at the door.

"Are you Mason Graves?" I asked.

"Yes. Did I win something?"

"No."

"Oh," he said, appearing unduly saddened by the lack of good news.

"I'm sorry," I said because it seemed like the right thing to do.

Before I met the real Mason Graves, I imagined a crafty man in collusion with an even more crafty man currently serving time. This Mason Graves brought to mind Lennie in *Of Mice and Men*.[1]

"Were you expecting to win something?" I asked.

"There's always a chance. I play the lottery every week."

"Well, I'm sorry I didn't bring you good news."

"That's okay. No one ever does."

"Can I ask you a question?" I asked redundantly.

"Sure."

"Do you know a Harvey Grunderman?"

"Yeah. He's my cousin Harvey. He helps take care of me."

"What do you mean?"

"He pays my bills and makes sure they bring me food every week."

"Harvey pays your bills?"

"I'm not good with money."

"Does he take care of your taxes and stuff?"

"Yes."

"Do you have a job?"

"I clean the building for less rent. I

1. Yeah, I read it. Well, I read the CliffsNotes.

vacuum and change lightbulbs and take out the trash and stuff."

"If you need money, where do you get it?"

"My mom cooks for me once a week and always makes sure I have sandwich money, and Harvey pays my rent."

"What's your mother's name?"

"Libby Graves."

There went one theory. I was really hoping he'd say Mrs. Enright.

"Do you know where Harvey is?"

"He took a vacation. He needed to go away," he said.

"Yes. He did. Where did he tell you he was going?"

"My memory isn't very good."

"Mason, do you have any other relatives in the area?"

"No. Just my mom and Harvey. My dad died a long time ago."

"I see. When's the last time you heard from Harvey?"

"Maybe a week ago," Mason replied. "He'll be home in a few months and then we can go back to our weekly card game."

I took out my card and handed it to the real Mason. "In the meantime, if you need something, give me a call."

Mason read the card. "Izzy Ellmanspay?"

"Oops. Sorry. That's the wrong card."

I handed him the one with my real name on it and said my good-bye.

Sometimes you just want a bad guy to be a bad guy. Someone you can take down alone. Harvey Grunderman came with an extra two hundred and fifty pounds of responsibility. I couldn't close the case the way I planned — with a police report. Something else had to be done.

I drove directly to the Winslow home after my Tenderloin visit. In any metropolitan demographic, the sharp contrast between the social strata can be alarming, but in San Francisco, within five minutes you're in a whole new world. My brief meeting with Mason Graves shot me with a strong dose of sadness. I wanted to sneak one of Mr. Winslow's pricy rugs out of his home, hock it on eBay, and leave the cash on Graves's doorstep. One fancy rug could buy a whole lot of sandwiches.

Len greeted me at the door.

"Ms. Spellman, why the long face?" he asked, shaking me into an entirely different world.

"Long day. That's all."

"But it's only just begun. Do you have news?" Len asked. And if you're wondering, no, he still hadn't lost his ridiculous accent.

"Case closed," I said.

"Did you find Mason?"

"Yes. His real name is Harvey Grunderman and he's currently doing time for neglecting to pay child support. I suspect his employment here was a long con on Mr. Winslow. Please have your employer contact his attorneys and make sure that if there are any stipulations in his will for Mason Graves that they be retracted. That's all I want you to tell Mr. Winslow. I will deal with Grunderman myself."

"I knew that butler was no good from the start," Len said.

"I'd like you to help Mr. Winslow interview for a new valet. We'll do a thorough background check on each one and hopefully he won't run into any problems in the future. I need to remind you that your time here is coming to an end."

"What if I wished to stay on?" Len asked.

"You want to talk in that voice for the next decade?"

"It wouldn't bother me in the slightest."

"How are things at home?" I asked.

"The same."

"Listen carefully, Len. This gig is over in a few weeks. You need to move on, and you and Christopher should have a long talk about whatever domestic war is going on here. Got it?"

"Sometimes, Isabel, you are so tiresome."

You know who else found me tiresome? Harvey Grunderman. I drove two hours to Folsom Prison for a personal meeting. Physically, Grunderman was average in every way. Approximately five foot ten, brown hair, brown eyes, even features, no scars or tattoos. He was the perfect physical specimen for a criminal: impossible to describe beyond his averageness. The one thing that set him apart was his overly dignified bearing. He sat straight up, looked you right in the eye, was well groomed, and spoke clearly, though he didn't waste the accent on me. Harvey had the look of civility, even in the orange uniform. That said, there was definitely something uncivil about the look he gave me when I informed him that his services would no longer be required in the Winslow home. (Once he was released, of course.)

I then informed Harvey that I would hold off on having Winslow press charges so long as I saw that he was continuing to take care of his cousin, the real Mason Graves.

Harvey tried to play on my sympathies.

"Everything I've done, I've done for Mason," Harvey said in a plain American accent.

"Sell that story to someone else. I'm glad to hear that you decided to break character for your prison time. I think it was a wise decision."

"I'm not so bad," Harvey said, still trying to defend his actions. "I bet you and me aren't so different."

"Trust me. We are. In fact, I've encountered very few people I have things in common with. Listen carefully, Mr. Grunderman: I'll be watching you. Don't do anything stupid."

# THE GIFT OF PROBATION

I didn't want Rae to do time, even in a juvenile facility. She would be destroyed within days. While her will is spectacularly stubborn, her body could withstand only so much abuse. And she would be the ultimate target in an environment where brawn wins out. However, I made it clear that I wanted her to get some serious probation time, and I wanted this infraction on her record. Of course, in a few months it would be expunged, but I needed payback. I think I got it.

The entire family, including the auxiliary members, Maggie and Henry, attended Rae's hearing.

The Honorable Judge Walter Groggins conducted the proceedings. I found great delight in the stern gaze he held on my sister. Even I would have wilted under that stare. Judge Groggins read Rae's verdict: guilty of false imprisonment, which, for an adult, can carry a term of three to five years. The DA met with Henry, the arresting officers, and my parents and negotiated a fair punishment for the act. While I could have filed a civil claim against my sister, my parents had derailed that option by granting my three punitive wishes against Rae (one of which had yet to be realized). And when Judge Groggins read the terms of her probation, it was like a fourth wish had been granted:

"Until the age of eighteen, you will volunteer fifteen hours a week at Greenfields, a community organic garden that donates produce to charitable organizations throughout the county."

For some people, gardening is a soothing, fun, spiritually nourishing activity. For my sister, who has never met a vegetable she liked, it would be hell on earth. Hard labor, patience, dirt, produce — all things she loathes — and now she would be spending over 13 percent[1] of her waking hours learning how to make things she hated grow. If that isn't justice, I don't know what is.

Rae looked as if she might cry or try to make a run for it across the border. Mom and Dad just seemed relieved that the

1. Yes, someone else did the math for me. Okay?

ordeal was over. Maggie and David kept to themselves, whispering whatever it is that they whispered. Those two could have their secrets so long as they stayed together.

Henry walked me to the door.

"How do you feel about the outcome?"

I turned to Henry. "I could kiss the person who came up with the organic gardening idea."

"Good to know."

I phoned Morty from the parking lot of the courthouse and shared my exciting news. The conversation was brief, however, since the movers were at their Florida condo and he was trying to have a conversation with me while dodging large pieces of furniture.

**Me:** What's your ETA?

**Morty:** I had a pastrami sandwich on rye today.

**Me:** Huh?

**Morty:** How many lamps do I need?

**Me:** I can't answer that question for you, Morty.

**Morty:** Izzele, are you there?

**Me:** Yes.

**Morty:** What were we talking about? There's lots of noise here.

**Me:** Pastrami sandwiches and lamps.

**Morty:** Speaking of pastrami, I want to go to Moishe's the second I arrive. Make a reservation.

**Me:** They don't take reservations.

**Morty:** Make one anyway.

**Me:** Fine. Morty, when are you arriving?

**Morty:** Watch out. I only got the two feet.

**Me:** When are you arriving?

**Morty:** What day is it?

**Me:** You should know what day it is.

**Morty:** What difference does it make?

**Me:** It's Tuesday.

**Morty:** I'll be in Frisco Thursday next week.

**Me:** Don't call it Frisco. Only tourists do that.

**Morty:** Stop telling me how to talk. I've been doing it a lot longer than you.

**Me:** Doesn't make you better at it.

**Morty:** See you Thursday in the Frisco, Isabel.

**Me:** Bye, Morty.

# FREE SOMEBODY ALREADY

The Schmidt case moved forward with the speed of light — at least that's how it seemed in comparison to the Merriweather case. The DNA results proved that the unidentified blood found on the victim and the skin particles found under the victim's fingernails did not match the DNA of Levi Schmidt. That DNA belonged to someone else, someone who conveniently was already in the system. His name was Jesse Harper, and he was currently doing a ten-year stint in San Quentin for rape.

Armed with this information, Maggie filed an immediate writ of habeas corpus.[1] While the evidence was compelling, the DA wanted a confession out of Jesse Harper to seal the deal, and that confession would take weeks of negotiation. Still, Rae was hopeful,

1. A petition to the court to question whether the person is lawfully imprisoned.

which had the unfortunate side effect of taking the edge off her gardening work.

As for Demetrius, I knew from the start his case wouldn't be so easy. I just didn't realize how not easy it would be. I presented what I believed was an irrefutable argument to Maggie, beginning with the absence of convincing physical evidence. If he'd murdered a woman, shouldn't he have had her blood all over him? If he was foolish enough to keep her television, how could he be so crafty as to hide a murder weapon so well that it was never discovered? There was also the ten-year-old witness, who saw a man who showed no signs of having just committed murder casually leave Ms. Collins's home. Aside from all that, Demetrius didn't have a single violent crime on his record. Nothing pointed to murder. But having no evidence pointing to a murder suspect isn't incontrovertible evidence that the suspect did not commit the murder. Once Demetrius was incarcerated, the burden of proof fell back on the defense. Turns out that my case hinged on circumstantial logic. And you can't free a man just because it makes sense.

After compiling all the data that I had on Merriweather's case, I returned to Maggie's office to see if it was enough. She shook her head and said, "No." Then she excused herself to use the restroom. Then she returned to her desk and consumed half a stack of saltines and drank some ginger ale. I did my best to pretend not to notice, which came off as more suspicious than just asking, "Are you feeling all right?" Maggie then reminded me of what I was up against.

To free a man who has been wrongly incarcerated, you need a really good reason and you need a reason that wasn't presented in the original defense. While I knew that Harkey had mishandled Merriweather's case, I also knew that police misconduct would be a hard sell and there wasn't enough evidence yet to convince a judge to even reopen the investigation.

My only chance of freeing Merriweather would be to look into all of Harkey's cases to see if there was a common thread. If I could cast doubt on Harkey's reputation, there was a chance that all of his cases would require some review.

Maggie could subpoena all of Harkey's cases, but that would draw direct attention to the case and to me. I told her to hold off. There might be an easier way.

I returned to the Spellman offices and immediately pounced on Dad.

"I need to see the police files on all of Harkey's cases when he was working homicide. Any chance you can get those for me?"

I had hoped for a simple yes or no answer, preferably yes, but my father said, "What's going on, Isabel?"

"Can't you just do this for me and not ask any questions?"

"Uh, no."

"It's very simple. Rick Harkey was the arresting officer on the Merriweather case."

"The convicted murderer that you're wearing on your shirt?" Dad asked.

"Yes, the innocent convicted murderer. The DNA evidence is conveniently missing, the case was purely circumstantial, has as many holes as a Wiffle ball, and it looks like Harkey coerced the alibi into retracting her testimony. If I can prove misconduct on other cases, then maybe we have a shot at proving a trend, which could result in a reinvestigation of Harkey's cases in general."

"So, you're not doing a good deed, looking into a wrongful conviction; you're still on a Harkey witch hunt."

"Why can't it be both?"

"What are you getting yourself into here?"

"There's no other way, Dad. And I just know Demetrius is innocent."

Dad said he'd think about it. But Dad uses the "thinking" excuse as a stalling tactic. He's done it for years. When I was twelve, I asked for a puppy. He's still "thinking" about that one. I took my father's response as a clear-cut no.

I'd hoped to escape the house before I ran into Mom, but she intercepted me in the foyer.

"Isabel! Just who I was looking for."

"Do I know you?" I asked.

"I believe you're due for another lawyer date. How's the hunt coming along?"

"Mom, are you aware that the doorknob to the dining room is now missing?"

"Yes. Now how is that date coming along?"

"I'm busy," I replied. "Why don't you go to the store and pick one out for me?"

"What's the catch?"

"No catch," I replied.

"Okay," Mom said, not losing her suspicion.

There was a catch, but I'll get to that later.

# Free Merriweather —

## CHAPTER 3

I needed ten years' worth of police files, which meant I needed either a cooperative DA or a cop who had access to police records. I went to the only other cop I thought might cooperate in my endeavor.

The door to Henry's office was slightly ajar. I shoved it a bit and said, "Are you busy?"

"What are you doing here?"

"I was in the neighborhood."

"You're always in some neighborhood," he replied.

"Isn't everyone?"

"Come in and close the door behind you."

I did. I was about to sit down when Henry said, "Don't sit."

I didn't.

Henry then circled his desk and proceeded to frisk me without even asking first. I slapped his hands away. His payback was reaching into my coat pocket and pulling out a dirty tissue.

"Ha," I said.

"Throw them out when you're done," Henry said, tossing the tissue into his trash and then searching his desk for hand sanitizer.

"What were you looking for?" I asked.

"Drugs, Isabel."

"Get over it. It was a one-time deal."

Once Henry was satisfied that I hadn't brought contraband into his office, he offered me a seat.

"I need a favor," I said.

"Of course you do. Why else would you visit me?"

There was enough of an edge to Henry's reply that I felt, well, guilty. And here's something that might surprise you: I don't feel guilty all that often.

"That's not true," I replied, even though as far as I could recollect, it was true.

"What do you need?" he snapped.

"Now I feel bad. I'm not going to ask."

"Go ahead," he said.

I quickly got to my feet and said, "I'll be back later." Then I made an abrupt exit.

## TWO HOURS LATER

I returned with a picnic basket (i.e., a large paper bag) full of farmer's market items —

anything I could find in the unprocessed food category, including organic cheese and crackers, since I can't make a meal of apples and whole-grain bread.

"Can you take a break?" I asked when I entered his office.

"What's in the bag?"

"Drugs," I replied. "And lots of them."

Henry rolled his eyes.

"A snack. I thought we could have an afternoon picnic."

"Seriously?"

"This picnic will include entertainment."

"They always do. In the form of ants."

"This entertainment I'm speaking of is better than any episode of *Doctor Who* in the history of *Doctor Who*."

"That's not possible."

"Get your coat. It's chilly outside."

An hour later Henry and I were seated on a wool blanket just outside the fence of the organic garden in which Rae was doing time. While the inspector and I dined on sustainably-grown nourishment, our afternoon's entertainment was the pained expression on Rae's face as she dug ditches, planted zucchini, and watered the tomato plants. The frozen look of disgust on her face carried an uplifting comedic edge. In fact, we both lost our appetites because we were laughing so hard. I hoped that as long as her probation lasted, she would rail against her punitive assignment. Henry, on the other hand, simply enjoyed the fact that Rae was forced out of her comfort zone and into a job that served society rather than manipulated it.

As we gathered our picnic remains, our spirits were considerably elevated, I imagine in the same way someone leaving a great theater production might feel.

"That was the best show ever," Henry said, smiling. He doesn't smile all that often, so it was a surprise.

"I know. I came here the other day, out of curiosity. Stayed an hour. Figured I shouldn't keep it all to myself."

"Kind of you," Henry replied.

On the car ride back to the precinct, Henry said, "Okay, what do you want?"

"I need to look at police files from when Harkey was on the job. Preferably before DNA evidence had really evolved and for anything that was a potential capital offense."

"I gather this is in regard to the Merriweather case?" Henry asked.

"You gathered correctly."

"Is this about freeing Merriweather or taking down Harkey?"

"Tomato, tomahto."

# Lawyer Date — The Final Chapter

If you found my relinquishment of choice in the lawyer-date matter suspicious, you were on the right track. I was simply making sure that when my final lawyer date went down in flames, Mom would take the brunt of the fallout.

In truth, I had kept the secret long enough. My mother had few weapons left beyond her knowledge of Prom Night 1994. It was time I took that sword away from her. But I get ahead of myself. First, may I introduce you to Jason Berendt, Lawyer #5, RIP?

We met at some swanky bar in the financial district. I wore my JUSTICE 4 MERRIWEATHER T-shirt, a corduroy jacket, and a knee-length skirt with boots. I ordered a whiskey on the rocks and waited at the bar.

[Partial transcript reads as follows:]

**Jason:** Isabel?

**Me:** Jason, the lawyer?

**Jason:** Yes. But Jason is just fine.

**Me:** Have a seat.

**Jason:** Thank you. Bartender, can I get a Budweiser?

**Me:** My mother didn't tell me you drank piss beer.

**Jason:** [long pause] I guess I never mentioned it to her.

**Me:** Interesting.

**Jason:** Who is Merri—

**Me:** Merriweather. Demetrius Merriweather. Wrongly convicted for murder twenty years ago.

**Jason:** I see. You want justice for him.

**Me:** Now that I know you can read, tell me something else about yourself.

**Jason:** I'm a lawyer.

**Me:** That I know. It's in the rule book.

**Jason:** Excuse me?

**Me:** Nothing. So what do you do for fun?

**Jason:** Golf. Snow sports. I'm a total gym rat.

**Me:** Why is it all you people play golf?

**Jason:** "You people"?

**Me:** You know, white, male lawyers.

**Jason:** I don't think we all play golf.

**Me:** Most of you do.

**Jason:** [hostility creeping in] What do *you*

do for fun?

**Me:** I don't have as much fun as I used to.

**Jason:** What did you use to do for fun?

**Me:** Rebel.

**Jason:** What were you rebelling against?

**Me:** What have you got?[1]

**Jason:** You're not like your mother described.

**Me:** Especially not today.

**Jason:** I'm beginning to doubt we have much in common.

**Me:** We have *nothing* in common.

**Jason:** This wins as the weirdest blind date in the history of my blind dates.

**Me:** Thank you.

**Jason:** Not a compliment.

**Me:** Did you know that in the Ice Age, giant beavers the size of grizzly bears roamed the earth? Can you imagine that?

**Jason:** No.

*[End of tape.]*

I studied my mother as she listened to the recording. Her scowl took a shape that only Botox could fix, and fortunately I have the kind of mother who won't submit to torture for her looks. Sadly, I knew that scowl would vanish the moment our conversation

---

1. I'm sorry. I had to quote Brando at least once on these dates.

came to a close.

"You know this doesn't count," my mother said. "Why waste your time sabotaging a date when you know you'll only have to redo it?"

"I'm done with all the secrets," I said.

"Really?" Mom replied skeptically.

"There's something you should know. Connor and I broke up."

"I'm sorry," Mom said, and she put her arm around me.

"You already knew, didn't you?"

"Yes."

"Did you know he was cheating on me?"

"I did."

"Why didn't you tell me?"

"You know why," Mom replied.

"Is that why you made me go on these lawyer dates?"

"That and I thought it would be fun."

"For whom?"

"Me, mostly."

"So, no more lawyer dates, Mom. I'm done."

"Are you?" Mom said, thinking she still held all the cards.

"I'm going to tell Dad what happened that night."

My mother suddenly became speechless. I could see her mind spinning, various scenarios playing out in her head.

"No, you're not," she said.

"Why?" I asked.

"Because it's not just *your* secret any-more."

# PART IV: SENTENCING

# PROM NIGHT 1994

If I really stretched the truth, I could blame the whole thing on Petra. She had come to school the week before junior prom with a Cheshire cat smile on her face.

"You are not going to believe what I discovered in the back of my mother's closet."

"What's its resale value?"

"We're not selling this shit."

Petra then handed me what appeared to be her lunch. Inside was a dime bag of marijuana.

"Smell it," she said.

I opened up the baggy inside and my sophisticated nose told me we were dealing with some prime Humboldt County weed.

"Oh my god," I said.

*"I know,"* Petra replied.

"Won't she know it's missing?"

"Maybe. But that's not even a fourth of what she had."

"I didn't know your mom was a pothead."

"She's been under a lot of job stress lately and she's got this new boyfriend. It could be his."

"We totally scored."

Fifteen minutes later, flanked by giant trash bins behind the cafeteria, Petra and I took a few hits before history class. We thought it might make the Declaration of Independence a little more interesting.[1]

While I fought back a coughing fit, Petra had an idea.

"You should search your parents' room."

"My dad's an ex-cop. There's no way he has any contraband in his room. No way."

"You're probably right," Petra replied.

The bell rang, Petra put her pipe away, and we headed to class.

That night, my parents went to a movie. David was studying at a friend's house and I was babysitting my three-year-old sister. I read from the *Encyclopedia Britannica* as her

1. Turns out, it was kind of interesting. Mr. Blank tried to get Petra's and my attention by pointing out that the document was written in a bar on 100 percent hemp paper. Unfortunately, the mentioning of hemp paper just got us paranoid.

bedtime story. I chose the entry on photosynthesis and she passed out within minutes. I watched some television, tried to pick the lock on the liquor cabinet, and then considered that maybe my parents kept some booze in their bedroom. And then searching their room didn't seem like a bad idea at all.

There was no booze to be found (and believe me, if it was there, I would have found it). I explored every inch of that room. But I didn't leave empty-handed. In the bottom dresser drawer, under my father's old police uniform, I found his badge. And I took it.

Flash-forward two weeks: Petra arrived at my house in a red velvet evening gown that was cut in such a way that it appeared the shoulders had made a run for it, as if in direct protest to the massive shoulder pads of the eighties. I was in an unfortunate forest-green number that my grammy Spellman had bought for me a month earlier. Wearing the dress was my punishment for some minor curfew infraction.[2] One picture

2. I returned home about eight hours late after a school excursion.

was taken, which I later destroyed.[3]

Before I left, my mom said, "Isabel, please stay out of trouble."

Her voice had a pleading tone. But that never stopped me.

Petra and I had no intention of going to prom. She picked me up at seven P.M., and we stopped at Mel's diner, had French fries and Cokes, and changed into street clothes in the bathroom. A few hours later, we were crossing the bridge to Berkeley. Petra had learned of a college party that night. And we were going to crash it.

The thing about college parties is that not everyone at them is in college. The house was easy to locate — revelers spilled out onto the sidewalk like sloppy drippings from a sundae. It was the parking that was impossible. Petra eventually settled her car in a red zone three blocks away and we hoped for the best.

We fought our way through the crowd and located the booze. A guy named Scott was doling out shots of Jägermeister. After we sank our first drink of the night, Petra

3. That was back in the divine days before the digital camera. All you needed was the photo and the negative and it was like erasing history.

418

switched to beer, since she was driving. I poured myself a tumbler of vodka, ice, and lemonade and we worked our way out onto the balcony.

I finished my vodka drink and filled the tumbler with beer from the keg, since it was parked right in front of me. At some point a guy named J. T. approached the two of us. He was attractive in a one-weekend-only kind of way. The sleaze factor would get old after a while. But I remember he was fine entertainment for the night.

"You ladies got some ID on you? Because I think you look like jailbait."

The last thing we wanted was to be pegged as high school students. I pulled my father's badge from my pocket, flashed it, and said, "Run along, now."

J. T. didn't run along. He held out his hand and identified himself, or his initials.

"You got a name?" he said.

"Nope," I replied.

"My kind of girl," J. T. said.

Now here is where things get fuzzy. Petra met a guy on the lawn bowling team. She'd never met anyone who actually played that sport and was taken with him immediately. Then she vanished, as far as I knew. J. T. kept filling my tumbler with a wide mix of alcoholic beverages and telling me tall tales of his travels in Europe. He was an art dealer, a talent scout, and briefly a spy. All lies, I knew.

I woke up in an empty bed in a cheap Oakland apartment, having almost no recollection of the night before. My clothes were scattered about the floor. I dressed quickly, despite the throbbing pain in my head, and made a quick escape. I never set eyes on J. T. again.

Without a cell phone or any other means of contacting Petra without phoning parental units and incriminating myself, I found my way to the closest BART station. I reached into my pocket for my wallet and was pleased to find I had enough cash to return home. When I reached into the other pocket, a jolt of adrenaline and fear shot through me. My father's badge was gone.

I arrived home and climbed through the window. On my bed was a note from my mother that informed me I was grounded for the next three weeks. I took a shower and got into bed. My mother took a boom box and a CD of Rae's sing-along tunes and planted my sister as a steady source of pain right outside my door. She stayed all morning.

I lived in fear for weeks, not knowing when, how, or in what form the discovery of my father's missing shield would take place. I decided that outright denial was my only option and I mentally prepared for my defense. It never occurred to me that the badge would turn up again.

Exactly four weeks after Prom Night, I returned to my bedroom and found my father's police badge on my pillow, accompanied by a note in my mother's hand: *I own you.*

And this is where it becomes my mother's story.

The day before, Mom had caught a call from the Redwood City Police Department. A man named J. T. Schaeffer had been arrested for possession of a controlled substance and impersonating a police officer. Schaeffer's record gave the arresting officers leverage, and Schaeffer agreed to cooperate, telling a tall tale of some fresh-faced, brown-haired woman selling him the badge for fifty dollars.

My mother arrived at the station and asked to speak with Schaeffer. He gave her a description of the woman; my mother filled in the blanks — including the blank that I probably slept with a stranger and he nicked the badge after I showed it off. She knew I wouldn't sell it. Or at least she knew

I'd ask for more than fifty bucks.

To keep my father out of it, my mom suggested to Schaeffer that he plea out on the drug charges and turn informant for the PD. She then tactfully asked the arresting officers if they could keep this incident quiet. She was vague about her reasons but persuasive, as she always is, and besides, cops like to look after other cops. No one ever knew what happened besides me, my mother, and J. T. Oh, and Petra. Because I told her.

For six months following the incident, I was on my best behavior. And when I started to slip again, my mother had other tools of coercion and we never really brought up Prom Night again.

Now, sixteen years later, I was ready to come clean. Turns out my mother wasn't.

"Hold on a second," Mom said, after I said I was going to tell Dad the truth. "You're not going to tell your father anything."

And this, my friends, is when the leverage in the relationship shifted. It never occurred to me before, but my mother's secret was far worse than mine.

"I really want to tell Dad the truth," I said.

"It would feel good to get this off my chest. But I'm willing to negotiate."

# THE $500 PAYBACK

What would have been extremely hard but satisfying labor for a single person ended up as a two-man job. Rae was at school and then gardening probation, which gave us a window of eight hours. We shopped for the necessities the day before, managing to stay just within my budget — $479.84, when you added up the receipts.

For two women with little experience in decorating — especially decorating out of their aesthetic — I think we did a brilliant job. My third and final attack on my sister would be realized that evening.

I sat in the living room, drinking a beer and watching television. My mother, wiped out from the day's labor, sipped a cocktail and put her feet up. Rae returned home, spirits crushed after a long afternoon of commingling with nature, and climbed the stairs to find solace in her own personal space.

The scream that emanated from upstairs was one of the most satisfying sounds I had ever heard in my life. As predicted, footsteps racing down the stairs followed the scream. Then Rae stood in front of me and Mom and gawked at us with a look of disbelief.

"What have you done?" she said.

Let me tell you what we had done: We painted Rae's bedroom canary yellow; we replaced her navy-blue corduroy comforter with a lacy pink duvet with ruffles and hearts. We plastered boy-band photos all over the walls; we hung mobiles with glitter; we painted her desk white and did a hideous decoupage with a mermaid theme.

There were tears in Rae's eyes.

"How am I supposed to sleep in that?"

"Guess what?" I said. "The fairies on the wall, they glow in the dark. You don't need a night-light anymore to find the bathroom."

Rae went to the kitchen and poured herself a ginger ale. My mother followed her in and laid out the parameters of the punishment.

"You live in it for two weeks. Then you can restore it how you wish. I saved your duvet and all your wall art."

Rae didn't talk to anyone for the rest of the evening. In the morning, she phoned me. I was prepared for a deluge of abuse.

Instead, all I got was this:
"I'm sorry, Isabel. I'm really, really sorry."

# Case Closed?

That afternoon, as I drove to the Winslow mansion to check on all things butler related, my cell phone rang. It was Connor. Or it was someone else calling from the Philosopher's Club. I let the call go to voice mail. But I had to admit: I missed that bar.

After I parked in the circular driveway, I listened to the message.

*"Is-a-bel. It's me again.[1] Pleeaase call me back this time. I miss ya. I'm sorry. Ya know, one of those women I kissed before we were officially together and the other one was just crazy and attacked me. I wan' ta talk to ya. I wan' ta see you again. Please. Call me back."*

Instead, I deleted the message and entered the Winslow home.

---

1. I guess I forgot to mention that Connor had called at least a dozen times since the opening of my photography/egg exhibit.

■ ■ ■ ■

"I'm afraid none of the applicants we have met so far are suitable for this position," Mr. Leonard said after we sat down for excellent tea and a chat in the butler's quarters.

"Did you use the domestic service that I recommended? I got the number from the rich old lady across the street. She's got a whole crew in that house and doesn't seem to run into any trouble."

"Well, Mr. Winslow's needs are very particular. He has a great love for the arts and he simply cannot abide having a cultural crude in his employ."

"Len, you've got to let this job go. It's not for you. Did you get the paperwork I asked for?"

Len rolled his eyes and handed me an envelope. "Yes. Here is Mr. Winslow's latest will. It took forever for us to locate it, as apparently his attorney is on vacation. You will be interested to learn that Winslow provided generously to the valet previously known as Mason Graves."

"What's 'generously'?"

"Five hundred thousand dollars."

"That's definitely generous. Anything else

428

in here I should know about?"

"Yes. He bequeathed approximately fifty thousand dollars to Mrs. Enright."

"He scowls every time she enters the room. Why would he leave her any money?" I asked.

"Apparently Mason was quite fond of her. On numerous occasions Mr. Winslow considered firing her and Mason always convinced him against it."

I honestly couldn't get a handle on that Enright woman; something funny was going on and I was missing it.

"That's all for now, Len. I'm giving you two weeks' notice."

"Only Mr. Winslow can do that," Len replied.

"Who pays your checks?"

"You do, but —"

"No buts. You're out of here in two weeks. Mark my words."

I should have left bread crumbs as I wormed my way through the Winslow home. As I traveled through the mansion maze, I got lost and ended up in an entirely separate wing, which held a separate, more modest kitchen, which I suppose was where most of the staff consumed their meals. Out of the corner of my eye, I caught the back of Mrs.

Enright's head. She was eating a sandwich — an innocent enough act. As I turned to find my way out, my coat rustled against the wall. Mrs. Enright twisted around in her chair and stared right at me.

"Excuse me," I said. "I seem to have gotten lost. How do I get out?"

"Ms. Spellman, can I help you?"

"I said, 'I'm lost,' " I replied, louder than before.

"You're what?" she said, competing with me for sheer volume.

I would have repeated myself again, only I was tired of the ruse. If she could hear fabric brush against a wall, she could hear me say at full volume that I was lost.

"Forget it," I said. "I'll find my way out."

That night I phoned Len and Christopher's house to get a status update on the dialect wars and to find out something else.

Christopher answered the phone in his regular English accent, which I would have taken as a fortuitous sign if it weren't for the content.

"This. Is. All. Your. Fault," Christopher said, long-jumping over all forms of pleasantries.

"If I had a dime for every time someone used that line on me . . . forget about the dime. I'm going to start charging people for saying it. Five bucks a pop. Listen, Christopher, I gave your boyfriend a job — not just any old job, an exciting acting-slash-spying job that most jobless people would shave their heads for. It's not my fault he took to it like Krazy Glue on . . . well, anything. Besides, there's something else going on that you haven't told me. Len isn't dedicating himself to this role just because he's found his calling in butlering. So either fess up or keep it to yourself."

There was a pause. You could even call it a lull.

"He's bartering," Christopher reluctantly replied.

"For what?" I asked.

"A move to New York or Los Angeles so that he can actively pursue his acting career."

"I've always thought Benson[2] was ripe for a feature film adaptation."

"You're not as funny as you think you are."

"I'm funnier, aren't I?"

"I'm going to hang up now."

2. I'm speaking of the Benson from *Soap,* the brilliant sitcom from the seventies. (I am also in favor of the spinoff *Benson* but not offering as strong a recommendation.)

"Oh, you're just cranky because you hate packing."

"Won't you miss us?" Christopher asked.

"You haven't gone anywhere yet."

"You'll miss us when we're gone."

"So you are moving?" I asked, suddenly saddened by the prospect of yet another friend skipping town.

"The way I see it," Christopher said, "is that either we move to New York or Los Angeles, Len and I break up, or my life partner spends the rest of his days as a black Jeeves impersonator. Obviously, we cannot go on as we are."

"Have you made a decision yet?"

"No," Christopher replied. It sounded as if the wind had been sucked out of him. "I take it you have business to discuss with Mr. Leonard?"

"Just a quick question," I replied.

A moment passed and Christopher passed the phone to Len.

"Isabel, darling, what can I do for you?"

"When Mrs. Enright takes a day off, does she sleep elsewhere?"

"Yes, I believe so."

"Does she have a car?"

"Yes. An old, dented Toyota. Hideous thing. She parks it in the back, out of sight."

"Do me a favor. Drop by the office tomorrow morning. I'm going to have you stick a GPS on her car. Okay?"

"It would be my pleasure," Mr. Leonard replied.

"Knock it off," I said, and quickly hung up the phone.

# FREE MERRIWEATHER —
## CHAPTER 4

Having been unable to free Merriweather, I figured the least I could do was visit him on occasion and let him know that someone was on the case. My fear, however, was that all my work would be in vain. It's a hard concept to wrap your head around — a man can be in prison for a murder he didn't commit and there's no way to fight the system. You have to fight it, of course, but in my research it's become obvious that sometimes justice isn't served. DNA evidence has freed many men and women, but in cases where DNA evidence has been lost or corrupted, the other avenues of appeal are incredibly limited. Especially so many years after the original crime took place.

"My angel," Demetrius said when he saw me through the plastic divider.

I couldn't help but wonder if it had special filters that made me appear more virtuous. I had no news for Merriweather. I was still hoping Henry would come through on the case files, but I figured incarcerated life had to make someone crazy — evidenced by my sister's insanity upon her release — so I paid my "pen" pal a visit. I even wore my shirt.

According to Rae (not that I'm crediting her with being an expert on anything), one of the primary complications for a newly released prisoner is adapting to a world that has drastically changed. Since Demetrius and I had little in common — he could quote scripture all day long; I'd memorized most of the Ramones' songs — I decided to use visiting hours to test him on his knowledge of the outside world. I made up a quiz and I am happy to report Demetrius passed with flying colors.

### Quiz for Merriweather[1]

1) What corresponds to a medium-sized cup of coffee?
   a. grande
   b. tall
   c. venti
   d. medium

2) People talk to themselves more than

1. For answers, see appendix.

they used to.[2]
a. True
b. False

3) How do you spell "See you later" in a text message?
a. See you later
b. See U later
c. c u l8r

4) What does phat-phree mean?
a. Something low in calories
b. Something that's not phat
c. Something that's uncool
d. B and C

5) Flying cars are . . .
a. Available to the very wealthy.
b. In Germany only.
c. Still only seen on *The Jetsons.*

6) Pay phones have all but disappeared.
a. True
b. False

7) Pilates is . . .

2. I wanted to prepare Demetrius for the experience of seeing people talk on their cell phones all the time.

a. A children's television program about pilots who have wooden legs and pet parrots.

b. A new wacky disease.

c. A type of exercise.

d. The largest cup of coffee in the world.

8) The U.S. will be switching over to the metric system

a. In one year.

b. In five years.

c. Never!

9) After going to the moon in 1969–1972, scientists used that knowledge to:[3]

a. Use the moon as a toxic-waste dump.

b. Go to Mars.

c. Build a luxury moon hotel.

d. Not go to the moon anymore.

10) A venti mocha with whipped cream costs:

a. Approximately $2.00.

b. Approximately $3.00.

c. Approximately $4.00.

Now this is where Merriweather and I got

3. Question #9 is courtesy of David. He's still really mad about the lack of current moon exploration.

into our first and only argument.

"I'd never pay four dollars for a fancy cup of coffee."

"You say that now, but things change, Demetrius."

"Never, Isabel. That's just wasteful."

"We'll see what happens when we get you out."

"Never," he said, shaking his head.

And then, when I was scoring his quiz (100 percent), Demetrius said, "Angel, I do appreciate your efforts to enlighten me on current events. But we do have access to the Internet and TV here. And you know how I love the television. Reality TV has been my porthole to the outside world. I know what's going on."

"That's the saddest thing I ever heard," I said.

"It's sad to watch," Demetrius replied. "Almost makes me want to stay on the inside."

Then he laughed.

"Just kidding, Angel. I still want out."

When it was time for me to leave, I told Demetrius to hang in there. Demetrius told me to "be good." I thought about it, but then I changed my mind.

Henry phoned me later that afternoon.

"I'll be home at seven. Come over then," he said, and then promptly disconnected the call.

I arrived at seven fifteen. Henry had a stack of files splayed across his kitchen table. Harkey files. It would be hard to convey the pleasure this vision brought to me. I guess it would be akin to another woman coming home to a room full of roses. "Did you look through them?" I asked hopefully.

"I glanced," Henry said, which meant he did more than glance.

"Your initial impression?" I asked.

"He was a bad cop," Henry replied. "See for yourself."

For the next two hours I reviewed all of Harkey's murder cases over a ten-year period, during the time he was a homicide inspector for the SFPD. By the time the two hours were up, I could tell you that Harkey can't spell, has trouble forming complete sentences, and definitely never looked beyond the obvious suspects.

"How did he even make it into homicide?" I asked Henry.

"He comes from a long line of cops."

"Right. I forgot."

When it came time to discuss what to do

with all this information, I drew a blank. I'm used to private investigative work, not legal research or criminal law.

"How would you proceed?" I asked Henry.

"I'd let it go," Henry replied.

"Let me rephrase the question: If you were me, how would you proceed?"

"Harkey's first partner — John Rooney — took an early retirement. From the outside, it looked like they were trying to avoid a scandal. At the same time, a forensics expert, Graham Daley, quit unexpectedly. There were rumors that they were tampering with evidence, but everything was hushed up. Remember, it was twenty years ago. If Harkey learned the job from Rooney, he might have taken certain matters into his own hands if he thought he had his suspect. I'd look into any case that Harkey was working on with Rooney. Also, I heard that he butted heads a lot with his last partner. A young guy, still on the job. His name is" — Henry shuffled through the paperwork to find it — "Andrew Fishman."

"What can you tell me about him?"

"A straight-up cop. The wrong partner for Harkey. They were together two years before Harkey retired. Fishman has a good reputation. But I don't know if he'll talk. You know how cops are."

I stared down at the mess of my papers and tried to unscramble my head; I had a flashback to my high school days, trying to write a ten-page term paper on the American Revolution — I spent most of my time widening the margins and playing with the font to make 2,200 words stretch.

Henry brought me a cup of coffee and a snack of carrots and celery and hummus, which he annoyingly called "brain food." My own brain functions better on a bag of salt-and-vinegar potato chips.

Speaking of potato chips, my sister and Fred showed up a short time later. Henry had grown accustomed to their regular drop-bys, but this time there was a new energy in the air.

"How'd you get here?" Henry asked, after he opened the door and peered outside for evidence of transportation.

"We took the bus," Fred said triumphantly.

"Excuse me," Rae said, brushing past Henry. "I need to wash my hands."

"So, how'd it go?" Henry asked anyone who would answer.

Rae sighed. Fred smiled and said, "We got to where we were going and nobody vomited on anybody."

"There's always next time," I chimed in.

Rae glared at me and then scoured the pantry looking for her not-so-secret-stash of junk food, which was not-so-secretly missing.

"You got rid of it again?" Rae said, betrayed.

"Yes, when you commit a felony, you lose junk-food storage privileges. That's how the world works."

"Whatever," Rae said, rolling her eyes. "Can we watch TV?"

"What's wrong with either of your homes?"

"Lost Wednesday," Rae replied. "And David is having a dinner party, which I'm not invited to. He told me to make myself scarce until ten."

"My parents don't have cable," Fred said, explaining his side of the bargain.

"Just keep the volume down," Henry said.

"I'm not driving anyone home," I announced ahead of time.

"Who asked you?" Rae replied.

Two hours later, the kids performed a quiet disappearing act. I got the feeling Henry was wondering when I would do the same. I suppose I should have asked him earlier.

"Can I sleep on your couch?"

"Something wrong with your home?" he replied.

"Yes. It's being fumigated tonight."

I doubt he believed me, but Henry made up the couch and offered me an extra toothbrush. I turned off my cell phone just to make sure that my sleep wasn't interrupted.

# REGRESSION

I met Bernie at the Hemlock the following afternoon. I think this was the first time in our history that I returned his bear hug with the same enthusiasm. Bernie and I sat down at the bar and I said for the first time in my life, "Get this man the finest bourbon you have."

Of course I didn't know that the finest bourbon would cost me ten dollars a shot, but still, it was worth it.

"You okay?" I asked Bernie, eyeing him for any visual injuries.

"I'm fine. Not sure I can say the same for the other guy, though," Bernie replied, chuckling to himself.

"Tell me *everything*."

"It's a short story, Izz. I arrived at your apartment at two A.M. on the dot. I put on my PJs and got into bed. Believe it or not, I nodded off. The next thing I know, some Irish guy hops into bed with me, just wearing his T-shirt and shorts. If I weren't so assured of my own manhood, I might have had an issue. Anyway, Irish guy screams like a girl, says, 'Bloody 'ell,' asks what I'm doing there. I says, 'What does it look like I'm doing?' He says, 'Where's Isabel?' I says, 'She's not here, but she gives you her best.' "

"That was a nice touch," I said.

"I thought so. Then he puts on his clothes, storms out of the apartment, and the rest, as you say, is history."

There's one final detail that I suppose will bring this matter to a close. Connor left a single voice mail message at three A.M.: *"Okay, Isabel. I hear ya loud and clear. Give my regards to the fat guy. You know, he's not so bad, come to think of it. At least he shows up when you make a date."*

And that was the last I ever heard from Connor O'Sullivan, Ex-boyfriend #12.

# THE CASE OF THE DISAPPEARING DOORKNOBS

I watched the exodus of stuff from the Spellman residence for over a month. I'd solved one piece of the puzzle, but there was another angle I couldn't figure out. Light fixtures vanishing, doorknobs departing, and now the hot-water nozzle in the downstairs bathroom sink had made an exit.

"All right. What gives?" I said to my parents when I returned to my desk after a quick bathroom break that required the use of my own personal doorknob.

"Excuse me?" Mom said innocently.

This time I was going for a direct approach.

"When are you going to tell me what's going on here?"

"I have no idea what you're talking about, Isabel," Mom replied dismissively.

Dad remained silent, as usual. I wasn't surprised to see my father keeping his distance from the conversation, but I knew

446

he was the weak link.

I used my doorknob as a pointer and turned to him. "Something fishy is going on here, Dad. Speak."

"Don't point that thing at me. It's rude," Dad replied.

"Evading as usual," I said.

I spun around in my chair and directed the doorknob at Mom.

"Are you happy living like this?"

"We're doing a little home improvement. That's all. It always involves some chaos. You have to go with the flow, Izzy."

Eventually I realized I wouldn't get anything out of these two impenetrable souls. I took my doorknob and the rest of the afternoon off.

To clear my mind and improve my spirits, I picked up a coffee and sat by the community garden watching Rae scowl her way through her green probation. She had, however, managed to convince all of her co-gardeners to wear FREE SCHMIDT! shirts.

While I was sipping coffee and delighting in my fantasy of Rae on an eco-friendly chain gang, I saw Fred out of the corner of my eye. He was hard to miss since he was wearing his usual FREE SCHMIDT! T-shirt with his army jacket uniform over it. Come to think of it, I never saw Fred in anything but that green jacket. I wondered if he had some odd clothing superstition like Uncle Ray did with his lucky shirt.[1]

When Fred saw me, he waved and came over.

"What are you doing here, Fred?"

"I was in the neighborhood," Fred replied.

Weren't we all?

He opened his brown-bag lunch and offered me half of a sandwich.

"What kind is it?" I asked.

"Ham and cheese," Fred replied.

"I thought you were lactose intolerant," I said.

"I just say that," Fred replied, "so that I can quit the drinking game whenever I want."

"Smart man."

"Thanks."

"Let me give you a piece of advice: If you're ever being followed, lose the jacket."

"I'll take that under advisement," Fred said. "I keep my inhaler[2] in it and it's got all sorts of handy pockets. Sometimes you

---

1. If you've been reading these documents in order, you get that reference.
2. Why is it that I liked him even more after I learned he had asthma?

just decide that one jacket is all you need."

That got me thinking about Demetrius and *his* jacket. Where was that denim jacket right now? I needed to double-check the evidence log in the file. But first, I had to finish eating my excellent sandwich.

"I had a feeling you'd be here," Fred said.

"Oh yeah?"

"Rae says you find pleasure in her pain."

"Well, wouldn't you, under the same set of circumstances?"

"I'm not judging," Fred replied.

"You seem like a nice guy, Fred. What are you doing with her?"

"She's not like anybody else," Fred replied.

He was right. I just hoped he had the mettle to handle that human tornado.

"Just be careful," I said.

"Will do," Fred replied.

"What we talked about the other day," I said. "You've no doubt kept quiet."

"I'm a man of my word," Fred replied.

"Sorry to doubt you. I just don't come across those very often."

Fred and I sat in silence, finishing our provisions and enjoying Rae's frozen expression of hostility — or at least I was enjoying that.

"Wow. She really hates this gardening," I said.

"I know," Fred replied. "And now your brother is making her plant perennials in his backyard."

"Really?"

"That's what she told me."

"Interesting."

# My Agenda

Sometimes I can barely keep track of the galaxy of investigations, deceit, turmoil, clashes, and chaos that I travel through every day. I had too many cases — professional, pro bono, and personal — to mentally catalog. I returned home and made a list of the dangling matters that I had to contend with so that I could come up with a clear plan for a solution. Here is my to-do list at the time, which I itemized in descending order of urgency.

- Free Merriweather.
- Destroy Harkey.
- Discover Mrs. Enright's angle.
- Solve the doorknob conspiracy at Spellman headquarters.
- Find out what dirt David has on Rae to explain extra gardening.
- Take shower.

I suppose the last item on the list wasn't necessary, but since I was writing things down . . .

After my shower, I reviewed the Merriweather police file again and focused primarily on the crime-scene photos. For years investigators have been familiar with the phenomenon of perps occasionally returning to the scene of the crime to glory in their handiwork. While reviewing the pictures, I was pretty sure I spotted Demetrius standing with the crowd behind the police tape. However, Demetrius, being Ms. Collins's neighbor, would naturally have been curious when teams of squad cars and ambulances pulled up right next to his home. What I noticed about the picture was that Demetrius was wearing a jean jacket. A jean jacket that looked just like the one Jack Weaver said he was wearing the night of the crime. Now, if Demetrius stole Mrs. Collins's TV and stabbed her fifteen times while wearing that jacket, shouldn't it have been covered in blood?[1] And would he have been foolish enough to return to the scene of the

1. Sure, he could have washed it; but it's really hard to get blood out of denim and Merriweather didn't strike me as an expert on stain removal.

crime in a jacket splattered with the victim's blood?

Also in the file was a brief mention of another witness. The name was Craig Phelps. The note on Craig was brief. "Saw white man leaving Elsie's house. Witness unreliable. Known drunk."

A witness who sees another person leaving Elsie's house and there's no follow-up? What kind of defense attorney did Mr. Merriweather have? I needed to consult Maggie on a few matters, so I put the file away and moved on to another item on my list.

I pulled out my computer to check on the tracking device that was placed on Elizabeth Enright's Toyota and watched her movements on her day off. Unfortunately, she drove her car to a parking garage off Van Ness, and it didn't move for twenty-four hours. So Mrs. Enright's vehicle wasn't going to tell me anything. Maybe a short tail on her would. But there was no time for that now.

I phoned Len and asked him how the valet interviews were going.

"Dreadfully," he replied.

"Can you put Christopher on the phone?"

"Hello," Christopher said.

"Are you moving to Los Angeles or New York?"

"I haven't decided."

"Decide. Mr. Winslow has Len's trust. He needs Len to help him find a replacement and Len won't get anything done until you have a clear plan in sight."

"Isabel, sounds to me like those are your troubles, not mine."

"Well then I'm going to tell Len he can keep his job with Mr. Winslow, and they don't need to look for a replacement. At least then I know my client will be in good hands."

"You've made your point, Isabel."

"Good night, Christopher."

# THURSDAYS WITH
## MORTY REDUX

I picked Morty up at the full-service condo that he and Ruthy were renting near the Embarcadero. It had only been seven months since I'd seen him, but those seven months had taken their toll. Florida will do that to you, I guess. He also had something of a tan. Mixed with his square Coke-bottle glasses, the tan made him look like a Miami natural, but he was glad to be home. I could see that.

I gave Morty a Bernie-style bear hug, but then I softened the embrace because it felt like he would crumble in my arms. When Ruthy came out of the kitchen to greet me, she also appeared tired, as if the months in Florida hadn't been as invigorating as she had hoped.

"Nice to see you again, Isabel."

"You too," I said, and kissed her on the cheek.

"Staying out of jail?" she asked.

"Not exactly," I replied truthfully.

"I don't want to hear another word," she said, and returned to the kitchen.

After she left, I squeezed Morty's weak bicep and said, "We need to get you back in a regular shuffleboard game," I said. "You're getting soft."

Morty ignored me and said, "Did you make a reservation?"

"Of course. We need to hurry if we're going to make the one o'clock seating."

Morty returned to the kitchen, where he said good-bye to Ruthy. I could overhear the tones of a mild disagreement, but I couldn't make out any of the content.

At Moishe's Pippic,[1] we took a table in the back. Morty ordered matzoball soup, which seemed odd since he was always talking up the pastrami. But maybe it's hard to find yourself in the mood for soup in Miami and he was ready for a change. When Morty unbuttoned his Pendleton shirt, I noticed that he was sporting a FREE SCHMIDT! T-shirt underneath.

"You're wearing the wrong shirt," I said.

"I thought we wanted Schmidt free," Morty said.

"Sure we want Schmidt free, but that

1. Morty's favorite deli.

looks like it's going to happen. Now we want to free Demetrius. He takes priority. I had another shirt made for you."

I gave Morty my offering.

" 'Justice 4 Merri-weather'?" Morty read as he held up his nice, new bright red shirt with black lettering. "Must have taken forever to iron on all those letters."

*"Forever,"* I replied, reliving the memory.

"They're crooked, you know."

"Not another word."

"So you're done hunting Harkey?" Morty said with a tone of disbelief. "And now you're searching for justice?"

"That sounds fairly close to the truth," I replied.

"Why don't you give me the whole truth and nothing but?"

And so I did. And by the time Morty was finished with his soup and two cups of decaf coffee, he agreed that the evidence against Merriweather was shamefully weak — and also agreed to wear the Team Merri-weather T-shirt.

# Free Merriweather —
## CHAPTER 5

I phoned Harkey's old partner, Inspector Andrew Fishman (now lieutenant), at least four times and left a message. I made a foolish mistake with the first phone call, mentioning that I wanted to discuss Harkey. This might have been the kiss of death — even when I followed him to work and then phoned his office, I was told that he was out for the day. There had to be another way. And the other way involved keeping me out of the picture.

Next up, I had to track down Craig Phelps. The file contained only his name and an El Cerrito address. But that was twenty years ago; Craig Phelps is a fairly common name, and tracking him down based on a previous address alone was next to impossible. The police file didn't even bother giving any other identifying information on Phelps, since he was so handily dismissed.

I ran a name search for every city in the Bay Area and narrowed down the list by eliminating any Craig Phelpses under the age of forty or over eighty. This left me with ten Craig Phelpses. I started making phone calls. With each call I identified myself as a representative of a close relative who was trying to make contact with a certain Craig Phelps. Then I explained that the relative in question had lost touch with Phelps after he moved from the El Cerrito address that I provided. Craig Phelps #6 was my man. I arranged for us to meet at a nearby diner so that I could have his full attention.

We met at a Denny's on Carolina Street. Craig Phelps was now sixty and, as far as I could tell, sober. Although based on his complexion, it might have taken him a few years to dry out. I ordered pancakes with a whipped cream face because I thought it would keep things light. It's hard to feel threatened by someone eating a happy face.

"I'm afraid I've brought you here under false pretenses," I said over my first bottomless cup of coffee.

"Oh yeah?" Craig replied.

"But really, it's not that bad. I'm going to pay for your breakfast and give you fifty bucks after we have a short chat. No harm can come of that, right?"

459

And so Craig and I chatted. I reminded him of the Merriweather case and did my best to jog his memory about the officer who interviewed him. The interview, he recalled, was short; the officer, based on his description alone, was Harkey.

Then I asked Craig what he saw that night. He said he saw a white male exit through Ms. Collins's back door sometime before dawn. Craig admitted to having been drunk at the time, but he was always drunk back then and it rarely incapacitated him. He stood by his original statement. He saw a white male, approximately twenty-five years of age, run off after exiting Elsie Collins's home. According to the report, the date of the interview was five days after Elsie was murdered. I asked Craig if it was possible that he was remembering a white male exit her home on a different night. But he said no. The following day was etched in his memory because the murder caused such a stir in the whole neighborhood.

I asked him if he knew Demetrius Merriweather.

"Not very well," Craig replied, "but I'm pretty sure he stole my hubcaps once."

I drove to Maggie's office after my meeting with Phelps. Same as my last visit, she was feasting on saltines and ginger ale and she had the general look of queasiness about her.

"How long are you going to pretend not to notice?" Maggie asked.

"As long as you'd like me to," I replied.

"Who knows?"

"I think just me and Fred."

"Fred?"

"Nothing slips past that kid. But, unlike Rae, he can be dealt with."

"You didn't threaten him, did you?"

"No. I wouldn't threaten Fred. I reasoned with him. He's reasonable. Listen, your secret is safe for a little while, but it would be wise for you to break the news on your own, if you know what I mean."

"We just want to wait a few more weeks."

"Congratulations. I'm really happy for you."

"You don't think it's too soon?" Maggie asked.

"Of course not."

"Will your mother?"

"My mother will be beside herself with joy. I have to say, however, I don't know how you're keeping this from Rae."

"Between gardening and the Schmidt case, her attention is otherwise occupied."

"Isn't Schmidt free yet?"

"All the legal work is done; we're just waiting for the court to make a decision on his release. Rae's convinced he's getting out. She spends most of her time here writing Schmidt letters about what has changed on the outside since his incarceration. I think she's currently working on a slang glossary and text-message spelling guide for him."

"How productive," I commented dryly.

"I assume you want to discuss the Merriweather case?" Maggie asked.

"How could you tell?"

"It's written all over your shirt."

And then we discussed Merriweather. I detailed my recent interviews and pointed out that the ten-year-old witness merely saw Merriweather exit Collins's home with a television set. I also told her that he described what Merriweather was wearing and showed her the photograph of Merriweather at the crime scene, wearing that same jacket, the following day. Then I mentioned my interview with Craig Phelps — a drunk, but a functioning drunk, who saw a white guy leaving Collins's home later that night. The witness and the possible subject had been summarily dismissed. Wasn't this enough evidence to reopen the investigation?

The short answer: no. The long answer is

that if the evidence was available at the time of the trial, it is not sufficient for an appeal. You need new evidence. And since all of the hard evidence in Merriweather's case had gone conveniently missing, we couldn't rely on DNA, which is the primary liberator of the wrongfully convicted. It makes you wonder how many people will remain behind bars who truly are innocent of the crimes for which they were convicted.

"Doesn't ignoring a witness's testimony qualify as police misconduct?"

"You don't have enough here," Maggie said. "And if I file an appeal now before we have something more substantial to go on, I can ruin Merriweather's chances for the future."

"What do I need?"

"If you could prove that the arresting officer had a history of manipulating witnesses or found evidence of other kinds of corruption, that *might* help us."

"So I need to get another police officer to talk, right?"

"It wouldn't hurt."

I sat in Maggie's office, dwelling on the sheer impossibility of this endeavor. Before I met Demetrius, I could have lived with the idea that there was nothing I could do to help him. But now, the concept that

Merriweather might never be freed was so hideous that I refused to even contemplate that possibility. Once I got his hopes up, it seemed unconscionable to quit before he was free. But I had to wonder if I would be spending the rest of his days fighting an impossible battle.

"Isabel, are you all right?" Maggie asked.

"Yes, I was just thinking."

"About what?"

"Nothing," I said. To be more precise, what I was thinking about was that I was out of ideas. However, I quickly wiped that idea out of my head. I just needed more time to think.

Before I left Maggie's office, I had to get to the bottom of one other matter.

"Why is David making Rae plant perennials in your backyard?"

"He's not making her," Maggie replied. "She offered."

"Excuse me?"

"We thought she had just sort of taken to the gardening thing."

"Didn't you think that was suspicious?"

"Sure. But people change."

"No, they don't," I replied as I made my quick departure.

# THE PERENNIAL PROBLEM

From the car, I phoned David. He was conveniently at home. Five minutes later, I pulled into his driveway and knocked on his door.

"Something very strange is going on," I said.

"Isn't it always?" David replied.

"By the way, congratulations. *Please* tell Mom and Dad before they figure it out on their own."

"How'd you find out?"

"I'm a detective," I replied. "Is there going to be a wedding? And, if so, please tell Maggie not to torture me with one of those crazy bridesmaid's dresses."

"She's not that kind of torturer."

"I didn't think so. But you never know."

"To what do I owe the pleasure?" David asked.

"Can you please show me where Rae has been 'gardening'?" I said, using finger quotes.

"Sure," David replied, eyeing me with the appropriate germ of suspicion.

I followed my brother through the back door and down the short steps to the small yard, which consists mostly of weeds, a patch of grass, and an old cypress tree. Along the side of the wooden fence that divides it from the neighboring property, I saw a long patch of dirt that was unsettled but dry.

"Aren't you supposed to water this?"

"Rae told me to leave it alone. She'd take care of it. She said overwatering perennials is the kiss of death."

I don't have a green thumb, but I can tell you that not watering a plant is also the kiss of death.

"Where's your shovel?" I asked.

David opened the door to a small tool shed and pulled out a shovel. I took it from him and immediately began digging into the unsettled dirt.

"Isabel. You're ruining my perennials."

"You can't be this stupid," I replied as I continued digging.

Within sixty seconds the shovel hit something hard. I got down on my hands and knees and brushed away the dirt, revealing a large paper bag. I pulled the bag out of the ground and opened it. Inside were three doorknobs and a sink handle. I continued digging, this time being more careful, since I knew I might hit a glass light fixture or two. Suffice it to say, within an hour's time, I'd unearthed the entire collection of missing Spellman hardware.

After we collected the items in a box and washed up, David and I sat in his living room, drinking bourbon (he let me have the good stuff) and mulling over possible explanations for his doorknob garden. I already had the answer, but I wanted to see whether David could figure it out on his own.

"If Mom and Dad knew that someone — and when I say 'someone' I mean one of their children — was stealing hardware from their house, why wouldn't they try to get to the bottom of it?" he asked.

I shrugged my shoulders, playing oblivious.

"Did they ever accuse you of anything?" David asked.

"They accuse me of things all the time. But no, not of this."

"That means they knew it was Rae."

"Yes, I'd have to agree," I replied.[1]

"Because Rae knows something that they don't want us to know," David replied.

1. They *totally* knew it was Rae.

"That sounds about right."

"Do you have any ideas?" David asked.

"I'm still working out the details," I replied.[2]

"Care to share?"

"Not yet."

2. Not really. I had them worked out.

# Etiquette Lesson #157

You might have noticed that I spared you etiquette lessons one through one hundred and fifty-six. Since I wish I'd been spared those, I assumed you would feel the same way. Besides, these lessons spanned two decades. However, this particular etiquette lesson is accompanied by further details of the tale I'm telling you, so I provide it for you here.

I knocked on Henry Stone's door around six or seven P.M. He answered as I expected him to.

"I need a favor," I said. "A huge favor."

Henry backed away from the door, silently agreeing to my entry.

"Of course you do. Why else would you drop by?"

"I drop by all the time for Rae extractions."

"It's been a while. Have you noticed?" Henry said.

Come to think of it, I hadn't noticed, but it was true.

"She's taking the bus now. Hasn't asked anyone for a ride in two weeks."

"That Fred is a miracle worker."

I followed Henry into his kitchen, where he was doing something that resembled cooking. I'm not all that familiar with the activity, so I could only speculate.

"Do you want to stay for dinner?" Henry asked, picking up a large knife.

"What are you making?" I asked.

Henry put down the knife, turned to me, and provided a solid expression of basic annoyance. "Excuse me?" Henry said. The way he furrowed his brow in disbelief was very distracting and amusing and so I didn't reply. "When someone invites you over for dinner," Henry said, "you don't ask what they're making unless you are on a severely restricted diet. You especially don't ask when you've already mentioned that you need a favor. Where did you learn your manners?" he asked.

"Take it up with my mother," I replied. "I'm doing my best."

A long silence followed while I waited to see whether my previous comment smoothed things over. It didn't. So I had to do some more smoothing.

In my perky voice, which I don't pull out all that often, I said, "I'd love to stay for dinner. Can I help with anything?"

Henry nodded his head in the direction of the cutting board.

"Can you dice that onion for me?"

"Yes," I said, without any further back talk.

While Henry prepared the marinade for the tofu,[1] I followed my orders. I could see Henry checking on me out of the corner of his eye as if he thought I was capable of destroying the entire meal through my one assignment.

"Where'd you learn to chop an onion like that?" Henry eventually asked, impressed.

"On television. Where I learn *everything*."

Over a less-bland-than-expected meal, I finally got around to asking for my favor. It was big, so I didn't know how Henry would handle it.

"Lieutenant Fishman refuses to return my calls. If he had good things to say about Harkey, he would have called me back just to get rid of me. I've left at least eight messages. He won't talk to me because I'm not

1. Which is why I asked what was for dinner in the first place.

a cop. Do you think he'd talk to you?"

"I don't know. Maybe," Henry replied, although he refused to make eye contact.

Cops stick together because when they're on the job, trust is essential. But sometimes that means a good cop will keep quiet about a bad cop to avoid breaking a link in that network. Without evidence of Harkey's mishandling of the case, there wasn't much I could do for Demetrius.

And so I launched into a Merriweather speech, not unlike Rae's previous Schmidt diatribe.

"Let me tell you about Demetrius Merriweather . . ."

By the time dinner and my Merriweather lecture were over, I'm fairly certain that Henry was moved by his story. I even did the dishes to seal the deal, even though I suspected Henry would rewash them later.

Before I departed, I said this: "I know you think this is still about Harkey, but it isn't. It wouldn't matter what dirty cop sent Merriweather to prison. I'd still want to help get him out. We have to do something."

Henry nodded his head, but he said no more. He'd been quiet that night. Something was in the air, but I couldn't put my finger on it.

# Mrs. Enright Revealed

On her one day off a week, Mrs. Enright drives her car to a parking lot and leaves it there overnight. To gain insight into her meager personal life, I had to resort to old-fashioned surveillance.

Saturday afternoon, Enright left the Winslow residence, drove three miles to a parking garage off of Van Ness, and then strolled a few blocks down to O'Farrell Street and entered a multiplex theater, where she remained most of the afternoon, on one ticket's purchase. I know this because I watched the movies with her, in disguise. Mrs. Enright, shockingly, is partial to comedies. In fact, her sharp, stinging laugh distinguished itself from the mass of other guffaws. The pleasure she received from the mediocre escape made the mediocrity of it seem less so. How could a film be so terrible if it could transform a person within minutes? I studied Mrs. Enright as she exited the first theater and made her way to the concession counter. It appeared as if her body was inhabited by someone else. Her features remained the same, but the way they were arranged was utterly changed.

Enright replenished her soda at the concession counter and then indulged in a warm pretzel. She had clearly planned ahead, checking her watch, taking the escalator up two floors, and finding her next two-hour vacation. The second film was a bromantic comedy. If you are unfamiliar with the newest film genre since the mockumentary, it's essentially a buddy film that emphasizes heterosexual man-love.[1] Enright enjoyed the second film as much as the first. I skipped the third film when I learned it was about a talking dog, figuring that six-plus hours in a multiplex would be her limit. I went to a café until the film let out.

As I predicted, Enright's movie marathon ended after the third feature. I watched her from a bus bench across the street as she exited the unusually ornate building. I picked up the tail as she began walking south down Van Ness. She turned left on

1. That reminds me. I should include this in a future Merriweather quiz.

Eddy Street and entered the Civic Center, where there's a weekly farmer's market. For an hour she tasted samples of fresh produce and purchased an assortment of locally grown items, and then, when her shopping was complete, she casually walked up to Jones Street and entered Mason Graves's building.

I'm going to use the defense that I was distracted by other matters. For instance, being locked in a file room overnight, warring fake accents, disinterred doorknobs, and my new obsession with justice for Demetrius. My original instincts were correct; I simply didn't follow through. Libby Graves, the real Mason's mother, is the one and only Elizabeth Enright, housekeeper to Mr. Franklin Winslow. She was also a human being with unusual responsibilities who may or may not have participated in a carefully calculated con against an extremely wealthy man. Either way, she had to be dealt with. She was certainly in on Harvey's con, but I had to find out the extent of her involvement and deal with her appropriately. If I went to the cops and they decided to press charges, she could go to prison. And if she went to prison, who would look out for her son?

I knocked on the real Mason Graves's

door. "Libby" opened it. The relaxed expression that a day of leisure had imparted vanished the moment she saw me. I felt like a cruel intruder, learning her secrets, taking her away from the few moments of her life that she could enjoy.

"I don't want trouble," I said. "But I know too much to let this thing go."

Libby silently invited me into the kitchen, where Mason was eating milk and cookies. He waved a friendly hello. His mother started coffee brewing. Once our cups were in hand, we negotiated a deal that would keep Mason in sandwiches, Harvey off the streets, and Libby in her current employment. As it turns out, Enright is her maiden name, and she was committing no real crime beyond allowing her nephew to take on her son's clean identity.

In case you're curious, I didn't tell my parents the whole story. They like to keep their cases out of the gray area. You serve the client and the client only. But I lived so many years of my life in that land where rules exist only to be broken that I still sympathize with those who can't seem to follow them all, including the law breakers. I was one of them once. I guess, if you think about it, I still am. I know that a world of people ignoring absolutes could create a society that cannot function, but I am so sure of my ideals that I make this choice. If, one day, I notice the world slipping and feel that I am truly part of it, I'll snap back in line. Until then, this is how I'm going to play the game.

The final phase of the Winslow story is almost complete. After a dozen interviews, Len found number thirteen, his lucky charm. The replacement to the temporary replacement for the man previously known as Mason Graves would be Arthur Hawkins. Hawkins has been a valet for forty years, since his midtwenties. His sole reference was the family of Gregory Normington, who employed Hawkins for forty years. Only the death of his employer could have ended their relationship. Since Mr. Hawkins was still in good health and all of his records checked out, Len finally agreed to leave his employment with Mr. Winslow. In turn, Christopher agreed to move to New York.

That's not quite the end of that story. There will be a good-bye party to attend. But I'll get to that. Later.

# THE SUNDAY-NIGHT DINNER MASSACRE

If ever there was a dinner to turn you off dinners for good, the next time the Spellmans congregated was that kind of occasion. I shouldn't even mention the food, since it was only a part of the peripheral nightmare, but it seems worth mentioning nonetheless. My father's cholesterol and blood pressure had begun to creep up again, noted after his last doctor's appointment. My mother, according to character, pulled out her health-nut whip and cracked down. The evening's repast consisted of a faux meatloaf made primarily out of bulgur wheat, lentils, and oats. A side salad of beets and Swiss chard rounded out the meal.

When Rae came downstairs, she was wearing her FREE SCHMIDT! shirt. I was wearing JUSTICE 4 MERRI-WEATHER. We'd each tried to get the unit to represent our respective causes, but since the last family meal the unit had agreed to remain mostly impartial, which meant Dad wore Merriweather (because he had more bulk to carry the letters) and Mom wore Schmidt.

Rae circled the kitchen, crinkled her nose, and asked, "What's for dinner?" But then she immediately retracted the question, went into the living room, and turned on the television.

When David and Maggie arrived, I pulled my brother aside and said, "I'm going to reveal everything over dinner. Just back me up."

"How about you just tell me first?" David suggested.

"Nah. It's more dramatic my way."

I then grabbed the digital recorder from the office to ensure we had an archive of the evening's proceedings. I think you'll agree it was an event worth archiving.

When the meal was served and explained, because it required explaining, the mood of the table darkened. Please note that whenever anyone asked for the "meat" loaf, finger quotes were used.

[Partial transcript reads as follows:]

**Olivia:** Anyone who feels like complaining about the meal should keep it to himself.
**David:** I have no interest in talking about

the food.

**Rae:** What's there to say, really? I think in juvie I could get a tastier meal than this.

**Isabel:** You spent one night. You're no expert.

**Olivia:** You haven't even tasted it yet.

**Rae:** Most of what we taste is directly connected to our sense of smell. I can smell.

**Isabel:** Where's Fred? I miss him already.

**Albert:** We invited him, didn't we?

**Rae:** Yes, but I caught him on the way over and told him to save himself. He's getting a slice at Village Pizzeria.

**Maggie:** Oh my god. That sounds so good. *[The serving dishes are soberly passed around the table. A long silence ensues.]*

**Albert:** Does anyone have news they'd like to share?

**Isabel:** I think you do, Dad. And Mom. *[The unit exchanges eye contact.]*

**Albert:** Well, I'm sure something of interest happened this week.

**Olivia:** I think Rae and Maggie have news to share about Schmidt.

**Rae:** In two weeks Schmidt will be a free man. How are things working out between you and Merriweather?

**Maggie:** Rae, it's not a competition.

**David:** Tonight, I'd like to shelve the Schmidt-Merriweather rivalry, if that's all right with everyone.

**Isabel:** Fine by me.

**Olivia:** But you have to admit, David, that freeing an innocent man is big news.

**David:** You know what else I think is big news? Items vanishing from your home and you doing nothing about it.

**Isabel:** More like suspicious news.

**David:** Agreed. Mom, Dad, do you know where your doorknobs are?

*[I observe another one of the unit's telepathic exchanges. Rae stares down at her plate of food and actually tries to eat the "meat" loaf.]*

**Olivia:** Oh, they're around here somewhere.

*[Dad, too, focuses his whole attention on his inedible meal and dives in with unnatural speed.]*

**Isabel:** I know where they are. Mom and Dad, would you like me to tell you? Or maybe it would be better if Rae told you.

*[You've never seen bad food consumed at such a clip.]*

**Rae:** I have no idea what you're talking about.

**Isabel:** Oh, so you don't remember burying over half a dozen doorknobs, a couple light fixtures, a sink handle, and one towel rod in David's backyard? She told David she was planting perennials; David was stupid enough to buy that excuse —

**David:** Yes, I was stupid enough to believe my sister wanted to do something nice for me.

**Albert:** Olivia, you've outdone yourself with this "meat" loaf.

**Olivia:** No need to be rude, Al. You're the one who can't keep his cholesterol down.

**Albert:** Like it's my fault.

**Olivia:** Losing a few pounds might improve matters.

**Albert:** I'm so tired of naturally thin people thinking they have all the answers.

**Rae:** *My* cholesterol is fine. Can I make myself some mac 'n' cheese and go to my room?

**Isabel:** You are staying right there, you little convict, and explaining to the table why you were trying to bury this house in David's backyard.

**Rae:** Like I said, I have no idea what you're talking about.

**David:** Why, Rae? It doesn't make any sense.

**Isabel:** Actually it does. Mom and Dad are planning on selling the house. They used the Lost Wednesday excuse to get us all out of here so they could consult with real estate agents and show it and do some home improvement. They fooled Rae for a while, but she lives here, so she figured it out. She started sabotaging the showings by stealing relevant household items to lower the house's value and compromise any viewings. Most of the doorknobs and fixtures are antiques. I don't know where she was hiding them at first, but eventually, she figured out a good place to store the mass of hardware.

**Maggie:** Wow. You people really have your own way of doing things.

**David:** "You people?" We're back to that again.

**Maggie:** Nobody has a conversation in this family.

**David:** I think we're having a conversation right now.

**Maggie:** Now that the cat's out of the bag . . .

**Isabel:** We're going to have a civilized conversation right now, if for no other reason than to show Maggie that we're capable of it.

*[Long, long silence.]*

**David:** Mom, Dad, is this true?

**Albert:** [to Rae] Young lady, I want every single household item shined, cleaned, and returned to its place.

**Rae:** If you even think about selling this house, I will handcuff myself to the pipes in the basement.

**Olivia:** I guess you've never heard of bolt cutters, then.

**Rae:** Excellent point. Perhaps more drastic measures will be taken.

**Albert:** Enough with your empty threats.

**Rae:** Now that Schmidt will be freed, there's no need for those shirts. I wonder what would happen if I cut them up and flushed them down the toilet.

**Albert:** Go to your room right now. If you do anything erratic, I swear to you, I will have you arrested on vandalism charges, and I will make sure you do some serious time in juvie. Got it?

*[Rae glares at my father and doesn't move.]*

**Olivia:** Rae, leave this table right now.

*[Rae stomps up the stairs to her bedroom.]*

**David:** Does anyone have Fred's phone number?

**Isabel:** I do.

**David:** Call him. She needs company right now. I don't trust her for one second.

**Albert:** Me neither.

The dinner table quieted while I made the call to Fred. He seemed to understand where I was coming from. Maggie excused herself and used the restroom. She looked a bit green when she returned to the table.

My mother circled the table and brushed Maggie's hair aside and kissed her on the cheek.

"Congratulations," Mom said. "Do you want me to get you some ginger ale and saltines?"

"Yes," Maggie replied.

My father also circled the table and offered Maggie a warm embrace.

"How did you know?" she asked.

"I didn't know," Dad replied cluelessly. "My wife told me."

And then there was the silent standoff. Who would speak first? What was there to say? The lull was brief. There were too many opinions for anyone to keep quiet for too long.

"Why do you want to sell the house?" I asked as calmly as I could.

"Isabel, do have any idea what's going on outside in the real world?" Dad asked.

"I get my news through the Internet. I've heard of the economy," I replied snappishly. "Don't try to twist this into a discussion about the gaping hole in my current-events knowledge. What's the bottom line?"

"We're selling the house as soon as we can get a decent price for it," Mom said.

"No, you're not," David flatly replied, and that is when the lengthy negotiations began.

Here's what you need to know: A third of my parents' retirement was demolished in the stock market last year. They had already taken a second mortgage out on the house. They wanted to leave me a business that was free and clear of debt and now they were looking at potentially having to fund an Ivy League education for Rae. Business had been slow. Private investigative work, no matter how you spin it, is a luxury. It's an easy thing to give up in a failing economy. Mom and Dad wanted to keep the secret as long as possible to avoid this exact drama. They had thought of everything, or so they thought, and this was the only answer. But they foolishly believed their children would sit back and agree to their terms. Of course, we didn't.

The night was long and loaded with negotiations. It also yielded the discovery that David had somehow been psychic about the stock market and liquidated his assets just in time. If I were on the board of the SEC, I would probably have him investigated, but I'm not. Also to be considered was Rae — the first Spellman spawn to actually figure out what was going on. Once she made her discovery, she wrote a letter to all of the Ivy League schools where she'd applied and explained to them that she had done time and they should not accept her under any circumstances. Rae was now determined to go to a state school, preferably in the Bay Area. Fred had gotten an early admission to Berkeley and now this was Rae's top choice.

Speaking of Fred, he arrived an hour after we phoned him. He brought Rae contraband (pizza and a soda). After all her antics, my mother almost confiscated the meal, but Rae's screams from above — "I'm hungry and I have a scissors and shirts up here" — convinced her otherwise. Mom sent Fred to Rae's room with a short list of his responsibilities. Later in the evening, after David explained the various ways he could help the family,[1] Fred came downstairs to negotiate for Rae. He simply handed a piece of paper to my father, who then passed the piece of paper to my mother, who shook her head with sad disappointment.

"Anything you'd like to share?" I asked.

"Rae insists that if she goes to college — the 'if' is capitalized — she will only attend a state school and live at home," my father said.

After Fred delivered his message, he returned to Rae's room. More practical

1. Primarily a zero-interest loan.

discussion ensued. I won't bore you with the details.

After fifteen minutes Fred returned to the conference area and said, "Rae would like to know how the negotiations are going."

"We've only just begun, Fred. Nothing will be decided tonight," said Dad.

"Is that what I should tell her?" Fred asked.

"Yes," my mother replied.

Upstairs, a toilet flushed. My parents turned to one another with a look of panic. As if on cue, Rae shouted downstairs.

"I was just peeing. That's all!"

We killed a few more hours casting out ideas but came to no hard conclusions that night. Still, having the secret revealed certainly erased some mysteries and other tensions.

I returned home, exhausted. I drank a glass of that special bourbon my brother gave me last Christmas[2] and then tried to erase all memories of the day as I went to sleep.

2. So I would drink less of his.

# SLEEP, INTERRUPTED

I was woken from a deep yet troubled sleep at two thirty in the morning. A knock at the door, followed by rhythmic doorbell ringing, jarred me out of a dream in which I was digging up doorknobs from some community garden under the watchful eye of a city official. The dream had this Sisyphean[1] element. I'd dig up a doorknob, put it on a stack, and then dig up another doorknob.

I tripped out of bed, checked the time on the alarm clock just to be sure, and stumbled to the door. After looking through the peephole, I opened the door and glared with sleepy eyes at my visitor.

"Do you know what time it is?" I asked, rubbing the sleep out of my eyes.

"Yes," Henry replied as he entered my apartment and closed the door behind him.

"Is there an emergency?"

1. A few things from high school stuck, okay?

"No."

"Then what are you doing here so late?"

"I needed you groggy for this," Henry replied.

"Huh?"

It was then I felt an arm slip around my waist and another arm behind my head. And the next thing you know, Henry was kissing me. I can't tell you how much time passed between the beginning and the end of the kiss. I was still half-asleep, remember? Well, I remember. My point is it took me a while to push Henry away and start saying stuff.

"Hey," was the first thing I said.

"What's going on here?" was the second.

"Are you drunk?" was the third.

Henry only answered the third question.

"No," he said.

Then he kissed me again. I got to the "hey" part faster the second time around.

"You said you wanted to be friends," I said.

"I lied," Henry replied.

"What?"

"You heard me."

"But all those drinks and dinner and forced friendliness. What was that about?"

"All part of my evil plan," Henry said.

"You're confusing me," I said, punching

Henry in the arm, although it was a weak punch with me being half-asleep and all.

"I was confused myself."

"You said I wasn't a grown-up!"

"You're better now."

"Not that much better."

"Yeah, I know," he said.

There I stood in my pajamas in the middle of the night, sleepy, confused, trying to muster up enough anger to pretend I wasn't weak in the knees.

"You can't come around here and change your mind. I've moved on."

"I made a mistake back then. You make mistakes all the time. Why can't this one be forgiven?"

"I have to think first," I said.

"Take your time," Henry replied.

Then he sat down on my couch.

"What are you doing?" I asked.

"I'm going to wait here," Henry replied. Then he took off his jacket, his shoes, and his socks, and then he asked for a blanket.

"You're going to sleep on the couch?"

"I'm too tired to drive home."

I grabbed a blanket from the closet and threw it at Henry.

"Thank you," he politely replied to the assault.

I went into my bedroom, shut the door,

and spent the next six hours in an unsatisfying and fitful sleep.

In the morning I woke up to coffee. Henry silently handed me a cup and then made me breakfast. And since he used the ingredients from my refrigerator, there was no tofu in sight. I ate the breakfast because I was hungry and normally no one is cooking me anything, except Mom, and frankly I wish she wouldn't.

"This doesn't change anything," I reminded Henry.

"I know," he replied.

I showered and changed for work. When I was ready to leave, Henry was still in the kitchen tidying up.

"Let me ask you a question," I said. "When did you change your mind?"

"About ten minutes after I told you I wasn't interested."

"Huh."

"I made a mistake," he said.

"I'm leaving now," I said, standing in the doorway to the kitchen, not-so-subtly hinting that it was time for Henry to leave as well.

Henry threw the dishtowel over his shoulder, approached me, and said, "Have a nice day."

"Whatever," I replied.

Then he kissed me again. I was super-fast pushing him away this time. I even followed it up with a solid punch in the arm.

"Ow," he said.

"Knock it off," I said.

Henry reached into his pocket and handed me a piece of paper with a phone number on it.

"This is Andrew Fishman's cell phone number. He'll talk to you and he has something to say."

"You should have led with that," I said, snatching the number out of his hand. "Thank you," I reluctantly added.

"You're welcome," Henry replied.

I left Henry in my apartment. I had thinking and work to do. And frankly, I thought there was a good chance that if I left him alone, I'd come home to a clean apartment.

# FREE MERRIWEATHER —
## CHAPTER 6

Lieutenant Fishman met me at a coffee shop south of Market. It was neutral territory where both of us would go unnoticed. We agreed that everything was off the record, so that I couldn't go around quoting him, and if I happened to mention something that might incriminate me, he couldn't follow up with an arrest.

Once we'd agreed upon the terms, I told him everything. I told him what I knew about Harkey's methods as a PI. I told him I had evidence that Harkey was illegally recording conversations. I also had to admit how I acquired that evidence.

Then I told him about Demetrius. About how the evidence in the case didn't match up. How Harkey ignored a solid witness, who may have also been a drunk. If a guy in prison can be a rat for the prosecution, why can't an alcoholic on the street be a witness for the defense? Harkey buried that witness so the defense wouldn't get their hands on him. The witness was in the police file but not the defense counsel's papers. I mentioned the jacket Demetrius wore all the time and the photos from the crime scene. I mentioned that all of the physical evidence had conveniently disappeared around the time DNA testing became widely available. I told him point-blank that Merriweather was innocent and that Harkey probably knew it.

Then I told him about the other cases I'd looked into.

Harkey would choose his prime suspect and never waver. These prime suspects usually had a couple of things in common — they were African-American or Hispanic and had a criminal record.

Then I asked Fishman about the last case he worked with Harkey. After reviewing the file, I knew I was missing something. It was a murder investigation that looked like it was going somewhere and then it went nowhere. They had a suspect, he was indicted, charges were dropped, and then Harkey retired. Five years later, Fishman revisited the old case and found a new suspect and the charges stuck.

This was when Fishman talked.

"I was young. I had only been in homicide

for two years and Harkey was my first partner. I noticed things and let them slide, but as they continued I couldn't let them slide anymore. Witnesses pushed to identify suspects, improper search-and-seizures . . . but the last case, Harkey took it too far. Both victim and suspect were dealers. Harkey had been after this guy Rollins for a while. The victim, Marcus Turner, also had a rap sheet. Not a nice guy. Shot with one of his own unregistered guns. Word on the street was that Rollins had threatened Turner. But that happens all the time. There was no evidence beyond that. Nothing that tied Rollins to the murder. Not until Harkey removed Turner's Rolex from the crime scene and conveniently found it after getting a court order to search Rollins's home.

"I had been watching Harkey for a while. Nothing he did slipped past me, although I pretended like it did. I documented everything. Just in case it came to that. But back then if you snitched on another cop, your career or your life was over. It's better now, but still. I had a family to support. I did what I thought was best."

"You blackmailed him into retiring?" I blurted out.

Fishman checked the restaurant to make sure no one had heard my exclamation.

"That's one way to put it," Fishman quietly replied.

"Did you ever think about all the suspects before Rollins? How many times Harkey might have tampered with evidence to get the result he wanted? I checked — he had the highest clearance rate on the force for five years."

"I thought about all of it," Fishman soberly replied.

The waitress refilled our coffee; we remained silent. She was the friendly kind of waitress who requires interaction. Our lack of interaction with her and each other apparently needed commenting on.

"I sure hope this isn't a date. You two seem to have nothing in common," she said as she sashayed away.

She was very wrong.

"I thought about it. But at the time, there was only so much I could prove. So I thought about the men and women who would come later. And I still have to think I did some good."

"So now what?" I asked.

"Do you know what you're getting yourself into?"

"A little bit," I replied. It was the truth, at least.

"I want you to think about it for a few

days. Consider every angle. You might not want to touch this mess, Ms. Spellman."

"What if I do?" I asked.

"I'll be in touch."

Before Fishman left, I gave him a copy of the Merriweather file.

"We could free him now if only the physical evidence would turn up," I said.

Fishman took the file and nodded his head. Our conversation was over. At least for now it was.

I needed to clear my head, so I went to the one place that gave me peace in those days: the community garden. On this particular afternoon, I picked up a cup of coffee and sat on the bench where I'd discovered the best view. The other bench perk was that Rae could see me watching her, which I knew she found utterly unnerving. Once she even dug the shovel into her own shoe. Good times.

This afternoon, Rae approached the chain-link fence and glared at me.

"Don't you have anything better to do?" she asked.

"Absolutely not," I replied.

She rolled her eyes, shrugged her shoulders, and got back to work.

Once my body was caffeinated and my

head was clear, Henry approached the park bench to muddle everything all up again.

"Haven't I seen you enough for one day?" I asked.

"I don't know. Have you?" he said, then he handed me a bag with a chocolate croissant inside.

"Is this from _____?" I asked.

"Yes," Henry replied.

There's this French bakery on None of Your Business Street. I won't tell you the name because then you'll go there and the lines are already long enough. Suffice it to say, you can't find a better croissant on this side of the Atlantic.[1]

"Thanks, but I'm all out of coffee."

Henry pulled a thermos out of nowhere, it seemed. I uncapped my to-go cup and Henry poured the piping-hot brew.

"You think you're so smart," I said with as much attitude as I could muster under the circumstances.

"I like to come here myself sometimes. I find it relaxing," Henry said in his own defense.

Then nothing was said for a while. I drank more coffee and ate that croissant from the

---

1. Not to suggest that I have any idea what's going on on the other side.

place I'm *so* not going to tell you about. And we watched Rae dig and give us dirty looks. It was like Shakespeare in the park, I bet. When I was done with my afternoon coffee break, I scrunched up the bag and gave my garbage to Henry.

"I'll walk you to your car," he said.

Henry tossed my trash into the appropriate recycling bins and followed me to my vehicle. I tried to pretend he wasn't there, but it was more of a performance piece.

"Thanks for the croissant," I said, trying to sound not all that thankful.

"You're welcome," he replied.

"Well, I'll be seeing you around," I said, unlocking my car door.

"There's been something I've been meaning to tell you," Henry said.

"What's that?" I said.

"You know this whole community-gardening probation?"

"Yes?" I said, turning around.

"My idea," Henry said.

You can only fight your feelings for so long. A hot cup of coffee and a pastry might warm your heart, but you can cool it down with memories of rejection and embarrassment. But there are some gifts that are too perfect to ignore, gifts that tell you that someone knows you deep down in your core. I could pretend for years that I didn't still love Henry Stone and I could tell myself every day that he was all wrong for me and I was all wrong for him — and we were most definitely wrong for each other. But I'm the sort of person who's always embraced wrong. So why not embrace it now?

This time I threw my arms around Henry and kissed him; this time, nobody broke away; this time, we accepted what lay ahead. We knew we were doomed. The kiss was a warm acceptance of years of bickering, years of me consuming foods that I found barely edible and Henry tidying up after someone who already thought she had tidied up. When I kissed Henry I wasn't imagining Ex-boyfriend #13; I was picturing Husband #1.

What ended the kiss was not any desire to end it but a hazy sense of being watched. At the same time, Henry and I broke away and looked toward the garden fence. Rae had her cell phone out and was shooting pictures. No doubt they were already being e-mailed to the unit.

Henry sighed and looked at me sheepishly. "I always imagined that we would tell them."

I quickly walked toward the entrance to the garden. Henry followed after me.

"Where are you going?" he asked.

"Oh, there's just something I need to do."

I found Rae's bike and let the air out of the tires. When I was almost done, Rae caught me.

"Hey, what are you doing!" she shouted through the fence.

"Consequences, Rae. Consequences."

# CONSEQUENCES

A flurry of events, negotiations, and family meals transpired over the next several days. In the interim, all of the doorknobs, light fixtures, and other transportable household necessities were returned to their proper places. What was odd about their sudden reappearance was the adjustment period required in returning to the norm. In fact, my dad had so gotten used to carrying around an extra doorknob that I caught him a few times, doorknob in hand, realizing that he could use the one that was already in its place.

As anticipated, Rae disseminated the photos of me and Henry to every relevant person in her address book, including Grammy Spellman, who found the whole thing quite sordid. The next time I saw my mother and Henry in the same room, I could've sworn she tried to give him a high five. In his defense, he shook his head scornfully at her. It got me thinking that maybe my mother was the ultimate puppet master. I had to admit, I really didn't care anymore.

If you know me at all, and you should probably know something by now, you know that I don't like beginnings. They feel awkward, strange, and unnatural to me. I understand the status quo; it's getting there I have trouble with. While I had shared many meals with Henry and been to his house on numerous occasions, we had never been on an official date. Neither of us quite knew how to proceed.

He phoned me the afternoon after the garden kiss.

"What are you doing later?" he asked.

"I have no plans," I replied.[1]

"I'll see you at eight," he said.

At eightish (I'm not a timely person) I arrived at Henry's house. At eight o'clock sharp, Henry arrived at my place. He waited patiently inside my foyer for ten minutes, then phoned my cell.

"Where are you?" I asked.

"Where are you?" he asked.

"At your place," I replied.

1. No, I never read that freakin' "rules" book, and let me tell you where you can stick it.

"I'm at your place too," he said.

"I thought you didn't like my place," I said.

"I thought you didn't like my place."

"I like your place fine. I just don't like the food there and since there's no food in my place, it doesn't make any difference, does it?" I said.

"Here's the plan —"

"It needs to involve food, because I'm starving," I said.

"I'll go to the store."

"Listen to me very carefully: I'm *not* eating tofu!"

"Calm down, Isabel."

See, beginnings suck. But as the night progressed, matters improved. Henry keeps a hide-a-key in a slot in his doormat.[2] Once I got a neighbor to let me into his building, I was able to get into his apartment, where I promptly ordered Chinese food before he could protest.

After dinner, there was a knock at the door. Henry quickly muted the television set and dimmed the lights. We sat in silence for ten minutes until we were certain that the person behind the door (Rae) had

2. Stupid, I know. But the slot is hard to find.

vanished. Then Henry cleaned up, because he likes cleaning up and I don't, although he did mention that if I was thinking this relationship was going to involve permanent maid service, I was very wrong. I didn't mention that I had a feeling he was very wrong.

Of course, other things happened during the evening and I did stay the night, but most of that stuff is none of your business. Henry claims I'm a blanket stealer, and he snores (on occasion), but in my experience they all snore at least a little bit. In the morning, he made the bed with me still in it.

"What are you doing?" I asked as he straightened out the blanket on top of me.

"Now all you have to do is slip out of your side and tuck in the covers."

"You're insane," I replied as he tucked in the covers on my side of the bed. He kissed my forehead while I was freeing my arms from the bedding trap.

"I'll make coffee," he said, leaving the room.

I slid out of bed when the mug was ready for me. I made toast and watched Henry eyeing the crumbs that sprinkled onto the kitchen table. When I was done eating, he wiped the table clean with a sponge.

"I was going to clean that up," I said.

"No, you weren't," he replied.

He was right. I wasn't. I had a feeling fights would come frequently and would last indefinitely, but that morning I got a glimpse of something very different than the list entries that preceded Henry.

# FREE MERRIWEATHER —
## CHAPTER 7

Lieutenant Fishman phoned me a few days later. He wanted to meet me again at that out-of-the-way diner. He'd had a chance to look over the Merriweather case and had a few insights. Especially since I didn't have any, I welcomed the meeting.

The case was beginning to weigh on me. Not only because an innocent man was doing time, but more because an innocent man was doing time and I had given him hope for freedom. That hope was beginning to feel more and more tenuous.

Fishman kept the pleasantries brief. He ordered coffee and oatmeal and explained that he had a cholesterol problem. I made a sympathetic order of oatmeal myself, even though I can't stand the stuff. Mostly I drank coffee.

Fishman slid the file back to me.

"Don't you think it's an interesting coincidence that the physical evidence went missing right around the time DNA evidence became a common tool in the legal system? Twenty years ago, when the murder took place, it was still in its early stages, but it wasn't regularly used and was still considered somewhat unreliable. For instance, people didn't even trust it in the O. J. case. But by then, it *was* solid and it could have freed Merriweather, if it was available and someone took the time to look into it."

"But it's missing," I said. "What can we do?"

"It's conveniently missing," Fishman replied.

"What are you getting at?"

"He might have been protecting himself," Fishman said without too much conviction. He said it as if he was hoping it wasn't true.

"You think Harkey might have taken the evidence?"

"He might have misplaced it. It's easy to misplace. It's just stuff with a label on it. We're human. It's not a file you can stick on a computer. Certainly evidence nowadays is easier to track down, but if you misplaced a box in the evidence room, it would be like finding a needle in a haystack to locate it again."

"Let me get this straight," I said. "You're suggesting that, years later, Harkey might have made the evidence disappear in the event someone revisited the case."

"All conjecture," Lieutenant Fishman replied.

"Why hasn't anyone ever done anything about him? How many other cases has he manipulated?"

"I don't think you understand the mess of trouble that could happen if we try to open an investigation into Harkey's old cases. He wasn't only involved in improper convictions. In fact, most of his cases were legit and the right person went to jail. All those convictions would be revisited if we could get the DA to reopen this one case, which is unlikely. What is more likely is that we could get shut down immediately because so far in these files there's nothing that can be easily proven — besides what I know."

"Isn't what you know enough?"

"Except that it happened fifteen years ago. And it could destroy my career."

"You can't tell me there's nothing we can do."

"Maybe there's something. But I should warn you now, it's a long shot."

That was my morning; I'm afraid to report that the afternoon only got worse.

# DIVINE INTERVENTION

When I arrived at Morty's house to pick
him up for lunch, Ruth was there, whispering something to him. He whispered something back in an agitated tone.

"Are you ready?" I asked.

"Not yet. Have a seat, Izzele."

I sat down on this impeccably white couch
that came with the furnished condo. I hated
that couch.

"What's up?" I asked.

"I got good news and I got bad news; what
do you want first?" Morty said.

"The good news."

"Today, you can pick the restaurant."

"Okay. Thank you," I replied.

"You want the bad news now?" he asked.

"Next week you get restaurant choice?" I
suggested.

"That's true, but that's not the bad news."

"Okay, give me the bad news."

Long pause.

"I'm sort of dying."

"What?"

"I'm sick. I don't have much time left."

"Like a normal eighty-five-year-old?"

"Sure. Like a normal eighty-five-year-old who has four to six months to live at the most."

"This is not how you tell someone that you're dying," I said, feeling my face flush red.

"How do you know? Have you done it before?"

"What's wrong with you?"

"I've got the cancer."

This was not the time to criticize Morty's excessive use of an article. I let it slide, sort of.

"What kind of *the* cancer do you have?"

Morty slowly got up from his chair, walked over to me, and pinched my cheek. "Now that, Izzele, is why I got to keep you around."

I took a deep breath.

"Where are we going for lunch?" Morty asked, trying to keep things casual.

"I don't know," I replied. I wasn't even sure I could drive, let alone eat.

"Izz, no crying. I need you to step up right now. I'm swimming in long faces. I got to have one person who can pretend this isn't happening. And that person is going to be you. If you think about it, you owe me. All that free legal work, when you got yourself in trouble? Did you get a single bill? Because I don't remember sending one. This is how you repay me. Pull yourself together right now. If you don't, I will refuse to see you."

"Seriously?" I said, fighting, and I mean fighting, back tears.

"Yes," Morty replied. "You can just forget about lunch."

"Excuse me," I said.

I rushed to the bathroom and splashed cold water on my face. And then I did exactly as I was told. I pulled it together. Well, just for lunch I did.

When I exited the bathroom Morty had his coat and scarf on.

"What are we eating?" he asked.

"Sushi," I said.

"What, are you trying to kill me?"

"You can order the teriyaki chicken," I calmly replied.

During lunch we talked about the weather, Gabe's upcoming wedding to "the shiksa," and then the Merriweather case, which seemed to be the subject that felt the least awkward, the least like we were doing everything in our power to not talk about what was going on. When I dropped Morty off at his house, he made one final serious comment to me.

"I'm old, Izzele. It's okay to be sad, but it's not a tragedy. This is part of life. Now next week we go to Moishe's as usual, we'll chat about the Merriweather case and your ridiculous romantic life, and you'll help with some of my funeral arrangements."

"Isn't that a bit premature?" I said.

"I want to go out with a bang," Morty replied. "So we'll have to plan ahead."

I didn't return to work after lunch. I went home and slept and maybe did that crying that Morty had forbidden. Then I had a couple (maybe more than a couple) drinks and fell asleep on the couch.

# SABOTAGE

There was a knock at my door a few hours after my bourbon nap. I peered through the peephole and saw it was Henry. I tiptoed away from the door and into my bedroom. I immediately turned off my cell phone and ignored all calls to the main line. After about a half hour, he went away. I drank more bourbon and watched bad television and tried to think about nothing at all, which is really hard, if you've ever tried to do it.

Much later in the evening, somewhere in the vicinity of eleven P.M., there was another knock at the door. This person kept knocking; then she started yelling. It was my mother. Through the door, she claimed she would call the cops if I didn't open up. So, I opened up.

Mom pushed her way inside, looked me up and down, and then said, "You smell like a distillery."

"It was only a matter of time."

"What are you doing?"

"What does it look like I'm doing?"

"Drinking yourself into a stupor."

"Now that we've got that cleared up, you can be on your way."

"Pour me a drink," my mother said.

After my nap, I couldn't remember where I last left the bottle, so I roamed my hardly roamable apartment, scanning for the booze. My mother found it first and served herself.

"I talked to Ruth Schilling," my mom said. "I'm sorry, Izzy."

I stopped roaming once the bottle was located and sat back down on the couch. Mom parked herself right next to me. The sympathy stuck in her voice, but there was something else there as well. I was drunk so I couldn't put my finger on it. It could have been disappointment or fear or guardedness. She wasn't sure who she was dealing with at that moment — old Isabel, new Isabel, or another mutation.

"I know this is hard, Isabel. If you need anything, I'm here for you. But try to hold yourself together, honey. Morty needs a friend now. You can shut down later."

"Don't worry; I'll manage," I said unconvincingly.

"Do you want me to stay?" my mom asked.

"Nah."

"I'll see you at work tomorrow," Mom said.

My mother left and sometime later I fell back asleep on the couch. I woke up at nine fifteen A.M. to my phone ringing.

"You're late," my dad said.

I looked at the clock.

"Not that late," I replied. Although I would be quite late once I made it in.

"You'll feel better if you come to work, Isabel."

"I'll feel better if I sleep another three hours," I replied.

"Honey, get in here right now."

"Should I take a shower first?"

Believe it or not, my dad yelled to my mom, "She's asking if she should shower."

My mom shouted a really loud "yes" in reply.

One hour, a shower, three aspirins, four slices of toast, and two cups of coffee later, I entered the offices of Spellman Investigations.

"You look like hell," Mom said.

"What were you expecting?" I asked.

My mother approached the whiteboard and drafted yet another rule.

# RULE #68 — ARRIVE AT WORK
## LOOKING WELL-GROOMED

I promptly vetoed the rule and assumed I could convince Rae to second it. It would soon be a moot rule. I charged my cell phone, which had died in the middle of the night, and soon it began chirping, alerting me to messages. I put the phone on mute.

"You have some calls to return?" my mother asked.

"Nope," I replied, trying to focus my attention on the credit report of Sheryl Magnuson, Zylor Corp. employee applicant. As I added the relevant and nonderogatory data into her main file, my head began throbbing again.

"Is there any coffee in the kitchen?" I asked.

"Yes," my mother flatly replied.

I poured the coffee and returned to the office, where I spotted my mother checking my cell phone and whispering to my dad. I snatched the phone from Mom's hands.

"This office isn't big enough for the three of us," I said.

"Why don't you go to the basement and shred some old files?" Mom replied.

"Why don't I go home?"

"Why don't I not pay you this week?"

Mom said.

"Why don't I go to the basement and shred some files?" I replied.

"Take your phone with you."

I walked down the rickety stairs of the dimly lit basement. Above our industrial-sized paper shredder is a sign that reads SUGGESTION BOX. Inside the box are all the files that are ready to shred. Once I stuck the first stack of pages through the shredder, I realized my head could not tolerate the grating din of the machine. There's a cot in the basement, which gives it a prison-cell quality but also makes it a good place to nap. You can't hear the shredder very well from the office, so I opted for a nap instead. It's nice to get paid to sleep.

I woke an hour later somewhat refreshed. At least it didn't feel like miners were trying to tunnel their way out of my skull. I shredded a few more files but decided I'd had enough. I walked up the steps to the office door and noticed that the doorknob was missing. The door, however, was latched.

I knocked on the office door.

"Hey! I'm locked in here," I said.

There was no answer. I shouted again. Still no answer.

Since I had my cell phone on me, I phoned my mother. Thankfully, she picked up.

"Hello?"

"Mom, it's me."

"Who?"

"So, so not funny right now."

"What do you need, Isabel?"

"I need you to get me out of the fucking basement. That's what I need. It had a doorknob when I came down here."

"We're at a lunch meeting right now."

"Where? In the kitchen? Walk ten paces forward and twenty to your left and let me out!"

"We'll be back in the office as soon as we can," Mom said, and hung up the phone.

Then I phoned Dad. His call went straight to voice mail, per my mother's instructions, I'm sure.

I called David after that.

"Can you come to the house and let me out of the basement?"

"Sorry, Izzy. Mom already phoned me and told me I couldn't let you out."

"What's the point of all this?" I asked. "I could have those two arrested and then they'd have to spend fifteen hours a week digging trenches at an organic garden."

"Isabel," David replied. "Just call him. Okay?"

I spent the next forty-five minutes trying to figure out a way to open the door without a knob, but apparently it's a finely tuned symbiotic relationship.

So I made the call.

"Hello?"

"Hi, Henry. It's Isabel."

"Where have you been? I was worried."

The hangover, the second false imprisonment, and the fact that I thought Henry should know exactly what he was dealing with forced an honest answer out of me.

"Morty told me he was dying and so I got tanked and didn't answer my door when you dropped by. My mother has locked me in the basement of the office. Can you please come to the house and both free me and arrest them?"

"Olivia locked you in the basement?"

"Yeah. And you know what? It's not like you get used to this sort of thing."

"I'll be right there. Is anyone home?"

"I'm pretty sure they're eating lunch in the kitchen."

Twenty minutes later, I was freed.

"Oh my goodness, Isabel," my mom said, playing innocent. "I don't know how that happened."

My dad stared at his shoes, unable to pull off any performance. Henry glared at my mother.

"Olivia, that's not how you handle things."

"Are you sure, Henry?" Mom replied. "Because it seems to have worked out exactly as I planned."

I didn't say anything, but she was dead right.

"Isabel, do you want me to take you home, or do you want to stay at work?" Henry asked.

"What do you think?"

"We're leaving," Henry said.

"Start the car," Mom replied. "Isabel will be right out."

My father walked Henry to the door while Mom cornered me in the office.

"Sweetie, it is now time to be a grown up. You've had thirty-two years — more time than most people. I don't expect you to wear sweater sets and have manners, but I do need you to not sabotage everything good in your life. I know you're tough. But sometimes you can ask people for help."

"Okay, Mom. You've made your point. But can you now scale back a bit on your interventions?"

Mom nodded her head in agreement. "I promise you, as of today, I'm done meddling."

My mother lied. She wasn't done meddling, not by a long shot. However, her future meddling took on a far less criminal air. And on that day her words did not fall on deaf ears.

# DECISIONS, DECISIONS

It wasn't my choice to make, but the way I
saw it, there were two options in the
Merriweather/Harkey situation. With Maggie's help and Fishman's testimony, we
could launch an all-out investigation on
Harkey. What fruits would come of this
inquiry were uncertain. If it panned out, it
could uncover more cases in which police
misconduct might have led to improper
convictions. In theory, we could free more
than one innocent man or woman. However, the court system does not make this
process easy — it fights against it at every
turn — and Harkey seemed to have covered
his tracks well, or well enough. If we
launched the investigation, there was also
a good chance that nothing good would
come of it. Perhaps there would be a shadow
over Harkey's reputation, but that shadow
was already there and didn't seem to affect
him.

There was another option, as Lieutenant Fishman explained to me. An option that had equally doubtful rewards but held more promise. We could convince Harkey that we were about to begin an investigation on all of his cases that went to conviction and try to barter with him.

A few days later, at Henry's house, I paced the night away trying to make the decision. I also hunted for snack food, which was hard to come by in Henry's house.

"You need more snacks."

"Look on the third shelf," Henry replied. "I got you some cheese puffs."

My heart warmed briefly until I saw the label on the bag.

"No, you bought me Karma Puffs."[1]

"Same difference."

I broke open the bag of Karma Puffs and continued pacing while snacking.

"I'm going to have to vacuum tomorrow," Henry said.

I ignored him. He could worry all he wanted about Karma Puff dust; I had more pressing matters to contemplate.

"What do I do, Henry?"

1. An organic cheese puff–like snack, which is not all that bad if there are no Cheetos around.

"You could eat those over the kitchen sink."

"No, about Merriweather."

"You do what you can live with," Henry replied.

And that was the right answer.

An hour later, Rae showed up. She was tired of the unit and wanted to watch TV. Henry asked her to leave; she refused. I asked her to leave; she rolled her eyes. Since I was staying the night at Henry's place, I was in no mood to drive her home. Briefly both Henry and I were at a loss as to how to get rid of her. We phoned Fred, but he was at some family dinner and didn't pick up.

Henry sat down on the couch next to Rae and politely asked her one last time to leave. She refused.

"That gives me no choice," I said as I approached Henry, straddled him on the couch, and planted a long, passionate kiss on his lips.

Within seconds Rae, struck with terror, screamed, almost vomited, and was out the door.

And that, my friends, is how we solved the Rae extraction situation once and for all.

■ ■ ■ ■

Over the next week, Maggie and I assembled our case against Harkey. We created a list of every questionable arrest and interrogation procedure and a spreadsheet of every witness Harkey had ever interviewed in consideration of the possibility that he had swayed their testimony. Everything that looked shady we pulled together into one nice, clean, threatening file.

Maggie made an appointment with Harkey on a Tuesday afternoon. She strolled into his office lugging the file and dropped it on his desk. She explained that she had enough evidence against him to bring to the DA to request a full investigation into Harkey's practices on the police force. However, she explained, her loyalty was to her client. All she really wanted was the evidence box on the Demetrius Merriweather case. Casually, Maggie mentioned that should that physical evidence suddenly be returned to its proper place, this file would go back into the file room and never see the light of day again.

However, if the physical evidence didn't turn up, she would have no choice but to approach the matter from a broader perspective. She left him a thick folder containing copies of the key elements in her case against Harkey to bring the threat home. She told Harkey to think about it. She told him that his thinking should take no more than a week.

One week later, the physical evidence in the Merriweather case miraculously reappeared in the evidence room. A day later, my car window was bashed in. Coincidence?

# DOING TIME

While Schmidt was being freed from San Quentin, Rae was unfortunately stuck in probation at the community garden. Maggie took pictures and sent them to Rae's cell phone. Unlike so many others who have had the misfortune of being falsely imprisoned, Levi Schmidt had a family that could welcome him home and give him time to breathe and learn to live in the outside world again. Schmidt would have a chance for a relatively normal life, at least what was left of it. That day at the garden, Rae planted carrots and zucchini and didn't mind so much that she was spending most of her free time on her hands and knees in the dirt. That was the last day she wore her FREE SCHMIDT! T-shirt. More than a few times I've wondered what happened to the hundreds of navy-blue tops — I guess they turned into sleepwear, cleaning rags, and landfill.

■ ■ ■ ■

I visited Demetrius as soon as we got the news on the evidence and told him to be patient. DNA testing takes time. Requesting the courts to test for DNA on a closed case takes even more time. But I reminded Merriweather that it was a step in the right direction. Then I had Merriweather take another quiz. He scored 100 percent again, so I figured, like I've always said, you can learn almost anything from television. Since we had some time to kill and I knew these visits helped kill the monotony, Merriweather and I played Mad Libs. (Our game options were limited because of the plastic divider.) Still, I think he enjoyed himself. Then it was time for us to say our good-byes.

"Angel, when I get out of here, I'm going to buy you a four-dollar cup of coffee," Merriweather said.

"I look forward to it," I replied.

Since I was crossing the bridge and not far from the Winslow residence, I decided to drop in and see how Mr. Winslow and his new valet were doing. I'm afraid I have nothing of interest to report. They were doing fine. Although Winslow did ask about Mr. Leonard and I could tell from the wistful tone of his voice that while the new valet had all the skills, manners, and attentiveness required for the position, Winslow clearly missed the dramatic presence and true friendship of Mr. Leonard.

I then checked on Mrs. Enright and inquired how her son was doing. She played no games this time. She shook my hand but avoided eye contact in the way that people avoid eye contact when they can't stand to be seen. I left quickly, knowing that I was making her uncomfortable. I had seen too much of her life and she didn't like it. I suppose it was the contrast of having just visited Demetrius, but it seemed fascinating to me that a man in prison could find more joy in life than a woman who was free to roam the streets. Our ability to adapt is amazing. Our ability to change isn't quite as spectacular.

# THE ATTACK OF
## SUNDAY-NIGHT DINNER

The attendance at family meals began to expand exponentially after Fred started showing up, though I got the feeling he always ate a slice of pizza before coming. I got that feeling because I noticed tomato sauce stains on his shirt and he made a big show of only eating the vegetables for my mom. This night, Henry made his first appearance.

My mother was always extra nice to Henry, as if she had to compensate for whatever trouble I inflicted in our private life. I think Henry enjoyed the deference. Truth be told, there was definitely some inflicting being done.

Also making an appearance that night were Morty and Ruth. When Morty saw Henry, he pulled me aside and said, "Finally, you gave the cop your number."

"Yes, Morty. He definitely has my number."

Morty pinched my nose. "Good girl," he said. "Don't blow it with your crazy shenanigans."

"I have no idea what you're talking about."

I tried not to notice how little my old friend ate these days and averted my gaze from the way his clothes hung loose off his bones. The glasses made him Morty. If he removed those, I don't think I could have borne to look at him.

Fortunately the evening's primary distraction was David and Maggie's announcement that they would be getting married in two months' time. I am happy to report that not a single person used the phrase "shotgun wedding." My mother insisted that Rae and I throw a combination baby/bridal shower. Rae and I exchanged a glance that mixed both terror and incomprehension, having only been to such things on rare and cruel occasions. However, my sister and I reverted to our poker faces and offered helpful suggestions.

"I can make Magic Punch," I said.

"How do you feel about pizza rolls?" Rae asked.

My mom interrupted us and said, "Don't worry, Maggie. We'll make sure it's tasteful."

I heard David mutter, "Because tasteful is

Isabel's middle name." Then I heard him say, "Ouch," which meant that Maggie had kicked him under the table.

After the minor assault, Maggie turned to me and said, "If I see anything pink or powder blue, or there's a pacifier or a baby bottle in sight, I will take you down right then and there. Do you hear me?"

"Loud and clear," I replied.

Maggie was going to make an excellent sister-in-law.

The next time Morty and I met for lunch, he wasn't up for an outside excursion, so I brought the deli to him. Still, he was only eating soup.

"Have you ever done any party planning before?" Morty asked, as if I were at a job interview.

"Well, I'm working on a baby/bridal shower right now," I replied.

"Good. Good," Morty said. "Take out a pen and paper."

I followed his instructions.

"First things first. I want you to do my eulogy."

"Huh?"

"You heard me," he said.

"I don't think that's a good idea," I replied. "I'm not really good with words that way."

"Who cares? I'm writing it."

"Oh," I replied. "So you're going to write

your own eulogy?"

"And you're going to deliver it."

"Can I say no?"

"You'd deny a dying man his last wish?"
*Sigh.*

"Good," Morty replied. "You're not a Jew, but the guilt still works. Now take out a pen and paper and let me dictate."

Morty ate a few more spoonfuls of chicken soup and contemplated the words he wanted to leave the world with.

"How should I begin?" he asked.

"I don't know," I replied.

" 'Friends and family' — no, that's too serious."

"It is a funeral, Morty."

"So? It doesn't mean we can't have a little fun."

"What's your goal with this speech?"

"I'd like you to impart some of my wisdom to my friends and family."

"Okay, let's start with the wisdom part," I said.

"Good thinking," Morty replied. Then he started thinking.

My pen was poised over the pad of paper for about five minutes until Morty broke the silence.

"Breakfast is the most important meal of the day."

"You don't say?" I replied.

"Why aren't you writing?" Morty asked.

"I'm not going to talk about breakfast in your eulogy."

"Let's not think of it as a eulogy. You'll be delivering my sage advice."

"Is that the kind of wisdom you want to leave people with? Breakfast? Really?"

"We're brainstorming, Izzele. Are you going to argue with me the entire time?"

"I hope not."

"I'd also like you to wear a dress. Something in a bright color that's festive."

"I can't wear a festive dress to a funeral."

"It's always 'no' with you."

"Let's get back to the speech," I suggested, mostly to detract from the subject of my wardrobe.

"Let's start at the beginning," Morty said. "We're losing focus."

"Okay," I replied.

"I just need a good opening line," Morty said.

"How about 'Ladies and germs,'" I said.

"That's good. I like it."


Unfortunately, that wasn't the only speech Morty and I had to prepare. Gabe and Petra's wedding was nearing and I was part of the modest bridal party. Petra has tattoos

and wore a silver 1920s flapper dress. As
you can imagine, we were given free rein
with our wardrobe, as I think it should be.
It was an evening wedding, so I got away
with wearing black. Henry told me I looked
lovely. Morty told me I looked like I was
going to a funeral.

"Don't even think of wearing that to
mine," he said when he saw me.

"We'll talk about this later," I replied. "Do
you have your toast prepared?"

Morty patted his breast pocket. Once the
festivities were under way and the revelers
were appropriately booze soaked, Morty got
up to the microphone and delivered verbatim
another speech we had tangled over for the
last few days. It was remarkably brief but
met the requirements I'd insisted upon — it
included the phrase "l'chaim" and excluded
the words "shiksa," "body piercings," "tattoos," and "let's see how long this lasts."

Morty lied at the end and said, "I couldn't
be happier for the two of you," then he
raised his glass, a toast was made, and
Henry made me dance with him, until I
stepped on his toe and told him that if he
felt particularly attached to his feet, we
should probably keep this activity to a minimum.

Even with Morty's reservations about the

couple in question, he looked happy that night. He worked the room at a snail's pace, but he said hello to each and every guest, which ultimately was good-bye.

A few weeks later, Morty entered the hospital for the last time. I was still allowed to bring him deli food. But he'd eat only a bite here and there.

The cancer Morty had was a brain tumor, a glioblastoma multiforme, they call it. One day, when I was visiting him, he showed me the brain scan.

"There it is, Izzele. The thing that's killing me. What does it look like to you?"

"A butterfly," I replied.

"Funny, isn't it?"

"Not so much."

"Let's work on my speech."

"I want to be clear on something, Morty. Just because you're writing it, don't forget that I have to deliver it."

"Remember when I went away the last time?"

"To Miami?"

"Remember that list I gave you?"

"Yes."[1]

1. "Morty's Last Words," it was called. See previous document for complete list.

"Maybe we should go with that list. Can you find it? We'll make some adjustments here and there."

"I'm not going to tell people to stay out of prison at a funeral."

"See? It's always 'no' with you."

Other good-byes had to be said, as well. Len and Christopher had packed up all of their belongings and their move to New York was only a week away.

I brought Henry to the good-bye party. Len, even after all these years, still had trouble with cops, so he didn't warm to him right away. However, he did manage to say that Henry was the most well-groomed man he'd ever seen me with.

"You have no idea," I replied.

Then we talked about his plans for New York. I suggested *Benson! The Musical.* Christopher suggested I pour myself another drink and stop talking about it. When we left, Len promised me orchestra seats for every theater production he was in. It was a promise he wouldn't keep. Thank god.

I would like to report that after the physical evidence in the Merriweather case miraculously reappeared, his release was imminent. I would like to report that, but I cannot. The steps in the legal process continue to keep Merriweather behind bars. First Maggie had to convince the DA to retest the evidence. Since it had been missing for eight years, the chain of evidence was in question. We needed the evidence tested to rule out Merriweather, but because it had been missing for so long, the prosecution could argue that it was in some way contaminated. Eventually, a judge agreed to have the clothing from the crime scene and Demetrius's jacket tested. Those tests took three months to complete. The result was that there was no DNA evidence connecting Merriweather to Elsie Collins.

However, in the court system, that doesn't mean he's innocent. Maggie filed a motion to vacate the original verdict and Merri-weather was released. But two weeks later, he was arrested again and new charges were filed, based on the same circumstantial and eyewitness testimony of the previous trial. The DA stood by his original conviction, which means that Merriweather will face yet another jury trial, in part because we never could come up with another viable suspect. The white male who was seen exiting Elsie's house was as useful to us as a ghost.

The trial is months away as I write this. One day I expect Demetrius to be free. But now he isn't. I continue to visit him, mostly to help kill the time. Sometimes I bring a quiz, but he always passes. I'm certain there are things about the real world that will shock him once he's out, but we'll worry about that when the time comes.

Here's another detail in my story that you might find interesting: A few months after the Merriweather verdict was vacated, Rick Harkey retired and moved to Florida. We noted a marked increase in business after that.

The goal of my job is to solve cases, uncover secrets, and get to the truth. Sometimes the truth unfolds perfectly, liked a quartered piece of paper. Sometimes, even, a mystery is solved. But mostly, the universe doesn't fit together like a jigsaw puzzle. Pieces will always be missing. In my work we look around and ask questions and find that, in the end, there are just more questions. If you're looking for a standard mystery, with a surprise ending and a villain, a punishment, and a wrap-up of events, I can't give it to you. That's not how the real world works. Most mysteries I've encountered remain unsolved. Most questions I ask are left unanswered.

What I can give you is this: a moment in time when questions hung in the air and lives felt whole and life-altering decisions were made. I can give you that. But that's all.

# BEGINNINGS AND ENDINGS

Rae and I somehow managed to pull off the bridal/baby shower. I wouldn't call it a brilliant success; "adequate" would be a more appropriate word. Having no knowledge of these sorts of things, and with my mother being curious about how we would manage without her, Rae and I were left to our own devices, which meant we were slaves to the Internet and relied heavily on our previous party-planning experiences.

I made Magic Punch. We couldn't find pink and light-blue Lifesavers, so we opted for Jelly Bellies. Only, instead of buying the candies in those specific colors, Rae purchased twenty variety boxes and made us pick through each and every box for the pinks and blues. Eventually, I refused to continue the painstaking task when I realized the point of it all was so Rae would have the remaining colors for her sugar stash. I drove directly to the Candy Store off Polk Street and bought the appropriate supplies.

Jelly beans dissolve faster than hard candy, we soon discovered. Dropped in a vat of vodka, limeade, and sparkling water, they reduced quickly and bled in such a fashion that the punch bowl looked more like a science experiment than a beverage. Still, it was the only booze we offered, so guests partook. After three almost-choking incidents, we decided to sift out the partially dissolved Jelly Bellies and rename the concoction "Lime Surprise."

We played bizarre games. One involved making wedding dresses out of toilet paper. Rae thought the idea was amusing but couldn't stand behind the waste, so she purchased the most earth-friendly recycled bathroom paper she could find. The result was a tragic mess of shredded light-brown squares, precariously connected by weakening serrated edges. The draping bore no resemblance to anything like formal wedding wear. In fact, it didn't even resemble a mummy or a shipwrecked person at the end of a long journey. It barely even resembled toilet paper wrapped around a person, to be honest.

Then we played a game Rae had found online in which we asked Maggie trivia about David and she had to put a piece of bubblegum in her mouth whenever she got an answer wrong. Being siblings of the groom, we had no problem in arriving at twenty difficult questions. We also saw this as an opportunity to semi-publicly humiliate our brother. After five questions and four giant gumballs down, my mother called a halt to the game, which was probably wise since Maggie appeared to have reached her gum capacity. In case you're curious about the questions, the ones we managed to get out before Mom put the kibosh on the game are as follows:[1]

1) What was David's first girlie magazine?
2) How many times has David had his teeth professionally whitened?
3) Given the choice between losing his hair or his little toe, what would David choose?
4) Why was David sent to the principal's office in the eighth grade?
5) What hair band did David worship in the midnineties?

Trust me, you don't want to know questions six through twenty.

1. For answers, see appendix.

Maggie seemed to have had a pretty good time, even though she couldn't partake of the Lime Surprise. She thanked us profusely and promised that there would be no bridesmaid-dress nightmares in our future. She kept her word.

# THE SUNDAY-NIGHT DINNER SMACKDOWN

If you've been paying attention, you know that certain family issues have remained unresolved. The weekend following the bridal shower, we had one more torturous meal and a lengthy dinner negotiation in which most primary matters were finally settled.

David had only one agenda item for the evening: figuring out how my parents could keep their house. He wrote down a number on a piece of paper and handed it to my father. David repeated his zero-interest loan offer to help with the mortgage, which my father rejected.

"How is it that you have all this money, David?" Mom asked.

David shrugged his shoulders as if it were also a mystery to him.

"We don't need all this space with Rae going away to college," Mom said.

"I'm not going away," Rae replied.

"You were accepted at Yale," Mom said. "That's quite a commute."

It's true. Yale did accept Rae, even after she informed them of her legal troubles.

"I sent them a rejection letter," Rae replied. "I'm going to Berkeley and living at home," she said with a tone of finality there was no point in arguing with.

"You can retract your rejection letter to Yale," my mom said.

Rae chuckled to herself. "You wouldn't say that if you read it."

My mother glared at Rae. "You should have consulted me first."

"Would it make you feel any better if I told you that Fred's going to Berkeley too?"

It made everyone feel better, but no one admitted it except Maggie.

"I think that's great. And I'd be happy to give you some part-time work if you behave yourself and stay out of my desk."

"See? Everything is going according to plan," Rae said.

If you thought about it, it was going according to Rae's plan.

"So, what do you say?" David asked. "According to Isabel, business has improved since Harkey skipped town. You can stay in the house if you want to."

I decided that someone had to be the

voice of reason and point out at least one drawback of this plan.

"That means four more years of Rae under the same roof."

My father sighed and nodded, as if taking in the full meaning of the situation. Rae was oblivious to the inherent insult in this line of conversation and interjected her own demands.

"I want to move into the attic apartment. I need more space," she said.

"Don't we all," I replied.

Over the blandest sponge cake in the history of desserts, a deal was brokered. Between Rae staying local, the new business from Harkey's absence, and a generous no-interest loan from David, 1799 Clay Street would remain in the Spellman name. While all our lives moved forward it was comforting to have one thing remain the same.

I suppose there are a few other things I should mention. I almost suffered a housing crisis of my own. Bernie and Daisy broke up for good. Although I never got the complete story, it had something to do with a poker game that went on for two weeks, and while it wasn't mentioned, I have a feeling hookers played into the saga as well. Just when my old friend tried to be "roomies" again, Henry suggested I move in with him.

I agreed and immediately bought one of those vacuums that look like science fiction pets. They roam your apartment sucking dirt on a random and endless loop. I figured that would partially compensate for any extra messes I made. I named it Arthur. I thought Henry would take a liking to Arthur, but he didn't. Still, Arthur seemed a key ingredient in the success of our relationship, so I insisted that he stick around. Sometimes I pet Arthur and talk to him like he's my dog.

Until the end of Rae's probation, I would go to the community garden at least once a week. On my last visit there, the entire staff was wearing JUSTICE 4 MERRI-WEATHER T-shirts. When I drove Rae home, she asked me if I finally forgave her for the "file-room incident," as we would forever call it. I told her I did. Then she told me that she'd left a hundred more T-shirts of varying sizes in the trunk of my car. I asked her how she got the keys, but she didn't answer. I did, however, finally discover how Rae always managed to have an unlimited supply of slogan wear. Fred Finkel's dad, it turns out, is the business-logo king of Oakland.

I was glad for the shirts, but in truth, they

were a constant reminder to me that Merriweather wasn't free.

Rae graduated high school without event. Although I'm fairly certain she was involved in an elaborate senior prank that turned the bushes in front of the school into papier-mâché igloos. As with almost everything she does, she got away with it. Fred took her to senior prom. I made sure dozens of photos were snapped. While she looked lovely in my estimation, I could only hope that years of fashion evolution would one day make this particular outfit an embarrassment worthy of blackmail. Perhaps you think I should be beyond all that, but I'm still me. Any more personal growth and I might become unrecognizable. We wouldn't want that, would we?

# THE EULOGY

Four months after he returned to San Francisco, Morty died in the hospital with his friends and family by his side. I don't know what his last words to Ruthy were, but his last ones to me were, "We have an agreement. *Capisce?*"

" *'Capisce'?*" I said. "When have you ever used that word before?"

"An agreement is an agreement."

I couldn't argue with him. About that agreement . . .

I wore a light-blue sundress in the middle of a particularly chilly fall. My attire was a shock amid the crowd full of dark mourning attire. Ruth understood that my clothing was a sign of respect, even if most of the congregation found it unusual. I stood in front of the synagogue and explained that the words I was about to speak were not mine but Morty's. I further explained that if anyone found the words inappropriate for the occasion, they should take it up with him.

Ladies and germs,[1]
I would like you to know that I had a good life. I also had a long life, for a man who had no interest in the[2] exercise and ate deli meats several times a week.

Here are some things I know for sure that I thought I'd share with you: If you haven't said "I love you" to someone today, do it. You won't always be happy, but you should try to be. Don't be too afraid of germs. Those people have no fun. Remember to look around sometimes. You might see something you haven't seen before or at the very least avoid being hit by a flying object. Speaking of flying objects, don't spend your life looking for extraterrestrial life, unless you work for NASA. Remember that you always have to cooperate with someone. Life is an endless negotiation. Play fair. Stay out of jail. Don't live in the past. Eat breakfast. It really is the most important meal of the day. Try to make new friends, even when

1. Oh, how I tried to change that opening line.
2. Yes, I tried to get rid of "the."

you think you're too old to do that. And remember me as that handsome, funny man who liked to have a good time. Do me a favor: Take care of Ruthy for me. Whatever she asks you to do, do it. I'm watching you.

And finally, remember this: "Yes" is always a better word than "no." Unless, of course, someone has just asked you to commit a felony.

When I stepped outside, a thick layer of fog had rolled in that sent a chill through me. Henry gave me his coat and we moved on to the next phase of Morty's memorial, which naturally involved consuming large amounts of deli food.

Because Morty wrote his own eulogy, I never had the chance to write my own. My eulogy would have been brief. I would have mentioned all the good work he had done in his lifetime, including keeping me out of jail. I would have thanked him for all the lunches, even the ones I didn't enjoy. And I would have told him that I learned many things from knowing him. For instance, you should keep dental floss on you at all times; when your eyesight goes, quit driving; don't keep too many secrets, eventually they'll eat away at you. But the most valuable lesson he taught me was this: Every day we get older, and some of us get wiser, but there's no end to our evolution. We are all a mess of contradictions; some of our traits work for us, some against us.

And this is what I figured out on my own: Over the course of a lifetime, people change, but not as much as you'd think. Nobody really grows up. At least that's my theory; you can have your own.

# APPENDIX

## DOSSIERS

*Albert Spellman*

Age: 65

Occupation: Private investigator

Physical characteristics: Six foot three; large (used to be larger, but doctor put him on a diet); oafish; mismatched features; thinning brown/gray hair; gives off the general air of a slob, but the kind that showers regularly.

History: Onetime SFPD forced into early retirement by a back injury. Went to work for another retired-cop-turned-private-investigator, Jimmy O'Malley. Met his future wife, Olivia Montgomery, while on the job. Bought the PI business from O'Malley and has kept it in the family for the last thirty-five years.

Bad Habits: Has lengthy conversations with the television; lunch.

## Olivia Spellman

Age: 57

Occupation: Private investigator

Physical characteristics: Extremely petite; appears young for her age; quite attractive; shoulder-length auburn hair (from a bottle); well groomed.

History: Met her husband while performing an amateur surveillance on her future brother-in-law (who ended up not being her future brother-in-law). Started Spellman Investigations with her husband. Excels in pretext calls and other friendly forms of deceit.

Bad Habits: Willing to break laws to meddle in children's lives; likes to record other people's conversations.

## Rae Spellman

Age: 17 1/2

Occupation: Senior in high school/assistant private investigator

Physical characteristics: Petite like her mother; appears a few years younger than her age; long, unkempt sandy blond hair; freckles; tends to wear sneakers so she can always make a run for it.

History: Blackmail; coercion; junk-food obsession; bribery.

Bad Habits: Too many to list.

## David Spellman

Age: 35

Occupation: Lawyer

Physical characteristics: Tall, dark, and handsome.

History: Honor student; class valedictorian; Berkeley undergrad; Stanford law. You know the sort.

Bad Habits: Makes his bed every morning; excessively fashionable; wears pricey cologne; drinks moderately; reads a lot; keeps up on current events; exercises.

## Henry Stone

Age: 45

Occupation: San Francisco police inspector

History: Was the detective on the Rae Spellman missing persons case three years ago. Before that, I guess he went to the police academy, passed some test, married some annoying woman, and did a lot of tidying up.

Bad Habits: Doesn't eat candy; keeps a clean home.

## Mort Schilling

Age: 85

Occupation: Semiretired defense attorney

Physical characteristics: Short with scrawny legs and small gut; enormous

Coke-bottle glasses; not much hair.

History: Worked as a defense attorney for forty years. Married to Ruth for almost sixty years.

Bad Habits: Sucks his teeth; talks too loud; stubborn.

## Maggie Mason

Age: 36

Occupation: Defense attorney

Physical characteristics: Tall; slender; long, unkempt brown hair.

History: Dated Henry Stone; they broke up. Rae introduced her to David, and they began dating.

Bad Habits: Keeping baked goods in pockets; saying "you people"; camping.

## Connor O'Sullivan (Ex-boyfriend #12)

Age: 39

Occupation: Barkeep

Physical characteristics: Tall; dark haired; blue eyed; a little too handsome for his own good.

History: Took over the Philosopher's Club from previous owner Milo.

## Bernie Peterson

Age: Old

Occupation: Drinking, gambling, smoking cigars, annoying sublet tenants.

Physical characteristics: A giant mass of human (sorry, I try not to look too closely).

History: Was a cop in San Francisco; retired; married an ex-showgirl; moved to Las Vegas; moved back to San Francisco when she cheated on him; reconciled; moved back to Las Vegas. Repeat.

Bad Habits: Imagine every bad habit you've ever recognized. Bernie probably has it.

And, for the hell of it, I'll do me:

*Isabel Spellman*

Age: 32

Occupation: Private investigator/one-time bartender

Physical characteristics: Tall; not skinny, not fat; long brown hair; nose; lips; eyes; ears. All the usual features. Fingers, legs, that sort of thing. I look okay, let's leave it at that.

History: Recovering delinquent; been working for Spellman Investigations since the age of twelve.

Bad Habits: None.

### ANSWERS TO DEMETRIUS QUIZ

1) A and D

2) True and False
3) C
4) D?
5) C
6) A
7) C
8) C!
9) D
10) C

## ANSWERS TO BRIDAL SHOWER QUIZ

1) *Penthouse*
2) Three times. However, he uses an at-home whitening kit at least once a month.
3) Little toe
4) I don't know. I'm still trying to find out.
5) Slayer

# ACKNOWLEDGMENTS

I've set a precedent for lengthy acknowledgments, but this time I'm going to cut back. Most of these people have been thanked at length in the previous documents. Please note: I am not in any way feeling less grateful this time around, I simply want you to get through this page without requiring a nap or a lunch break.

First and foremost, I must thank my brilliant editor, Marysue Rucci, and my amazing agent, Stephanie Kip Rostan. You both are not just colleagues, but friends. I am very lucky.

Many other wonderful people at S&S must be acknowledged: Carolyn Reidy, David Rosenthal (aka Dr. Ira), Victoria Meyer, Deb Darrock, Aileen Boyle, Sophie Epstein, Michael Selleck, Leah Wasielewski, Jonathan Evans, and Nicole De Jackmo; and my new publicity team, Julia Prosser and Danielle Lynn. You all have been very good to me and I am extremely grateful.

At Levine Greenberg Literary Agency: Jim Levine, Dan Greenberg, Monika Verma, Melissa Rowland, Elizabeth Fisher, Miek Coccia, Sasha Raskin, Lindsay Edgecomb. You are all far too wonderful.

My mother, Sharlene Lauretz: thank you for everything.

My family: Bev Fienberg, Mark Fienberg (reluctantly, I'm still holding a grudge), Dan Fienberg, Jay Fienberg, Anastasia Fuller, Uncle Jeff, and Aunt Eve. If I haven't mentioned you, that doesn't mean we're not related or that I don't appreciate you.

My friends, who help me survive everything: Morgan Dox, Steve Kim, Julie Ulmer, Peter Kim, Carol Young, Frank Marquardt, Stephanie Dennis, and Charlie R. Merci. This list could be endless, so I'm merely mentioning the people that I've harassed the most in the past year.

Other people: Once again, I must thank the booksellers who shove my book into unsuspecting customers' hands, as if not reading it might cause a severe rash to break out. As promised, thank you, Scott Butki for your endless support. Also, thank you to the wonderful media escorts who help me survive the tour and remind me where I am and where I'm supposed to go.

Last but not least in any way: Dave Hayward, my friend/subordinate: I'm pleased to announce you have been named employee of the year. A fruit basket will be forthcoming.

The employees of Thorndike Press hope you have enjoyed this Large Print book. All our Thorndike, Wheeler, and Kennebec Large Print titles are designed for easy reading, and all our books are made to last. Other Thorndike Press Large Print books are available at your library, through selected bookstores, or directly from us.

For information about titles, please call:
  (800) 223-1244

or visit our Web site at:
  http://gale.cengage.com/thorndike

To share your comments, please write:
  Publisher
  Thorndike Press
  295 Kennedy Memorial Drive
  Waterville, ME 04901